DATE DUE

MASTERPLOTS II

SHORT STORY SERIES

MASTERPLOTS II

SHORT STORY SERIES SUPPLEMENT

10

Spi-Z

Edited by

FRANK N. MAGILL

Consulting Editor

CHARLES E. MAY
CALIFORNIA STATE UNIVERSITY, LONG BEACH

SALEM PRESS

Pasadena, California   Englewood Cliffs, New Jersey

∞ The paper used in these volumes conforms to the American National Standard for Permanence of Paper for Printed Library Materials, Z39.48-1984.

Library of Congress Cataloging-in-Publication Data
Masterplots II: Short story series.
Bibliography: p.
Includes index.
Summary: Examines the theme, characters, plot, style and technique of more than 1,200 nineteenth- and twentieth-century works by prominent authors from around the world.
1. Fiction—19th century—Stories, plots, etc. 2. Fiction—19th century—History and criticism. 3. Fiction—20th century—Stories, plots, etc. 4. Fiction—20th century—History and criticism. 5. Short story. [1. Short stories—Stories, plots, etc. 2. Short story] I. Magill, Frank Northen, 1907- . II. Title: Masterplots 2. III. Title: Masterplots two.
PN3326.M27 1986 809.3 86-22025
Supplement.
ISBN 0-89356-769-8 (set)
ISBN 0-89356-773-6 (volume 10)

PRINTED IN THE UNITED STATES OF AMERICA

LIST OF TITLES IN VOLUME 10

LIST OF TITLES IN VOLUME 10

MASTERPLOTS II

SHORT STORY SERIES

SPIRIT WOMAN

Author: Paula Gunn Allen (1939-)
Type of plot: Fantasy
Time of plot: The 1970's to 1980's
Locale: San Francisco
First published: 1983

Principal characters:
EPHANIE, a Native American woman living in San Francisco
THE SPIRIT WOMAN, a vision who appears to her

The Story

Ephanie, a woman of unspecified age and circumstance, is a Native American living in San Francisco. One morning, she is awakened by the presence of a shadowy form, cloaked in a swirl of vapor, at the foot of her bed. The form slowly assumes the shape of a woman, small, with "something of bird, a hawk perhaps, about her." Her eyes have a strange gleam, and her clothes and appearance are those of a traditional southwestern Pueblo Indian woman. Her hair is cut traditionally, falling in a straight line from crown to jaw, forming perfect square corners on either side, with straight bangs cut at the eyebrows, in the ancient arrangement that signifies the arms of the galaxy, "the Spider." She wears a finely woven shawl, embroidered with spider symbols, and buckskin leggings wrapped around her calves. The woman announced that she has come to tell a story, one that Ephanie has long wanted to hear.

Knowing that this is no mortal visitor but a spirit woman, Ephanie raises herself in her bed and performs the traditional ritual of greeting, the sign of the sunrise, by taking a pinch of corn pollen between her fingers and thumb and opening them as though to free the pollen.

The spirit woman begins to speak, chanting the creation story of the Keres people. Old Spider Woman—known also as Sussistinaku, Thinking Woman, because she creates by thinking things into existence—is the creator of the world. First she creates two sisters to help her, and she structures her creation in the pattern she brings with her from the center of the galaxy, a pattern of corners, turnings, and multidimensional arrangings that "is the sign and the order of the power that informs this life and leads back to Shipap," the home of Iyatiku (Corn Woman), the goddess who governs the spiritual affairs of the Keres people.

Next, the spirit woman explains the relationships and natures of the Keres deities. After Sussistinaku created her two sisters, Uretsete and Naotsete, Uretsete was known as the father, Utset, because Naotsete had become pregnant and had a child. Uretsete is the woman who was known as father, the Sun, and Naotsete is the Woman of the Sun. Iyatiku is another name for Uretsete, and "The One was the unity, the source, Shipap, where Naiya ['our dear mother'] Iyatiku lived."

In the patterns of the spirit woman's stories, Ephanie finds something that she has long sought, a truth and a meaning, an imperative to shape her life in the ancient manner. In addition to explaining the origin and nature of the universe to Ephanie, the spirit woman gives her a prophecy. She explains that the time of ending is coming to Indians, but tells her not to weep, because this is as it should be. In the Keres story of the origin of humankind, humans evolved through a series of four underground worlds before emerging on the earth's surface in this, the fifth world. The spirit people will now leave this world and go on to another place, the sixth world.

The spirit woman explains that there is another earth, almost like this one, but with a new way of looking at reality that is more valid, more real, more vital than the old way. She says that she is in that other world, where there is also a San Francisco, but a different version of the place than the one Ephanie inhabits. She invites Ephanie to visit her in her city. She is confident Ephanie will like it there, and will be surprised to see that there is no death—life and being are the only truth.

Long ago, the people knew death was not possible because they could actually see the person make the transition, leaving the flesh behind, like seeing a person strip off clothes. Then Old Coyote, the Keres trickster figure, said there would be death: Instead of seeing the whole transformation in its entirety, people only would see the body, first alive, then still. The spirit woman tells Ephanie that she must jump and fall into the new world just like Anciena, the sky woman of Iroquois myth, who fell through a hole in the sky and began the human race on earth. With this, the spirit woman seems to dissolve, and Ephanie sleeps and dreams.

Prompted by the spirit woman's visit, Ephanie dreams of women who lived long ago, who knew magic, directed people upon their true life paths, and healed them. These were the women of the Spider Medicine Society, "the double women, the women who never married, who held power like the Clanuncle, like the power of the priests, the medicine men. Who were not mothers, but who were sisters, born of the same mind, the same spirit. They called each other sister." Ephanie's room begins to fill with shapes, which turn into women who sing and dance in the ancient way. Ephanie picks a heavily embroidered shawl from the bottom of her bed, wraps it around her shoulders, and joins the dance.

Themes and Meanings

Although "Spirit Woman" constitutes the conclusion of Paula Gunn Allen's novel *The Woman Who Owned the Shadows* (1983), its self-contained unity justifies its separate treatment as a short story. In it, Allen develops her own idiosyncratic interpretation of traditional Keres myths, especially those dealing with creation and death. Through the character of Ephanie, Allen demonstrates the need for a return to the principles, if not the exact rituals, that patterned ancient Native American life. Although most of her myths come from her own Keres people, she imagines these principles as being pervasive throughout pre-Columbian North America.

Most notable among these principles is that of matriarchy. Allen has argued that traditional Indian cultures across the continent were originally gynocentric and matrilineal. The Keres creation story told by the spirit woman to Ephanie pictures Thinking

Woman as the first creator, and sees her two sisters (Uretsete and Naotsete) as containing within themselves both male (Utset/the Sun) and female (Naotsete/the Woman of the Sun) natures, making the male a derivative of, and secondary to, the female.

A second theme is the idea that the essential relationship for any woman to achieve is not that of wife or mother but that of sister. It is through her discovery of her sisterhood with the women of the Spider Medicine Society and her participation in their ritual dance that Ephanie finds the true meaning and purpose of her existence. The story concludes with the words of the song, "I am walking—Alive . . . I am Entering—Not alone," indicating that Ephanie has found true life and meaning in the company of women.

Style and Technique

Allen is of mixed Keres, Sioux, and Lebanese heritage, and was brought up at the Keres pueblo of Laguna in New Mexico. Allen's fiction derives not only from Keres beliefs and myths, but also frequently, as in "Spirit Woman," incorporates into the plot materials from the oral tradition, such as the creation story and the explanation of Coyote's responsibility for the entry of death into human experience. The story's structure is that first the myth is presented, followed by Allen's interpretation and the application of that interpretation to the life and situation of the story's main characters.

The physical action of the story is minimal: waking, a gesture of greeting, a dream, a final physical and spiritual waking. The sentences tend to be short and fragmentary, the diction simple and straightforward, but the content is influenced heavily by surrealistic techniques, as when Ephanie's room "filled with shadows. And the shadows became shapes. And the shapes became women singing. . . . With her shawl wrapped around her shoulders in the way of the women since time immemorial . . . she joined the dance. She heard the singing. She entered the song."

Dennis Hoilman

SPUNK

Author: Zora Neale Hurston (1891-1960)
Type of plot: Sketch
Time of plot: The 1920's
Locale: Florida
First published: 1925

Principal characters:
SPUNK BANKS, a giant of a man who loves Lena Kanty
LENA KANTY, a pretty woman
JOE KANTY, her timid husband
WALTER THOMAS and
ELIJAH MOSLEY, gossipy townsmen

The Story

In a small town in central Florida that is populated exclusively by African Americans, Walter Thomas and Elijah Mosley are sitting on the porch of a store. They notice that Lena Kanty has disappeared into the nearby palmetto bushes with Spunk Banks, who is not her husband.

Unconcerned about town gossip, Spunk and Lena continue down their brazen path, oblivious to the fact that Joe Kanty, Lena's beleaguered husband, has entered the store. Walter and Elijah, who function like a Greek chorus, mock the shy husband and warn him that he is about to be cuckolded. Joe is fully aware of the implications of Spunk and Lena's behavior; he knows that the men at the store have seen her, and he knows they know he knows. Joe pulls out a razor and claims that Spunk has gone too far.

After Joe leaves in search of Lena and Spunk, Walter and Elijah reflect on their role in this family drama. Walter criticizes Elijah for mocking Joe and taunting him to action. Elijah defends himself by saying it is not decent for a man to accept such behavior. Walter then points out Spunk's physical superiority and prowess as a fighter: Spunk is the only man in the village brave enough to ride the circle saw at the sawmill. If Spunk and Joe were to tangle, Joe would not fare well.

Lena's role in this triangle is obvious to all the observers, except Joe. She is in love with Spunk and wants to leave her husband for him. Spunk claims her for his own. The issue is settled definitively when Joe, after following the couple into the palmetto bushes, is killed by Spunk in self-defense.

Spunk and Lena do not live happily ever after, even though the main barrier to their happiness has been eliminated. In another one of their gossip sessions, Elijah asserts that Joe has returned as a ghost to haunt Spunk. The incident had occurred just as Spunk and Lena were preparing for bed. Elijah says that a big, black bobcat had walked around the house howling. When Spunk grabbed his gun, the bobcat stood still, looking at him and howling. Spunk realizes that it is not a bobcat, but Joe.

The townsmen believe in the story about the ghost without question. It causes them to reflect on the relative bravery of the two men. Walter concludes that Joe was the braver, because even though he was frightened of Spunk and knew he had a gun, he still pursued him. Spunk, on the other hand, a natural-born fighter, was scared of nothing. In Walter and Elijah's estimation, it was nothing for Spunk to fight when he was never scared.

A few days later, the ghost appears for the second time. Once again, the story is told from the townsmen's perspective. The men were at work in the sawmill when Spunk inexplicably slipped and fell into the circle saw. As he was dying, the men reached him and heard his last words: "It was Joe, 'Lige . . . the dirty sneak shoved me." Elijah concludes: "If spirits kin fight, there's a powerful tussle goin' on somewhere ovah Jordan 'cause Ah b'leeve Joe's ready for Spunk an' ain't skeered any more."

At Spunk's wake, all the townspeople have gathered to pay their respects to Lena, who is lamenting her loss. Even Joe's father has come. Significantly, old Jeff Kanty, "who a few hours before would have been afraid to come within ten feet of him, stood leering triumphantly down upon the fallen giant as if his fingers had been the teeth of steel that laid him low." As they are eating at the wake, the other mourners speculate on who will be Lena's next lover.

Themes and Meanings

Zora Neale Hurston's fiction centers on the people, events, and customs of her hometown, Eatonville, Florida—which is distinguished for being the first incorporated African American township in the United States. Author Alice Walker strongly praises Hurston for the "racial health" that Hurston exhibits in her work and "for exposing not simply an adequate culture, but a superior one." Hurston believed that the greatest cultural wealth of the continent could be mined in towns of the black South, such as Eatonville. There, one could show how the "Negro farthest down" was "the god-maker, the creator of everything that lasts."

These beliefs explain why Hurston became an anthropologist and sought to preserve the Eatonville folktales, anecdotes, and beliefs in her book, *Mules and Men* (1935). In her fiction, however, Hurston portrays the townfolk in a much more realistic manner. Joe's bravery in going after the much larger man is undercut by the fact that he attacks Spunk from behind. Walter's compassion toward the Kantys is undercut by Elijah's mean-spirited, nosy, loud-mouthed behavior. Elijah slaps his leg gleefully when he sees Spunk and Lena head for the bushes in the beginning of the story. Later, through his taunts and teasing, he all but pushes Joe to seek revenge, knowing that Joe is the much weaker opponent.

The townspeople fare no better. From the porch of the store, they view the whole incident as a form of entertainment. When they see Joe head into the bushes after Spunk, they laugh boisterously behind his back. At the end of the story, their attitude does not change even as Spunk lies in front of them at the wake: "The women ate heartily of the funeral baked meats and wondered who would be Lena's next. The men whispered coarse conjectures between guzzles of whiskey."

Hurston pleased no one by portraying the townfolk in this manner. The people of Eatonville were angered at her when they recognized themselves in her stories; she did little to disguise their identities and used their real names. Other famous black writers, such as Richard Wright and Ralph Ellison, did not like Hurston's minstrel-like characters. Hurston knew that she had not made herself popular by what she had written. Her autobiography, *Dust Tracks on a Road* (1942), states: "I sensed early, that the Negro race was not one band of heavenly love. There was stress and strain inside as well as out. Being black was not enough. It took more than a community of skin color to make your love come down on you."

Style and Technique

In *Dust Tracks on a Road*, Hurston relates her mother's dying moments:

> As I crowded in, they lifted up the bed and turned it around so that Mama's eyes would face east. I thought that she looked to me as the head of the bed reversed. Her mouth was slightly open, but her breathing took up so much of her strength that she could not talk. But she looked at me, or so I felt, to speak for her. She depended on me for a voice.

Hurston fulfilled this destiny in her stories and novels; the African American voice is the first thing that a reader notices when reading Hurston's work. In her article "Characteristics of Negro Expression" (1934), Hurston describes African Americans' urge to adorn language and lists their linguistic techniques, such as metaphors and similes ("mule blood—black molasses"); double descriptives ("low-down"); verbal nouns ("funeralize"); and nouns from verbs ("he won't stand straightening"). She disproves the notion that the black idiom is spoken by people of inferior intellect and sensibility. Instead, she asserts that their skill at embellishing the English language is the result of their belief that there can never be enough beauty, let alone too much.

The outcome of "Spunk" turns on the townspeople's ability to manipulate Joe Kanty through their verbal dexterity. When Elijah first spots Spunk and Lena sauntering off to be alone, he cries out for all to hear: "Theah they go, big as life an' brassy as tacks." His judgment shapes the villagers' perception of the situation. He reinforces his message by using colorful language. He tells the other men that Spunk is not afraid of anything on "God's green footstool"; that by strutting around with another man's wife, Spunk does not "give a kitty." Joe, on the other hand, is "a rabbit-foot colored man." When it is Spunk's turn to be frightened of the bobcat, he gets so "nervoused up" that he cannot shoot. Elijah, by first introducing the story of the bobcat and making the others—perhaps even Spunk himself—believe in it, helps to move the story to its grim conclusion.

Anna Lillios

STALKING

Author: Joyce Carol Oates (1938-   )
Type of plot: Psychological realism
Time of plot: The early 1970's
Locale: Apparently a U.S. suburb
First published: 1972

Principal characters:
GRETCHEN, the thirteen-year-old protagonist
THE INVISIBLE ADVERSARY, the taunting figure that she follows

The Story

On a cold, gritty November day, Gretchen follows the Invisible Adversary through muddy fields and past vacant buildings to a shopping mall, then to a Big Boy restaurant, and, finally, to her own suburban home. It is a landscape littered with the debris of a burgeoning middle America, with its developing tract home subdivisions, detouring traffic, gas stations, banks, restaurants, and stores. The realistic portrayal of the landscape is infused with the sensibility of a young teenager who is so detached from her surroundings and other people that she displays an utter disregard for the consequences of her actions.

Gretchen has hours for her game of stalking on this Saturday afternoon, and her sheer plodding determination is menacing in its relentlessness. In contrast to the Invisible Adversary, who has "long spiky legs brisk as colts' legs," Gretchen "is dressed for the hunt, her solid legs crammed into old blue jeans, her big, square, strong feet jammed into white leather boots that cost her mother forty dollars not long ago, but are now scuffed and filthy with mud. Hopeless to get them clean again, Gretchen doesn't give a damn." Her face, too, is strong, yet neutral and detached. More than just teenage angst, Gretchen's impassivity seems to reflect a deeper discontent and the possibility for destruction.

As the Adversary taunts her, Gretchen follows him through a field to a new gas station that has not opened in the six months that her family has lived in the town. The new building now has broken windows, and snakelike tar has been smeared on the white wall. Cars move past her as they detour because of construction on storm sewer pipes. She remembers the Adversary, and after jumping over a concrete ditch stained with rust-colored water, she contemplates a closed bank before entering the Buckingham Mall. She always seems to notice her surroundings, especially the geometric shape of signs and the vacancy of buildings, with an aloof impartiality. She barely acknowledges the few people who enter her consciousness. Instead, she plods along, following the Adversary with quiet excitement and with a cunning, patient attitude.

Once inside the mall's drugstore, as a salesgirl's attention is diverted by another customer, Gretchen shoplifts a tube of light pink lipstick. Despite the Adversary's finger-wagging admonishment, she steals a package from a cardboard barrel without knowing or caring what it is. With the Adversary trotting ahead of her, Gretchen calmly enters another store. In the bathroom, she smears the lipstick onto the mirror and then tosses the tube, shoplifted toothpaste, toilet paper, and a cloth towel down the toilet until it clogs. Gretchen's next act of quiet destruction occurs when a boy bumps her into a trash can; she methodically spills its contents. After a ritual stop in Sampson Furniture, she enters Dodi's Boutique where she takes several dresses into a dressing room. She steps on a white wool dress, smearing mud on it, and breaks the zipper on another.

With the same methodical pursuit of the Adversary, she next enters a department store. She catches a glimpse of her mother on an escalator. Gretchen's mother does not see her, and Gretchen makes no effort to make contact with her mother. This stalking is just between the Adversary and the girl. Gretchen eats at a Big Boy restaurant while the Adversary waits outside. After eating, she follows the Adversary to the highway. She waits and then sees the Adversary dart out in front of a car. She follows the staggering and bleeding Adversary to an upper-middle-class neighborhood, giggling that he walks like a drunken man. He leads her to a large colonial house, and she is entranced at the blood spots the Adversary has left in the foyer. Her boots leave a trail of mud in her empty house; her mother must still be shopping, and her father is out of town. Gretchen settles down on the goatskin sofa to watch a rerun of a "Shotgun Steve" show. Chillingly, with the stalking game at an impasse, Gretchen decides, "If the Adversary comes crawling behind her, groaning in pain, weeping, she won't even bother to glance at him."

Themes and Meanings

Joyce Carol Oates has stated in a *Chicago Tribune Book World* article that a single dominant theme runs throughout her work: "I am concerned with only one thing: the moral and social conditions of my generation." During the course of her prolific career, Oates has often taken the ordinary conditions of day-to-day living, and, while presenting the realism of that world, she has also shown the terrifying conditions that lurk just below consciousness. Gretchen is a character who plays an imaginary stalking game, but her game with the Invisible Adversary becomes hauntingly nightmarish because of the utter lack of empathy and emotion that she feels toward others. Gretchen herself becomes almost a mechanical animal as she stalks her prey.

In Scripture, Satan is often referred to as the Adversary, which is no doubt alluded to in this story with the Adversary's taunting and influence to maliciousness. Here, the Invisible Adversary is also Gretchen's psychological projection of her own need to feel something in a gritty suburban world filled with "a jumbled, bulldozed field of mud," "no sidewalks," "gigantic concrete pipes," "geometric areas," and "artificial hills." It is not the Adversary but Gretchen who enacts the petty theft, destroys property, and leaves a trail of mud with her scuffed and expensive boots. The plodding and insistent stalking is menacing in its utter disregard for the broken trail it leaves behind. Gretchen's undefined malaise and anger are very possibly only the prelude for future and more damaging devastation, and this is what suggests the underlying terror in the story.

For Gretchen, the world is devoid of any human contact; even her mother does not see her in the department store. Gretchen's reaction to other people—if she notices them at all—is one of physical violence. In gym class, she runs heavily, sometimes bumping into other girls, even hurting them. When a boy in a group at the mall bumps into her, she does not look at them, but coldly and angrily knocks the trash can over onto the sidewalk. While many critics have commented upon the violence that is inherent in so many of Oates's stories, Oates herself does not graphically display the violent acts in her work. In "Stalking," the Adversary is hit by a car and then described as stumbling home. It is Gretchen's initial reaction to this event—the feeling of satisfaction bordering on pleasure—and her ultimate lack of compassion for the Adversary that is so chilling. The Adversary is, after all, her own creation, and her renunciation of this embodiment of her disturbed psychological state leaves her even more empty of human emotion.

Style and Technique

Although Oates has tried many techniques in various genres during her prolific career, she stated in an interview that she has "done a good deal of experimentation with very short stories—'miniature narratives,' I call them. I would like some day to assemble them into a book. They are, in a sense, 'minimalist'; in another sense a species of prose poetry." "Stalking" is barely more than eight pages long, yet the realistic depiction of the suburban wasteland—striking because of its exactness of detail and haunting familiarity—is only the façade for the disturbing psychological repercussions to this environment as they are demonstrated through the character of Gretchen.

Gretchen is an adolescent from an upper-middle-class family, yet she spends her November Saturday in a bizarre game of stalking the demon: her own *Doppelgänger*, her other self. She is a product of the American Dream, and she is also heir to the liabilities that can turn that dream into a nightmare. With her characteristic use of italicized thoughts and feelings, Oates, as always, demonstrates a great fidelity to the American condition, both as it is described realistically and as it is portrayed through those thoughts and feelings that lurk below consciousness. It is the image of the muddy boots that leave their footprints throughout the story with no sidewalks that remains: "Entranced, she follows the splashes of blood into the hall, to the stairs . . . forgets her own boots, which are muddy . . . but she doesn't feel like going back to wipe her feet. The hell with it."

Laurie Lisa

THE STAR

Author: Arthur C. Clarke (1917-)
Type of plot: Science fiction
Time of plot: Twenty-sixth century
Locale: Aboard an exploratory spacecraft
First published: 1955

Principal character:
THE NARRATOR, a Jesuit priest and astrophysicist

The Story

The unnamed narrator, a Jesuit priest, is the astrophysicist on an exploratory scientific spacecraft. He is constantly reminded of this duality by his shipmates and by the very decorations and features of his room. The Jesuit speaks throughout the story to an unnamed "you" who is often unknown, sometimes himself, at times St. Ignatius Loyola (founder of the Jesuits), and finally, God. The narrator's several brief asides show his distress over something the ship has discovered.

The ship has come to the Phoenix Nebula, the remains of a star that became a supernova, to try to reconstruct the events that led up to the catastrophe and, if possible, to learn its cause. Expecting to find only the burned star, the ship makes a much more exciting, and ultimately poignant, discovery. The last planet of the star's system survived the burning, and an artifact is sending out a beacon from its surface. Although untrained for this unexpected archaeological work, the crew enthusiastically sets out to discover what secrets and treasures have been waiting through the centuries for discovery and rescue.

A monolithic marker leads the men to the hopes of the race doomed by the supernova, a civilization that knew it was about to die and had made a last bid for immortality. The artifact contains artwork, recordings, and written works, including keys for their translation. It also contains photographs of beautiful cities and happy children playing on beaches under the then-quiet sun. Although the vanished people most likely left only their best, as the narrator acknowledges they had a right to do, their remains show the men from Earth a civilization that could reach neighboring planets, that possessed beauty and culture, but that ran out of time and was destroyed on the brink of interstellar travel, which might have allowed some of its people to survive. To add to the sorrow the men feel, the race looks humanlike, inviting even more empathy.

The men, who teased their astrophysicist on the journey to the nebula about his religious beliefs, ask him how such destruction can be reconciled with God's mercy. The Jesuit tries to accept this questioning and answer it, but cannot. He wonders if even St. Ignatius could have reconciled this situation, although he recognizes that God has no need to justify his actions to humankind. When, as the ship's astrophysicist, he makes his calculations, he finds something that severely tests his own deep faith. He calculates the date of the supernova and when its light reached the Earth.

The reason for the narrator's doubt and seeming despair becomes clear in the final line of the story. Every day stars go nova and every day races die, but this tragedy has a horrific irony for the theologian: "What was the need to give these people to the fire, that the symbol of their passing might shine above Bethlehem?"

Themes and Meanings

The issues in "The Star" relate to the concept of theodicy, which is an attempt to answer the question of the problem of evil that is summed up by three statements: God is good, God is omnipotent or omniscient, and there is evil. The last statement is the easiest to prove and is usually accepted as a given. If God is good, but not omnipotent, he wants to stop evil, but cannot. If God is omnipotent, but not good, he could stop evil, but does not choose to do so. The Judeo-Christian ethic, however, sees God as both good and omnipotent, so some other answer for the existence of evil is necessary. One theodicy is that God has no need to justify himself to humanity; that humanity's free will causes evil is another. Most religious people accept a theodicy that allows them to reconcile their faith in God with the tragic events of everyday life.

The unnamed narrator of "The Star" claims to have reached a point at which his faith is shaken. The nova's date will not be ignored by either his shipmates or his fellow scientists back on Earth, nor can he himself ignore it. He recognizes God's mystery, but can no longer accept it on faith; he has been driven to question all that he had believed.

One may speculate, however, that the Jesuit has not thoroughly lost his faith because the last lines of the story are a plea, almost a prayer, to the God he has tried to claim he no longer accepted. A test of faith may not be the same thing as a loss of faith, and the man, by clinging to his previous dependence on God, may yet save and salvage his understanding of God's mysteries. The reader is free to speculate whether or not the Jesuit—like the biblical Job who first received the answer that God did not need to justify himself—will be reconciled, or can be.

Style and Technique

Arthur C. Clarke's "The Star" won a Hugo Award for best short story of the year. First published in *Infinity Science Fiction*, it has been widely anthologized since then. Many of Clarke's stories have religious themes or elements.

"The Star" makes ample use of symbols. It opens with a description of the juxtaposition of the Jesuit's crucifix with the astrophysicist's computer. The dichotomies of the narrator's life are thus immediately apparent. The narrator's picture of St. Ignatius, the founder of the Jesuit order, which historically has been dedicated to education—bringing light—is juxtaposed with the tracings from his spectrophotometer, which measures another kind of light. The two concepts of light and enlightenment have come together. The narrator even wonders what the pictured man would have made of the pictured tracings.

Another important symbol in the work is the phoenix. The Phoenix Nebula is the supernova the ship has come to study. In mythology, the phoenix is a bird that dies and is reborn out of the ashes of its pyre. The phoenix has been used as a symbol for Jesus and for Christianity because it seems to die but, rather than remaining ashes, it rises from the dead to live again. This is the hope that Christians have for themselves and a major part of the belief they have in Jesus as the Christ. One might argue that out of the funeral pyre of this lost race came the birth of the new race of Christians on Earth, although the Jesuit narrator does not seem able to see this hopeful interpretation of the nebula's catastrophe.

One of Clarke's strengths as a writer of short fiction is his ability to write single-sentence concluding paragraphs that make the reader rethink an entire story. Clarke has used this type of surprise twist ending in other stories, notably "Rescue Party." In "The Star," this final line tells the reader that the light of this nebula was the star seen above Bethlehem, signaling the birth of Jesus. Until this moment, it is the death of this lovely race that seems to drive the priest's despair, despite the answers he seeks to prepare for the questions of others. The clash of his two positions finds a climax in the discovery that he, as an astrophysicist, makes about the date of the nebula and what he, as a priest, knows about that historical date on Earth.

Susan Jaye Dauer

STAR FOOD

Author: Ethan Canin (1960-   )
Type of plot: Psychological realism
Time of plot: Probably late twentieth century
Locale: Arcade, California
First published: 1986

Principal characters:
DADE, the eighteen-year-old narrator
HIS MOTHER
HIS FATHER
A SHOPLIFTER

The Story

Dade, the sensitive young narrator, recalls how he disappointed both of his parents for the first time the summer that he turned eighteen. Perhaps he has disappointed himself too, for throughout the story he slowly realizes that he does not know what direction his life should take. Dade has been told by his father that if he does not take his work seriously, he will end up poor. The father—who owns the grocery store of the title—is a practical man who works hard, runs a clean, thriving business, and maintains good relationships with the community. When he proposed marriage to Dade's mother, he probably saw right to the end of his life, Dade thinks. Dade works in the store and is sometimes industrious, but often he spends his time daydreaming on the store's roof. He disappoints his father by not being earnest enough about his work in the store. Instead he gazes at clouds, stars, and the sky for hours, trying to make the discovery his mother has always thought he would make. She reminds him that he will someday inherit the store, yet she encourages him to think and dream because she is sure he will someday become a person of limited fame. It is her theory that men like Leonardo da Vinci and Thomas Edison simply stared at regular objects until they saw new things.

Dade initially goes to the roof to clean the large, incandescent star that sits atop the store to advertise its presence. He sometimes stays there for hours to think about the clouds and their shapes. He has studied the names and properties of clouds and gives precise, detailed descriptions. Sometimes his father joins him on the roof. When Dade looks off the roof to the ground, he gazes west to the affluent parts of town where sparkling swimming pools may be seen among the trees and where the girls who drive their own convertibles to high school live. His father, however, forces him to look in the other direction to the neighborhoods populated by rusted old cars and men who sit on curbs all day. Dade, he says, will become one of these men if he does not take business more seriously. Yet because Dade is so young, both parents want to give him some space to find himself and his own direction.

A shoplifter forces matters to a crisis. Dade has apprehended shoplifting children on several occasions. One day, however, a middle-aged woman in a gray plaid dress walks out of the store with a cut-rate loaf of rye bread. Dade feels powerless to act under her stare. Later she steals pineapple juice. The thief somehow inspires his pity. His mother explains that he must feel sorry for her. Understanding the son's sensitive nature and reluctance, the father hires a guard. One day on the roof, Dade sees some Air Force jets in the sky. His response to them makes him feel he has seen a sign. Dade tells his dad he is ready to catch the shoplifter, and soon he does. While they are waiting for the father to come to the back room to deal with the shoplifter, Dade changes his mind and allows her to escape, as his mother had sometimes done with children before. In shame or guilt, Dade leaves too, walking with the woman for a while. They do not speak to each other. Later that night as he walks, he realizes that he has disappointed his father and his mother and that he feels alone in the world, like the shoplifter. Moreover, he still has no definite ideas about what direction his life should take.

Themes and Meanings

The primary theme of Ethan Canin's story rests in the conflict between the practical spirit that wants to accomplish concrete and worthwhile things and the tendency for creativity, insight, and romantic dreaming. These two opposing spirits are personified by Dade's businessman father and his hopeful, romantic mother. Their hopes for Dade and his future are played out on the roof and in the store. Down in the store he works hard at the checkout counter and in the stockroom, but sometimes he neglects his work, even when his father needs him, in order to gaze at stars and clouds, which are food for his thoughts. He is an extremely introspective eighteen-year-old, but his musings never seem to come to much. He has no definite goals of his own. Unlike many boys his age, he does not fantasize about cars, girls, sports, or even escaping from his town or his family. He does not think about the drudgery or rewards of running a business, nor mention any friends or pastimes.

As a thoughtful young man, he recognizes his indecisiveness. The family often goes to the movies on Friday evenings. Dade's self-awareness is reflected in his comments about the movies:

> I liked the movies because I imagined myself doing everything the heroes did—deciding to invade at daybreak, swimming half the night against the seaward current—but whenever we left the theater I was disappointed. From the front row, life seemed like a clear set of decisions, but on the street afterward, I realized that the world existed all around me and I didn't know what I wanted. The quiet of evening and the ordinariness of human voices startled me.

In an interview published in *Contemporary Authors*, Ethan Canin admits that he closely identifies with the character Dade. He thinks the tension between the romantic and practical views of the world creates a driving force that he sees in himself. It is these forces that propel Dade first one way and then the other. Finally, he realizes that he will not make the kind of discoveries his mother is hoping for, and he will also not feel the zeal for stock work and business that his father wishes he did. At one point, Dade shouts to the highway and the cars, "Tell me what I want." He waits expectantly, but no answer comes. At the story's end, he still has not decided where he thinks he should be directing his efforts. Perhaps by realizing that he cannot satisfy either of his parents and recognizing that each person is essentially alone, he has made a start in finding his own direction.

Style and Technique

The story is narrated in the first person by Dade. The style is deceptively simple, and the language is perfectly appropriate to the thoughts of a young person. Introspection and subdued emotion dominate the tone of the story. There is little conversation; much of the story consists of Dade's reflections. One of the characteristics of the story is its use of abundant detail and precise description. Canin has a wonderful sense of the particulars that make up a scene, shown when he describes the layout of the store, the produce, and the characters. Dade's description of his father illustrates the author's skill in description: "He was a short man with direct habits and an understanding of how to get along in the world, and he believed that God rewarded only two things, courtesy and hard work." The description goes on for several more sentences, but readers can get a clear picture of the father just from this one deft sentence.

Another example of Canin's style is illustrated in Dade's comparison of the sky to the sea: "When I looked closely [the sky] was a sea with waves and shifting colors, wind seams and denials of distance, and after a while I learned to look at it so that it entered my eye whole. It was blue liquid. I spent hours looking into its pale wash, looking for things, though I didn't know what." This sort of controlled extended metaphor is not unusual. Shorter lively comparisons such as "my thoughts piled into one another" and "apricot-size balls of hail" abound. This carefully crafted story employs a consistent narrative voice and vivid imagery appropriate to a sensitive, observant young man.

To symbolize the conflict between the parents' views and the son's inner thoughts as well, Canin uses the grocery store ceiling. The father invents a grid system for easy location of foods, which he paints on the ceiling. A few days later, the mother pastes up fluorescent stars among the grid squares, accurately showing constellations even though they could not be seen because of the bright store lights. It seems useless, but the idea appeals to her nevertheless.

Toni J. Morris

STEADY GOING UP

Author: Maya Angelou (1928-   )
Type of plot: Social realism
Time of plot: The late 1950's or early 1960's
Locale: A bus traveling from Memphis, Tennessee, to Cincinnati, Ohio
First published: 1972

Principal characters:

ROBERT (BUDDY), a twenty-two-year-old African American man traveling north on a bus
AN ELDERLY WOMAN, who befriends him
ABE and
SLIM, two drunken white passengers
THE BUS DRIVER

The Story

Robert, a young African American man, is having trouble sleeping on the bus taking him north, from Memphis to Ohio, as it moves through the rain. He is tired and worries about his sister, who, he has recently learned, is ill in Cincinnati.

As he dozes, preoccupied with his concern for his sister's welfare, he recalls their history together. Since his parents died when he was fifteen, he has reared his sister himself. Apprenticing at an auto repair shop trained him to become an excellent mechanic. Meanwhile he cared for his sister and supported her when she reached college age and chose to pursue a career in nursing. Robert also has a fiancée, Barbara, who has helped him see the importance of his sister's career choice and of the pride that will come to the family when Baby Sister enters the caring profession and is in a position to help those like their own parents, who died before their time.

Giving up on finding a comfortable resting position, Robert rises from his seat to move forward on the bus but stops when an elderly woman—the only other black passenger—speaks to him. Taking a maternal interest in him, the woman cautions him that two white men (later identified as Abe and Slim) who are drinking were discussing him as he slept. Following the woman's advice, Robert returns to the back of the bus rather than risk confrontation.

When the bus stops, Robert must go to the restroom, so he exits the bus, even though the drunken white men also disembark. He is in the "colored" restroom when Abe and Slim burst in and trap him. Accusing him of going north to pursue white women, they threaten him, making lewd references to his genitals. Robert acts quickly. He knees one man in the groin, seizes a bottle, and hits the other over the head with it. After disguising the blood covering the front of his shirt with a coat belonging to one of the men, he leaves the restroom and bumps into the bus driver, who is looking for his missing passengers. As Robert boards the bus, the woman waiting inside expresses her relief to see him again. The bus continues its journey to Cincinnati, leaving the secret of the missing men in the restroom.

Themes and Meanings

The major theme of "Steady Going Up" is the vulnerability of innocent black men to white violence. Maya Angelou wrote the story out of the consciousness that African American women feel toward the endangerment that black men face, suggesting what the men might do to bolster and protect their manhood. Angelou draws implicitly on a long history of white violence against black men, false accusations that black men lust after white women, and the white stereotyping of black sexuality. In having her young African American protagonist persevere and conquer the white racists who seek to harm him, she reverses the pattern of victimization inherent in decades of lynchings and racial violence.

The story is written in the African American reform tradition of uplift, with the title a version of the motto of the black women's movement, Lifting As We Climb, meaning that each individual black person's achievements and contributions help to lift the race as a whole and aid other African Americans in seizing opportunities historically denied to them.

Style and Technique

Angelou re-creates stereotypes that are emblematic of different segments of the black and white populations. Robert is a good, responsible, caring young man who has been "steady going up." Since the death of his parents he has taken responsibility for the family by learning a trade, making himself a master mechanic, and rearing his younger sister. In looking after her interests, he has assumed the role of a father figure and best friend (as Buddy, her nickname for him, connotes). He has been a kind of guardian angel for her, helping her to attend nursing school and heading north to get her when he hears that she is ill.

Robert is a fine man physically as well as a person of good moral character. His tall physique makes it hard for him to get comfortable on the cramped seats of the bus, and when the elderly woman speaks to him, he is polite and deferential to her in response. The woman, meanwhile, also represents an important social type in the black community. She is the respected elder, what sociologists have called an "other mother," in reference to women who care for all the children in their neighborhoods as if they were their own, and who look out for the welfare of young black people even if they are strangers, offering advice and wisdom. Her religious faith, part of the paradigm of the respected elder, is represented in the Bible that she has on her lap. Her warning to Robert about the white men is based on a cognizance of what can happen to young black men at the hands of white racists. The two vile white men embody white Southern lower-class male racism—what the elderly black woman terms trash coming from trash.

Angelou creates a tension that grows throughout the story between Robert's goodness (manifested in his selfless concern for his sister, his polite respect for the elderly woman, and his love for his fiancée) and the ominous presence of the two drunken white men, who eye Robert and move closer to his seat as they drink liquor while the bus travels north. This tension builds to the scene when the bus stops. The tension, which develops out of the reader's fear for Robert and the physical harm that may come to him, is heightened by the use of claustrophobic imagery. Robert's body does not fit into the seats; he cannot move to more commodious seating in the front of the bus because of the white men, so he spends much of his time cramped into a semifetal position. Even outside the confines of the bus he is trapped within the narrow and filthy walls of the "colored-only" restroom that he must use when the white men corner him. The turning point of the story, and the release of tension, comes with Robert's victory over his would-be oppressors and his success in regaining his seat on the bus with his bloody shirt undetected. Ironically, it is the segregated institutions created by whites that protect Robert because the bus driver does not think to look for the missing white men in the nonwhite restroom.

Robert's success against his attackers is more than a personal triumph. It is classic in its dimensions—a David and Goliath story, or a dragonslayer tale in which the good and common hero turns the tables and prevails over forces that seek to destroy him. It also has a political moral as a reversal of the historical pattern of white violence directed at black men. The relief in tension comes when Robert proves himself able to avert disaster, defend himself, and continue on his intended journey to Cincinnati to help his sister. His ability to free himself from the restroom and reenter the bus is by extension his ability to continue through his own volition and capabilities on the "upward" journey of his life. Robert has been steady going up: He has been steadfast and hardworking as he has matured to young adulthood, determined to make a better life for himself and his sister. He proves steady going up north, as well, handling the life-threatening incident with the white racists well. He thus symbolizes a new generation of black people in the United States, coming of age in the era when Jim Crow rules began to fall and a call for rights and dignified self-protection replaced older systems of deference toward whites and victimization of blacks at the hands of whites. Robert represents a whole generation of black men and women steadily rising up.

Barbara J. Bair

A STORY

Author: Dylan Thomas (1914-1953)
Type of plot: Social realism
Time of plot: Early twentieth century
Locale: Wales
First published: 1953

Principal characters:
THE NARRATOR, a boy on the threshhold of adolescence
MR. THOMAS, his uncle
SARAH THOMAS, his aunt
BENJAMIN FRANKLYN,
MR. WEAZLEY,
NOAH BOWEN,
ENOCH DAVIES,
WILL SENTRY, and
O. JONES, his uncle's mates

The Story

In an attempt to provide a momentary respite from the rigors of work and the limits of domesticity, a group of men in West Wales go on an annual outing. It has as its ostensible destination the town of Porthcawl, but it is actually designed to stop at every inviting public house along the way. During the course of the year, a fund is gradually accumulated sufficient to purchase twenty cases of pale ale to supplement the fare of the local pubs and to hire a sightseeing bus for transportation. The story is told from the perspective of a young boy with a poet's flair for descriptive language and a fascination with the eccentricities of the men he accompanies. Since the boy lives in relatively meager circumstances with his uncle's family in a small house adjoining their tiny shop, his range of social circumstances is limited to the intricate detail of the shop, his observations of the peculiarities of his uncle's friends, and the energetically inventive stretch of his imagination. He first hears of the event when he reads an advertisement for sheep-dip, "which was all there was to read."

Because he spends so much time with his relatives, he has created an image of them that gives them a dimension beyond the mundane facts of their lives. His uncle is described as a huge old buffalo bursting the bounds of the little house; his aunt is reduced to a tiny mouselike creature. When his uncle's friends gather to plan their yearly outing, the boy turns his enthusiasm for local mythmaking toward their individualistic turns of speech, rendering their banter as the declarations of men with a singular capability, each exhibiting a skill appreciated and encouraged by the others, and each with a local history that includes some memorable feat from past excursions. There are certain conventions that have become a part of the preparation for the trip, including a temporary tiff in which the boy's aunt, Sarah Thomas, withdraws to her mother's house for the weekend. The uncle's decision to include the boy is a change in the routine, although not without some historical precedent, greeted predictably with good-natured, characteristic complaints before the men subside into tacit acceptance and find other things about which to disagree.

The tour bus leaves the village on a beautiful August morning, making a brief return to collect old O. Jones who, typically, has missed the bus. With impeccable timing, the men arrive at the first public house just as it opens. The boy is instructed to guard the bus against thieves—a preposterous notion—and occupies himself by wistfully looking at the cows while the men carouse in the bar, feeling a familiar sense of isolation ("on the lonely road, the lost, unwanted boy, and the lake-eyed cows") that is at the root of his poetic portraiture. When the men emerge, they are already becoming garrulous and boisterous, a mode of behavior that is compounded by further stops at a series of such exotically named pubs as the Twll in the Wall, the Sour Grapes, the Shepherd's Arms, and the Bells of Aberdovey. The boy remains an observer as the procession continues; he records the men's joyous exclamations, which reveal them in the spirit of freedom that is the goal of their journey. At the close of the day, he describes them as "thirty wild, wet, pickled, splashing men," whose company he has subtly joined through active observation.

At the last stop, a stranger tries to impress everyone with spurious boasts, only to be devastatingly exposed through the rapier wit of Enoch Davies, evidence of the bountiful effects of the entire enterprise. As the bus heads home through the moonlight, the men continue their idiosyncratic behavior with hilarious persistence. Mr. Weazley demands they stop for another drink, while Jones begins to cook supper on his portable stove. Since all the pubs are closed, the party stops and Jones sets up a makeshift kitchen in a field. While he prepares a classic Welsh meal of sausage and mash, his contribution to the gathering, the men drink and sing, their dull cares banished momentarily. The wonderful mood of celebration and ease is evoked in an image of serenity as the boy recalls that he drifted to sleep, feeling safe against his uncle's large waistcoat. For a moment, separated from the obligations of their lives and wives, the company of men has come in contact with eternity.

Themes and Meanings

Dylan Thomas developed "A Story" as a presentation for Welsh television during the last year of his life. Like his well-known poem "Fern Hill," it recalls a joyous time in his youth from the perspective of his mature years. By re-creating the sensory excitement, the almost delicious loneliness, and the feeling of a cosmos of infinite possibilities waiting to be explored, Thomas reaches back to a time in his life prior to the onset of the disappointments that plagued his adult years. Whereas "Fern Hill" depends upon a vision of the natural world as a source of wonder and delight, "A Story" is closer to *Under Milk Wood* (1954), his drama about the singular characters of the small Welsh town of Laugharne, which also presents a view of the adult world from a relatively innocent observer who is astonished and highly amused by the antics and odd speech of grownups. There are a number of images of an inspiring landscape, but most of the details are designed to convey the moods of the characters and the atmosphere of the shop, bus, and pubs where the action occurs.

The narrator's introduction to the mysterious world of men is presented as a readjustment of self-perception. At first, the boy's uncle is described in terms of his daunting size and physical presence, while his aunt is depicted as a quaint mouse-figure. There is a distinct separation between the boy and his family, since they are rendered in surreal terms. The shop is less a place of commerce than a magical child's realm, with hiding places, strange creatures, and no responsibilities. The uncle's decision to include the boy on the outing is a recognition that he is on the edge of adolescence, and his gradual involvement in the company of men is presented as a part of a ritual that is rooted in ancient customs and folk traditions. The men know their roles, but have room for verbal improvisation; the sentimentality that tends to weaken *Under Milk Wood* is replaced by an acerbic wit and an eye for human foibles. The tremendous enthusiasm for drink and song that marks the narrative, however, keeps the story within the child's inclination for delight. The men themselves are liberated by everything so that they may momentarily frolic again as the boys they once were. As in a child's dream, time itself seems to stop as food, drink, wit, and friendship transform the scene to "the end of the world in the west of Wales"—a charmed landscape akin to the countryside of "Fern Hill" and "Poem in October" (1946) to which Thomas always longed to return.

Style and Technique

The love of language and the mastery of craft that inform Dylan Thomas' finest poems are the source of the stylistic strength that gives "A Story" its unique narrative voice. According to poet and critic Donald Hall, Thomas was "the maddest of word-mad young poets," and his descriptions of the locations and characters of "A Story" are developed from the same long chains of adjectives that mark this poetry. The boy's uncle, in particular, is a figure of imposing dimensions, "a steaming hulk of an uncle, his braces straining like hawsers, crammed behind the counter of the tiny shop at the front of the house, and breathing like a brass band; or guzzling and blustery in the kitchen over his gutsy supper, too big for everything except the great black boats of his boots." Like a line from "Poem in October," the continual employment of qualifying and advancing terms, words recoiling off other words, gives the story its flavor. The mind of the boy is merged with the mind of the mature writer through the use of poetic language that expresses an outlook as well as a skill.

The pleasing peculiarities of the men on the outing are presented through Thomas' deft utilization of vernacular speech, itself poetic in its qualities and features. The story is a homage to the people Thomas lived among when at home in Wales, and the rhythms of his writing may be seen as emerging from the patterns and flow of the conversations he heard in pubs and shops. The dry, laconic humor and the verbal exuberance of men speaking before an appreciative audience effectively convey the boozy amiability that Thomas treasured.

Leon Lewis

THE STORYTELLERS

Author: Fred Chappell (1936-)
Type of plot: Psychological realism
Time of plot: The 1940's
Locale: Western North Carolina
First published: 1985

Principal characters:
JESS, the narrator, a young boy
JOE ROBERT, his father
UNCLE ZENO, a master storyteller

The Story

The narrator begins by questioning whether the events he is about to recount actually occurred. Certainly, Jess says, there was an Uncle Zeno in his Appalachian childhood, but he cannot remember much about him as a person. What lingers in his memory is primarily a voice, telling stories. Uncle Zeno then takes over the narrative.

Zeno's first story concerns a great hunter, Lacey Joe Blackman, whose dearest possession is an heirloom watch; a retired farmer, Setback Williams, who now spends his time growing apples; and a bear who is protected by the park service, even though he steals Setback's apples and destroys his trees. The tale has a surprising ending. When the bear finally has to be shot, his body gets caught on a tree limb, and as it swings, Lacey times it with his prized watch and comments that it is slow. Jess's father, Joe Robert, does not understand the story, but when he asks for an explanation, Zeno simply ignores him.

Jess now describes the efforts of his father, Joe Robert, to compete with Uncle Zeno. Feverishly, Joe Robert searches for stories to tell. He looks in the books around the house for old fairy tales and legends, and he collects anecdotes from people in the community. With a fine flourish, he tries out his discoveries on the family. Joe Robert always spoils even the best stories with his own embellishments and his theatrical endings. In contrast, Zeno seems to be a mere vehicle through which stories tell themselves.

The narrative now returns to Uncle Zeno, who is reminded of Buford Rhodes and his favorite coonhound, who is so smart that he can find a coon whose skin will fit any flat surface he sees. Unfortunately, seeing the ironing board, the hound sets off on an impossible quest, and Buford has to go in search of him.

By now, Joe Robert is so frustrated over Uncle Zeno's inconclusive endings and so jealous of his skill that he cannot let his guest continue. Despite his mother-in-law's expostulations, Joe Robert leaves to find the real Buford Rhodes, in order to ask him whether Zeno's account is a true one. During his father's absence, Jess happens upon Uncle Zeno, sitting all alone, and finds that he is continuing with the story in progress, which now involves a cave and a Cherokee woman.

Late that afternoon, Jess's father returns, reporting that he has not been able to find any trace of Rhodes. Joe Robert is sure that by casting doubt on Zeno's truthfulness, he has invalidated his story of Buford and maybe all the others. As usual, he has missed the point. Unlike his father, Jess understands that the value of a story does not depend upon its being factual. Jess, however, now has a rather unsettling theory about the relationship between fact and fiction. Since Buford Rhodes has disappeared as surely as the characters in Homer's *Iliad* and *Odyssey*, Jess now suspects that any individual who appears in fiction will promptly disappear from the real world.

At the supper table, Zeno's story brings Buford home to his family, who are being supported by Elmer, now a teacher at the high school. Joe Robert has had enough. First he confronts Zeno with the news about Buford Rhodes, and then he launches angrily into the tale of a man who married a mountain girl and enjoyed entertaining her family, except for his wife's storytelling relative, who drove him crazy.

After Joe Robert leaves the table, the mother and the grandmother try to understand his rude behavior toward Uncle Zeno, who they agree is harmless. Then Uncle Zeno begins another story. This time, to Jess's dismay, the main character is his father. Recalling his theory about what fiction does to real people who are incorporated into it, Jess goes out to the porch to check on Joe Robert, who indeed admits that he feels a bit weak. When Jess says that some apple pie might help, Joe Robert gets up to go indoors. Just as Uncle Zeno's voice falls silent, Jess sees his father disappearing into the darkness.

Themes and Meanings

"The Storytellers" is one of Fred Chappell's ten short stories about Jess's childhood in North Carolina that make up the novel *I Am One of You Forever* (1985). Throughout the novel, the adult Jess tries to come to terms with his past, to deal with the question that even the dead come back to ask him: "Are you one of us?" The volume ends with Jess's affirmation, which is the title of the book.

This affirmation is much more than just an assurance that Jess will always remember the place and the people who made him what he is. One could do that while still maintaining a comfortable emotional distance. What Jess means is that he has become incorporated into the life of his people, so that there is now no distinction between the subject and the object: They are one. In "The Storytellers," Chappell suggests that such a mystical surrender of the self is essential if one is to deal effectively with personal memories or, through the creative imagination, to produce a work of art.

Thus the two storytellers of Chappell's own story can be seen as symbols of the right way and the wrong way to approach both art and life. Jess's father is not a bad man; he has a good heart and an abundance of charm. Nevertheless, the same lack of self-discipline that sends him off to fish when he needs to work the farm, and impels him to play practical jokes without contemplating the consequences, also makes it impossible for him to become an artist. He cannot give himself to his story. When he recounts Homer's *Iliad*, Joe Robert adds props, such as the photograph of the film actress Betty Grable, whom he casts as the legendary beauty Helen of Troy; he interpolates his own comments on the action; and he concludes with a wild chase, with a sofa pillow used as the body of Hector. None of this is in the spirit of the original; all of it seems to be just an opportunity for Joe Robert to show off, like a schoolboy.

In contrast, Uncle Zeno acts as a medium through which his stories tell themselves. The fact that his art controls him, instead of the reverse, is evident in the way he starts and stops talking, without regard to the needs of his listeners, and even, as Jess discovers, without any listeners at all. The secret of Uncle Zeno's power, as well as of his serenity, is his capacity for surrender to a higher power. At the end of the story, the young Jess sees that his father will never understand the lesson to be learned from Uncle Zeno; however, in the way he stands aside to let "The Storytellers" be told by his narrators, the adult Jess shows that he is living by Uncle Zeno's rules.

Style and Technique

Like the other stories in *I Am One of You Forever*, "The Storytellers" is firmly rooted in a literary tradition that pervades Southern literature, that of the Old Southwest humorists, who set their stories in the frontier settlements of Alabama, Georgia, Mississippi, and Tennessee. Their humor, which often involved accounts of coarse practical jokes, and their tall tales, based on folklore and merging into myth and fantasy, influenced writers from Mark Twain, the author of *Huckleberry Finn* (1884), to William Faulkner.

Uncle Zeno's final story refers to a practical joke, described in detail in "The Good Time," which involved substituting pullet eggs for the fillings in some fine chocolates that Annie Barbara Sorrells would naturally bring out on the next social occasion. Such anecdotes, showing a triumph of crude nature over what pioneers saw as pretentious and artificial gentility, are typical of the Old Southwest humorists. Like them, the author of "The Storytellers" also delights in tall tales, such as Uncle Zeno's accounts of the clocklike bear and the analytical dog.

It is just a step from such comic exaggerations to more serious fantasy, and here Chappell's technique most clearly reflects his theme. In Jess's confusion about Uncle Zeno's actual visits, in his final description of his father's disappearance, and even in Zeno's unstructured stories themselves, there is more mystery than certainty in "The Storytellers." Thus Chappell illustrates his belief that, as the true artist knows, there is no real distinction between the seen and the unseen, the world of fact and the world of fiction.

Rosemary M. Canfield Reisman

A SUDDEN TRIP HOME IN THE SPRING

Author: Alice Walker (1944-)
Type of plot: Psychological realism
Time of plot: Late twentieth century
Locale: New York and Georgia
First published: 1971

Principal character:
SARAH DAVIS, one of two African American students attending a prestigious women's college in New York

The Story

An external narrator presents a few days in the life of Sarah Davis, a popular college student, one of the only two black students at a prestigious women's college in New York. Sarah faces many conflicts, both external and internal. Her environment is perfect for her in some ways, but also troubling. She is studying art at a college with the best teachers, yet she has difficulty with her art because there are few models for the black faces she wants to draw. She particularly feels unable to draw black males, because she cannot bear to trace defeat on her blank pages. Although she is popular with the other students, they do not understand her or her culture and unknowingly patronize her. One day, Sarah receives a telegram telling of her father's death and has to make a sudden trip home to Georgia to attend her father's funeral. Her father's death precipitates another conflict: Sarah begins to wonder about a child's duty to her parents after they have died. As she packs for her trip home, she talks to a suitemate about the difficulties that the black novelist Richard Wright had with his father.

Sarah's old bedroom at home now houses her father's body. As she looks at her father lying in his casket, Sarah reflects on her feelings about him and her mother. She blames him for her mother's death; her mother died in her sleep, seemingly from exhaustion from the difficult life that she led. Sarah views her father as the weak parent, the one not able to care properly for the family. Yet as she looks into her father's face and tries to find there the answer to her question of what a child owes to her dead parents, she begins to realize that perhaps her views are faulty. She begins to doubt if she is taking the correct route in her life by attending a college in the north.

While home, Sarah spends time with her grandmother, grandfather, and older brother. Her genuine interest in art and education becomes clear as she gently deflects her grandmother from looking too soon for a great-grandchild. Her interaction with her grandfather begins the resolution of Sarah's conflicts. Watching the strength in her grandfather's dignified face as he stands at his son's grave, Sarah wonders why it never occurred to her to paint his face. She promises her grandfather to make such a portrait, but he asks instead to be done "up in stone." Talking with her older brother furthers the resolution of Sarah's conflicts. He assures her that her interest in art is a worthy pursuit, and that once she learns to draw his face and sculpt her grandfather's, she can return to the South or go anywhere she wants. With the knowledge that her grandmother is looking to her to continue the generations and that her grandfather and brother have faith in her ability to fulfill her artistic dreams, Sarah returns to college. When a student who does not know the reason for Sarah's trip south asks her how her trip home was, Sarah responds that it was fine.

Themes and Meanings

"A Sudden Trip Home in the Spring" is an initiation story about a young woman coming to terms with adulthood, both by resolving the conflicted feelings she has about her father and by becoming more confident about her own artistic endeavors and life. The story implies that by coming to terms with her own inner struggles, she will be better able to deal with the external difficulty of living in an atmosphere in which her heritage is not valued or even understood. Sarah's internal and external struggles are connected: She doubts her father's strength because of the way he was treated by his white employers; envisioning her father as a weak man, she feels unable to portray strong men in her art; once she recognizes the strength in the males of her family, her artistry is released and her connection with her own culture becomes healthier, making her more able to deal with external obstacles. Although the story is cyclical, in that it begins and ends with Sarah at the northern college, it is cyclical geographically, not psychologically. The doubts and questions Sarah has at the beginning are resolved by the end. She is back at the college to master her creative abilities, but she is now more confident about the direction of her life. Sarah identifies her life with that of the black novelist Richard Wright, an important novelist to her, yet one that the other women at Cresselton do not know; in Sarah's mind, they are identified more by the world of the writer F. Scott Fitzgerald, whose novel *The Great Gatsby* (1925) presents the lives of the leisured rich.

Style and Technique

Alice Walker clearly focuses on Sarah in "A Sudden Trip Home in the Spring." Although Sarah's family members are important in helping her come to a healthy acceptance of her heritage and a confidence in her own artistic abilities, Walker keeps the grandmother, brother, and grandfather in minor roles, in part by not giving them names.

Twice in the story, Walker refers to a rat that Sarah must stare down. The first reference to the rat is when Sarah is alone in her bedroom with her father's body lying in the casket. She calls to her brother that there is a rat under the casket, but her brother does not hear anything, leaving Sarah alone to deal with it. The rat here is both literal and symbolic. Sarah stares straight at it until it finally runs away, but her thoughts just before she notices the rat are also important. As her father lies dead, Sarah is also forced to face the unpleasant feelings she harbors about him and their somewhat estranged relationship. After her mother's death, Sarah avoided her father as much as she could, spending much of her time in her own room. Thinking now about how Richard Wright came to terms with a father who betrayed him, Sarah wonders whether unresolved feelings about her own father may keep her from achieving a healthy connection with her own roots and with herself. As an adult, understanding the hardships her father endured working as a farmhand for white farmers, Sarah begins to see that what she felt was her father's weakness may have actually been a strength. By this point in her life, Sarah herself has been placed in uncomfortable and humiliating circumstances by her white friends at college. Her father endured humiliations and hardships in order to keep the family together so that her generation could prosper; his and her mother's difficult life brought forth a daughter who received a scholarship to attend a first-rate college. Sarah does not now see her father as a perfect man, but she begins to question her youthful assumptions about his weakness and what she saw as a lack of love for her mother. She recognizes now that he understood love much better than she did.

At the story's end, Walker again writes of the rat. A collegemate, who does not know the reason for Sarah's journey home, asks how her trip was. Sarah knows she is back in a world that has no comprehension of her own; she is back in an environment peopled by young women whose hair blows freely in the wind as they travel to the tennis courts and back. Sarah now is able to accept that world and yet hold tight to her own: "Stare the rat down, thought Sarah; and whether it disappears or not, I am a woman in the world. I have buried my father, and shall soon know how to make my grandpa up in stone." Just as Sarah stares down the literal rat, she learns to accept both the strengths and the flaws of her father's life and to tolerate the superficial view her college acquaintances have about her own life.

Marion Boyle Petrillo

SUICIDES

Author: Cesare Pavese (1908-1950)
Type of plot: Psychological realism
Time of plot: 1938
Locale: Turin, Italy
First published: "Suicidi," 1953 (English translation, 1964)

Principal characters:
THE NARRATOR, a civil servant
CARLOTTA, his deceased lover
JEAN, a boyhood friend

The Story

As the narrator sits at a café watching people pass, he falls into a guilt-stricken sense of loneliness. A solitary, brooding character quick to revert to memories of the past, he has suffered for years from delusions and remorse, but now he merely wishes to maintain his self-control and observe as life goes on all around him. This is one of the simple pleasures of his life, although at times it leaves bitter aftertastes. He wishes he were more astute or clever as, for example, women are in justifying their actions even to themselves.

On this particular morning, the narrator is amused by two café customers who are playing a trick on the young woman at the cash register. He is suddenly reminded of his own stupidity in certain situations and that when he reacts against other people, it is usually in a cruel fashion. These thoughts recall memories of Carlotta.

It has been a year since Carlotta died, but the narrator is constantly reminded of her. Carlotta was a simple person who worked as a cashier and lived in a little two-room apartment. He went to her house one evening, made love to her, told her he wished to be alone afterward, and went away for three days. On his return, he treated her coldly and spoke to her very little. When he first met Carlotta, he had just been humiliated by another woman, a bitter blow that had almost driven him to suicide. He understood that he was taking his revenge for one woman's cruel and unjust treatment on another woman, but continued to see Carlotta and leave her in the evenings after indulging his passion. He liked to walk the deserted streets at night; they reminded him of his youth, and allowed him to feel the resentment he harbored against women at its fullest. He thought that Carlotta was naïve and, since she was separated from her husband, merely turned to him for some comfort.

One evening, however, they went to the cinema together, they stopped for a drink at a café, and the narrator ended up spending the entire night with Carlotta. This intimacy made him feel tender toward her, but soon he reproached himself for this. It made him furious to see Carlotta looking blissful and content, since the woman he really loved never showed such happiness to him. On such occasions, he would walk in the cool morning air and promise himself to be firmer and harsher. On his return, he would tell her that their relationship was strictly physical and that she would never be a part of his life. Often, he would try to avoid Carlotta, and when they did get together he would be cold and distant. Although this made her think of leaving him, she lacked the courage to do so.

Some evenings the narrator talked and talked to Carlotta to the point that he forgot his bitterness and became like a boy again. On these occasions, Carlotta served as an audience and he would offer his opinions on love ("To enjoy love to the full, it must also be a betrayal") and youth ("We fell nobly in love with an actress or a girlfriend and devoted all our finest thoughts to her"). One evening, he tells Carlotta about a boyhood friend, Jean, who committed suicide.

Jean and the narrator loved the same girl, and they often talked together about love and death. Because they were both unhappy youths, the narrator suggested that they kill themselves. They had a revolver, which they took to the hillside to fire one winter day. In a deserted lane, Jean put the revolver into his mouth. The gun went off and killed him.

As the affair with Carlotta dragged on, the narrator became more sullen and cruel. He told Carlotta to go with anyone she wished as long as she does not catch a venereal disease. When she told him that her husband came to see her, he responded that she should try to get him back. After that, they saw each other sparingly at the café or talked briefly on the phone, until one evening when he visited her at her apartment. When he left her, they both knew that it was final. For weeks the narrator waited for a telephone call from Carlotta, but it never came. One day he went to the café where Carlotta worked and noticed that there was another woman at the cash register. He went to her apartment and learned from the concierge that a month earlier they had found her dead in bed, with the gas turned on.

Themes and Meanings

Cesare Pavese was obsessed with the idea of suicide, a recurring theme in his works. When he was still in school, a close friend of his killed himself with a revolver in the manner described in "Suicides." At his funeral, Pavese, wild with grief, was prevented at the last moment from following his friend's example. The subject was constantly in his thoughts, as many entries in his personal diary attest. The protagonist in "Suicides" is, in effect, a neutral version of Pavese himself.

Pavese's work expresses with painful clarity the crises and despair of modern man. A major theme in all of his works is that of solitude or alienation. Pavese wrote in his diary that the "greatest misfortune is loneliness. The whole problem of life, then, is how to break out of one's own loneliness, how to communicate with others." The protagonist in "Suicides" is continuously seeking to be alone with his innermost thoughts. His efforts at integrating into the city fail, and the only comfort he derives from it is to wander its deserted streets or to gaze unseen at its inhabitants. With Carlotta, the protagonist jealously preserves his privacy and attempts at all costs not to strive for any kind of human bond, since he knows that this is impossible with the human condition.

Love also becomes a marginal aspect of man's solitude. When Pavese was at the university, he fell in love with a woman with whom he had an affair that lasted five years. In 1935, he was arrested for alleged anti-Fascist activities and spent ten months in exile. Upon his return, the woman he loved abruptly left him and married another man. A hatred for women as deceitful, self-centered, and treacherous subsequently appears in almost all of his works. He portrays women savagely and with a certain degree of violence. In "Suicides," his brooding spirit of revenge against women reaches its extreme limit when the protagonist not only makes Carlotta suffer but suggests to her the idea of suicide by telling her how his young friend had killed himself. Love is not a solution, and the narrator in "Suicides" reproaches himself for even a kind thought or tender moment shared with Carlotta.

Style and Technique

"The style of the twentieth century expresses but does not explain. It is a never-ending revelation of inner life, manifesting it in moments when the subject of the story is the link between reality and imagination." These words from Pavese's diary hold the key to the author's style in "Suicides." It is objective, rather than descriptive or moralistic, in nature. The narrator's views on love and Carlotta as a symbol of all women are seen through his actions, which reflect his inner thoughts. It is his actions, the solitary walks or the cruel words to Carlotta, that reveal his pessimistic ideas on the human condition.

The manner in which the protagonist treats Carlotta also reflects the author's opinion of the impossibility of communication, of any sincere human relationship. Pavese does not treat the problem of the inability to communicate from a philosophical point of view; he describes what he sees around him, in the atmosphere and social surroundings. Thus the introspective nature of the narrator in "Suicides," his lack of participation in the life of others, conveys a basic division between self and the world, between individual and society. This expresses in painful clarity the crises and despair of modern man.

Victor A. Santi

THE SUITOR

Author: Larry Woiwode (1941-)
Type of plot: Domestic realism
Time of plot: 1939
Locale: North Dakota
First published: 1969

Principal characters:
MARTIN NEUMILLER, a young Catholic man
ALPHA JONES, his intended bride
CHARLES NEUMILLER, his father
ED JONES, Alpha's father

The Story

The Neumiller and Jones families live on neighboring farms in rural North Dakota. Martin Neumiller, in love with Alpha Jones, visits her parents' home on New Year's Eve to propose marriage. A fierce winter storm kicks up, the wind howls, the temperature drops below zero, and snow piles up to the axle hubs on Martin's Model A Ford. Alpha Jones accepts her suitor's proposal, but Martin is still uneasy about what her parents think of him. Because of the bad weather, Alpha's mother reluctantly agrees to let Martin sleep overnight on the sofa. Martin's anxiety over Alpha's parents confuses him, causing him to doubt whether Alpha has actually accepted his marriage offer. As he drops off, he thinks about what has happened that day and during all the time he has known Alpha.

Martin says prayers before going to sleep: Hail Marys, a decade of the rosary, the Our Father, and an Act of Contrition. The Neumillers are a devout Roman Catholic family—which may explain why Martin's and Alpha's parents have never been in each others' houses although they live only five miles apart. Martin's mother thinks Alpha's father, Ed, is a devil and an insane atheist. Martin's parents have often seen Ed Jones walking along the railroad tracks into town, his gray hair wildly flying in the wind and his eyes full of devious animal energy as he sings obscene songs and disrupts the quiet countryside. Charles Neumiller, Martin's father, has intercepted Ed when his wife has asked him to do something.

Ed walks into town because he does not have a car and does not want to wear out his horses just so he can go out and get drunk. Ed has told Charles that getting drunk is his only release; Ed says he is killing himself trying to rid his farm of the quack grass that is choking the wheat crop. He has tried cutting, burning, and digging, but nothing seems to help. Ed feels he was taken after buying the old Hollingsworth farm and discovering its poor soil. The farm has been put under the plow for only ten years and needs more work to make it productive. Drinking is Ed's way of running away from his problems on the farm—the impending loss of his daughter, a difficult relationship with his wife, the lack of sons to help him, and his inability to fight quack grass. After hearing this, Charles tells his family nothing is wrong with Ed Jones.

Martin's mother disagrees and tells Charles and Martin to stay away from Ed because they will be judged by the company they keep.

Alpha's mother was raised in the Missouri Synod Lutheran Church, known for its strict observance of ritual. She believes that every Catholic is up to no good. Ed Jones seems outwardly nonreligious and more open to Martin's courtship of Alpha. Ed claps Martin on the shoulder during his visits and calls him "boy." Outside the house, Ed discusses politics, government, horses, and his low opinion of mechanized farming. Ed thinks horses can do all farmwork and is proud of his team; he even worries over the condition of the barn where the horses sleep. Inside the Joneses' home, however, Ed is taciturn and silent.

Ed once caught Alpha and Martin kissing in Martin's car. Ed threw pebbles at the windshield but said nothing to Alpha's mother about the incident.

Ed echoed his wife's anti-Catholic feelings once as Martin listened in the next room. Ed may have been getting drunk with one of his friends when he yelled that Catholics were sanctimonious and hypocritical. Ed has warned Alpha against marriage to a Catholic, because the union would create many children. Alpha has told Martin that her father's angry remarks do not mean anything.

When Martin wakes up the morning after the storm, Ed is stomping around the house; he has been awake since 4 A.M. fixing a rattling windmill and sheltering the livestock. Ed wakes Martin up so he can help him pull his car out of a snowdrift. Ed irritates Martin because he turns Martin out before he has a chance to say good-bye to Alpha and confirm her acceptance of his proposal. Ed protests that Martin moves too slowly and the day is getting on.

Martin dresses and goes outside with Ed. It is still nearly dark, despite Ed's frenzied call to arms. Martin's fingertip becomes frozen to a metal buckle on his overshoes as he tries to put them on, further angering him. Martin decides now is the time to speak to Ed about his desire to marry Alpha.

Ed stops Martin short, saying he already knows about Martin's plans to marry. Alpha stayed up all night because of her excitement and told her family. The reason Ed has roused Martin so early, which was not obvious to the suitor, was to get Martin to church on time. Ed assures Martin that their marriage will work out, despite the two families' differences. Ironically, it is Ed, not his churchgoing wife, who remembers it is the Sabbath. The story ends with the apparently atheistic, possibly alcoholic father asking the pious Martin, "Do you think I might be Christian?"

Themes and Meanings

The story of the young man who falls in love with a young woman and asks her antagonistic father for her hand in marriage is universal in appeal. One theme is how love transcends family differences in its patience, kindness, and strength. The background of the family discord between the Neumillers and Joneses presents another thematic issue: a confident, educated, successful, faithful Roman Catholic family confronts a suffering, semitransient, regressive Protestant family. "The Suitor" echoes William Shakespeare's star-crossed lovers in *Romeo and Juliet* (c. 1596) and even the legend of Tristan and Isolde; each of these stories concerns young people who must reconcile cultural differences in order to love each other.

Yet the enigmatic Ed Jones, not the lovers, stands as the emotional and thematic center of "The Suitor." He represents the guardian of old ways (symbolized by traditional farming) and the keeper of the treasure (Alpha), but suffers from personal difficulties with drinking and trying to support his family. Despite his problems, Ed attempts to celebrate life in his drinking and singing, evading his problems on the wings of a different type of love—narcissism.

"The Suitor" explores the spiritual potential of the half-beaten Ed Jones. Darkness and light are mixed in equal proportions in him, making his a dynamic, complex personality. Ed's love of animals, his pride in his horses, and his painful battle with weeds place him close to nature. Although Ed is partially defeated, he lives life to its fullest and enjoys harassing the youthful Martin Neumiller. Ed's proper role is resistance to the kind of change Martin represents: education, business, machinery, and marriage. Metaphorically, Ed guards his fortress by protecting the things dearest to him, but his complexity allows him to transcend his own limitations.

Ed resents the dogmatic religion of both his wife and Martin's family. "The Suitor" suggests the possibility that this rebellious and unpredictable character is, in fact, the most genuinely spiritual. This is proven by his "offices," such as care for animals, and his observance of Sunday despite the storm and Martin's apathy. Ed accepts Martin as a surrogate son and receiver of his daughter, despite the fact the Neumillers have rejected him. Martin's mother is judgmental of Ed's behavior, while Ed suspends his biases in favor of giving his blessings to the marriage of Martin and Alpha. Ed thus shows the true path of unconditional love.

Style and Technique

To understand "The Suitor" fully, one must study the mythology of the Neumiller family in other stories. Larry Woiwode's stories create a system of family history and a complex web of relationships among people spanning several generations.

"The Suitor" is traditional and realistic in style, based largely on the author's autobiographical memories. The character of Martin Neumiller is modeled after Larry Woiwode's father. Critics have written that in his stories and novels, Woiwode revives a neglected literary form—the family album. Many of Woiwode's stories describe the plight of the Neumillers living in North Dakota, their German ancestors who emigrated to the United States, and the life of their children as they move on to various professions in Illinois and New York.

Woiwode uses rich description, limited dialogue, and an omniscient narrator in "The Suitor." The word choice is clean and especially beautiful and poetic when Martin reflects on his feelings toward Alpha. The story uses nonchronological organization, freely moving from the present to Martin's memories about what his family knows about the Jones family.

Jonathan L. Thorndike

SUMMER LEAGUE

Author: Danny Romero
Type of plot: Realism
Time of plot: The 1960's
Locale: Southern California
First published: 1989

Principal characters:
MICHAEL, an eight-year-old Chicano boy
ANTONIO and
PAUL, his friends
MR. GARCIA, his softball coach

The Story

Three young Chicano friends meet at a baseball field on the first Saturday after school closes for the summer. Although Antonio and Paul decide to sign up for a summer softball league, Michael hesitates to commit himself. When he gets home, it becomes clear that his reluctance to sign up is due solely to the fact that his family can ill afford the two dollars that joining the team will cost. Michael's mother cannot buy him a glove, but he is permitted to join the team.

When practice begins two days later, Michael and Antonio show up but discover that Paul has gone to Tijuana. The boys are placed on two different teams, with Michael being coached by Mr. Garcia, a dark, sweating man with a strong accent, bloodshot eyes, and a silver front tooth. On the first day of practice, the boys play no ball at all, but instead do jumping jacks and run laps. As the summer wears on, Michael plays mainly in the outfield, where there is little action, and he gets only one or two hits during the whole season. After Michael plays Antonio's team, he goes to Antonio's house for lunch, and the boys talk about who is the best pitcher in the major leagues. They also talk about who would win if the two of them had a fight and then playfully wrestle.

Just before the season ends, Michael's mother takes him to a sporting goods store and buys him an inexpensive glove, which he wears during the last game of the season. Because the pitcher on Michael's team walks ten batters in a row, Michael has nothing to do in the outfield. His team loses by a score of 23-0, with the game being called after the third inning. Michael decides not to attend the awards ceremony the following week, but thinks that maybe he will play again next season.

The story ends as Michael looks at his new glove and reads the name of some left-handed ballplayer that no one would recognize—"much like himself," he thinks.

Themes and Meanings

Danny Romero's brief story of a boy playing in a summer softball league seems simple and straightforward. It is about a young Chicano who spends an uneventful summer playing softball on a Little League-type team. However, it is precisely this lack of significant events that defines the boy and his summer. In fact, it hardly seems a story at all, more like a realistic slice of life with little or no thematic importance. What gives the story its significance is just the feeling of insignificance that Michael feels.

Romero chooses the summer sport of softball—a variation of baseball—purposely, for baseball, more than any other sport, takes on almost mythic significance as the great American pastime. As such novels as Bernard Malamud's *The Natural* (1952) and W. P. Kinsella's *Shoeless Joe Comes to Iowa* (1983; adapted into the film *Field of Dreams* in 1984) demonstrate, there is a heroic potential, typically American, about the "boys of summer" that does not characterize football or basketball. The fact that a young Chicano wants to play the game so he can feel like "big stuff" is thus ironic, for it signifies the immigrant's efforts to carve out an identity for himself by means of his adopted culture's icons and conventions.

The ultimate failure of the game to provide a sense of importance and identity for Michael is emphasized throughout the story. It begins with his sister's teasing him for being in the "tiny league" and yet acting as if he were so "big." It continues when Michael gets Mr. Garcia as his coach, a stereotype of the unkempt Chicano who wears baggy pants and drinks too much beer. There is no indication in the story that Michael has a father, for it is only his mother who attends to his needs; his coach certainly does not provide a strong male image for him. Indeed, Garcia seems more interested in selling firecrackers to the boys for the Fourth of July celebration—another allusion to ironic images of heroism in a story about Mexican immigrants, for the framers of the Declaration of Independence are not Michael's own forefathers. The fact that Michael may be missing a father image to emulate is also suggested by how pleased he is at the attention that Antonio's father pays to him when he goes to his friend's home for lunch. This lack of a father is an important thematic element in this story that centers on a sport in which a father and son playing "catch" is a conventional stereotype.

The image of Michael stranded in the outfield, having to tear off his borrowed right-hander's glove so he can throw the ball with his left hand during the few moments that it comes his way symbolizes the failure of the game to fulfill Michael's needs. It is a further irony that only one game remains in the season when his mother, who knows little about the game, finally takes him to the Big Five Sporting Goods store (another reference to the "big stuff"/"tiny league" dichotomy introduced early in the story) to buy him a glove.

The failure of the game to meet Michael's needs to have a father/hero figure and to feel important is finally emphasized at the conclusion of the story, when Michael tries to read the name of the left-handed pitcher in the center of his glove and realizes that the name is one that no one would recognize, "much like himself." However, in spite of this realization, the story ends on a note of hope with Michael thinking that he will return for the summer league next season.

Style and Technique

While the theme of "Summer League" focuses on the loneliness and lack of identity of a young Chicano immigrant seeking importance by means of the great American mythic sport of baseball (Romero uses softball because it is a diminutive of hardball, just as Tiny League is even smaller than Little League), the subtle way in which Romero communicates the thematic significance of this seemingly insignificant story places it within the modern short-story tradition of lyrical realism.

In the tradition of Anton Chekhov, the great late nineteenth century Russian short-story writer, Danny Romero knows that it is better to say too little than too much. "Summer League" is written in an economical and straightforward narrative style, with no exposition, explanation, or commentary. What readers know about Michael's situation, they infer from the apparently realistic details of the story. They guess that Michael has no father because no father is ever introduced and because Michael goes to his mother for what he needs. They know that his search for a heroic father figure in the league meets with failure because Mr. Gomez, who should provide an image of the surrogate father as coach, is merely a stereotype of a sloven drunk.

Other details in the story subtly suggest the strife and tentativeness of Michael's life as an immigrant. A brief scene in which a group of black children taunt a Latino snack truck vendor by calling him a "honky-ass" and the vendor responds by calling the children "jungle bunnies" establishes the ethnic isolation and conflict that serves as a backdrop for the story. The simple fact that the friend Paul cannot play ball because he has abruptly left for Tijuana suggests that he and his family may have been deported by immigrant officials.

Perhaps the most poignant scene in the story occurs when Michael goes to eat lunch at his friend Antonio's house in Antonio's father's new car. As Michael goes to the bathroom, he looks at the pictures on the hallway wall of Antonio and his family—who are all smiles at the beach, at Disneyland, at the circus, and in the mountain snow. When Antonio's father pats Michael on the shoulder and tells him that he has real heart, Michael almost burns his tongue on his soup. The fact that Michael is acutely aware of his lack of a father to make his family whole is finally suggested at the conclusion by Mr. Garcia's asking the boys to attend the awards banquet on Tuesday night and to "be sure to bring your family." As Michael turns to head for home, he knows that he will not show up on Tuesday night.

Danny Romero is not only keenly aware of the sense of isolation of the young Chicano in the United States, he is also skillful in using an economical writing technique that communicates what Frank O'Connor once called "the lonely voice" of the short-story form.

Charles E. May

A SUMMER TRAGEDY

Author: Arna Bontemps (1902-1973)
Type of plot: Domestic realism
Time of plot: c. 1930
Locale: Mississippi River Delta
First published: 1933

Principal characters:
JEFF PATTON, an elderly, black sharecropper
JENNIE, his elderly, blind wife

The Story

Jeff Patton has farmed the same acres on Greenbriar Plantation for forty-five years. He loves the land, but life has been physically demanding and the shares system has kept him locked in poverty. A recent stroke has left him lame, and he fears that another will make him a helpless burden on his wife, Jennie, who has been blind for years and is now frail. Both are sound of mind, but their life has been reduced to a series of losses, including the deaths of five adult children in the last two years. They share a state of constant grief and anxiety.

Jeff struggles to don the moth-eaten formal attire that he wears only on rare occasions, such as weddings. He feels excitement and fear as he and Jennie prepare for a trip. A short time later, driving through the countryside with Jennie in their old Model T Ford, Jeff feels a familiar thrill, as he surveys the vitality of the crops and natural vegetation. He feels again the determination and pride that always have accompanied his sense of his mental and physical strengths, required for survival on the land, but if he takes his hands from the steering wheel, they shake violently.

Jennie has repeatedly prompted Jeff to make this trip, relying on his courage to match her belief in the rightness of their decision. As they near their destination, however, she becomes wracked by grief at the thought of leaving everything behind. Crying like a child, she questions whether they should continue. Jeff is tortured by his knowledge of what they are about to do and would like to turn back, but he assures his wife that they must be strong. He knows that they have fully considered their fate, and that more reflection would merely lead to the same, inevitable conclusion. They both know that life has become intolerable, and would only get worse. After they regain their resolve and composure, Jeff drives the car into the deep water of the Mississippi.

Themes and Meanings

The story's title words, "summer" and "tragedy," suggest its theme: the shock of recognition that the cyclical fullness of life inevitably depletes the lives of individuals, calling into question the significance and nobility of human existence.

Historically, the concept of tragedy has implied that human life is very valuable, and that suffering, especially when it results inevitably from the pursuit of happiness, reveals that human life is richly meaningful. The combination of positive and negative connotations in the title hints at the potential for such irony. The author generalizes the truth of his perception by illustrating it with an instance from the common lives of simple people, even persons whose fated suffering would typically be ignored. The universality of what his characters face makes the story broadly applicable, and the way they face their fate demonstrates the possibility of heroic action, even by ordinary people.

The suffering experienced by the characters is easily recognizable by readers as something that could happen to them or someone dear to them. The author gains the reader's sympathy and even admiration for the tragic protagonist, Jeff Patton, by showing his affectionate goodwill, ability and dedication, mental strength, moral innocence, goodness of purpose throughout his adult life and in his final action, and pain and courageous struggle. Given his world of natural and societal forces that require strengths that those same forces limit and finally take away, Jeff's purposes—to provide happiness for his family and prevent further suffering by his wife—are likely to be interpreted by readers as reasonable, understandable, and courageous. His tragic decisions to kill his wife and himself, and then in fact driving into the river, challenge the reader to understand these characters' thoughts, place a value on their lives, and finally make a moral judgment regarding suicide, particularly a suicide and murder that might be interpreted as euthanasia.

Both Jeff and Jennie are grieving over the loss of their own children, the difficulty that daily life poses for persons who are infirm and are becoming a burden on others, the casting off of what good they yet find in their present life, the realization that they do not have the potential of an enjoyable future, and the prospect of death of their beloved partners and themselves, within the hour. Jeff's suffering is especially significant, because ultimately he must make the decision, exercise the will, and accomplish the action that brings about his own death and his beloved's.

The African American heritage of these characters, in a racist locale, is important within the context of the principle that labor and life are cheap. Slaves, and then sharecroppers, like mules, have provided inexpensive labor, and therefore have been considered expendable. This story, however, suggests that its characters share with readers, of whatever ancestry, a common human reality of fatal suffering. It elevates the psychological and moral status of its characters by showing them taking ultimate control of their lives through difficult and decisive action. While the author leaves it for the reader to judge whether his characters' actions are wise, their thoughts and feelings serve as an enlightening model of what readers might observe or experience under a similar crisis of age and health.

Style and Technique

In simple and straightforward language, such as his characters would use in their thought and conversation, Arna Bontemps tells a deceptively unassuming story about the last day in the life of an elderly couple. Only the literary and quasi-philosophical word "tragedy" in the title signals an alert reader that something portentous might be coming. That word places the story's protagonist in the company of characters such as Aeschylus' Agamemnon, William Shakespeare's King Lear, and Arthur Miller's Willy Loman, men who in old age take fatal action with more or less awareness of what they are doing, and more or less wisdom about the inevitability of human suffering.

Within his first few sentences, however, Bontemps cues the reader not only to his characters' age and health, but also to their social status, more like a Loman than like a king or conquering general. With a few early details and images, the author foreshadows their impending deaths: Jeff Patton is turning away from vanities, his coat is moth-eaten, his mouth twists "into a hideous toothless grimace" like a skull, his wife's voice comes like an echo, and she has a "wasted, dead-leaf appearance." Conversation, like life for this couple, is sparse, and therefore dialogue is used sparingly in the telling of their story, but when it comes, with a touch of the African American dialect of the Delta, the reader hears the direct, plain emotions of affection and fear that permeate the characterization and plot. The way the author establishes the decline and impending loss of life, paralleling the understated, ironic nobility of his characters, evokes the reader's sympathy and acquiescence in a violent death.

Simplicity of language and detail also creates an unpretentious, realist style of storytelling that makes the reader feel like a neighbor watching this couple pass by. There is nothing unusual or unnatural in the setting; the world is presented just as the Pattons would see it. When Jeff's or Jennie's emotions are revealed, they seem normal to the situation. Their thoughts then seem appropriate to both the situation and emotions; and the story's line of action follows convincingly from the characters' inner motivation.

There is also a touch of naturalism in the style, as the characters are so driven by the socioeconomic system and the effects of time that the fate of such simple lives might appear to be determined by external forces beyond their control. On the other hand, the author deftly uses mythic motifs of cyclical vitality; the eros of the vegetation of the countryside and of Jeff's love of the land, his wife, and life itself; the journey that the Pattons are taking; and even the donning of formal attire for a heroic task, to provide an epic dimension to his story, raising his characters above naturalistic victimhood into a conscious acceptance of suffering that glorifies them.

Tom Koontz

A SUMMER'S READING

Author: Bernard Malamud (1914-1986)
Type of plot: Social realism
Time of plot: Mid-twentieth century
Locale: New York City
First published: 1956

Principal characters:
George Stoyonovich, a nineteen-year-old high-school dropout
Sophie Stoyonovich, his twenty-three-year-old sister
His father
Mr. Cattanzara, a change-maker in a subway booth

The Story

Since George Stoyonovich left school on an impulse when he was sixteen, he has been through a string of unsatisfying jobs. Now he is almost twenty years old and unemployed. He does not go to summer school because he feels that the other students will be too young. He does not go to night school because he does not want the teachers to tell him what to do. Instead, he stays in his room most of the day, sometimes cleaning the apartment, which is located over a butcher store. His father is poor, and his sister Sophie earns little, so George has little money to spend.

Sophie, who works in a cafeteria in the Bronx, brings home magazines and newspapers that have been left on tables. George sometimes reads them along with old copies of the *World Almanac* that he owns. He has begun to dislike fictional stories, which now get on his nerves. At night, he roams the streets, avoiding his old friends and seeking relief in a small park that is blocks beyond his neighborhood, where no one will recognize him. In the park, he thinks of the disappointing jobs that he has held and dreams of the life he would like to lead: He wants a good job, a house of his own, some extra money, and a girlfriend. Around midnight, he wanders back to his own neighborhood.

On one of his night walks, George meets Mr. Cattanzara, a man who lives in the neighborhood and works in a change booth in a subway station. George likes Cattanzara because he sometimes gave George a nickel for lemon ice when George was a child. Cattanzara sometimes comes home drunk, but on this night, he is sober. He asks George what he is doing with himself, and George, ashamed to admit the truth, says he is staying home and reading to further his education. He then claims he has a list of approximately one hundred books that he is going to read during the summer. George feels strange and a little unhappy about what he has said, but he wants Cattanzara's respect. After commenting that a hundred books is a big load for one summer, Cattanzara invites George to talk with him about some of the books when George finishes reading them, and then walks on.

After that night, George notices that people in the neighborhood start showing respect for him and telling him what a good boy he is. His father and Sophie also seem to have found out about the reading. Sophie starts giving him an extra dollar allowance each week. With the extra money, George occasionally buys paperback books, but reads none of them.

George starts cleaning the apartment daily. He spends his nights walking through the neighborhood, enjoying his newfound respect. His mood is better. He talks to Cattanzara only once during the next few weeks; although the man asks George nothing about the books, George feels uneasy. He starts avoiding Cattanzara, once even crossing the street to keep from walking by him as he sits in front of his house, reading *The New York Times* from cover to cover. On that occasion, Cattanzara shows no sign that he is aware of George's presence. George stops reading entirely, even neglecting the newspapers and magazines that Sophie brings home.

One night, Cattanzara, obviously drunk, approaches George. He walks silently past George but then calls George's name. He offers George a nickel to buy some lemon ice. When George tries to explain that he is grown-up now, Cattanzara argues that he is not. He challenges George to name one book he has read that summer. When George cannot, Cattanzara tells George not to do what he did, then walks on.

The next night, Sophie asks George where he keeps the books he is reading, since she sees only a few trashy books in his room. When George cannot answer, she says she will no longer give him the extra dollar, calls him a bum, and tells him to get a job.

George stays in his room for almost a week, in spite of the sweltering weather and the pleas of Sophie and his father. One night, he goes out into the neighborhood and discovers that the people there still show him respect; Cattanzara has not told anyone that George is not reading. George feels his confidence slowly coming back to him. He learns that the rumor has gone through the neighborhood that he has finished reading all the books, and wonders whether Cattanzara has started the rumor.

One fall evening, George leaves the apartment and runs to the library. After counting off a hundred books, he sits down at a table to read.

Themes and Meanings

A central theme of "A Summer's Reading" is George's lack of self-confidence and self-respect. Early in the story, Bernard Malamud says that George believes that teachers do not respect him, but the one who really does not respect him is himself. He is so ashamed about quitting high school on an impulse that he hesitates to hunt for jobs, feels dissatisfied with the jobs he gets, avoids his old friends, and does not date the neighborhood girls. He is so uncomfortable in his neighborhood that he seeks escape in a park blocks away from where he lives. His lack of self-confidence and self-respect also keeps him from returning to school, going to night school, or even beginning to read the hundred books.

By telling people that George is reading one hundred books, Mr. Cattanzara helps create a sense of self-confidence and a feeling of self-worth in George. He enjoys being respected by his sister, his father, and the people in his neighborhood. When

Cattanzara discovers that George is doing no reading, he helps George even more by cautioning him not to make the same mistake that he made, and by not telling anyone that George is not reading. George thinks that Cattanzara is the one who has spread the rumor that George has finished the hundred books, a rumor that enables him to save his pride and feeling of self-worth and eventually enables him to begin reading. With the support of Cattanzara and of the neighborhood, George learns that it is all right for him not only to dream of a better future but to try to make that dream come true.

The story also emphasizes the importance of an education and of reading. George is uncomfortable with formal education, but Malamud indicates that the alternative of independent reading is available. At first, George feels unable to take advantage of that possibility, but at the end of the story, he begins to work on advancing his education.

Style and Technique

Irony lies at the heart of "A Summer's Reading," beginning with the story's title. During the summer, George reads none of the books he has planned to. As critic Robert Solotaroff points out, he instead reads his own psyche and the psyches of the people in the neighborhood. He learns that the people in the neighborhood support him, and that with their support, he just might be successful in his planned reading and thus in his life.

The greatest irony lies in Cattanzara's not telling the people of the neighborhood that George has done no reading; instead, George thinks that Cattanzara is the one who spreads the rumor that he has done all the reading he planned. This rumor enables him to retain the respect of the people in the neighborhood and, finally, to do something to make himself worthy of that respect.

Malamud uses a third-person narrative in "A Summer's Reading," but often the narrative seems to reflect what George is thinking. For example, Malamud writes of George's neighborhood, "George had never exactly disliked the people in it, yet he had never liked them very much either. It was the fault of the neighborhood." The rest of the story makes it clear that the sentence about fault reflects George's ideas rather than reality. Before the story is over, George finds himself liking the people of his neighborhood, largely because they begin showing that they like, support, and respect him. As a result, he begins to respect himself and finally is able to begin the process of reading that may lead to his being worthy of that respect and to his bettering his life.

Richard Tuerk

SUNDAY DINNER IN BROOKLYN

Author: Anatole Broyard (1920-1990)
Type of plot: Social realism
Time of plot: 1954
Locale: Brooklyn
First published: 1968

Principal characters:
PAUL, the narrator and protagonist
HIS MOTHER
HIS FATHER

The Story

A young man named Paul, who is apparently in his twenties, travels from his Greenwich Village apartment to his parents' Brooklyn home for Sunday dinner. As he walks toward a subway station, he glimpses the colorful characters who populate his path and draws vivid correlations among them, the local landmarks, and the associations they inspire in him. Among an almost circuslike array of people, the reader sees "the Italians . . . all outside on stoops and chairs or standing along the curb in their Sunday clothes . . . mothers with their hair pulled back and their hands folded in their laps . . . like Neanderthal madonnas . . . [and] girls [with] long pegged skirts which made their feet move incredibly fast."

The subway itself is an exotic realm. Paul states, "I took a long breath like a deep-sea diver and went reluctantly underground." In the subway train the passengers ignore one another, yet exhibit an uncanny attunement to one another's movements as they silently exchange seats in an undulating, almost somnambulistic underground ballet.

The scene surrounding Paul's arrival in Brooklyn proves that he has transported himself to still another world. The borough's empty streets remind him that in stable, middle-class Brooklyn, everyone conforms by eating dinner at the same hour. Paul walks to his parents' house where they greet him as a prodigal son. His mother and father strive to please him by providing him every comfort and by filling him with the food they hope will sustain him. In their eagerness to provide a perfect Sunday evening, Paul's parents revise and repress their own beliefs and desires, a fact that Paul understands, and a truth that ironically increases, rather than decreases, his anxieties.

Following dinner and conversation, Paul's father accompanies him back to the subway station. As the father starts to descend the subway steps, Paul stops him, telling him to remain where he is so as not to overexert himself or to breathe in the station's polluted fumes. Paul's father protests, but finally acquiesces, and as the disaffected son disappears down the underground stairs, he feels his father's sadness.

Themes and Meanings

"Sunday Dinner in Brooklyn" is a story about the bittersweet nature of love. Concentrating on the awkward, often painful, affection between parents and their adult children, Anatole Broyard's central theme is an exploration of how parent-child relationships evolve, rather than remain static, as children enter adulthood. Just how such relationships evolve is what interests Broyard; rarely can even the most psychologically well-adjusted families suspend their emotionally symbiotic attachment to one another in lieu of some sort of traumatically sanitized affection, and Broyard suggests they should not even if they could. Broyard's theme also extends to encompass the pain inherent in all types of love—physical, divine, and societal—as time necessarily transforms love into longing.

The story reverberates with subtle sexual messages. For example, the narrator describes a group of adolescent girls: "All of their movements seemed to be geared to this same tempo, and their faces were alert with the necessity of defending the one prize they had against mother and brother alike . . ." and " . . . the uninteresting boys they would eventually wind up with, older girls between affairs, older boys on the lookout for younger girls . . . [where] they stood, Fifth Avenue dribbled to its conclusion after penetrating Washington Arch." These sad observations show love—and society—not at its apex, but in its decline, a decline almost akin to dissipation.

Similarly, Broyard writes of religion, if not of spirituality:

> There was a tremendous vacuum left by God. In contrast to the kitchen-like intimacy of the church on Thompson Street—which in its ugliness succeeded in projecting its flock's image on the universe—the spiky shells on these blocks had a cold, punitive look, and seemed empty except for those few hours in the morning when people came with neutralized faces to pay their respects to a dead and departed deity.

As time withers passions into memories and human frailty erodes faith into duty, Paul's love for his parents and theirs for him evolves from a playlike existence wherein actors infuse life into lines written for them, to a more experimental scene in which the actors anxiously improvise in the hope of creating meaning. Paul travels to his parents' house as a gesture of respect, but more important he visits his family because he seeks the unencumbered, primary affections of his youth. As he arrives in Brooklyn, the sun hits him in the eye and he reflects, "It seemed to me that the sun was always shining in Brooklyn, drying clothes, curing rickets, evaporating puddles, inviting children out to play, and encouraging artificial-looking flowers in front yards." In other words, the Brooklyn in which Paul was raised, and where his parents still reside, nurtures Paul and his imagination more in his imagination than in reality. For in reality, just as clouds often shadow Brooklyn's sun—which cannot, after all, cure rickets—Paul and his parents' thwarted attempts to communicate with one another make them ache from their mutual desire so intense that pathos practically smothers them.

When Paul's mother declines the rocker—the home's prize chair—for him, he leans back to appease her, despite his desire to remain erect. When Paul eats his mother's food he recalls how, as a child, his first restaurant meal made him realize that she was not the world's best cook. Now, however, as he finishes his Sunday dinner he becomes "flatulent with affection." He knows, "belly to belly, that was the only true way to talk."

According to Broyard, after love's language loses its distinct expression, as it must, only the instincts that constitute love's metaphors can comfort. The failure satisfactorily to communicate as love struggles to transcend life's transformations is not a matter of fault, but of fate. Paul muses:

> When I was a boy, these streets had quickness and life for me, each detail daring me to do something to match my wits, my strength, my speed, against them. Then I was always running. I saw things on the run and made my running commentary on them without breaking my stride, hurdling, skipping, dodging, but still racing forward . . . until one day I ran full tilt into myself and blocked my own path.

So it is with love in all of its manifestations. Growth involves change, and the most painful aspect of that change, Broyard notes, is that those who are loved realize the intentions and needs of those who love them, but cannot adequately acknowledge or fulfill them. As it is with an individual such as Paul, so it is with society itself. Like a moth hovering too close to a flame, individuals and societies consume themselves by seeking the light that shines brightest in their fantasies.

Style and Technique

Broyard's decision to write "Sunday Dinner in Brooklyn" in the first person and in the past tense provides the intimacy and perspective necessary to convey the story's theme. Paul's surname is not mentioned, nor are the first or last names of his parents. Such names are not only unnecessary for the purpose of communicating the story, they are even inappropriate designations when perceived from the narrator's viewpoint. The lack of such names reinforces the idea that Paul is indeed Everyman. Like most young adults, Paul is incapable of conceiving of his parents as entities whose identities can be separate from his; to him they are "my father" and "my mother," not "Mr. and Mrs."

To achieve a rich, yet declarative style punctuated by subtle humor, slight ennui, and startling imagery, Broyard loads his language with similes, metaphors, and personifications. The story's first sentence reads: "I took a roundabout route to the subway, and because I was going to Brooklyn the Village seemed to have at the moment all the charm of a Utrillo." Comparing Greenwich Village to a Maurice Utrillo painting creates a specific visual image, while also allowing Broyard to suggest something of Paul's eager worldliness, education, and self-conscious, youthful snobbery.

The story's second paragraph begins: "Since it was summer, the Italians were all outside on stoops and chairs or standing along the curb in their Sunday clothes, the old men in navy blue and the young men in powder blue suits, as though their generation was more washed out than the last." Broyard's simile here reinforces his theme that Paul's generation relinquishes stability for seemingly less-substantial individuality. This is especially true of those like Paul who seek their identities away from the steady sameness of their parents' solid lives in favor of finding new, post-World War II identities in such teeming communities as Greenwich Village.

Broyard's dependence on figurative language permits him to avoid overwriting so that what remains unstated is implicit, ensuring that his occasional short, simple sentences deliver a punch.

L. Elisabeth Beattie

SUNDAY IN THE PARK

Author: Bel Kaufman
Type of plot: Domestic realism
Time of plot: The 1980's
Locale: A city, probably New York
First published: 1985

Principal characters:
A WIFE AND MOTHER, the protagonist
MORTON, her husband, a university professor
LARRY, their three-year-old son
JOE, a boy about Larry's age
JOE'S FATHER

The Story

The title suggests how ordinary a scene this brief story presents. In a quiet corner of an unnamed park in an unnamed city, an unnamed woman sits in the sun with her family—what could be more typical, more universal? Her husband, Morton, who works at a university, is pale and intelligent, enjoying some time out-of-doors with the Sunday paper. Their three-year-old son Larry is playing in the sandbox, earnestly digging a tunnel. The mother sighs, content with her life.

Suddenly another child about Larry's age throws a shovel of sand at Larry's head, narrowly missing him. Clearly, he does this on purpose, and he stands with feet planted, waiting for Larry's reaction, but Larry barely notices. His mother scolds the child as she would her own, reminding him kindly that throwing sand is unsafe. In response, the child throws more sand, and this time some lands in Larry's hair.

Larry now comes out of his concentrated stupor and notices the boy's behavior, but he waits for his mother to act. She speaks sharply, scolding more forcefully, while the two boys continue to look expectantly at her. Morton is still reading his newspaper, not paying any attention. The other boy's father does react, however. He announces that because they are all in a public park, his son Joe can throw sand if he wants to.

Now, as the mother has run out of resources, Morton finally becomes aware of what is going on. He tries to reason pleasantly with the other father, as he would reason with an erring student. However, the other man is not impressed with his calm manner, his "civilized" intellectual approach. He would rather settle the dispute with blows.

As the two men stand facing each other, the mother wonders how she can stop the inevitable battle. Morton is clearly off balance, not used to settling things this way. He stands unsteadily, and his voice trembles. "This is ridiculous," he says. "I must ask you. . . ."

"You and who else?" the man asks.

Finally, Morton turns his back and walks away awkwardly, gathering up his family as he heads out of the park. For reasons that she cannot articulate, even to herself, the mother is angry and ashamed. Always before she has been proud of her husband's and her son's sensitivity and delicateness. Now, although she is relieved that the confrontation was resolved without a fight and agrees with her husband that a fight would not have solved anything, she feels defeated.

As they leave the park, Larry struggles and cries. He does not want to go home. The mother cannot calm him, and Morton finally threatens that if she cannot discipline the boy he will do it himself. "Indeed?" she replies. "You and who else?"

Themes and Meanings

The story of the two boys and the two fathers is a story of the conflict between reason and force, between man and beast. Larry is smaller, quieter, weaker than Joe; the two boys ignore each other and manage to play side-by-side for a time. Morton is smaller and weaker than the other father, and he, too, ignores the scene in front of him at first. So long as neither engages, they are safe.

The family's security and contentedness is built, however, on a false view of the world. Morton is in his element at the university, out of the sun, where all disagreements are rational, where reason has power. On an ordinary Sunday in the park, however, he confronts a man who is not like him, who relies on physical power. The fact is, there are both kinds of people in the world. When push comes to shove (in this case, a literal possibility), force can beat reason every time, at least over the short term. Although Morton walks away from the fight and no one is physically hurt, his views of the world and himself have changed.

The role of women in this conflict is a complex one. The only person whose thoughts and feelings are presented is the mother; the reader can judge the other characters' thoughts only by their actions. Yet the mother's part in the external events is a passive one. She is the one who first notices Joe's aggressive actions, and she feels comfortable scolding the three-year-old boy, but as soon as Joe's father joins in the confrontation, she steps aside, leaving her husband to deal with both bullies. Interestingly, the only other female characters in the story are two women and a little girl on roller skates, who leave the park just after the first spadeful of sand is thrown.

Women have traditionally left brute force to men—not necessarily repudiating violence themselves, but relying on their men to deal with it for them. The mother in this story does not consider fighting herself, but she comes to wish her menfolk were more forceful and less exclusively rational.

With whom, then, is the mother angry at the end of the story? Why does she, at least in words, take on the role of the bully? It seems too simple to say that she is angry at Morton for not defending the family honor. She has always been proud of him before; she agrees that reason should be used instead of force. If she is disappointed in Morton for appearing weak, she must also be disappointed in herself—not because she should have punched the other father herself, but because she now doubts whether wisdom and intellect can really hold their own against brute force. If they cannot, what grounds has she for her secure contentment at the beginning of the story? If they cannot, what chance does a woman have in this world?

Style and Technique

"Sunday in the Park" relies heavily on sharp contrasts to make its points, beginning with the conflict between what the reader expects from the peaceful title and the brutality that lurks in that park. The peaceful scene becomes a battle between the forces of civility and barbarity, and Bel Kaufman plays up the differences in the two families to the point that they are almost allegorical figures.

At first glance, the two boys seem much alike. They are about the same age, and they are squatting calmly side-by-side in the sandbox. The boys are not sharing or playing together, but happily ignoring each other, in what child development experts call "parallel play." As soon as sand is thrown, however, the differences are made clear. Larry has a pointed little face and a small frame; Joe is chubby, husky, with "none of Larry's quickness and sensitivity in his face." After the mother scolds Joe, Larry looks to her to see how he ought to react, but Joe (whose name is pointedly not the diminutive "Joey") never looks at his father.

The fathers might also appear similar at first. Both men are sitting on park benches reading, ignoring their young sons playing in the sandbox. However, Morton is small, able comfortably to share a park bench with his wife, while the other father is big, taking up an entire bench himself. Morton reads the Sunday *Times Magazine* while the other man reads the comics. Morton speaks pleasantly and shows his anger by tightening his jaw, while the other speaks rudely and scornfully, flexing his arms and waiting for a punch.

No fight ever develops; the only fists in the story are the boys', and their fists are clutching sand shovels. The boys listen and stare, but the conflict soon stops being about them. In fact, Larry does not want to leave the park; the sand-throwing that starts the disagreement does not affect him.

Kaufman uses these contrasting details to shift the reader's focus, first to the boys, then to the fathers. The mother, the observer, is not paired with anyone, just as she plays no part in the potential fight. As details of her thoughts and actions reveal, she carries within her elements of both fathers. She can speak civilly or brutally, she can move gently or sharply. Ultimately, the conflict between reason and force is not between people, but within them.

Cynthia A. Bily

SUSANNA AT THE BEACH

Author: Herbert Gold (1924-)
Type of plot: Parable
Time of plot: The 1950's
Locale: Lake Erie, near Cleveland, Ohio
First published: 1954

Principal characters:
THE DIVING GIRL
A FAT SWIMMER
FREDDY, his friend
AN OLD POLISH WOMAN
HER PLUMP FRIEND
A PRETTY GIRL ON THE BEACH
HER MOTHER

The Story

As an unnamed adolescent girl practices diving into Lake Erie, a crowd of people watch her on the beach. The girl concentrates so fully on perfecting her dive that she does not notice a tear developing in the side of the worn, black bathing suit that she is outgrowing.

One of those watching the girl is a fat man who lolls in the water talking to his friend Freddy about business; both ogle the girl lustfully, making remarks about "biting off a piece" of her. Other watchers include an old Polish woman and her overweight friend, who talk about caring for their parents and who criticize the girl for having no shame. Also on the beach is a pretty young girl with a junior-miss nose who hugs herself the way her favorite starlet does. The men are not interested in the pretty girl on the beach; they sense that she would fear to dive into the tricky, polluted lake water. Her mother declares, with some satisfaction, that the diving girl will get an earache because of the organisms in the water.

The diving girl has fled all the billboard schemes of a pretty girl in order to focus on a grand design: perfecting her dive. Although her exercises are simple, she has an idea of what they should be and she has the will of perfection. The men who watch her from the beach think that her self-sufficiency is a pity and a waste, and it makes them sad. The women on the beach envy her youth and devotion to her art, but consider themselves morally superior to her.

As the girl repeatedly dives into the murky water, the tear in her worn suit lengthens, revealing the side of her budding breast and threatening to show more. The girl feels the rip just once, but she is so intent on the demands of perfection that she closes the split with her fingers, then forgets it and lets it go. If she thinks of her body at all, it is only to think of her skill and her practice for her body's sake, for she is an expert.

Finally, the girl's breast is fully revealed, "its pink sprouting from the girl's body like a delicate thing nurtured in the dark." The old Polish woman screams, "You're nekked, girlie! Nekked!" and the fat man and his friend cheer her on. When the girl finally notices the observers, she is at first incredulous, then, turning from them toward the water, she runs into the lake. Thinking that she wants to drown herself, several men swim after her. However, although the "righteousness" of the mob's laughter urges them on, the girl is strong, skillful, gifted, and "encumbered by nothing but her single thought."

Themes and Meanings

The title of Herbert Gold's story and its basic situation clearly signal his intention to retell the story of Susanna and the elders from the Book of Daniel in the Apocrypha. The biblical story is a simple account of Susanna, a young married woman who walks daily in her garden, where she is seen by two elders who lust after her. One day when she is alone in the garden, the elders rush up to her and tell her that if she does not yield to their desires they will say that a young man has been with her. However, Susanna is a righteous woman who says that she would rather be at their mercy than lie with them and sin against the Lord. Susanna is vindicated when Daniel tricks the elders into giving conflicting testimony. The biblical story embodies the conflict between the sacred and the profane and exemplifies the triumph of the spirit over the things of the world.

In giving this universal situation and theme a modern setting, Gold has no trouble creating a similitude for the lusting elders in the men on the beach who watch the girl and wait for her suit to rip. However, Gold transforms Susanna's trust in God in the Apocrypha story to the diving girl's single-minded demand for perfection, and he also expands the profane world to include not only the lustful men, but also the women who envy the girl's innocence, purity, and quest for perfection.

The girl is obviously elevated from the crowd on the beach, sufficient unto herself, dedicated to her discipline, concerned only with the demands of perfection. Her ambition has no practical purpose and thus seems madness to the watchers. Although the watchers focus on the body of the girl, which is desired by the men and envied by the women, the girl herself is seemingly unaware that she even has a body; the complete perfection of her dive, if such were possible, would mean the use of the body as a means of its own transcendence; she wishes to create an alternate world superior to ordinary reality. As a modern-day treatment of the Susanna and the elders story, the end of the story is a vindication of the girl's innocence and superiority.

Style and Technique

Although "Susanna at the Beach" focuses on a modern-day event and seems to feature realistic characters engaged in everyday activities, both the title and the style of the story suggest its parable nature. The story's point of view is that of an anonymous observer who watches the events but does not place himself in the story. Because the narrator does not know the girl's name, the only reason he gives her the name “Susanna” in the title is to identify her situation thematically with that of the beautiful and devout Jewish woman in the story of Susanna and the elders.

The style of the story is like a parable in that its single-minded focus throughout is on the meaning of the girl’s elevation above those people on the beach because of her devotion to her craft. Whereas the people on the beach are real and fleshly, the girl herself—although her body is an object of desire and envy—has no consciousness of the physical. Gold’s style makes it clear that her diving symbolizes her devotion to an idea: “The girl used herself hard, used her lightness hard.” Moreover, like Susanna in the story in the Apocrypha, the girl is the embodiment of innocence, not responsible that she is the object of fleshly desire. “Her innocence—an innocence of lessons—was informed by the heart and by the pressure of her blood.”

Gold’s language also makes it clear that what motivates the people on the beach is not merely physical desire and prudery, but also an intense jealousy that they do not have the same dedication and single-minded focus on an ideal that the girl has. For example, as the old Polish woman looks at the girl, she shivers “at her own memories of paleness, of resiliency, of pink colors.” And the fat man and his friend Freddy are not interested solely in sexual attractiveness; they ignore the pretty girl on the beach, for they know that despite her prettiness she has put herself apart from “risks of pleasure.”

The rip in the bathing suit makes it possible for Gold to emphasize a fundamental difference between the girl and the people on the beach: While the people cannot ignore her body as mere flesh, the girl thinks of her own body, if at all, as only that which must be transcended to perfect her art. In his elevated parable style, Gold says that all the people on the beach lean together to watch the tear widen, “sharing the girl and sharing each other, waiting for their world’s confirmation against the challenge she brought it, an assurance of which they were in need before the return to autumn and the years rapid upon them.”

“Susanna at the Beach” is an effective example of a writer’s ability to transform a simple everyday event into a moral parable by paralleling to a traditional mythic tale and by maintaining a style that emphasizes the transcendent significance of events.

Charles E. May

SWADDLING CLOTHES

Author: Yukio Mishima (Kimitake Hiraoka, 1925-1970)
Type of plot: Horror
Time of plot: An April evening in modern times
Locale: Tokyo, Japan, near the Imperial Palace
First published: "Shimbungami," 1953 (English translation, 1966)

Principal characters:
TOSHIKO, a twenty-three-year-old mother of a new son
HER HUSBAND, an actor
A NURSE, who gives birth to a son in Toshiko's home

The Story

After a shocking incident in their home two days earlier, Toshiko and her actor husband meet friends in a Tokyo nightclub. The young wife and mother is dumbfounded to hear her husband recounting the incident—which has disturbed her greatly—as merely an amusing story for their companions' entertainment. Troubled and vulnerable, Toshiko feels acutely aware of her husband's insensitivity, neglect, and lack of consideration for her. Her mind swells with loneliness and her fears of the future provoked by her horror at the scene she has so recently encountered in her son's nursery.

The story that so horrifies Toshiko began with the arrival of a new nurse, a woman with an oddly distended stomach and a prodigious appetite. Not long after she arrived, loud moans came from the nursery. Toshiko and her husband rushed in to discover the nurse giving birth on the floor. Toshiko's husband rescued the family's good rug and placed a blanket under the nurse to prevent damage to the parquet floor. Nonetheless, a terrible mess was made; bloodstains can still be seen in their son's room.

Although two days have passed, Toshiko, in contrast to her husband, is still preoccupied by this experience. In particular, she obsesses about one scene that she alone witnessed. The doctor who finally arrived to attend the nurse derided her and her bastard child so strongly that he had his attendant wrap the newborn boy in newspaper. Appalled by the doctor's cruelty, Toshiko rewrapped the child in new flannel. The image of the innocent child in his soiled paper wrappings, however, is still imprinted on her mind. She alone witnessed his shame.

As Toshiko's husband sets out from the nightclub for other engagements, she goes home alone in a taxi. Riding through the darkened streets of Tokyo, she reflects on the nurse's child and the secret shame of his birth. What if this boy, twenty years hence, should meet her own son? The one, reared in solid comfort, might be savagely attacked by the other who will have been turned into a brute by a life of deprivation and disgrace. The bloody newspapers in which that newborn was briefly wrapped would mark him for life; they would be a blight on his being, the secret emblem of his entire existence, his inescapable doom. She imagines one day going to the boy to tell him of her secret knowledge of his first moments of life.

On impulse, Toshiko leaves her taxi and walks beneath the cherry blossoms in the dark deserted park near the Imperial Palace. She wanders until she encounters the form of a man, asleep on a bench, wrapped in newspapers. Standing beside the dirty anonymous figure, she imagines this young man as the future manifestation of the baby recently born in her house. With a rustle of newspaper, a powerful hand seizes her wrist. Instantly, Toshiko realizes that both her foreboding and her powerful sense of connection to the baby in newspaper swaddling have been realized. Her meeting with him has come to pass.

Themes and Meanings

"Swaddling Clothes" explores the barren geography of the alienated human. On one level, the story maps the painful terrain of an empty Japanese marriage, a union characterized by a husband absent emotionally and physically. The wife is ignored and the child tended by a surrogate. The devaluing of human life is boldly marked by the image of a child alone on the floor, wrapped like trash, degraded. The protagonist, suffering in silence, half mad with loneliness, vulnerable to her own thwarted sensitivity and caring, devalued and disregarded, falls prey to morbid preoccupations, obsessive fantasies, and a powerful pull to self-destruction.

The bastard child that will become the brutal killer of the future is perhaps a projection of Toshiko's own husband's domination of her spirit as well as the outward sign of the murderous oppression of her culture's patriarchy. In this tale women and children are ignored and demeaned by adult males. The bastard child imagined as killer of her own son and assassin of herself is the true offspring of her man's inhumanity to man.

Also implicit is an indictment of the social order in which Toshiko resides. The doctor, the supposed epitome of compassion and caring, disdains an innocent life, degrades it, dishonors it. The whole society is characterized by willful disregard for human dignity. The locale that Mishima chooses for the climax of his story suggests that this evil, this menace, is asleep at the very heart of Japanese culture, beside the Imperial Palace at the hub of the ethos of Japanese life. In the enigmatic ending it is the female who is threatened, the silent but sole source of compassion. The grip of the mysterious male hand is a death grip; Toshiko's fate is to be destroyed by the homeless disfranchised offspring of her own heartless and mercenary society.

Style and Technique

Scholars say that a literal translation of the title of this story is "waste newspapers." Although the English title, "Swaddling Clothes," is not entirely accurate, ironically, it captures a central tension of the tale. With this title the warm white flannel evoked by the English term is conflated with the dirty newspapers which first swathe the newborn child. The child in the dramatic birthing scene is visible throughout the tale in a series of tensions; the cherished child in clean flannel contrasts with the bloodied paper wrappings which declare this child trash, a piece of meat, a throwaway life.

As the pristine flannel and the soiled papers are held in tension, so are other objects and persons united. Two powerful images are conflated in the story: images of cherry blossoms and images of newspapers. To Toshiko the artificial cherry blossoms on the theater marquee are revealed to be shreds of paper; she walks down the park path beneath an umbrella of blossoming trees with heaps of waste paper at her feet, and at first the sheets of paper draping the vagrant on the bench glow in the darkness like a blanket of cherry blossoms. Both the blossoms and the newspapers suggest transience, one the transience of events natural, the other the transience of events humanmade. The blossoms evoke an entire genteel aesthetic and the most ancient traditions of Japan. The other suggests the blaring emptiness of modern Western lifestyles of conspicuous consumption. Most dramatically, the newspapers unite the bastard child born in Toshiko's nursery with the malign force of the shadowy figure of her future destruction. This small tale of horror lifts a corner of the veneer of Japanese contemporary life and reveals the madness and violence beneath.

The conjunction of oppositions is a pattern woven in the very fabric of the story. The boundaries of familiar dualities are broken as the commonplace becomes the bizarre and the domestic transforms into the public. East and West, traditional and modern, birth and death, past and present, nature and humankind unite until inner and outer realities merge at a park bench. Doubles people the landscape of Toshiko's life: two babies, one legitimate and one a bastard; two mothers, united in silence and powerlessness; two males, powerful forces of personal and social control; and finally the bastard and the vagrant, both swaddled in newspapers, both social discards. Two acts of personal violation mirror each other as well. The dishonoring of the newborn is the psychic seed of the impending violation of Toshiko. The horrific union of the wraithlike female protagonist and the menacing phantom embodiment of the newborn suggests Japan's fate, an impending destruction of personal, social, economic, and political orders.

Part of the dramatic power of this tale arises in its use of point of view. The narrative voice is omniscient, yet the narrator's power to reveal people and the world is not employed. In the tale the reader never goes outside Toshiko's mind. One does not hear others' words or views; one sees other people's actions in the indistinct impressions that they register on Toshiko's consciousness. Certainly the mode of presentation conveys the alienation and isolation of Toshiko in her world. More important still, the point of view suggests Toshiko's alienation from herself. Lost, she bumps into her own thoughts and feelings like strangers on a crowded street. The effect of this narrative technique on the reader is profound. One cannot identify with the protagonist. She walks like an automaton into a death grip, seemingly never speaking and never being spoken to, scarcely seen or felt. As she is estranged from herself so she is estranged from the reader. An omniscience which could tell all but reveals nothing is a strategy for creating that paradoxical preternatural quality of events. The narrator can show and tell all but reveals nothing. Is Toshiko a mad housewife intent on suicide? Or is she a symbol of the fragile spirit of a nation inexorably, blindly, walking into the hands of its own murderer? In the context of the social, economic, political, and moral upheavals of post-World War II Japan, after the incineration of Hiroshima and Nagasaki, Mishima sought to ring an alarm for his people, to cry for renewal of human dignity and compassion for others in both personal and social realms.

Virginia M. Crane

THE SWIMMERS

Author: Joyce Carol Oates (1938-   )
Type of plot: Social realism
Time of plot: 1959 to 1971
Locale: The Chautauqua Mountains of New York State
First published: 1989

Principal characters:
SYLVIE, the narrator, a woman recalling an incident during her youth
JOAN LUNT, an attractive woman in her mid-thirties
CLYDE FARRELL, Joan's lover, Sylvie's uncle
ROBERT WAXMAN, Joan's former husband

The Story

Sylvie looks back at a sequence of events that occurred in 1959 when she was thirteen years old and observed the relationship between her uncle, Clyde Farrell, and Joan Lunt, a mysterious new woman in town.

Clyde and Joan meet when both are swimming one early morning at the YMCA. Clyde admires Joan's style of swimming even before he sees her up close. Although they swim together in the pool, they do not speak to each other. The next time he sees her at the pool, he introduces himself. Strongly attracted to each other, Clyde and Joan soon begin spending most of their time together.

Clyde is a good-looking man, an athlete, with well-defined shoulder and arm muscles, who had been a boxer in the Navy and has worked as a truck driver, factory foreman, and manager of a sporting-goods store. He likes to gamble at cards and horses. Although he is powerfully attracted to women, no one expects him to marry.

Joan Lunt is a good-looking woman with dark eyes, thick dark hair, and a thin scar at the corner of her mouth. She has been in Yewville about a month when she meets Clyde. She lives in a tiny furnished apartment and works at the most prestigious department store in town. The townspeople perceive her as arrogant because she is independent and values her privacy. She attends church, but leaves without speaking to anyone, and she drinks alone at the Yewville Bar and Grill. She remains a mystery to the townspeople, who grow suspicious of her.

Sylvie's relationship with Joan also begins at the YMCA pool. One day after their swim, Joan waits in the lobby for Sylvie and invites her to her apartment. Although the apartment is shabby, to Sylvie, who is pleased to be Joan's first guest, it has a makeshift glamour. Sylvie thinks it strange that although Joan has been living in the apartment for weeks, she still has not unpacked the two suitcases that lie opened on the floor. When she asks Joan about the scar beside her mouth, Joan tells her that a man once hit her and warns Sylvie never to let a man hit her.

The relationship between Clyde and Joan becomes more serious as they spend time at Clyde's cabin, the racetrack, and the local bars and restaurants. They are happy in each other's company, but when Joan disappears for a day or two without an explanation, Clyde becomes angry and upset. The real trouble comes when Rob Waxman, Joan's former husband, shows up, and Clyde sees that Joan is terrified of him. When Clyde steps between Joan and Rob, the two men scuffle, and Rob pulls a gun and shoots Clyde in the shoulder. Despite the wound, Clyde attacks Waxman and beats him until someone pulls him off. Joan is upset by the fight. Although she loves Clyde, she has such a fear of violence that seeing him beat Waxman terrifies her. Clyde wants to forget the incident, and the two discuss their situation at length. Clyde thinks that they will continue their relationship, but Joan leaves town and the two never see each other again.

Although Clyde searches for Joan, he never finds her. Sylvie goes away to college and never sees Joan again either. Clyde lives a typical bachelor lifestyle for a time, but eventually retreats to a solitary life. The last time Sylvie speaks with Clyde about Joan it is 1971, twelve years after the end of the affair. Clyde's face, with its "look of furious compression" and the dents that resemble animal tracks, shows his unhappiness. Observing him closely, Sylvie wonders if she is "seeing the man Joan Lunt had fled from or the man her flight had made." Sylvia and Clyde never learn what became of Joan.

Themes and Meanings

As in many of Joyce Carol Oates's works, violence is an underlying theme of "The Swimmers." The violence that took place in the past is an ominous presence, and fear of more violence is at the core of the story. Joan Lunt is a wounded person, struggling to build a new life for herself, still held captive by the fears of her past. Just as her relationship with Clyde is strengthening, an act of violence breaks them apart. When Clyde hits Joan's former husband, he is reacting as many men would in the same situation. It may be said that he is actually acting as her protector. Joan, however, sees only the act of violence and runs away.

Another characteristic of Oates's characters is their fear of commitment. Joan is fighting to overcome her past, to survive on her own, unencumbered by possessions or people. Her suitcases remain packed so that she can flee quickly if necessary. The contradiction in her personality is shown in the contrast between her clean, strong, self-confident strokes as a swimmer and the frightened woman who drinks alone at the bar, always watching for trouble. She is suspended between her love for Clyde and her fear of involvement. Her previous experience has left her unable fully to commit to a new relationship. Although Clyde has a number of friends, he has never made a serious commitment to anyone either. A powerful attraction draws them together, and their feelings for each other are intense. The tension in their relationship charges the atmosphere. The failure of the relationship is a result of a lack of understanding and an inability to make a commitment.

Isolation is another theme that pervades "The Swimmers." Joan is an outsider, different, an object of curiosity. The townspeople regard Joan with suspicion, and she does not want to become involved with the community. Joan guards her privacy, and

Clyde leads a solitary life. These people who swim so expertly in the safety of the YMCA pool seem unable to deal with the forces of life on the outside.

Style and Technique

By using the device of an observer-narrator, Oates is able to tell the story from the point of view of a young girl, but with an emphasis on the actions of the adults. Sylvie observes and records the actions of the main characters, but she does not see into their minds. There are gaps in the story because of Joan's flight and the narrator's confusion about what has happened. Although Sylvie continues to observe her uncle, she never really understands him either.

Oates describes the small details of ordinary contemporary scenes. The love story begins in the harsh, cold light of the swimming pool of the YMCA with its antiquated white tiles, wired glass skylight, and sharp medicinal smell of chlorine. Joan's apartment building is shabby and worn with a "weedy back yard of tilting clotheslines and wind-blown trash."

The sentence structure itself reflects the action. In two long, smooth sentences of almost eighty words each, Oates describes Joan's style of swimming as "a single graceful motion that took her a considerable distance." Oates uses a long, graceful sentence to describe this type of stroke. The only scene of violence in the story comes up suddenly. Waxman appears without warning and the situation explodes in violence almost immediately. Oates describes this scene with speed. Clyde reacts with quick actions, animal-like responses. She uses phrases such as "Waxman leapt after her" and "Clyde . . . scrambled forward . . . bent double . . . and managed to throw himself on Waxman." Everything happens so fast that, in retrospect, Clyde cannot even remember his "lightning-swift action."

Oates's choices of images and metaphors show her underlying concern with violence. In the opening paragraph of the story, the narrator says that this story lodges in the memory "like an old wound never entirely healed." The inanimate objects in Joan's apartment are described in terms of violence, "battered-looking furniture" and "injured-looking Venetian blinds." The pool, on the other hand, is a symbol of security and safety. The water provides an environment in which Joan is "sealed off and invulnerable." Later, Oates juxtaposes the shelter of the pool where Joan and Sylvie are "snug and safe" with the icy "pelting" rain that hits the skylight overhead.

In describing Joan, Oates piles up details of physical description to show that she is a cautious person, trying to get her life under control. Joan focuses on the details as a way of establishing some sense of order in her life. Joan's face is "carefully made up" with an "expertly reddened mouth." Her hair is "carefully waved," and her nails are "perfectly manicured, polished an enamel-hard red." Joan's appearance provides a picture of a person who is in control, as if these details of grooming protect her from intrusion. In contrast to these details, the small scar "is like a sliver of glass" that shows her vulnerability.

Judith Barton Williamson

SYLVIE

Author: Gérard de Nerval (Gérard Labrunie, 1808-1855)
Type of plot: Fantasy
Time of plot: Around 1838
Locale: France
First published: 1853 (English translation, 1922)

Principal characters:
THE UNNAMED NARRATOR
ADRIENNE, a girl he loved as a youth
AURÉLIE, an actress in Paris
SYLVIE, the girl he might have married

The Story

The narrator goes night after night to a theater in Paris to sit at the feet of Aurélie, an actress who approximates his distant feminine ideal. Aurélie remains distant. She is said to love a pale young man who echoes the romantic ideal then in fashion in a society where the narrator seems to be a marginal participant. When the narrator leaves Paris and returns to the Valois in the countryside, he remains equally an outsider, referred to by his old friends as "the Parisian."

Several associations, begun when a newspaper headline reminds him of a country festival from his past, have prompted the narrator to hasten to the Valois in time to see his childhood friend Sylvie at an all-night dance honoring Saint Bartholomew's Day. His destination, however, recalls another festival, at which he once abandoned Sylvie for the fascinating but unattainable Adrienne. A daughter of a noble family of the region, Adrienne had enchanted him with her singing, but her family expected her to follow a religious vocation.

Back in the country, the narrator quickly finds Sylvie. Once again he is torn between two societies, a somewhat mythic past that he associates with Adrienne and the traditions she represented, and the present, where Sylvie lives. Alone on a path at night, he alternately races toward a convent that may house Adrienne and the village where, in the morning, he is reunited with Sylvie.

Sylvie seems to appropriate some of the traditional past. She once tried on her aunt's old wedding dress and costumed the narrator as her bridegroom. This masquerade is now past. He must recognize that Sylvie has redecorated her house in a modern style and no longer keeps up her traditional craft of lacemaking. In one last scene of intimacy, Sylvie sings an old folk song to him. The song, a story of three beautiful girls, parallels the narrator's situation.

There is no indication which of the women in his life would be the most beautiful. Sylvie reveals to him that Adrienne had had bad luck, without giving further details. Sylvie also becomes inaccessible. Upon hearing of her impending marriage to one of their old friends, the narrator abruptly returns to Paris.

The story then moves ahead in time. The narrator does have a chance at the love of Aurélie, but the actress must have a man who is totally devoted to her. When the narrator avows his continuing fascination with Adrienne, Aurélie abandons him. At the very end Sylvie, now happily married, reveals to him that Adrienne had died in the convent many years before. He has lost both the women he might have loved because of the memory of a woman who no longer existed.

Themes and Meanings

The nature of this story, composed in the first person and consisting largely of the narrator's thoughts, makes it perfect as a vehicle for extensive descriptions. Through his choice of material in the descriptive passages, Gérard de Nerval introduces a series of value judgments on the people and places described.

At first the presence of description seems ironic. In the first scene at the theater, after commenting on the dress and jewels of members of the audience, the narrator asserts his lack of interest in them. The ensuing description of Aurélie, however, already contains elements calculated to enhance the reader's perception of her by specific associations.

Aurélie is as beautiful as "the divine Hours . . . of the frescoes at Herculanum." This analogy with the recently discovered classical paintings heightens the degree of beauty ascribed to Aurélie, but by the distance implied, reinforces the idea of her inaccessibility.

In the case of these romantic allusions, Nerval draws on concepts popular in his day with which his readers would already have specific associations. In his portraits of Adrienne and Sylvie, he creates a more personal system of association where older, traditional things appear good, while their modern replacements seem crass and uninteresting. Adrienne's strong link to the traditions of her aristocratic forebears establishes her as having a superiority to which Sylvie can only briefly aspire.

The chapter that introduces Adrienne presents a brief glimpse of her in the context of a traditional local festival. Before she appears, a lengthy description of a chateau from the time of Henri IV, with young girls dancing and singing, establishes the important role of girls and singing in this landscape. Thus when Adrienne sings, her beauty and mystery captivate the narrator. She has become his only link to the desired, mythic past.

In contrast to this invocation of authentic French culture, the narrator's encounters with Sylvie are marked by two temples of neoclassical style, ornaments of the past century now falling into ruin. He recalls previously escorting Sylvie to a festival on an island where such a temple formed a part of the setting. Recalling the image of Antoine Watteau's painting *Voyage à Cythère* (1717), he characterizes this as the temple of love. When he seeks Sylvie again later, he comes across the temple of philosophy. This temple marks an end to festivity, for the narrator notes that the young girls dressed in white are absent from it. This, together with the distressingly modern objects he observes in Sylvie's house, portrays Sylvie in a context that is cut off from the beauties of the past.

Style and Technique

The events of "Sylvie," composed largely of an erratic journey the narrator makes through the Valois region of France, are of secondary importance to the memories that the places he visits evoke. The central element of the story involves the narrator's mental and emotional travels, of which his actual physical movement gives only a limited approximation.

Contrasting social customs serve to distance the narrator from the women he loves. At first readers see the contrast of Paris with the provinces. Chapters set in Paris at the beginning and end of the story form an enclosure for the narrator's trip, showing him as traveling away from Paris, even though he is returning to the scenes of his youth. In fact, the narrator remains an outsider in both settings.

The descriptive flashbacks in "Sylvie" go beyond mere decoration. Through them Nerval re-creates an entire past society, much as Marcel Proust later did in *Remembrance of Things Past* (1913-1928), but with the exception that, lacking Proust's linking device of the madeleine, Nerval's associations remain essentially visual.

The society of late medieval France had a special importance for Nerval who, seeing himself descended from heroes of that time, felt that he had a continuing association with them. This dual perception of himself seems to have figured in his crises of mental illness, but his intimate association with the past was also something that he valued greatly.

The transition from a present to a past life may be irresistible, but it is not easy. The narrator easily slips into remembering scenes from his past, but his true enchantment with Adrienne comes through a series of initiatory steps that recall the entry of a knight into an adventure. While he begins by imagining a chateau and many girls dancing, his attention narrows until he loves only one. As they are drawn together by the ritual pattern of the dance, it becomes appropriate for him to kiss Adrienne. With his kiss, even before Adrienne begins her enchanting song, he declares that an unknown trouble took hold of him.

This kiss as turning point recalls Nerval's line from "El Desdichado," the sonnet that reflects his descent into the hell of his madness. After that experience, he declared that his forehead was "still red from the queen's kiss." The identity of this queen, linked in the poem to both pagan and Christian tales, remains unclear. Still, the important image of the woman marking him with a kiss parallels Adrienne.

Although elements of episodes with Sylvie also parallel chivalric antecedents, the crossing over water to reach the temple on the island for example, they do not result in the same evocation of the past. The trip to the island produces the relatively modern image of a painting by Watteau.

Engagement with the past, as represented by the narrator's infatuation with Adrienne, corresponds to Nerval's overwhelming wish. Its dangers are apparent in that it costs the narrator the happiness he could have had with either of the two women who might have loved him.

Dorothy M. Betz

THE SYMBOL

Author: Virginia Woolf (1882-1941)
Type of plot: Sketch
Time of plot: Late nineteenth or early twentieth century
Locale: An alpine resort, possibly in Switzerland
First published: 1985

Principal character:
THE NARRATOR, an elderly English woman

The Story

This brief story begins with a description of the mountain, the focal point of the alpine village in which the story is set. The mountaintop is like a crater on the moon, filled with iridescent snow whose color changes from dead white to blood red. The mountainside is a vast descent from pure rock and a clutching pine to the village and graves in the valley.

An elderly English woman sits on her hotel room balcony. She starts to write to her sister in England that the mountain "is a symbol," but she pauses to observe the mountain, as if to think about its symbolic significance. While the woman is musing, the omniscient narrator comments on the theatrical nature of the alpine resort: The hotel balcony is like a box at a theater and human behavior appears as "curtain raisers." From this omniscient perspective, life looks artificial and temporary: "Entertainments to pass the time; seldom leading to any conclusion." When the English woman sees young men on the street below, she recognizes one of them as a relative of the mistress of her daughter's school. She remembers that young men in the past have died climbing the nearby mountain and becomes again mindful of its symbolic presence and power.

Continuing her letter to her sister, the woman recalls the time that she spent with their dying mother on the Isle of Wight. This remembrance stirs her to disclose that she longed to hear the doctor say that her mother would die soon, when in fact she lived another eighteen months. She writes that she regarded the mother's death as a symbol—a symbol of freedom. She goes on to say that "a cloud then would do instead of the mountain" as a sign of having reached the top. Her memory then turns to her Anglo-Indian uncles and cousins who were explorers, and she reveals her own great desire to explore though marrying was a more sensible choice.

After turning her attention to a woman routinely shaking out a rug on another balcony, the woman resumes her letter to her sister. After mentioning the local villas, food, and hotel, she returns to the subject of the mountain and what a splendid view she has of it, as well as of everyone else in the village. She says that the mountain is always the center of conversation; people discuss whether it is clear and seems close, or it looks like a cloud and seems farther away.

Just the night before, she confesses, she hoped the storm would hide the mountain, and then asks if she is being selfish to want it concealed in the face of so much suffering. Admitting that this suffering afflicts visitors and natives equally, she quotes the hotel proprietor as saying that only an earthquake could destroy the mountain and that no such threat exists there.

The woman again notices the young men, who are now roped together and climbing the mountain; she stops her letter midsentence: "They are now crossing a crevasse. . . ." The pen falls from her hand as the men disappear.

Later that night the men's bodies are uncovered by a search party. The story ends with the woman finding her unfinished letter and writing that the old clichés seem appropriate: The men tried "to climb the mountain"; peasants put flowers on their graves; and the young men have "died in an attempt to discover . . . ." Because no conclusion seems fitting, the woman tacks on the conventional line, "Love to the children," and signs her pet name, closing the letter and the story.

Themes and Meanings

Virginia Woolf finished "The Symbol" less than a month before her death in 1941. The story explores the issues associated with her experimental interests in the novel—how to blend objective and subjective reality in ways that capture the sensuous and tangible qualities of experience, while suggesting its ephemeral and elusive nature. In essays such as "Modern Fiction" and "Mr. Bennett and Mrs. Brown," Woolf explores the new aesthetics involved in presenting a fiction reflective of modern behavior. For the twentieth century sensibility, as Woolf and other modernists perceive it, life is in a constant state of flux where nothing is stable and the mind constantly receives "myriad impressions." Life, unlike its treatment by Edwardian novelist Arnold Bennett, is not a tightly plotted Aristotelian drama with a clean beginning, middle, and end. Instead, life—like character—is always in a state of becoming—a state of uncertainty and change in which decisive moments are internal and subjective, moving the individual upward in a spiritual quest of self-knowledge.

Woolf's concerns lay the groundwork for understanding how "The Symbol" reflects themes characteristic of her experimental art. Her unnamed woman writer, an outsider in the alpine village who is removed from its street bustle, muses on what a symbol is and how it relates to the mountain—the recurring focus of her thoughts. The mountain becomes identified here with the human quest, the "longing" to reach the top and whatever the perceived goal suggests. For the protagonist, it is a desire to be free of traditional restraints—first her mother and then her sensible marriage. It is a longing to transgress conventional boundaries like the male explorers in her family—her Anglo-Indian uncles and cousins. This family is a blend of the West and the East, of British pragmatism and Indian spirituality, a mix conducive to successful exploration. The young alpine explorers, distinguished in the past by their valley graves and in the present by being roped in their upward climb of the mountain, are not so different from the woman's own uncles and cousins in their quest for the unknown. The protagonist, through apparently limited by gender expectations, manages to eke out a life of adventure through her role as writer/observer—the onlooker who records the life and death of the young explorers as well as the ups and downs of her own emotional life.

Many of Woolf's characters, particularly in her novels, are imaged as being on literal and symbolic journeys leading to something that continually beckons and eludes the human imagination. The symbol, like the quest, escapes definition and summary. The suggestive and abstract significance of a mountain, cloud, letter, or death depends on the changing context of the perceiver. When the protagonist is responsible to her dying mother, she says that a cloud signifies freedom as well as a mountain and that death itself becomes a symbol of release. For Woolf, the process of questing, of scaling the mountain, of writing the letter seems more important than the goal itself. Indeed, the process of discovery seems to take precedence over physical death as the protagonist closes her comments on the young male mountain climbers with the unfinished line, "They died in an attempt to discover . . . ." This inconclusive ending reaffirms death as yet part of the discovery process that may continue beyond material life as humans know it.

Style and Technique

Woolf constantly experimented with style, searching for ways of presenting character that explore the unconscious self. Dissatisfied with the summary treatment of character in terms of external events, she was primarily interested in character as a fluctuating interplay of the mind in response to ordinary experience. Physical sensation, as described in her fiction, provokes thought and memory, and the latter also nudge each other, unfolding in a series of images. In "The Symbol" the protagonist is suggested largely by her thoughts and memories, which are spurred initially by the view of the mountain and the village life and subsequently revealed in the letter. For her, the past, present, and future clearly shape who she is. As she reflects on the mountain and the aspiring climbers, she remembers an earlier balcony on the Isle of Wight. There she entertained her mother by describing the travelers who disembarked on the isle after an ocean journey. Like a dutiful daughter, the young protagonist attended to the requests of her dying mother, perceiving death then as a symbol of freedom, of unlimited possibility to be explored.

The protagonist's past and present experiences, subjective and objective reality, are connected by her musing on the symbol and trying to understand its significance. Woolf's characteristic style is to shift the narrative back and forth between memory and present experience, as mediated through the protagonist's perceptions and the omniscient narrator's description. The shifting narration symbolizes Woolf's notion of how to describe character in terms of a fluctuating play between external sensation and internal reaction. Ultimately, the story itself can be read as a symbol of how character depends on, and is shaped by, imaginative desire and longing.

Chella Courington

TAKE PITY

Author: Bernard Malamud (1914-1986)
Type of plot: Fable
Time of plot: The early 1950's
Locale: New York City
First published: 1956

Principal characters:
ROSEN, a former coffee salesman
DAVIDOV, a census-taker
EVA KALISH, a widow

The Story

Rosen, an elderly former coffee salesman, lives in a drab and spartan room, into which Davidov, a census-taker, has limped without knocking. Davidov is surprised that the worn, black shade over the single narrow window is closed, but Rosen grumbles that he does not need light. After cryptic—and, for Rosen, uncomfortable—preliminary exchanges, Davidov opens a notebook and prepares to write. Finding his pen empty, the census-taker pulls out a pencil stub and sharpens it with a razor blade, letting the flakes fall to the floor.

Davidov finally prods Rosen into revealing the nature of his acquaintance with Eva Kalish and the charities that Rosen extended to her. Eva, thirty-eight years old and the mother of two young girls, is the recent widow of a nearly bankrupt immigrant Jewish grocer who died at Rosen's feet. Rosen's subsequent efforts to aid the new widow clearly play a critical role in the census-taker's inquiry.

Rosen is made to relate his persistent attempts to help Eva and her children as she struggles, and fails, to keep her dead husband's business afloat. Drawing on his own experience, he repeats to Eva the advice that he once gave her husband: The store is in a bad neighborhood; it was a mistake to begin with; it will be a grave for him and his family; they should get out. After Mr. Kalish's capital was exhausted, he had agreed with Rosen, just as he fell dead. Rosen tells the widow to take the insurance money bequeathed to her, leave the business to creditors, and go to relatives.

Rosen is secretly in love with Eva, and his pleading becomes more insistent, but Eva is deaf to him. She cannot go to relatives; Hitler has killed them. She refuses his offer of credit. She even becomes upset when he brings her a piece of sirloin. She will not consider rent-free living in part of a house Rosen owns. She will not even allow him to pay for someone to watch her children while she looks for a job. Rosen fails, too, when proposing a platonic marriage, from which he seeks nothing but to care for her. Eva steadfastly rejects each of Rosen's overt and covert offers of charity.

Each rejection, none of which he comprehends, plunges Rosen more deeply into despair. Nevertheless, he is determined. Drafting his will, Rosen leaves all of his worldly goods to Eva and her girls, turns on the gas, sticks his head in the stove, and commits suicide.

Rosen is a suicide looking out the window of his coffin; Davidov is an angel sent to record Rosen's charities. When Eva appears at the coffin window to apologize, Rosen screams at her: "Whore, bastard, bitch. Go 'way from here."

Themes and Meanings

Best known as a Jewish American writer, Bernard Malamud frequently created characters that are poor, sad, benighted, and living on the margin. Yet they somehow manage to preserve, maintain, or regain a semblance of self-worth in the teeth of implacable circumstance. Rosen's suicide represents an assertion of a sadly comic human dignity in a chaotic, often merciless and incomprehensible world. Rosen has literally killed himself trying to succeed in what he believes is a worthy effort. Feeling that he has been pained and abased by endlessly entreating Eva to accept his unselfish help, Rosen salvages something of himself by angrily rejecting the apologetic and beseeching Eva when she appears outside his coffin window. As he lies in limbo awaiting judgment, he may even meet the angel Davidov's standards.

"Take Pity" is one of several stories appearing in *The Magic Barrel and Other Stories* (1958), Malamud's first collection, most of which are tragicomic tales of long-suffering Jews. Although they are that, it would be superficial to see them as that alone. While his characters often are Jewish, they are created less to realistically chronicle aspects of traditional Jewish life than to serve as moral metaphors. In "Take Pity," for example, Malamud emphasizes the horror and comedy of Rosen's frustrated need to share, to enjoy a communion prized by many people throughout most cultures. The story, then, is a moral fable with near-universal spiritual relevance.

Within this context, however, Malamud fills his tale with ironies. The angel, Davidov, like the people he scrutinizes, is shabby, poorly equipped, somewhat frazzled and bored. Kalish, the grocer, saddles Rosen with his burdens as he dies at the feet of the old, sick, lonely coffee salesman. It is ironic that Rosen, a skeptical and experienced person, is willing to visit all of his money and goods upon a widow whom he scarcely knows. Woven throughout the story is the crowning irony that those who are eager to savor the joy of giving unselfishly must suffer from the would-be recipient's hatred and endure personal anguish and humiliation. Even worse, with the Holocaust still excruciatingly etched in Jewish memories, Rosen dies by gas. When Rosen is stripped of everything with nothing remaining to give, proud Eva appears, repentant and importuning.

Ironies aside, however, "Take Pity" stands as a testament to the enduring Jewish, enduring human spirit.

Style and Technique

This is the first of Malamud's stories to be written from an omniscient point of view. This device more readily evokes a gothic mood, one characterized, that is, by desolate settings and macabre, mysterious, and violent events. The dialogue superbly demonstrates the Yiddish idiom. One example is when Davidov asks Rosen how the grocer died. "On this I am not an expert," Rosen replies. "You know better than me." "Say in one word how he died," Davidov impatiently demands. Rosen answers, "From what he died?—he died, that's all." Davidov presses, "Answer, please, this question." Laconically Rosen responds, "Broke in him something. That's how." Davidov asks, "Broke what?" and Rosen retorts, "Broke what breaks."

Malamud masterfully blends the banal and commonplace with the mystical and the spiritual. Through the first part of "Take Pity," for example, Rosen speaks with an angel whose appearance, speech, and demeanor are anything but angelic. Davidov behaves like a drab, ordinary, Yiddish-speaking mortal. Rosen also speaks and acts as if, despite his death, he were alive. The reader accepts these characterizations until Malamud reveals, smoothly and without explicit explanations, Davidov's real identity and Rosen's true condition.

In "Take Pity," Malamud facilitates this merger of the real and the unreal by using a spare setting and employing almost cryptic prose. This allows his characters to move easily between worlds—a device that Malamud often employed—without things seeming in the least out of the ordinary. Neither Rosen's nor Davidov's actions or speech betray their incongruities to the reader, and Malamud introduces no digressions or distractions. His writing rivets on the essential. Rosen and Davidov are not engaged in chit-chat. Rosen is not interested in the latest news, gossip, trends, fads, fashions, or politics. He is grappling with frightening glimpses of his own inner nature. Through his intense concentration upon the essentials of Rosen's inner struggle, Malamud permits Rosen to discover an inner resilience and depth, although partly discovered in death, that Rosen never knew he possessed.

Critics generally do not rank "Take Pity" among the finest of Malamud's short stories. Some find that it suffers from the author's omniscient narration, that is, from the absence of Malamud's own voice. Others find it too gothic and pessimistic. Still others question the discrepancy between its supporting structure and its abrupt ending—Rosen's cursing of Eva. There is general agreement, however, that "Take Pity," like much of Malamud's writing, is powerful, distinctive, and rare in its ability to join the commonplace with the mystical and spiritual and, by doing so, encourages readers to explore their own inner realms.

Clifton K. Yearley

THE TALE

Author: Joseph Conrad (Jósef Teodor Konrad Nałęcz Korzeniowski, 1857-1924)
Type of plot: Psychological realism
Time of plot: World War I
Locale: At sea
First published: 1917

Principal characters:
THE COMMANDING OFFICER, the protagonist and narrator of the tale
THE NORTHMAN, the master of a cargo ship
THE WOMAN, who listens to the officer's tale

The Story

Twilight is falling through the window of a long, gloomy room. In the gathering darkness, a woman asks her companion, a man of the sea, for a tale. He begins, awkwardly, deliberately, reminding her that what he is about to relate is a story of duty, war, and horror.

During the early days of the "bad" war, a commanding officer—the narrator himself—is taking his ship past a dangerous rocky coast. The weather is foul, a thick, impenetrable fog obscuring the coast so that the commanding officer can see nothing and can only sense the danger before him. What he can see is small flotsam, perhaps cargo from a ship sunk by an enemy submarine reported to be near. The officer suspects that the cargo may be intended for the enemy, left there for the submarine by another ship. He knows that certain supposedly neutral ships have violated their neutrality for profit, and that one of these may be close by.

As the fog thickens, the commanding officer orders the ship to be brought closer to land and to lower anchor in the shadow of the coast and wait for the weather to clear. Here he sees another ship, sitting quietly at anchor, as if in hiding. He begins to wonder if this ship is an innocent neutral or if, indeed, it is guilty of providing the submarine with supplies. Does it intend to sneak out when the fog lifts?

Alarmed yet puzzled by his suspicions, the commanding officer boards the mysterious cargo ship. The master, a Northman, is congenial, even loquacious. He insists he really is lost. The Northman tells his own tale, a brief account of his getting lost in the fog and of having engine failure. This voyage was his first in these waters. The ship is his own, providing a meager living for his family. The Northman's tale is credible enough, but the commanding officer is unconvinced. Cleverly he implies that the Northman is making a profit from the war, but the Northman denies trading with the enemy, insisting that his cargo is bound for an English port.

Although the Northman has given a good account of himself—even his manifest is clear—the commanding officer is increasingly suspicious. Looking firmly into the Northman's face, the commanding officer suddenly becomes convinced that this honest-seeming, slightly drunk captain has forged an enormous lie. Seeing no way out, convinced of some monstrous villainy, the commanding officer declares that he is letting the Northman go and orders him to steer south by southeast, which would take him past the rocks and into the safety of the open sea. Tired but trusting, the Northman steams off.

The commanding officer ends his tale here, but in a final summation to the woman in the darkening room he declares that the course he gave the Northman led not to safety but to destruction on the rocks. The Northman had been telling the truth; he had been lost. The commanding officer has been left bitter and despairing of never knowing the real truth.

Themes and Meanings

As in so many of Joseph Conrad's works, meaning is at once contained in and amplified by the setting. In "The Tale," the setting of the sea in fog takes on metaphorical and symbolic significance. The crux of the story is the commanding officer's attempt and ultimate failure to find certitude. Has the Northman violated his neutrality by supplying the enemy? The commanding officer is unable to verify his suspicions. The Northman seems to be telling the truth—he is, indeed, at sea, unable to find his way out of the fog. The commanding officer is also fog-bound, unable to see, to distinguish truth from falsity. A philosophical dilemma faces the commanding officer, a dilemma pertinent to all humankind: How can one know the truth in a world in which the truth is obscured by the fog of human fallibility?

The commanding officer is at war not only with the enemy submarine or the mysterious cargo ship, but also with himself, with his frailty as a creature fog-bound by intellectual limitations. Although in command of his ship, he is full of doubts, prejudices, capable even of mean-spiritedness. When he sends the Northman to destruction on the rocks, he is guilty of a cleverness verging on the diabolic. The truth as he learns it is that the Northman really was lost, but the commanding officer realizes that he will never know whether he committed murder or exacted justice.

The commanding officer discovers that his actions and motives are shrouded in fog, that the controlling agency of his endeavors is ignorance. Such fog, such ignorance, pervades not just the sea but the room in which he tells the tale. The twilight setting makes his companion only a disembodied voice. He cannot see her clearly, can only respond to her questions. The relationship thus implicit between them is as uncertain as the darkening room. When the commanding officer turns away from her at the conclusion of his tale, he signifies his despair. The enormous lie that he perceived as part of the faithlessness of war has now become for him part of the faithlessness of human conduct, even in acts of compassion and love.

Style and Technique

Conrad's technique of the frame narrative is integral to the story's meaning. The central story of the commanding officer is told as part of a larger narrative, the frame, involving the narrator of the tale and the woman who asks him to tell it. Such a device, awkward as it may be in lesser works, is at least as old as Giovanni Boccaccio's

Decameron (1353) or Geoffrey Chaucer's *The Canterbury Tales* (1386-1400), works in which short tales appeared as independent narratives supporting an overall plan. In "The Tale," the device is used not only to create suspense, but also to reinforce the theme of uncertainty and confusion. By connecting the wartime experience of the narrator with the personal relationship implied between him and the woman listener, the device emphasizes the narrator's inability to trust or to love. The narrator's revelation of guilt and uncertainty at the end of his story connects with the end of the frame narrative when the woman compassionately seeks to comfort him. The narrator cannot accept her comfort. He merely turns away, suggesting that he has carried his doubt into his personal life, shutting him off from her tenderness and, perhaps, her love.

Within the narrator's tale, the Northman relates his own story. Brief as it is, the account provides still a deeper obscurity to the narrator's attempt to see the light. Credible as the Northman's tale appears, its presence within the narrator's tale to the woman merely emphasizes confusion. "The Tale" is thus constructed like a nest of Chinese boxes: a tale within a tale within a tale, obscurity within an enigma within a puzzle.

Finally, the sentence structure reinforces the theme of uncertainty and forms a kind of rhetorical subtext to the settings of fog and twilight. The commanding officer speaks deliberately, haltingly; his opening narrative to the woman is awkward, filled with pauses, punctuated with unfinished declarations and cryptic remarks. In turn, the woman's own dialogue comprises a series of questions, probings into the narrator's halting observations. Even when the tale has advanced, the narrator is still speculative, his remarks circling around the puzzle, seeking certainty. Both style and technique, then, are not merely reflections of Conrad's Victorian manner of storytelling, but are directly integrated with the theme and meaning of the tale itself.

Edward Fiorelli

TALL TALES FROM THE MEKONG DELTA

Author: Kate Braverman (1950-)
Type of plot: Psychological realism
Time of plot: The late 1980's
Locale: West Hollywood, California
First published: 1990

Principal characters:

THE UNNAMED NARRATOR, a recovering alcoholic divorcée who teaches creative writing
LENNY, a Vietnam veteran, former drug addict, and former convict

The Story

The unnamed protagonist is a thirty-eight-year-old California woman who is divorced and raising a young daughter, has been a recovering alcoholic for five months, and is currently seeing an analyst. As she walks across a parking lot in West Hollywood one day on her way to an Alcoholics Anonymous meeting, she is accosted by a short, fat, pale man with bad teeth who introduces himself as Lenny. He invites her for coffee, inquires about her life, and tells her that he will show her the other side and give her the ride of her life. She turns him down. The next day, Lenny is at the narrator's noon Alcoholics Anonymous meeting and has brought her a bouquet of roses. Again he invites her out, and again she refuses, but Lenny persists. After watching her for two weeks, he knows every move that she makes. Lenny calls it "recon," the kind of reconnaissance he used to do in Vietnam, and promises to tell her some tall tales from the Mekong Delta. She again cuts him off, but later, sitting in her car, she notices the sky in a different way. It is China blue, and Lenny's talk of Asia has given her exotic fantasies of emperors and concubines.

At her meeting the following day, she finds herself looking for Lenny. Sure enough, he is there, holding two cups of coffee as though awaiting her arrival, and he seems younger and tanner than she remembers. Walking out later, she looks at her watch, but Lenny admonishes her, and makes her take it off and give it to him. Time is not important, he says; besides, he will give her something better, a Rolex. He claims to have a drawerful of them, along with a bundle of cash in a safe-deposit box. He offers to take her for a ride around the block on his motorcycle and extends his hand. She takes it, and fantasizes once again about blue Asian skies and China seas.

Over the next week, the narrator tries to avoid Lenny. She changes the times and locations of her meetings, but trembles when she thinks of him and is irresistibly drawn back to the earlier meeting place. She finds him sitting on the front steps of the community center as though he were expecting her. She begins to cry. Lenny consoles her, offers to buy her dinner, and tells her not to worry about the way he looks. He is in disguise, on the run from Colombian drug dealers, and he shows her a knife he has hidden in his sock. He has another under his shirt and is carrying guns. The narrator feels dizzy, lost, but Lenny reassures her: He is in her dreams; he is her ticket to the other side, and she can never get away from him. She lives in a dreamlike state, another time almost, since she no longer has a watch.

Days later, when Lenny says he wants to have sex with her, she finds herself helpless, although rationally she knows better. He needs to get an AIDS test, he is a drug addict, he is pathological, and he has spent time in prison. Lenny reassures her by telling her that if she contracts a disease, he will see that she never suffers. He will take her to Bangkok, keep her loaded up with dope, and will kill her with his own hands before she suffers too much. With Lenny, she is like a child, frozen in time as though under a spell, and she allows him to take her to a place in Bel Air vacated by one of his acquaintances. On the way there, Lenny tells her about his experiences as a drug runner, flying planes from Arizona to Colombia. In fact, that is how he got into trouble with the Colombians. The narrator now fantasizes about living with Lenny in Colombia, dancing barefoot in bars and fanning herself with handfuls of hundred-dollar bills. At the Bel Air mansion, she and Lenny swim naked in the pool and make love in the bedroom, her body draped with expensive diamonds.

The narrator does not see Lenny for a while, but on Christmas Eve he shows up on her doorstep in blue jeans and a black leather jacket, riding a motorcycle. The Colombians are after him, and he is on his way out of town. He needs a drink; despite the fact that the narrator is in Alcoholics Anonymous, she agrees to have one with him. He wants her to come with him, but she refuses. She has a daughter to think about. Nervous and anxious to leave, Lenny heads for the door, tells her it was some ride and that he gave her a glimpse of the other side, and roars off into the darkness. She takes another sip of vodka and knows that when the bottle is empty, she will buy another and another. The air seems a pool of blue shadows, an enormity that will enter her, finding out where she lives and never letting her forget.

Themes and Meanings

"Tall Tales from the Mekong Delta" concerns a woman whose inner emptiness makes her vulnerable to a crude and dangerous man who taps into her deepest fantasies. She is a bored, upper-middle-class Beverly Hills woman who, at the age of thirty-eight, has fallen prey to the conventional twentieth century modes of self-destruction—divorce, alcoholism, and drugs—and is trying to patch things back together through Alcoholics Anonymous and psychotherapy. She is, however, a woman of intelligence and rich imagination; she teaches creative writing and is a writer herself. It is precisely this inner life that makes her vulnerable.

Lenny, for all of his vulgarity and physical unattractiveness, comes from another side of life about which the woman has only fantasized. He is the rebel, the outlaw, who offers her a glimpse of the forbidden, the dangerous, and the deadly. He knows exotic places such as Vietnam, Colombia, and Thailand, has experienced war and adventure, has been in prison and smuggled drugs, and has access to luxurious homes, cars, and diamonds. He even wears black leather jackets and rides a motorcycle, conjuring up images of an aging James Dean, Marlon Brando, or Elvis Presley. When Lenny is with her, the narrator envisions blue skies with sunsets of absinthe yellow and burnt orange, warlords and concubines, and villages on the China Sea. He is an exotic passport into a world about which she has only dreamed—a Mekong Delta of possibilities that fill the emptiness of her life.

Lenny proves to be no better than the alcohol that once removed her from the painful reality of her life, however, and after she has a farewell drink with him, there is every indication that she will return once again to the bottle for her fantasies. The color blue, used throughout the story, has become an infected blue at the end, a kind of contagion that fills up the protagonist. Her dreams of a richer, fuller life depart with Lenny, and the emptiness within her is still there. He has become just a tall tale to tell her friends, like his own tall tales of the Mekong Delta, and while she may have gotten a glimpse of the other side, she knows she will never reach it. The China blue sky of possibility will always be inside her, never letting her forget.

Style and Technique

Kate Braverman has written "Tall Tales from the Mekong Delta" as a series of dramatized encounters between the protagonist and Lenny, each involving them more deeply in their relationship with each other. After the initial meeting in the parking lot, there are encounters in the meeting room of the community center, in the basement of a church, in a public park, and in a Bel Air mansion. The more open settings—the park, the mansion's swimming pool—are appropriate for the fantasies of the protagonist, who envisions skies, rivers, sunsets, and flowers. The dramatic encounters also point up the differences between the woman and Lenny. Lenny's speech is crude, profane, bullying, and selfish; the protagonist's is direct, defensive, apologetic, and spare. The most poetic passages are the protagonist's fantasies, gracefully written passages that are full of color and beauty, a stark contrast to her simple speech.

Braverman places the final scene on Christmas Eve. While there are other religious references in the story, such as an AA meeting that takes place in the basement of a church, the final encounter between the protagonist and Lenny suggests the Christian virtues that are lacking between them: love, charity, and selflessness. Lenny's departure takes place on an evening of tall tales about Santa Claus and flying reindeer, an appropriate setting for his final appearance in the woman's life and for the tall tales he leaves behind.

Kenneth Seib

TEARS, IDLE TEARS

Author: Elizabeth Bowen (1899-1973)
Type of plot: Social realism
Time of plot: The 1930's
Locale: London
First published: 1937

Principal characters:
MRS. DICKINSON, a widowed mother who tries always to do the right thing
FREDERICK, her seven-year-old son, who cries constantly
A YOUNG WOMAN, who befriends Frederick

The Story

Seven-year-old Frederick bursts into tears in the middle of Regent's Park on a beautiful, sunny May afternoon as he and his mother are on their way to the zoo. His elegantly dressed mother is mortified at his crying, yet it is her reproach that draws the attention of the passing people to the scene. She has been so troubled by her son's frequent crying that she is unable to speak about it with any of her friends or relatives. Once she had started to write to a mother's advice column for assistance, but never sent the letter because she could not think of the correct way to sign it.

Frederick cries often and long. He never knows why or what happens to make him cry. He just cries. Nothing matters to him when the tears take over; this day in the park his mother refuses to take him to the zoo, but he does not care. His lack of self-respect makes others look at him and respond in unkind ways; he gets no sympathy. His mother tells him at least once a week that she does not know how he will fit in at school because of his crying. Mrs. Dickinson hates the fact that when she takes a privilege away from him for crying, he seems not to care. She seldom openly punishes him, but she rebukes and belittles him almost constantly. When he seems to feel no emotion about not going to the zoo, she tells him she wonders what his father would think of him. She goes on to say that his father, a pilot who had died after an airplane crash, used to be so proud of him that she is almost glad that he is no longer with them. After this strong reprimand, Mrs. Dickinson walks on ahead so as not to be embarrassed. She tells Frederick to pull himself together before he catches up to her.

Frederick stays behind, knowing that his mother is really ashamed of him. He makes little noise as he sits composing himself and watching a duck. Mrs. Dickinson keeps walking and as the distance extends, so do her emotions. She had been a pillar of strength when her husband died five years ago. While she sat by his bed for two days waiting for him to die, she never shed a tear. After his death, she remained unnaturally composed, only crying once when she went to see her baby, Frederick. At the age of two, Frederick lay awake while his mother's tears had put her to sleep. The look in Frederick's eyes caused the servant to comment that it seemed as if he knew what had happened. Since then, however, Mrs. Dickinson has stood straight and tall, accepted no pity, and needed no support. Her response to men who wanted to marry her was always that Frederick was now the man in her life, and she had to put him first.

Once Frederick stopped crying, he knew he could go after his mother, but he did not want to. Instead, he climbed over the rail to go down and pat the duck. As he reaches out and the duck swims away, he hears a voice warning him about being over the rail and on the grass. He looks and sees a young woman sitting on the park bench, and he thinks that she does not really look or act like a woman. He is intrigued. She gives him an apple and asks about his crying. She has been sitting on the bench during the whole crying fit and wants to know what makes him cry. Something in her tone and her remarks comfort Frederick and make him talk with her: She is not demeaning to him; she really wants to understand. She tells him a story about a boy named George who used to live in a place where she worked. He was a boy, older than Frederick, who also cried out of control. She says he cried as if he knew about something that he should not know. She tells Frederick that he should stop crying so that he does not become like George. Frederick's mother comes into view, and the young woman tells him to go to her before there is more trouble. They shake hands and part.

Mrs. Dickinson is coming down the walk, being careful not to look or seem anxious because Frederick has been gone so long. Appearance is everything to Mrs. Dickinson; she remains calm and unflustered at any cost. As she waits for Frederick to come, the young woman stays on the bench and thinks about George and Frederick; their eyes "seemed to her to be wounds, in the world's surface, through which its inner, terrible unassuageable, necessary sorrow constantly bled away and as constantly welled up." As the young woman is thinking about her meeting with Frederick, he is running toward his mother shouting that he has nearly caught a duck.

Although years later Frederick still recalls with pleasure the afternoon that he spent trying to catch the duck, he has never again thought about the young woman or George.

Themes and Meanings

"Tears, Idle Tears" is about innocence versus experience; it is a coming-of-age story about a young boy's feelings being ignored by one member of the adult world and being restored by a stranger. Frederick is made to feel so bad about disgracing his mother when he cries that he withdraws within himself and becomes apathetic, but he overcomes the disgrace of crying when a young woman on a park bench is friendly to him. The years of being badgered have started to affect Frederick. He never knows why he cries, it just happens. He is a sad little boy.

Mrs. Dickinson must have everything in her life appear to be proper. She dresses and behaves in an elegant manner; she also dresses Frederick elegantly, and expects him to behave accordingly. The expectations she places on Frederick are too cumbersome for him to carry. He has become the man in her life; therefore, she expects him to act like a man. She cannot understand where the tears come from when he cries, nor does she want to understand. Frederick behaves like a child because he is seven years old. Mrs. Dickinson shut down her emotions five years ago and now performs rather than lives life. She is incapable of feeling; she acts rather than reacts.

Tears are viewed as a bad thing. When Mrs. Dickinson's husband lay dying, the chaplain and the doctor gave thanks that Mrs. Dickinson was so brave. In the five years since her husband's death, Mrs. Dickinson has alienated women, but attracted men. Elizabeth Bowen is showing a social difference between men and women by their reactions to the crying.

The title comes from Alfred, Lord Tennyson's poem "Tears, Idle Tears":

> Tears, idle tears, I know not what they mean,
> Tears from the depth of some divine despair
> Rise in the heart, and gather to the eyes,
> In looking on the happy autumn-fields,
> And thinking of the days that are no more.

Frederick's idle tears are not understood by most of the adult world.

Style and Technique

Elizabeth Bowen is known as an exceptionally descriptive and detailed writer. Landscapes and colors are very important to her stories. Frederick cries in the middle of Regent's Park where "Poplars stood up like delicate green brooms; diaphanous willows whose weeping was not shocking quivered over the lake. May sun spattered gold through the breezy trees; the tulips though falling open were still gay; three girls in a long boat shot under the bridge." At once, the reader is in the park with Frederick and his mother. Bowen's description of her characters manages to present their attitude as well as their appearance. Mrs. Dickinson is "a gallant-looking, correct woman, wearing today in London a coat and skirt, a silver fox, white gloves and a dark-blue toque put on exactly right." Frederick's "crying made him so abject, so outcast from other people that he went on crying out of despair. His crying was not just reflex, like a baby's; it dragged up all unseemliness into view. No wonder everyone was repelled." The young woman in the park has a smile and a cock of the head that was "pungent and energetic, not like a girl's at all."

This detail and description help make it possible for Bowen to weave the difficulty of love throughout her story. The boy's hysteria and the mother's coldness can be explained by the fact that the boy's father died five years earlier. Because Bowen has realistically presented the past and present experiences of her characters, the reader can see how previous wounds have scarred them and made them who they are today.

Rosanne Fraine Donahue

TEENAGE WASTELAND

Author: Anne Tyler (1941-)
Type of plot: Psychological realism
Time of plot: The early 1970's
Locale: An unnamed city
First published: 1984

Principal characters:
DONNY COBLE, a troubled fifteen-year-old boy
DAISY and
MATT COBLE, his parents
CALVIN BEADLE, his tutor

The Story

When Daisy Coble receives a telephone call from the principal of her son Donny's private school, the boy's problems do not seem serious. He is described as "noisy, lazy, disruptive, always fooling around with his friends." At a conference with the school's principal, Daisy is ashamed to be regarded as a delinquent, unseeing, or uncaring parent. She describes the restrictions that she and her husband have placed on Donny: no television on school nights, limited telephone calls, and so on. Following the conference, Daisy conscientiously follows the principal's suggestion that she personally supervise Donny's homework and is discouraged by the weaknesses she finds in Donny's work.

In December, the school reports that Donny shows slight progress, as well as new problems: cutting class, smoking in the furnace room, leaving the school grounds, and returning with beer on his breath. Psychological testing is undertaken and a tutor recommended. "Cal" Beadle, the tutor—whom Donny resists at first—quickly establishes himself as being on the boy's side: against the school, which he calls punitive, and the parents, whom Donny calls controlling and competitive—words which he has obviously picked up from Cal.

Donny apparently enjoys his sessions with Cal, who encourages his students to hang around by listening to records and shooting baskets at the backboard on his garage. Donny's grades do not improve, but the school notes that his attitude is more cooperative. This proves to be an illusion, however, as in April Donny is expelled after beer and cigarettes are found in his locker.

Instead of coming home after his expulsion, Donny goes to his tutor's house, where Daisy finds him looking upset and angry. When Donny refuses to accept any blame for the incident, Daisy recalls the bold-faced, wide-eyed look on his face when, as a small boy, he denied little mischiefs, despite all the evidence pointing to his guilt.

Donny proposes that he apply to another school, an idea about which Cal is enthusiastic, saying that he works with many students at the other school. Cal adds that this other school knows "where a kid is coming from." Daisy does not like the sound of the school and is troubled by Cal's smile, which strikes her as "feverish and avid—a smile of hunger."

Shortly after this conference, Donny's parents enroll him in a public school and terminate his tutoring sessions. Although both decisions are against Donny's wishes, he plods off to his new school each morning, without friends, looking worn out and beaten.

In June, Donny disappears. The police try to find him, but their remarks about the hundreds of young people who run away every year are not reassuring. Three months pass without word from Donny. Both his parents have aged, and his younger sister tries to stay away from home as much as she can. Daisy lies awake at night going over Donny's life, trying to understand their mistakes and wondering who to blame.

The story ends as Daisy, falling asleep, glimpses a basketball sinking through the hoop, onto a yard littered with leaves and striped "with bands of sunlight as white as bones, bleached and parched and cleanly picked."

Themes and Meanings

Anne Tyler's focus in this story is the gradual disintegration of the relationship between a teenage boy and his parents. The title of the story, taken from the lyrics of "Baba O'Reilly," a song popularized by The Who in the early 1970's, clearly suggests Tyler's theme, although in an oblique way. "Teenage Wasteland" is a metaphor for the place where Donny's parents see him when they pick him up at Cal's: Students there are idly shooting baskets; loud music pours out through the windows; and Donny, "spiky and excited," looks like someone they do not know. To Daisy and Matt, all the students look like hoodlums. When Daisy murmurs, "Teenage Wasteland," recognizing the song, Matt, misunderstanding, replies, "It certainly is." Thus in only a few lines, Tyler encapsulates the enormous distance between them and the youngsters playing in Cal's backyard. The distance increases as Donny moves further from them, until communication between them nearly ceases. When Donny is expelled, the fact that he heads for Cal's house instead of home signifies both his preference for his tutor and his inability to make his mother accept his lame explanation of the incident which precipitated the expulsion.

The image with which Tyler closes the story is subtle and moving. Lying awake at night, Daisy tries to understand what has happened and has a vision of Cal's yard, where a neighbor's fence casts narrow shadow bars across the spring grass. As she drifts off to sleep, she recalls that scene, the stripes of sunlight "as white as bones, bleached and parched and cleanly picked." It is a fearful image, one which Tyler does not explain, leaving it to the reader to interpret as an expression of Daisy's defeat and despair.

Style and Technique

The narrative viewpoint of "Teenage Wasteland" is that of Donny Coble's mother, Daisy. The entire story is told in the third person as an omniscient author might tell it, but one who knows only the thoughts and feelings of Daisy. All events are presented as Daisy experiences or observes them and the dialogue always includes her.

Daisy is not given to introspection and emotionalism, as one may expect, considering the disappearance of her son, with whom she cannot communicate. The boy wants to be trusted and treated as an adult, even as he behaves in childish and self-indulgent ways. These are judgments that the author's style leads the reader to make; Tyler herself does not judge. Her style is unemotional, detached, and objective. Her characteristic use of brief, telling descriptions and natural, credible dialogue keeps the pace of the story swift; there is not an unnecessary word. For example, when Daisy catches up with Donny at his tutor's home after his expulsion, she merely says, "Hello, Donny," a simple greeting that conveys her inability to express her deep feeling of relief, her uncertainty about how to approach her son, who replies by simply flicking his eyes at her.

In addition to concise, sketchy narration, and dialogue that seems exactly suited to the speakers' personalities, Tyler uses images to convey tone and mood. The brief scene in Cal's backyard, for example, is made visible and meaningful through the image of a fence casting shadows across the grass in narrow bars. The suggestion of a prison is not made, but the connection is undeniable. The scene is echoed in the closing sentence of the story as Daisy sighs and tosses sleeplessly, unable to come to a clear understanding of what has happened.

It is possible to read this story in terms of superficial facts. However, the reader who searches for what those facts suggest beneath the surface of brief conversations and simple, straightforward narration in which every word is essential, will be rewarded. As usual, Tyler transforms ordinary people in familiar situations into a moving tale that can appeal to readers who recognize themselves or someone they know.

Natalie Harper

TELL THEM NOT TO KILL ME!

Author: Juan Rulfo (1918-1986)
Type of plot: Social realism
Time of plot: Early twentieth century
Locale: Jalisco, Mexico
First published: "¡Díles que no me maten!" 1953 (English translation, 1959)

Principal characters:
JUVENCIO NAVA, the owner of a small farm and herd, an escaped criminal
JUSTINO, his son
COLONEL TERREROS, the son of a man whom he murdered

The Story

Juvencio Nava cries out, "Tell them not to kill me!" pleading with his son, Justino, to help him. Juvencio, who is in his sixties, has just been arrested for a crime he had committed thirty-five or forty years earlier. At first, Justino is reluctant to interfere, fearing that the police or the soldiers may arrest him too or even shoot him. Then there will be no one left to care for his wife and children. He finally relents and offers to see what he can do to assist his father.

As he waits, tied to a post, Juvencio recalls the past events that led up to his present predicament and circumstances. Years earlier he killed Don Lupe, his neighbor and the landowner in the areas of Alima and Puerta de Piedras. The two men had been feuding over grazing and water rights during a particularly dry spell. Don Lupe refused to let Juvencio's animals graze on his property. After several warnings, Don Lupe finally killed one of Juvencio's animals for wandering onto his land. In retaliation, Juvencio killed Don Lupe.

Juvencio then bribed the judge to release him and bribed the posse not to follow him, but they came after him anyway. He finally escaped and went into hiding with his son in Palo de Venado. He later learned that Don Lupe's widow had soon died; their two small children had been sent far away to live with relatives. Thus Juvencio thought that he might be relatively safe and that the incident would gradually be forgotten. He still lived in fear of detection, however, hiding out or going on the run whenever he heard that outsiders or strangers were in the area.

Meanwhile, Juvencio's son grew up, married a woman named Ignacia, and fathered eight children. Juvencio's own wife abruptly left him one day, but he dared not go searching for her, since he still feared capture. He did not want to leave his hiding place to go into town. All he had left to save was his own life. He thought and hoped that after so much time, he would finally be left in peace, an old man in his last years, a threat to no one.

Now they have arrested him after all. They have even tied him up, even though he is too old and weak to try to escape. They say that they will execute him. After so many years of dodging capture and death, he cannot imagine being caught and dying so suddenly now. He simply cannot accept the dreadful idea. He continues to think and to hope, pondering a possible way out, but he can find none. He wonders if he can convince his captors to release him, but is afraid to speak to them. He remembers when he first saw the men coming, back on his own land, as they came trampling his field. Instead of hiding or fleeing, he went down to tell them not to damage his bit of property. That was a very serious mistake, a very foolish and costly error. He was caught and none of the four men would respond to his pleas for mercy.

The group's sergeant finally stands up in front of the door to the headquarters, speaking with his colonel, who remains inside. Only the colonel's voice can be heard as the sergeant relays his questions to Juvencio about the town of Alima and the Terreros family. Eventually the colonel reveals that he is the son of Don Lupe, that he grew up as an orphan, deprived of his father's protection. He learned several facts about the brutal nature of his father's murder. He tried to forget this information but could not. He had vowed to capture his father's murderer because he could not forgive such a man; he could not permit him to continue living.

The colonel then orders that Juvencio be shot by the firing squad. Juvencio pleads for his life, repeating that he is no threat, since he is so old and worthless; he says that he has been punished enough through all the years of living in fear and hiding, plagued by constant dread. The colonel finally tells his men to get Juvencio drunk first, before the time of execution, so that he will not feel the bullets.

In the final scene, Justino returns to collect Juvencio's body. The son places his father's body on a burro and covers his father's head with a sack, because the corpse is shocking to see. As he departs, heading home to arrange his father's funeral, Justino thinks that the family will hardly recognize the old man, he was so full of holes.

Themes and Meanings

This work is from Juan Rulfo's 1950's collection of short stories *El llano en llamas*, which presents scenes from life in rural Jalisco, Rulfo's native region of Mexico. The collection has been translated by George D. Schade as *The Burning Plain* (1967). Many of its stories, like this one, involve family relationships in difficult situations. Juan Rulfo himself was an orphan; his father was killed in the long years of the *cristero* revolts during the time of the Mexican Revolution and his mother died several years later. The theme of the search for the father, for family roots, and for personal or even national identity permeates Rulfo's writings.

Both sons in this story, the colonel and Justino, feel a sense of family loyalty and duty. The colonel is seeking justice as well as revenge for his father's murder. He does not attempt to face the guilty man directly, lest he feel some sense of compassion for him. Justino is hesitant, yet he tries to help his father. He seems to accept Juvencio's admitted guilt, and he finally claims the body for burial. Although Justino had his father with him during his youth, he felt the fear of a life constantly in dread of his father's potential capture and death. The colonel spent most of his life without a father; he came to be overwhelmed by the desire to see his father's murderer punished, perhaps as much to avenge his own lost childhood as to avenge his father.

Juvencio tries to avoid death almost up to the very end, as he has all of his life. Yet there is a certain inevitability and fatalism in his ultimate demise. He knows that his family suffered along with him all those years, but his primary thought is for self-preservation. The reader is left to ponder the limits of rights and responsibilities, of justice and revenge, of mercy and forgiveness. The story offers a strongly evoked regional setting, vividly described, which is elevated to a broader level by the sobering consideration of deep, universal themes.

Style and Technique

Juan Rulfo is noted for his powerful evocation of scene, for the sense of place created in his work. He employs dialogue and popular speech to add to the realism of the social situations depicted. All five senses are invoked as the sights, sounds, smells, textures, and tastes of the landscape are described. The reader can feel the impact of the hard, rugged life of the region. Rulfo's literary devices include some repetition, as in this story, to underscore a character's desperate psychological state. The reader can feel Juvencio's fear and dread as he thinks about the events leading up to his capture. The heat, the dust, the harshness of the scene are all conjured up for the reader's imaginative consideration.

Rulfo also varies verb tenses in order to illustrate alternations between past and present, between memory and current reality; events are not revealed in a directly linear, chronological order. A character's memory is used to portray the past, while dialogue among characters is interspersed with the protagonist's own thoughts. Rulfo utilizes language in a disciplined, economical style. His setting often is one of intense and grinding poverty, desperation, and desolation; towns are seen to be depopulating as people seek a better life elsewhere. Sometimes only the dead are left behind, as in his novel *Pedro Páramo* (1955), with its use of Magical Realism (joining the possible with the imaginary). His stories, in contrast, are predominantly and truly realistic.

Margaret V. Ekstrom

TENNESSEE'S PARTNER

Author: Bret Harte (1836-1902)
Type of plot: Social realism
Time of plot: 1853-1854
Locale: Sandy Bar, a fictional western mining town
First published: 1869

Principal characters:
THE NARRATOR, an unnamed resident of Sandy Bar
TENNESSEE'S PARTNER, a devoted friend of Tennessee
TENNESSEE, a notorious gambler and thief who is hanged
JUDGE LYNCH, who captures Tennessee and presides at his trial

The Story

The unnamed narrator explains that the real name of Tennessee's Partner has—in accordance with Sandy Bar's quixotic practice of rechristening new arrivals—never been known in the mining town. The locals have dubbed the man "Tennessee's Partner" because he teamed up with Tennessee, a wholly disreputable character whose own real name has been similarly obliterated from communal memory.

The narrator goes on to relate the story of Tennessee's Partner's search for a bride. A year earlier, in 1853, the man set out for San Francisco from Poker Flat, but got no farther than Stockton, where he was attracted by a waitress in a hotel. During a courtship, the waitress broke a plate of toast over Tennessee's Partner's head, then agreed to marry him before a justice of the peace. With his new bride in tow, the man returned to Poker Flat, and then went to Sandy Bar, where the couple took up residence with Tennessee.

Some time after his partner's return, Tennessee began making indecent advances to the new bride until she ran off to Marysville. He then followed her there and set up housekeeping without the aid of a justice of the peace. A few months later their relationship ended; the woman took up with yet another man and Tennessee returned to Sandy Bar. To the disappointment of the townspeople, who gathered to witness a shooting, Tennessee's Partner was the first man to shake Tennessee's hand and he greeted him with affection. With no trace of bitterness, and without apology, Tennessee and his partner resumed their former relationship as if the woman had never existed.

The narrator goes on to explain that the residents of Sandy Bar suspect that Tennessee—already known to be a gambler—is also a thief. These rumors are confirmed when Tennessee is caught red-handed after robbing at gunpoint a stranger traveling between Sandy Bar and Red Dog.

After frantically escaping from Sandy Bar, Tennessee is cornered in a canyon, where Judge Lynch finds him. Armed with a better "hand" than Tennessee—two revolvers and a bowie knife—the judge calls Tennessee's bluff and takes him prisoner.

During the ensuing trial, conducted by Lynch, Tennessee's Partner tries to buy his friend's freedom, offering a watch and seventeen hundred dollars in raw gold, his only belongings of any real worth. This offer is construed as a bribe, so rather than help the accused, it merely hastens his date with the "ominous tree" atop Marley's Hill. Tennessee is convicted and sentenced to hang.

Tennessee's Partner does not attend the hanging. Afterward, he arrives with a crudely decorated donkey cart and rough coffin to claim Tennessee's body. Followed by a curious crowd, he drives the makeshift hearse through Grizzly Canyon to an open grave near his cabin. There he gives a brief, rustic funeral oration, thanks those in attendance, and buries Tennessee.

After this primitive funeral, the health of Tennessee's Partner declines. He visibly wastes away until he takes to a sickbed and dies. In his final delirious moments, he envisions his reunion with Tennessee in death: "Thar! I told you so!—that he is—coming this way, too—all by himself, sober, and his face a-shining. Tennessee! Pardner!"

Themes and Meanings

"Tennessee's Partner" chronicles an inexplicable bond between two men, Tennessee and his partner, both crude, unlettered mining camp men. The basis for their bond is never explained, but its durable strength is revealed in the fact that their friendship survives a breach of its faith: After Tennessee runs off with his partner's wife, he returns to Sandy Bar and is welcomed back by his friend without rancor or resentment. Theirs is a friendship that transcends marriage ties—at least for the protagonist, Tennessee's Partner.

Although Bret Harte's story is in the tradition of local-color realism, its essential idea is romantic in origin. It argues that no matter how primitive a man appears to be, he may still possess some indelible virtue, such as loyalty. The devotion of Tennessee's Partner to his friend is not contingent upon refined sensibilities honed through schooling or sophisticated social codes. In fact, Tennessee's Partner cannot even articulate the code by which he lives or the feelings that bind him to his friend. When he is asked to speak on Tennessee's behalf at his friend's trial, he can only ask, "What should a man know of his pardner?" To him, loyalty is simply a fact of his life—one as unfathomable to him as it is to the reader.

The fact that rough and tumble frontier mining camp existence scarcely seems a promising incubator for the kind of sensibilities that underlie the protagonist's behavior makes his loyalty all the more remarkable. It is also unique in the story, for the citizens of Sandy Bar do not share Tennessee's Partner's simple virtue. In contrast, they tend to be cruel spectators. When Tennessee returns to Sandy Bar after having been jilted by his partner's wife, the townspeople gather in Grizzly Canyon, not because they hope there will be an amiable reunion between Tennessee and his partner, but because they assume there will be a shooting. And when Tennessee's Partner takes his friend home for burial, the townspeople follow, not from respect for the dead, but from idle curiosity. Some even jest, mocking the ceremony.

From the community's point of view, Tennessee's Partner's selfless devotion is an aberration, to be ridiculed, not admired. He has no other relationship, no friends; outside his relation with Tennessee he is basically a pariah figure, a familiar sort in the fiction of Bret Harte. Presumably, the bond between the two men is forged in part because, in reality, frontier life could be desperately lonely. No matter how wretched a man Tennessee is, he fills the fundamental need for human companionship that his partner and any sensitive person might feel in such an environment.

Style and Technique

Although some modern commentators have complained that "Tennessee's Partner" strains credibility and borders on the maudlin, it remains one of the best pieces of short fiction to come out of the western, local-color tradition in which Harte played such an important part. Its sentimentality is balanced by the sort of rawboned, understated humor, borrowed from the tall-tale oral tradition, that marks the stories of Harte's contemporary and one-time acolyte, Mark Twain. Harte uses a variety of comic elements, such as malapropisms, verbal irony, and inappropriate tone, to good effect, offsetting the sentimentality that otherwise might overburden the reader.

By employing an unidentified narrator who plays no other role in the story, Harte also distances the reader from the inward feelings and thoughts of his main character, making a psychological probing of his consciousness impossible. The narrator offers no explanation for the friendship of Tennessee and his partner; it is just there, inexplicable and mysterious. A simple, uncultured man, Tennessee's Partner cannot articulate his feelings, except, by implication, in his artless but quaint funeral oration and his rhapsodic meandering in his death throes. Only the narrator, who is the thinly veiled author, and Judge Lynch are articulate. In fact, the story's main flaw is perhaps the tendency of the author to editorialize, to orchestrate the reader's feelings in an attempt to evoke pathos. Harte also strains in some of the descriptive passages, using the pathetic fallacy familiar from romantic literature to achieve a desired mood. For example, the forlorn plight of Tennessee, on the eve of his trial, is heightened by the vastness of the surroundings. Harte describes the nearby Sierra Nevada as being "etched on the dark firmament . . . remote and passionless, crowned with remoter passionless stars." To the contemporary reader, such writing may seem turgid, but it would hardly have seemed excessive to the readers of Harte's own period.

By carefully blending humor and pathos, Harte manages to skirt emotional clichés, keeping readers intrigued with his story. One may complain that he never really investigates the motives behind Tennessee's Partner's devotion to his friend, but that objection arises in the wake of modern psychological theories that did not impact fiction until some decades after Harte wrote the story. In his fictional world, characters are often what they are by virtue of an innate proclivity that circumstances can only reveal but not necessarily explain.

John W. Fiero

TESTIMONY OF PILOT

Author: Barry Hannah (1942-   )
Type of plot: Social realism
Time of plot: The 1950's to 1970's
Locale: Clinton, Mississippi
First published: 1974

Principal characters:
WILLIAM HOWLY, the narrator
ARDEN QUADBERRY, a saxophone player and pilot
LILIAN FIELD, Arden's girlfriend
EDITH FIELD, her sister

The Story

In a rambling but effective manner, William Howly recalls the story of his odd friend, Arden Quadberry. They first meet by accident. Seeking to punish a nearby black family for what he believes was the savage treatment of a pig, William and another boy, Radcleve, shell the black family's home with Radcleve's homemade mortar. The shells, actually batteries, fall short, landing on the house occupied by the Quadberrys. Mr. Quadberry is a history professor, his wife is a musician; their son, Ard, with his Arab nose, saxophone, and mud-caked shoes, is not accepted by the other boys. Sent by his parents to tell the boys to stop the shelling, Ard is nearly blinded on the return trip when Radcleve nonchalantly tosses an M-80 firecracker packed in mud in his direction.

Made uneasy by his own silent complicity in the act as well as by Ard's strangeness, Howly keeps his distance until their senior year, when Ard joins the school band. As their lives begin to intersect, Howly, the band's drummer, has the opportunity to observe Ard more closely. Once he enters the band room and comes upon Ard and a small, red-faced ninth-grade euphonium player who calls him "Queerberry," and is beaten for his temerity. At the state championship, held in nearby Jackson, Howly sees a different side of his unusual friend. When Prender, the much-loved band director, is killed en route to Jackson in a head-on crash with an ambulance, Quadberry takes charge. Not only does he direct the others, he plays so brilliantly that the judges applaud, an attractive woman in her thirties walks up to Ard and introduces herself, and the beautiful Lilian, the majorette and third-chair clarinetist who missed the start of the performance because she was drowning her sorrow in two beers, offers Ard both her apologies and herself.

Howly's band, the Bop Fiends, which includes Ard, becomes well known, able to command twelve hundred dollars a night. Howly's success is also his undoing, as his loud drum playing soon makes him deaf. Ard goes off to the United States Naval Academy, the only school that wants him, charging Howly with looking after Lilian, who, like Howly, will attend the local college. Six years later, Ard, having given up his saxophone for a much bigger gleaming metal tube, a Navy fighter plane, arranges to meet Lilian at the Jackson airbase. He touches down and, without even bothering to deplane, delivers to Lilian, and through her to Howly, this one-size-fits-all message: "I am a dragon. America the beautiful, like you will never know."

In Vietnam, much the same good technique that had made him so fine a saxophonist makes him a successful fighter pilot, flying escort for B-52's on bombing missions. Immediately after downing his first enemy plane, killing its pilot, Ard's luck changes. Hit by a ground missile, he flies back to sea, ejects, and lands right on the carrier's flight deck. He spends a month recovering from a back injury. Returning to action, his plane fails on takeoff and drops off the end of the carrier's deck into the ocean. Again he ejects, this time under water, after waiting for the ship to pass over him. Again he hurts his back, this time so severely as to preclude his ever flying or playing again.

Sometime later, Lilian, now an airline stewardess, dies when a hijacker's inept bomb explodes a few miles off the Cuban coast. Two weeks after the memorial service, the handicapped and previously abstemious Quadberry returns home to Clinton, drunk and smoking a cigar. Howly is there to greet him and to tell him of Lilian's death. His mother shows up and his father, who had opposed Ard's participation in the war, is waiting in the car. Seven months later, Ard calls Howley, who now lives with Lilian's younger sister, Edith, to ask whether he should undergo a new surgical procedure that has a 75 percent chance of curing him, but a 25 percent chance of killing him. Howly tells him to trust his luck and have the operation. Quadberry does and dies, his luck having run out.

Themes and Meanings

"In Mississippi, it is difficult to achieve a vista." This line, delivered early in the story, proves doubly important. First, it underscores the strong Southernness of Barry Hannah's fiction, its links to a particular region and culture and to certain of the South's most important writers: Edgar Allan Poe, Mark Twain, William Faulkner, and Flannery O'Connor. Second, the line underscores the story's concern with how well one sees and how one is seen. How well one sees is highlighted in the opening pages in the number of times the narrator as a boy of ten or so manages to misjudge the small world that makes up his rather limited vista. How one is perceived proves especially significant in the case of the story's titular subject, with his Arab nose, white halo, and odd name. While Quadberry's inspired saxophone playing represents the school's best hope for winning the state championship, it also represents, at least to Howly, a "desperate oralness" that neither he, nor Lilian, nor the small, red-faced, ninth-grade boy can satisfy. That Ard is, or may be, homosexual only compounds his difficulty in trying to find a place either in his small Mississippi town or in the aggressively male world of Annapolis and Navy pilots during the Vietnam War.

When he goes to Annapolis, he begins the process that will take him from playing the saxophone to flying fighter aircraft, from soloist and musical genius to the no less intense but certainly more deadly isolation of a plane's cockpit. In the sky, he achieves the widest vista possible and the greatest distance from all that is merely human.

Howly moves in a parallel but opposite direction. Just as Ard must give up his saxophone because of his bad back, Howly must give up his drums because of his deafness. Howly's deafness, however, brings him closer to people, including Edith Field, Lilian's younger sister, "a second-rate version of her and a wayward overcompensating nymphomaniac." With Howly, she finds what Ard, with his chronic sneer and Arab nose up in the air, and the haughty Lilian never do, a measure of happiness, some relief for her desperate loneliness. In Hannah's world of odd characters, freakish accidents, and thwarted lives, the moral seems to be that less is often more.

Style and Technique

The one exception to the less-is-more rule is the narrator's style. The aptly named William Howly is a latter-day Huck Finn, although older, wiser, and better educated, who, instead of lighting out for the Territory, has settled into the relative comfort of a job as lead writer at a Jackson advertising agency. The story is told in the vernacular and follows a more or less straightforward chronological line. The delivery may be deadpan but the phrasings are often startling: hyperbolic, comically grotesque, the matter-of-fact rendered with a manic touch of Southern gothicism. Ard's "ugly ocher Chrysler," for example, "was a failed, gay experimental shade from the Chrysler people." Syntax is at times decidedly and comically colloquial ("I didn't know but what he was having a seizure"). The narrative often swerves from one scene to another; one section, for example, ends, "Now Quadberry's back was really hurt. He was out of this war and all wars for good," and the next begins, "Lilian, the stewardess, was killed in a crash."

Hannah's art is one of stark juxtapositions rather than intricate designs, an art of extravagant verbal effects and broad, cartoonlike strokes rather than the careful building-up of realistic detail. It is an art in which comic antics are deployed to keep despair at least momentarily at bay, and in which finely tuned psychological motivation plays a less important role than raw emotional force. "Testimony of Pilot" thus resembles Quadberry's playing, which combines technical brilliance with sudden transcendence: "desperate oralness" and a private ecstasy, dignified because of what came out of his horn. The story follows essentially the same dramatic idea that the Bop Fiends do—to "release Quadberry on a very soft sweet ballad right in the middle of a long ear-piercing run of rock-and-roll tunes"—and achieves precisely the same result, astonishing its audience with its tenderness.

Robert A. Morace

TEXTS FOR NOTHING 3

Author: Samuel Beckett (1906-1989)
Type of plot: Absurdist
Time of plot: Mid-twentieth century
Locale: Dublin, Ireland
First published: "Textes pour rien 3," 1955 (English translation, 1967)

Principal characters:
THE NARRATOR
VINCENT, his friend

The Story

This is one of Samuel Beckett's intellectually and perversely teasing monologues about existence, which are quite common in his later work. As the unnamed narrator considers what he should do, he seems to be trying to prove his own reality by constructing a story which he keeps chopping and changing. It may be a story of a journey, out and back, that takes place in the spring. There is to be no serious action, so the voice assures itself that there is nothing to fear. Nevertheless, there is a constant sense of anxiety and reluctance involved. The voice decides to be the character in the story, and there is a sense that it is to be a male character, an old man, cared for by a nanny called Bibby.

The narrator faces the problem of how to describe himself, perhaps with the help of memory, although he admits that he cannot remember much, so he abandons that idea. He will instead write of the future. As an example of that method, he thinks about how sometimes at night he says to himself that on the morrow he will put on his dark blue tie with the yellow stars. This thought seems to upset him, but he hurries on with his proposed action and decides to be accompanied by an old naval veteran, who may have fought under Admiral Jellicoe in the British navy in World War I. There is considerable gritty detail about this proposed companion, and about the narrator's physical state. The veteran's lungs are bad, and the narrator himself suffers from a prostate condition, which he alleviates in unpleasant detail. There is a sense that what he is saying is not simply being made up, but, in fact, actually occurred in the past, as numerous minor acts in his characters' lives are recorded with tangible details. The narrator imagines spending time with his companion trying to keep warm, and their pleasure in betting on horses and, occasionally, on dog races.

The narrator thinks for a moment of going alone, but reconsiders and decides to take his old friend, whom he calls Vincent, with him. He spends some time imagining what it would be like to start off with Vincent stumbling along behind him. But this consideration of how to make something of himself outside his loneliness fails, and he abandons the idea of making his trip with Vincent.

He tries again, thinking about how to describe himself physically, and concludes that he might find it easier just to be a head, rolling along, but with some sort of leg to deal with the hills, starting out from Duggan's (which may be a name for a Dublin betting shop) on a rainy spring morning. The voice admits that it is all for naught—that none of this exists, that his attempt to make flesh of his plight of being nothing but a voice fails him. He is reduced to his state of seeming nothingness, in which nothing will happen. There will be no departure or stories about tomorrow, and the voices he seems to hear have "no life in them."

Themes and Meanings

Samuel Beckett was always interested in problems of existence, particularly the simple fact that human beings have no certainty that anything or anyone exists outside their own consciousness. Beckett's characters, therefore, are battling against the nightmare of solipsism. He often expresses the battle to discover existence in stories about characters who try to give themselves life by contemplating existence in invented stories. There is something appropriate, if maddeningly circular, in the idea of Beckett writing about characters who are trying to confirm their existence by writing about making up stories about themselves.

In this story, the narratorial voice goes quickly to the problem as if one were writing a story, choosing a character, a plot, a setting, and a time-frame. There is some specificity in the naming of two characters, and the suggestion that the story is taking place in Dublin. For example, the reference to "the Green" may mean St. Stephen's Green, a park in the center of Dublin. There is also specificity in various graphic descriptions of the physical states of the narrator and his friend Vincent.

The story may be seen as a metaphor for the human condition, which Beckett always views with considerable pessimism as physically difficult at best, psychologically not worth the bother, and, ultimately, impossible to make any sense of, however hard one tries. For Beckett's characters, life is also difficult to prove. The philosopher René Descartes was assured by the proposition "I think, therefore I am." Beckett, by contrast, seems to think that the idea would be more accurately expressed as, "I think, but I am not so sure that I exist, and thinking does not necessarily clear up the problem or make things any better."

The story may be taken also as a metaphor for the difficulty of artistic creation—a frequent theme with Beckett narrators, who often weave it into their attempts to discover who and where they are. Beckett is called an "absurdist" because his stories are absurd in the sense of seeming to be meaningless, and they are absurd in the sense of reflecting his belief that life has no meaning.

Style and Technique

Beckett's fiction looks much more difficult than it actually is, but it does require careful attention, almost word to word, and certainly sentence to sentence, since his narrators are constantly changing their minds. Beckett's strength lies not in telling the usual narrative with a beginning, middle, and end, although there is a rudimentary structure of such in this tale, but in the texture of his monologues. His characters (if they can be called such) may be down and out, both physically and socially, but that is sometimes taken to suggest that they are stupid—which they are not. His is a plain, oral style, but the content and manner of his expression are often highly intelligent.

From early in Beckett's career, he was interested in the nature of human existence. By the time he got to this kind of work, he was almost exclusively concerned with the question of how one knows things, and particularly, with how one exists within one's own mind. This story is best read in the context of the other tales in *Stories and Texts for Nothing* (*Nouvelles et textes pour rien*, 1955; English translation, 1967), since, as a group, they form a kind of tone poem of musings, sometimes poignant, sometimes angry, sometimes self-pitying, about the nature of living at the lowest level of self-perception, cut off from most normal social connection, and living a bare-bones existence. The story can also be read by itself, with the understanding that there is no action, no plot, no resolution as one expects in the usual short story. What there is must be read carefully and slowly to keep track of the constant changes. Simply, it seems to be the musings of an old man, though his bodily aspects are clearly played down, who seems to be trying to make sense of his life by inventing it in the form of a story, but cannot make up his mind what or who or where or when to do it.

The aesthetic pleasure in this story lies not in its conclusion, nor in its incidents, but in listening to its cranky, eccentric, but intelligently wayward voice. As a result, the standards for judging the quality of the tale lie not in plot, or in characterization in the ordinary sense, but in the act of entering the mind of this odd creature. It requires, in a sense, an abandonment of the usual touchstones of short-story judgment, although it can be argued that Beckett is using a rather narrow form of the "dramatic monologue" in which the speaker reveals problems, and sometimes solutions thereof, while often inadvertently revealing character. It is an old literary form, which can be seen in Geoffrey Chaucer's Pardoner, in William Shakespeare's soliloquies, and in some of the poems of Robert Browning, T. S. Eliot, and W. H. Auden. The real standard for its credibility as a work of art lies in the experience of keeping track of what is happening in the mind of an interesting character. It is quite possible to do so, but it demands the reader's close attention, patience, and willing suspension of disbelief in much of what is ordinarily presumed to be the normal elements of the short-story form and content. Form illustrates meaning.

Charles Pullen

THANKSGIVING DAY

Author: Susan Minot (1956-   )
Type of plot: Social realism
Time of plot: The mid-1960's
Locale: Motley, Massachusetts
First published: 1984

Principal characters:
MA and PA VINCENT, the grandparents
GUS, their son
ROSIE, Gus's wife
UNCLE CHARLES, another son
AUNT GINNY, Uncle Charles's wife

The Story

Gus and Rosie Vincent arrive at Ma and Pa Vincent's home, followed by the other aunts and uncles and cousins. Coats are taken off, there are greetings, and then the adults line all of the young cousins up outside for the annual photograph. After the picture has been taken, Rosie Vincent instructs her children to go to the kitchen and greet Livia, the large, sweating woman cooking the family's holiday dinner. Livia drills the Vincent children in the catechism, and when they do not respond, she answers her own questions.

Sophie, Bit, and Churly snitch candy from the dinner table while the adults, except for Rosie, have cocktails in the living room. Some of the children drift into this adult sphere, keeping silent while their parents and grandparents talk. Readers see the details of the room through the wandering eyes of the quiet children: books, a photograph of Ma when she was young, the portrait of Dr. Vincent over the mantelpiece, the fancy shoes with flat bows that Ma is wearing and that her granddaughters like best. Interwoven through these details is the superficial, anecdotal conversation of the adults, who talk without looking at one another.

Delilah, sticking close to her mother in this uncertain adult world, says she wants to go look at the lion. Rosie tells her daughter to ask Pa, but Delilah and Sophie cross the room to examine a shadow box rather than address their grandfather. Finally Rosie speaks for her daughter, telling Pa that the children would like to go see the lion. His affirmative response is snapped out as a threat: "Watch out it doesn't bite you."

A troop of cousins ascends the stairs to the third floor, where the lion lies on the floor of the farthest attic room. In the thin light, amidst the scent of cedar, the cousins approach the dead animal. Bit is the only one who will dare touch the tongue, made of fired clay, and Sophie lies down next to it to touch her cheek to the lion's soft ears.

Leaving Caitlin and Churly at the red-leather bar, Sophie, Bit, and Delilah proceed to the owl room, some of the boy cousins following. In this room are all kinds of ornamental owls. Along the hallway, stretching away from the owl room, are photographs and silhouettes of Vincent family members: Pa's pictures of himself from his sporting, Harvard, and political speechwriting days; a picture of Pa's famous brother. When the wandering children return to the living room, the grown-ups are arguing over whether the lawn at the grandparents' house had ever frozen over and the kids skated on it. Uncle Charles remembers this and is corroborated by Gus and Ma, but Pa, in the stubbornness of his old age and contrariness, says no.

Dinner is served. Most of the cousins sit at the wobbly children's table. Plates arrive at their places with everything already on them. Sophie leaves the table to go to the bathroom, and she stands in the hallway for a moment, listening to the sounds of the meal in the other room—the sounds of silverware on plates, voices, echoes. She returns to the table in the middle of a conversation that the adults are attempting to squelch, but that Churly wants to know more about. Ma has called someone a crook and Churly wants to know who it is and what he stole.

At this point Ma makes a strategic turn, changing the subject to the vacation house in Maine. This also turns out to be an unsafe topic of discussion: There is an argument about a porch that the house used to have. Was it torn down or did it burn down? Pa insists that it was torn down, but Aunt Fran says she thought it burned. Ma agrees and gives the signal to end the conversation. True to form, Churly disregards Ma's cue and presses the subject, asking how it burned down. There is tension at the table; Sophie feels flushed. Pa repeats that it was torn down. Ma explains that the remainder was torn down. Pa glares at Ma.

Ma starts to stack dishes on the turkey platter, getting ready to remove the dinner things from the table. Pa and Ma argue over whether he is finished eating. Aunt Fran tries to move forward by tempting Pa with dessert. Pa obstinately curses Livia's pies and then follows with a nonsequitur that silences the table: "Only occasionally you will disguise a voyage and cancel all that crap." The children are uncertain amidst this tension. As the family eats dessert, Pa mumbles a series of phrases that seem unconnected to anything presently going on. When his wife whispers something in his ear, he loudly responds, "Why don't you go shoot yourself?"

The family dinner ends and the family members disperse. Ma and Aunt Fran take Pa upstairs and then join the other grown-ups for coffee in the living room. To Uncle Charles's query, Ma answers with finality that everything is fine. This time it is Delilah, not Churly, who challenges the signal to be silent. Unlike Churly, who pushes argumentatively, Delilah challenges out of bravery. Delilah asks whether Pa was mad at them. The question forces the issue of Pa and the family's treatment of him. Gus says Pa didn't know what he was saying. Rosie keeps silent, pouring the coffee. Ma says Pa wasn't mad at Delilah. Aunt Ginny says that the turkey was delicious. Uncle Charles tells her to shut up. The family exchanges compliments over the meal. Ma gives all credit to Livia. Rosie says that Ma arranged it beautifully, to which Ma replies, "Actually, I don't think I've ever arranged anything beautifully in my whole life." Silence reasserts itself, and the vignette of the Vincent family Thanksgiving Day ends on a note of strained quiet and stillness.

Themes and Meanings

Susan Minot's story, which does not have a conventional plot, derives its meaning from the rich collection of details depicting the Vincent family. Carefully selected and skillfully expressed, these details work together to describe various family members and, most important, the habits and rules of the family's interaction. The occasion for the family gathering is an annual holiday, and this, coupled with Minot's use of language and verb tense, suggests that readers are witnessing a ritual that has occurred before and will come again.

The economical, minimalist style used to narrate the story of the Vincent family's holiday communicates more about the characters than an initial read might suggest. The story reveals the peculiar habits and roles of several family members: Churly is argumentative; Rosie is patient and a peacemaker; Sophie is pensive and sensitive; and Pa's senility is filled with anger. The details about the family members and snippets of their conversation also provide a blueprint for the family's dynamics—who talks and who does not, who has the power to stop a conversation, how the three generations interact. Minot reveals that much of the power in the family now resides in Ma, which contains implications for Pa's deep anger. Also, the aunts and uncles function fairly rigidly within the confines of the family blueprint; but Churly challenges it aggressively, Delilah questions quietly, and Sophie studies it. Ma's retort at the end of the story is another breach of the family contract; the unexpected comment throws the family so effectively off-center that they are unable to respond.

Style and Technique

Minot's economical use of language and detail does not withhold information; readers should not conclude that there is no meaning beyond these details, that is, that the surface is all there is. The narrative economy forces one deeper into these details in any attempt to extract meaning.

Minot's style encourages readers to mine the surface and reveal the profundity of the ordinary. For example, Sophie's trip to the bathroom during dinner is not an irrelevant detail. Minot tempts the reader with such facts, in effect asking what one can make of them. Treated this way, the ordinary detail becomes metaphoric, and the reader must explore the possibilities of meaning that these metaphors might contain. When Sophie walks down the hall to the bathroom, she leaves the family. This separation can be seen as merely physical, but it may also signify deeper distances between this pensive girl and her family. When she listens to the noise of the family, she is studying these people with her ear. Perhaps Minot is suggesting a role for this little girl—a role of family observer, the one who pays attention, although from a safe distance.

Julie Thompson

THAT IN ALEPPO ONCE

Author: Vladimir Nabokov (1899-1977)
Type of plot: Sketch
Time of plot: Around 1941
Locale: Nice, France
First published: 1943

Principal characters:
THE NARRATOR, a former poet, fleeing from the Germans
HIS WIFE, a younger woman

The Story

The narrative of the struggle of a nameless man to preserve his sanity, this story is told through a letter that he addresses to a literary colleague whom he seems to have known since an early age. His letter tells the bizarre story of his marriage to a seemingly nonexistent wife, their eventful flight from Paris to Nice to escape the Germans, and the strange events that arise from their unfortunate separation in Faugères, so close to their destination.

When the narrator gets off the train to get food in Faugères, the train leaves without him—several minutes ahead of schedule. He leaves messages at the train station for his wife, has the station call other stations, and leaves messages with several station agents, all to no avail. He cannot find his wife in Faugères, Montpelier, or Nice, where he finally stays to look for her.

A week later, after the police try to convince the narrator that they have found his wife, he sees her, by coincidence, standing in line outside a store in Nice. She tells him of her misfortunes with the train, how she joined a group of refugees who lent her money to get to Nice, how she boarded the wrong train, but finally made it to Nice.

Reunited, they start the task of applying for exit visas to the United States. Soon afterward, however, the narrator's wife tells him that she lied about her disappearance. She admits that she had really been staying with "a brute of a man" whom she met on the train. This throws their relationship into disarray, as the narrator tries to find out every detail of her infidelity, believing that the truth will make it easier for him to bear.

Meanwhile, their quest for visas goes on. One day, the narrator's wife confesses "with a vehemence that, for a second, almost made a real person of her," that she had not done it.

Their wait for visas continues until, finally, the narrator comes home carrying two exit visas and two tickets for a boat to New York. When he gets home, however, he finds his wife has gone, along with her suitcase and clothing. The only memento she has left is a rose in a glass.

After several inquiries, the narrator finally finds an old Russian woman who tells him what his wife has told everyone else—that she has met a wealthy aristocrat and that she wants a divorce, but that her husband would not give his consent. On the narrator's way out, the old lady tells him she will never forgive him for killing his wife's dog before they left Paris. She is referring to the same dog the narrator's wife told him she would have missed had they had a dog.

After deciding to go on alone, the narrator goes to Marseilles to catch a ship for New York. Four days later, he goes on deck and runs into an acquaintance from Paris, who says he saw the narrator's wife a few days before in Marseilles, with her bag, saying that her husband would be along shortly. Taking this in, the narrator decides to write to his former colleague, who is also in New York now. He realizes that somewhere he has made a fatal mistake. This reminds him of Othello's similar situation, and he realizes that he may end up a victim of his own delusions—or worse—if he is not careful.

At the end, the story loops back to the beginning and explains the title. From the title it did apparently end in Aleppo for the narrator.

Themes and Meanings

Only Vladimir Nabokov could have written "That in Aleppo Once," an unusually complex short story with several levels of meaning. Chief among these are geometric patterns, word games, human relationships, and allusions to other authors. From its title through its end, "That in Aleppo Once" mimics the pattern of William Shakespeare's *Othello* (1604), and Nabokov's story follows a similar theme of love, perceived betrayal, and the progressive decline of the hero until he is consumed, like Othello, by despair and delusion.

When he is late for a train, he loses his wife for a week. When his wife shows up, she tells him that she has slept with three refugee women. Later, she changes her story to having slept with a hair-lotion salesman. Shortly afterward, she tells other people that an aristocrat was courting her, and that the narrator had threatened to shoot her and himself if she left him. On another level, the narrator marries (gains) her, loses her on the train, gets her back, loses her again when she leaves, almost gets her back through the friend on the boat who saw her in Marseilles, and loses her definitively when he sails without her.

In his quest for a visa, the narrator talks about the hopeless spiral: "We were trying to get . . . certain papers which in their turn would make it lawful to apply for a third kind which would serve as a steppingstone towards a permit enabling the holder to apply for yet other papers. . . ."

The narrator refers to an embankment on which he pictures his wife standing. It first appears as an "endless wind-swept embankment." Later, at the end of the story, it becomes "the hot stone slabs" with "tiny pale bits of broken fish scales" on which he pictures his wife walking.

Even the narrator's choice of words shows a devolving pattern: He starts the letter with sublime prose: "the sonorous souls of Russian verbs would lend a meaning to the wild gesticulation of trees . . . , " but, by the end, he is reduced to inane, slanted rhymes: "How is Ines? How are the twins. . . . How are the lichens?"

To make matters worse, the narrator's wife lives in her own world, and the narrator's attempts to understand her lead him to further confusion. For example, on the train from Paris, she starts crying about the dog they have left behind. When the narrator tells her they had never had a dog, she replies, "I know, but I tried to imagine we had actually bought that setter." The narrator does not recall ever talking about buying a setter. And yet, the dog takes on a life of its own, so that, near the end of his stay in Nice, the narrator is rebuked by an old Russian matron for hanging "that poor beast . . . with your own hands before leaving Paris."

The downward spiral ends in the narrator's recognition that he has made "a fatal mistake," just as Othello had in killing Desdemona, and the subsequent realization that he must pay for this mistake. The unfortunate implication of the title is that, as the author himself fears, he will ultimately lose control and end up killing himself—hence the line, "It may all end in *Aleppo* if I am not careful."

Style and Technique

Nabokov uses a variety of literary devices in this story. Most obvious to the reader is the first-person "confessional" narrative, seen in several other Nabokov works, notably *Lolita* (1958), and *Pale Fire* (1962). In "That in Aleppo Once," this device allows the author to express his own opinions without signing his name. Thus, when the narrator recalls "With all her many black sins, Germany was still bound to remain forever and ever the laughing stock of the world," it is really Nabokov expressing his contempt.

The title is an innovative example of foreshadowing: Readers familiar with *Othello* will recognize the line as a symbol of the impending death of a man whose illusions have overtaken him.

The narrator, being a poet, has a natural tendency to write in a descriptive manner, and, although he claims he is not a poet just now, he manages to slip in several rhymes and poetic allusions. The repetition and variation on certain themes, such as the loss of love and the embankment, seem like stanzas of a long, complex poem. In the middle of the story, when the narrator finds that his wife has gone with all of her belongings but has left a rose on the table, the narrator (and the astute reader) see this as what French rhymesters call *une cheville*—a word used to maintain the meter in a line of poetry.

In using so many literary devices and allusions, Nabokov is asking his readers to be as well educated as he. Without a knowledge of *Othello*, for example, the reader will miss the references throughout to that play, which reinforce the title's meaning. Furthermore, without a knowledge of some French, Russian, and historical background, the reader is equally blocked. Perhaps Nabokov's message, therefore, is that all of life depends on interwoven pieces and chance occurrences, and the more one knows, the better one can understand—and prevent—tragedy.

Gregory Harris

THEATER

Author: Jean Toomer (1894-1967)
Type of plot: Social realism
Time of plot: The 1920's
Locale: Harlem, New York City
First published: 1923

Principal characters:
JOHN, the brother of a theater manager
DORRIS, a chorus girl

The Story

The "theater" of the title is Howard Theater, an urban cabaret in the 1920's, set amid the "life of nigger alleys, of pool rooms and restaurants and near-beer saloons." As its afternoon rehearsal begins, the manager's brother John sits in the center of the theater and watches. He is a light-skinned African American, educated, urbane, and conscious of his social status.

The chorus girls themselves hold no interest for John. He coldly contemplates them and rejects them. They are beautiful, but beneath him socially; all of their movements are studied and routine. Although the women are unworthy of John and of his attention, the music and the glitter and the artificial passion soon begin to excite him. He wills his mind to put the excitement down, but when he sees Dorris appear on stage, he senses that there is something different about her. Unlike the other dancers, she is really engaged, really "throwing herself into it." He cannot help noticing and desiring her. Dorris has bushy black hair, a lemon-colored face, and full red lips. John tries to suppress his desire for her; she is beneath him socially, despite her beauty. It would never work.

Dorris notices John noticing her. She desires him as well, and asks her partner about him. He identifies John as the manager's brother, and "dictie" (slang for blacks who are overconscious of their social class). This makes Dorris angry. She knows she is just as good as John is, even if she is not educated or working in a respectable profession. She doubles her efforts in the dance, trying her best to impress John. If he is to refuse her, he may as well know what he is passing up. Soon her involvement takes her beyond trying to impress. The dance takes over her mind and body. All the men in the theater, and even in the alleyway, stop what they are doing to watch. Her spontaneity and energy are contagious; the other dancers start to move more freely as well.

John cannot take his eyes off Dorris as she swings her body and bobs her head. Beautiful and exciting, she is clearly dancing and singing for him now. No longer can he use his intellect to control his feelings for her. For her part, Dorris is imagining what she might have with John: passion, love, marriage, a family, and a stable home. He seems to be the sort of man who can give her all that. Her dance expresses the joy of possibility. John gazes at her and daydreams about meeting her, touching her, and watching her dance in private.

When the music finally ends, John is still dreaming about Dorris and does not realize that the dance is over. Dorris looks at him for approval, but he is not looking at her because he is staring off into space, seeing her in his dreams. Hurt to think that John has become indifferent to her so quickly, and saddened at the death of her own dreams, Dorris flees the stage in tears. The story ends. The two never even speak.

Themes and Meanings

In the sketches and stories that make up his collection *Cane* (1923), Jean Toomer often returns to the idea that African Americans who live in cities have lost an important part of themselves. A connection with the soil is, in an essential way, a connection with the soul. John, the "dictie" black man, is an example of this. Urbane and educated, he is also emotionless and controlled. When he begins to feel excited by the music and the dancers, he wills himself to ignore or suppress his excitement. He has developed the ability to control his feelings through his intellect, and Toomer shows that this trait, while it may be useful for urban life, is ultimately sterile and self-defeating. What excites John about Dorris is her spontaneity, her willingness to surrender control (or her inability to control herself). Her singing makes him think of "canebrake loves and mangrove feastings"—of earthy, rural pleasures that John's inner self craves. Every time that he rejects spontaneous pleasure because it "wouldn't work," he denies himself an opportunity to be a whole person.

Although Dorris is beautiful and can help John reconnect with his own soul, he talks himself out of wanting her. Because of the difference in their social classes, he will not approach her. Instead, he will touch her only in his mind, passing up what the reader realizes may be an important chance for his own happiness.

Dorris understands social class in the same way that John does, although she resents it. Because of the difference in their social standing—because he is "respectable" and she is not—she also will not approach him, and she can think of only one reason for his not approaching her. Dorris and John might be able to find a lasting and fulfilling relationship with each other, but the urban concept of social class—a bankrupt concept, Toomer believes—stands between them.

The theater is one place in a city where the two worlds meet, where "black-skinned life" will not be pushed aside. It is the only place where John can, for a time, connect with the world of feeling and spontaneity, and in fact there seems to be no other reason for him to be there. (He is not working at the theater and he never speaks to his brother, the manager.) But it is only a place, and he can leave it any time. For Dorris, there is no escape if John rejects her. The dazzling theater is a symbol of the city, glittering but essentially artificial and unsatisfying for everyone.

Style and Technique

Stylistically, "Theater" can be confusing at first, because its points of view are fluid, changing every few paragraphs. A narrator of sorts opens the story, but this voice changes from objective reporting to speaking for the characters. John and Dorris also speak for themselves, and many of their speeches begin with their names followed by a colon, as with lines in a play. Many lines are fragmented sentences, with spaces and repetitions: "Arms of the girls, and their limbs, which . . . jazz, jazz . . . by lifting up their tight street skirts they set free . . . (Lift your skirts, Baby, and talk t papa!)" The dream passage comes in short phrases and sharp images. Clearly, Toomer is manipulating point of view and language to capture the feeling of the music, and to force the reader to surrender intellect to feeling, just as John is asked to do.

A device that ties everything together is the image of walls. The opening paragraph describes the walls of the city buildings that seem to have a life and a music of their own. The singing and shouting of jazz mixes with the "tick and trill" of the walls. During the day the walls sleep, but at night they become soaked with songs. When John walks into the theater, "they start throbbing with a subtle syncopation."

As the pianist begins rehearsal, the walls awaken; as the men and women dance, the walls begin to sing and press inward. It is this pressing inward, toward him, that John first notices as his excitement builds, and his blood starts to press in also. As Dorris dances for John, the walls press in toward them both, until they feel as though they are in the same small space. John feels walls pressing within him also, pressing his mind within his heart—containing his intellect but not his emotions.

The image of the walls echoes Toomer's themes of boundaries, between social classes, between heart and mind, and between city life and country life. Here, the walls are boundaries, but living ones, with their own songs. If John would listen to the right songs, if he would wall up the right things, he and Dorris could build a room of their own together.

Similarly, images of light and darkness echo John's involvement with Dorris and with his emotional center. As he first sits in his seat, a shaft of light from above illuminates half his face. Dorris is backstage, in the shadows. When Dorris begins to dance, she glows herself, and as her intensity increases she moves to the front of the stage where she is in the brightest light. (The rest of the dancers are in shadow.) In his ecstasy, John feels himself rising on the shaft of light, and his dream is full of soft warm lights. But John's dream is just a dream—a shadow—and he is turning toward it instead of toward the real Dorris. When she looks to him, his face is entirely in shadow, and there he stays.

Cynthia A. Bily

THEFT

Author: Katherine Anne Porter (1890-1980)
Type of plot: Psychological realism
Time of plot: The late 1920's
Locale: New York City
First published: 1929

Principal characters:
THE UNNAMED NARRATOR, a woman who has lost her purse
CAMILO, her rejected Spanish escort
ROGER, her long-time friend
BILL, her drama collaborator, who cheats her
THE JANITOR, the woman who steals her purse

The Story

A woman living alone in New York City's bohemian area during the late 1920's discovers that her treasured gold cloth purse is missing. Aware that she had the purse in her hand when she came in the night before and dried it with her handkerchief, the woman recollects the events leading up to its loss.

The previous evening, the woman attended a cocktail party. When she left, she had the purse and it contained forty cents in a coin envelope. It was raining and she was accompanied by Camilo, who was escorting her to the train. Observing that Camilo's new hat was being destroyed by the downpour, she compared him to her sweetheart, Eddie, whose hat never looked out of place, no matter the weather or the hat's general shabbiness.

At the stairwell to the train, Camilo left, to her relief. She immediately met up with Roger, a long-time friend, who suggested a taxi for the trip home. Soon they were in a cab making small talk. Roger casually mentioned that his wife, Stella, had written and would be coming back to him. The woman told him about a letter she had received. He asked her for ten cents to pay for the cab and commented on her purse's beautiful appearance. She gave him the dime and remarked that her purse was a birthday present. Their last comments were on Roger's new play and his determination not to compromise his integrity.

Upon entering her apartment building, the woman was met by Bill, a struggling playwright, who offered her a drink while he unloaded his personal problems. He told her that his latest work was in trouble. The play's director had rejected the script after casting and rehearsing it for three days. Bill then began to criticize his estranged wife because she demanded ten dollars a week for their baby.

The woman attempted to change the subject by commenting on Bill's pretty rug. Bill told her it cost fifteen hundred dollars when it belonged to a celebrated actress, but he had paid only ninety-five dollars. She then asked him about the fifty dollars he had promised her for revising part of his third act. Angered, Bill chastised her. She reminded him that he was paid seven hundred dollars, but he did not relent. Despite herself, she told him to forget the money, had another drink, and left for her upstairs apartment.

The woman remembered taking the letter out of the purse before drying it. She again read the letter, which was from a lover (possibly Eddie). The letter writer blamed her for the collapse of the relationship. She tore the letter into narrow strips and burned them in the coal grate. The following morning, while she was in the bathroom, the female janitor came into her unlocked apartment, called out that she was examining the radiators, and left abruptly, closing the door sharply.

The woman remembers all these events while she dresses, smokes a cigarette, and drinks her coffee. She determines it was the janitor who stole the purse. Angry, she goes down to the basement, confronts the culprit, and demands the purse's return, stating that it was a present she did not want to lose. The janitor swears that she did not take the purse, so the disbelieving woman tells her to keep it. Climbing the stairs, the woman reflects on rejection, the ownership of possessions, and the loss of love.

The janitor follows her upstairs and hands her purse back to her. She claims that she took it for her teenage niece and thought it would not be missed. The owner retorts it was missed because it was a present from someone. The thief replies that the owner could easily get another one, but the niece might not; besides, the older woman has had her chance at love. The owner holds out the purse and tells the thief to take it. The janitor now refuses, saying her niece is pretty and young, but the woman needs it more. After another exchange of recriminations, the janitor leaves and the woman puts the purse down and reflects that it is she who will end up with nothing.

Themes and Meanings

"Theft," despite its brevity, contains several interlocking themes that lie at the core of Katherine Anne Porter's work. Foremost is the theme of alienation that permeates the story. Porter creates a modern alienated wasteland, populated by characters suffering from empty human relationships. None of the individuals portrayed connects emotionally to another. Of the five marriages or love affairs to which the story alludes, for example, none is successful.

Paralleling the theme of alienation is that of rejection. The woman, nameless because she has lost her identity, experiences rejection of one sort or another from all the characters. She rejects Camilo as unworthy of her and, in turn, is rejected by Roger, possibly a current lover, who chooses reconciliation with his wife. When she arrives at her apartment building, Bill rejects her contributions to his script by refusing to pay her the promised money. Rereading the letter from a lover who blames her for the deterioration of their relationship, she symbolically rejects him by destroying the letter. Her final rejection involves the loss of the purse and the janitor's unwillingness to take it once it is freely given.

Porter underlines the themes of alienation and rejection with another one involving loss—the loss of the stolen purse and the woman's feelings regarding it. On one level, the purse signifies a material possession that she is willing to give up; on another, deeper level, it is not just her possession, but an extension of her personality. It probably was given to her by Eddie and symbolizes not only their love and life together, but also her youth. Now older, she is forced to face this painful reality when the janitor throws the purse back and taunts her about no longer being young, thereby precipitating her spiritual isolation. Her latent feelings of isolation, loss, and rejection merge by story's end. She is left with an empty purse and cold coffee, devoid of love.

Style and Technique

"Theft" is a unique short story in the Porter canon for several reasons. It is the first effort at incorporating autobiographical elements into her work. Porter developed an intense relationship with Matthew Josephson, her literary mentor and lover. His wife, after discovering the affair, told him to choose between them. Josephson chose his wife and wrote Porter a letter detailing the decision and the fervent hope they could continue working together and remain friends. Porter was crushed and humiliated by the rejection, which is echoed in the experience of this story's protagonist.

Porter creates an atmosphere entirely different from those of her earlier efforts by placing "Theft" in a contemporaneous urban setting. She also uses flashbacks more extensively than in her previous work, and as integral parts of the story. Most of it takes place in the woman's mind. Her heroine is defined slowly and with a myriad of small details not present in her earlier characters.

Porter employs a number of effective stylistic devices. She uses the weather to set the story's tone through her use of the rain, establishing the bleak mood that distorts vision. Her use of material objects, such as the purse, hats, letters, and a cup of coffee, are skillfully and symbolically woven into the story. Camilo's hat being destroyed by the driving rain is contrasted to Eddie's stylish wearing of a hat under any circumstances and Roger's protection of his. Porter uses the letter device for both reconciliation and termination. For Roger, the letter means the renewal of the severed relationship with his wife; for the nameless protagonist, a letter triggers a rejection of part of her past and precipitates her feelings toward the thief and the stolen purse. The use of the cup of coffee is masterful. The woman had a hot cup of coffee before descending into the infernolike basement to confront the janitor. By story's end, after her heated altercation with the janitor and the realization that she is fully alone, the now-cold cup of coffee, combined with the rejected purse, symbolically drives home the sense of isolation and loss of love. It is easy to understand why most literary critics hail the subtle and complicated "Theft" as one of Porter's minor masterpieces of short-story writing.

Terry Theodore

THEY WON'T CRACK IT OPEN

Author: Yong-Ik Kim (1920-   )
Type of plot: Social realism
Time of plot: The 1950's
Locale: Sarasota, Florida
First published: 1969

Principal characters:
CHO, the narrator, a Korean school teacher visiting the United States as a student
DICK, an American who served in the Korean War
MA, Dick's mother, a first-generation Romanian immigrant to the United States

The Story

A school teacher from a village close to Pusan, South Korea, Cho comes to the United States to further his education. Before reporting to campus, he decides to visit his American friend, Dick—a soldier who was stationed in South Korea during the Korean War. Dick often visited the blind children's school where Cho was teaching and entertained students with stories about America. He told students that he came from a town where they had "the greatest show on earth" and once took a circus issue of *Life* magazine to show children its colorful pages. Cho described to the blind children what they themselves could not see: an elephant dancing, lions obeying their trainer, odd-looking animals with stripes, and the circus parade.

The blind students had trouble distinguishing the words "clown" and "crown." Cho tried to explain the difference to them but to no avail. After one student with limited vision touched Dick's big nose, the word "crown" stuck. Dick thereafter was known to the students as "Crown Dick."

Cho is surprised that Dick is not at the bus station to meet him. He takes a taxi and discovers that Dick does not live in one of those homes "whose large glass windows seemed to hold an underwater richness," homes with "shiny cars in the driveways and televisions inside." Instead, he lives in a worn clapboard shed with a battered old car parked outside.

During the visit, Cho learns that Dick's parents are first-generation Romanian immigrants. His family moved from Iowa to Florida after Dick's father passed away. Cho witnesses squabbles between Dick and his mother over jobs and money. Dick's mother, for example, does not want Dick to pay Cho's cab fare because they need the money for Christmas. But Dick worries about what Cho will think of them and insists on paying it. Dick's mother tells Cho that Dick is a good boy, but he always wants to show off. Dick's friends have offered him jobs, but he has been trying to find a "big job" by himself.

As they drive back to the bus station, Dick starts drinking. They take a detour to the beach where Dick tells Cho that one reason he decided to visit Cho's school was that his mother complained to the army about her eyes and asked them to send him home. He wanted to learn what people with weak eyes look like and fell in love with the students. Dick confesses that he told Cho's students "fairy stories" about what he would do when he returned home, and he asks Cho to promise not to tell them anything to disillusion them. He loves them now more than ever.

After Dick passes out, Cho decides to leave by himself. Walking back to the foot of a long, white bridge, he sees a pile of coconuts for sale and buys one. Carrying the strange fruit under his arm, he makes his way back to the city and finds the street where Dick said the greatest show on earth marched.

There Cho mails the coconut to his students in Korea and imagines them putting their heads together, touching and hugging the strange fruit and even its shadow. He can hear them say: "No, no! We will not crack it open to see what is inside. We want to keep it whole."

Themes and Meanings

The thematic concern of this story revolves around the conflict between illusion and reality. Dick is a complicated character, who is amusing, kind, and generous. His affection for the blind Korean students is sincere. He makes them laugh with his stories about the circus and gives them hope by describing what they cannot physically see. He promises the children that once he gets home, he will buy them candies, clothes, and shoes. By misleading the students into believing that everything in America is rosy and by painting a glorified picture of his own life, Dick instills false hopes into their hearts. The conflict between lies and truth is emphatically pronounced by Cho's discovery that not all Americans live in "beautiful homes with shiny cars in the driveways." It is also expediently demonstrated and accentuated by the physical conditions of the students. Their physical blindness mirrors and underlines their mental blindness. Their naïveté reveals their vulnerability.

Dick is not weaving "fairy stories" merely for the Korean children's benefit. He also wants to create an unreality for himself to block out unpleasant memories and to hide from reality. Dick is not happy at home. His parents are poor first-generation Romanian immigrants, who have been struggling to establish themselves in America. The squabbles between Dick and his mother are also often occasioned by cultural conflicts. Dick is more in tune with the mainstream American culture than with the culture that his parents brought with them to America. He is independent and lives in his dreams. He does not worry about finance and often takes his guests out to buy them dinner and drinks. Dick's mother, on the other hand, is pragmatic and frugal. She once asks Dick to pick up cow dung from the street. It can be used as fuel in winter. She believes Dick is ashamed of her, ashamed of her secondhand clothes, and ashamed of her broken English.

Telling "fairy stories" is one way for Dick to avoid facing reality. Alcohol is the other. Dick's mother has complained to Cho that Dick has been drinking heavily lately. On the way to the beach, Dick never stops drinking. He finally passes out in front of Cho, leaving the latter to figure out how to get back to the bus station.

The complexity of the story, however, lies in the fact that Dick is doing the wrong deed for the right reason. The blind Korean students remind him of his mother. He knows that they have been through a lot in life. He does not want to disappoint them by sharing the miseries of his own life with them. He wants to hear them laugh. He wants to inculcate and rekindle hopes in their tormented young hearts. As Cho recalls, their school "was in a bleak building that had once been a warehouse. Everything at the home for the blind children of refugees was bleak." But when Dick walked into that school, he "had heard for the first time" the blind students' "laughing shouts."

It is apparently for the same reason that Cho decides to send a coconut home. He can see in his imagination the children touching and hugging the strange fruit and its shadow while laughing and shouting: "We will not crack it open to see what is inside. We want to keep it whole."

Style and Technique

A first-generation Korean immigrant, Yong-Ik Kim came to the United States in 1948. He has published many stories and three novels, *The Happy Days* (1960), *The Diving Gourd* (1962), and *Blue in the Seed* (1964). The novels have been published in several languages. Several of Kim's works describe a first-generation immigrant's observations and experiences in the United States. They enable readers to look at America through the perspective of a new immigrant.

Typical of Kim's writing style, "They Won't Crack It Open" intermingles memory with reality. The narrative jumps back and forth from the present to the past and from America to Korea. The approach is effective. By juxtaposing the "fairy stories" about the circus Dick tells the blind Korean students and what Cho discovers in America, Kim is able to highlight the conflict between illusion and truth and between memory and reality. It also reveals the narrator's concerns for his students and his strong tie with his home country.

The narrative pace of the story is slow, deliberate, and almost leisurely. It follows the narrator's innocent view as he struggles to determine which America is the real and which one is the fake: the America he has heard in Dick's stories and the America he sees with his own eyes. Cho's misconception about America is subtly suggested in the beginning of the story. When he is waiting for Dick, he thinks that his Asian face should get someone's attention at the bus station. He is forced to face his own false conceptions of America, however, when "no one at the station" gives him "even a curious stare that might invite a foreigner to ask a question."

Qun Wang

THIEF

Author: Robley Wilson (1930-)
Type of plot: Fable
Time of plot: The 1980's
Locale: An airport
First published: 1980

Principal characters:
AN UNNAMED MAN waiting for a plane
A WOMAN WITH BLACK HAIR
A WOMAN WITH BLONDE HAIR

The Story

A man waiting at an airline ticket counter sees a beautiful, black-haired young woman and stares at her in an openly admiring way. She sees him and looks away. Later, while having a drink in the airport bar, he sees her again, this time talking to a blonde woman. He wants to attract her attention and buy her a drink, but cannot catch her eye. The third time he sees her, he is buying a magazine and she jostles him. When he remarks, "busy place," she blushes, frowns, and vanishes in the crowd.

This seems like the end of the encounter, until the man reaches in his back pocket for his wallet and realizes that it is missing. He thinks about the credit cards, the money, and the identification in it, and all at once knows that the black-haired woman has picked his pocket. As he considers the difficult process of canceling the cards and getting new identification, he feels suffocated and wonders what he should do. He curses the woman for pretending to be attentive to him, for letting herself stand so close, and for blushing—not out of shyness—but out of anxiety over being caught. Just as he decides to report the incident to a guard, he sees the woman sitting in the terminal reading a book.

When the man sits down and says he has been looking for her, she claims that she does not know him and accuses him of trying to pick her up. He accuses her of stealing his wallet and demands its return. Although the woman first denies it, she then takes a wallet out of her purse, gives it to the man, and runs away. Realizing that it is not his wallet, the man chases her through the crowd, until he hears a woman's voice behind him crying, "Stop, thief! Stop that man." A young marine trips him and he falls. The woman who has been chasing him is the blonde who he saw the brunette talking to earlier, and she has a policeman with her. The blonde accuses the man of stealing her wallet, and indeed the wallet the black-haired woman has given him belongs to the blonde.

Two weeks later, after the embarrassment and rage are gone and his lawyer has been paid, the man gets his wallet back in the mail, with no money or credit cards missing. Although he is relieved, he knows that he will feel guilty around policemen and ashamed in the presence of women for the rest of his life.

Themes and Meanings

Although "Thief" at first seems like a realistic story about real people in a real situation, it is actually an ironic fable about how men treat women as if they were anonymous things and steal their identity when they stare at them and have sexual fantasies about them in public places. The fable nature of the story is initially suggested by the implausible nature of the events that take place. Rather than being realistic, they have been calculated purposely by the author to illustrate his ironic theme. It is unlikely, for example, that the two women haunt the airport just to trap men who stare at them; it is also unlikely that they have just met at the airport and plan their revenge on the man spontaneously. Thus, if we cannot account for the actions of the story realistically, we must account for them in terms of the author's purposeful plan for the story's illustrative point.

The thematic significance of what the women do depends on the reader's realization of the fact that the man has first stolen something from the black-haired woman; thus her stealing his wallet so he can then be accused of stealing from the other woman becomes an ironic example of poetic justice. What the man steals from the woman by staring at her is her identity as an individual, since he is interested in her only as a conquest or as a sexual object. As the black-haired woman says when the man sits down and accuses her of stealing his wallet: "Is this all you characters think about—picking up girls like we were stray animals? What do you think I am?"

Although the man, like many men, may feel that his admiration of the woman and his desire to have a drink with her is innocent and harmless, the story seeks to illustrate that women may feel differently; indeed, they may deeply resent someone openly staring at them or trying to pick them up. Such an action is an invasion of a woman's freedom to be in public without being the victim of some man's sexual fantasies, for such fantasies drain a woman of her personal identity and transform her into a mere object. Wilson's story is about how two women turn the tables on such a man and steal his identity instead.

Style and Technique

Because the generic type of this story is ironic fable, its basic technique is ironic reversal and poetic justice. Indeed, its plot is a carefully controlled narrative about the two women who give the man a taste of his own medicine. The story's parable nature is also suggested by its being told completely in present tense, a point of view that conveys the sense of an illustrative picture. The point of view suggests the working out of a sequence of events to support a premise. For example, the story begins, "He is waiting at the airline counter when he first notices the young woman." The illustrative nature of the story is further emphasized in the chase scene, which the narrator says is like a scene in a motion picture, for as he chases her, the bystanders go scattering and she zig-zags to avoid a collision. The scene also resembles a film in that present tense is the basic time frame of all film. The man is not telling about a remembered event from which he has learned something, nor is some disinterested party who witnessed the scene recounting it in a narrative. Rather, the point of view suggests something taking place before the reader's eyes as a purely illustrative incident. That the story is like a film or lurid little drama for the tabloids is also suggested by the man's thinking how the newspapers will refer to the woman as an "Ebony-Tressed Thief" and by his feeling pleased with himself by his use of the word "lifted" instead of "stole," "took," or even "ripped off" to describe what the woman did, for it sounds more like a word used in a film.

Everything that happens in the story is ironically appropriate to illustrate the poetic justice of the man having his own identity taken from him (his credit cards, driver's license, and identification cards) in revenge for his trying to steal the identity of the black-haired woman by staring at her as an object of his own sexual desire. It is ironically appropriate that the blonde woman says to the policeman, "He lifted my billfold," thus echoing the word the man was so pleased with using earlier. It is also ironically appropriate that the man cannot even prove his identity to the policeman, because that which proves his identity has been stolen from him.

At the end of the story, the man is embarrassed but cannot really tell anyone why, for he knows that he has brought the incident upon himself. He only knows that since he deserved what happened to him, he will feel guilty around policemen and ashamed in the presence of women for the rest of his life. This final awareness emphasizes the story's parable nature.

Robley Wilson has called his fiction "premise fiction," a genre that occupies something of a middle ground between realistic fiction and dream fiction. Even as the event he describes seems real, there is something wildly improbable and fabulistic about it. Like much of Wilson's fiction, "Thief" is based on following an idea out to its logical conclusion, not on following real people as they interact with one another in actual life. The events of the story proceed along highly improbable lines, even as Wilson uses simple realism to recount them. In such a way, Wilson can take advantage of the techniques of both fantasy and realism simultaneously, and thus illustrate the themes of his premise fiction in an economical and uncluttered way.

Charles E. May

THE THINGS THEY CARRIED

Author: Tim O'Brien (1946-　　)
Type of plot: Psychological realism
Time of plot: The late 1960's
Locale: Vietnam
First published: 1986

Principal characters:
First Lieutenant Jimmy Cross, a boyish army platoon leader
Martha, a college student who writes to him
Kiowa, a Native American soldier
Ted Lavender, a terrified soldier

The Story

A platoon of seventeen American foot soldiers is on the march in the booby-trapped swamps and hills of Vietnam. They have been ordered to set ambushes, execute night patrols, and search out and destroy the massive tunnel complexes south of Chu Lai constructed by Viet Cong guerrillas. Young and frightened, most of the Americans are ill prepared emotionally for the stresses of war. The story does not follow a traditional linear plot but instead offers fragments of their experience, including seemingly unending lists of gear and personal effects that they carry with them. What they carry links them, yet distinguishes them.

Chief among the men and one of the oldest is First Lieutenant Jimmy Cross, twenty-four years old and not long out of college, who is smitten with love for a girl back home. He carries with him two photographs of Martha, an English major from Mount Sebastian College in New Jersey, whom he briefly dated. He yearns for her sweatless perfection, her white skin and clear gray eyes, fantasizing a relationship with her that never existed. Although she writes to him and he carries her letters, rereading them each night, it is clear that his passion for her is not reciprocated. When Martha sends him a talisman, a white pebble from the Jersey shore, Lieutenant Cross carries it in his mouth, savoring its salty taste as something almost holy. Dreams of Martha help him to escape Vietnam.

On April 16, the men draw lots to see who will wire a Viet Cong tunnel with explosives. The soldier selected to search the tunnel is the one about whom they are concerned, for his risks are great. When he finally emerges, covered with filth, all are relieved, but just as the tension eases they hear a shot. Ted Lavender, who stepped away from the group to relieve himself, is killed without warning by an enemy sniper. The incident stuns the platoon. Death in a firefight is one thing, but this swift and meaningless death is quite another.

Ted Lavender has always carried tranquilizers and top-grade marijuana to numb himself against his own terror, but his obsessive fear and caution do not help him; the twenty pounds of ammunition that he has carried makes no difference. He dies, as his friend Kiowa marvels, without time to react. His horrified comrades place him in a body bag and summon a helicopter. While they wait, they smoke Lavender's marijuana and crack jokes to mask their emotions. Then they burn a nearby Vietnamese village in retaliation, shooting the dogs and chickens.

That night Kiowa, who carries moccasins and his grandfather's hunting hatchet, tries to make sense of Lavender's death and to grieve, but he feels nothing. He pillows his head on the New Testament that he carries with him, a birthday gift from his father, and is glad simply to be alive. This fact comforts him, and he sleeps soundly.

Lieutenant Cross, on the other hand, weeps; he accepts full blame for Lavender's death, although in truth there is no blame. He suffers with guilt because he was thinking of Martha at the moment that Lavender was killed—he has loved her more than his men. He realizes now that his distant Anglo-Saxon virgin is nothing more than a dream. In his foxhole he burns her letters and photos, surrendering his illusions, and determines to conduct himself as an officer, a leader. He will be strong, tough, and silent—a man's man. He will protect his men, maintaining discipline and order so that they will live.

Themes and Meanings

A major theme that this story explores is the initiation of young men in wartime, when youths must become men. Pranksters must become killers, dreamers must become realists—or someone dies. The world of the intellect (Lieutenant Cross is a college graduate, Martha's letters express her admiration for Geoffrey Chaucer and Virginia Woolf) is of little relevance here; neither is romance or idealism. Courage becomes a concept without meaning. Getting through the experience alive is the important thing, as Kiowa knows too well. Fear paralyzes them all, yet somehow they manage to continue their march, to put themselves at risk, to carry out their orders. The trick is to survive.

The weight of their burdens is real. What these men have to nourish and protect them is only what they bear on their backs. Scarcely past boyhood, a medic packs his comic books and M&M candies for the relief of particularly bad wounds. A gentle soldier carries a rubbery brown thumb cut from a Viet Cong corpse. A third, a big, stolid man, packs with him the delicacy of canned peaches and his girlfriend's pantyhose. The men also carry infection, disease, and the land itself in the particles of dust and mud. They carry fear. They carry the weight of memory; they carry ghosts. They carry the burden of being alive; they carry "all they could bear, and then some."

Each man likewise carries within himself a longing for escape from the senseless and terrible reality of war. Some make their escape through sleep, as Kiowa does. Others manage to survive through daydreams, like Lieutenant Cross, or through drugs, like Ted Lavender. Every man waits for the blessed moment when a plane, or "freedom bird," will lift him above the ruined earth, the sordidness and death, his own shameful acts, into the lightness of air and the promise of home. The phrase "Sin loi! . . . I'm gone!" echoes in their real and imagined nightmares.

Style and Technique

This story is not told in chronological sequence. Rather, the random observation of one character after another alternates with a deliberate litany of weights and masses, the things they carry. Tim O'Brien's style here is fragmentary, close at times to pure stream of consciousness. His language is largely flat and understated, except where it is salted with slang, military jargon, and obscene black humor. The men's conversations are brief, punctuated by dashes rather than quotation marks, so that their spoken words are not easily distinguished from narrative.

Lavender's death is announced matter-of-factly in the second paragraph. Again and again the story returns to this event, each time revealing a little more detail, a new perspective, almost as if in a dream. The story spirals away from, circles around, focuses momentarily on this death.

The style is the story—a plodding, monotonous narrative punctuated by brief flashes of action. The catalog of objects carried, the accumulating weight of things, extends in steady, numbing procession. Gradually the repetition of weights and measures acquires meaning. This is what their lives have become, step after step, ounce after ounce.

Even the names seem symbolic. Jimmy, a boy's name, is paired with a man's title, lieutenant; these two qualities meet or cross in the protagonist. The boy inside the man's body is forced to become an adult and shoulder the burdens of an adult. Kiowa is also one in whom past and present views of race, war, and religion collide. His Indian grandmother remained an enemy of white people during her lifetime, yet his father now teaches Baptist Sunday school in Oklahoma City. Although Kiowa still carries his moccasins and an ancestral hatchet, he also carries boots and modern weapons. Finally, the delicacy of lavender, both scene and hue, suggests Lavender, the fragile youth who cannot bear to meet war face to face, and who quite literally loses his mind when he is shot in the head.

Tim O'Brien's story is heavy with irony. Lavender, weighted down by extra ammunition and sheer panic, is the only American to die. Jimmy Cross leaves behind his love for Martha, choosing instead to bear responsibility and guilt for a death that could not have been foreseen. The story's emphasis on their innocence and vulnerability, coupled with the repeated date of Lavender's death, suggests poet T. S. Eliot's opening lines from *The Waste Land* (1922):

> April is the cruellest month, breeding
> Lilacs out of the dead land, mixing
> Memory and desire, stirring
> Dull roots with spring rain.

In this cruel month, in this cruel war, all of these young men carry in their hands and on their backs their damaged, terrified, desperate lives.

Joanne McCarthy

THIS INDOLENCE OF MINE

Author: Italo Svevo (Ettore Schmitz, 1861-1928)
Type of plot: Psychological realism
Time of plot: The 1920's
Locale: Trieste, an Austrian town occupied by Italy
First published: "Il mio ozio," 1957 (English translation, 1969)

Principal characters:
ZENO, the narrator, an aging bourgeois man
FELICITA, his enterprising mistress
CARLO, his nephew, a medical man
MISCELI, a rival for Felicita's "affections"

The Story

The narration begins with a pronouncement that the present established by calendars and clocks is merely arbitrary; that the self and the people around the self constitute the true present. The reader is thus introduced to the ensuing interior monologue and its obsession with time.

The narrator's present is dominated by his retirement from business and an impending inertia. It is also largely dedicated to medicine. In arming himself against disease, the narrator, Zeno, is aided by his nephew Carlo, just out of the university and conversant with the most up-to-date remedies. Guided by Carlo, Zeno is committed to preventive treatments. Having determined that Mother Nature will maintain life in an organism only so long as there is hope that it will reproduce, he prescribes a mistress for himself.

Zeno and the tobacconist, Felicita, to whom he becomes attracted, agree at the outset on a monthly allowance. Felicita rarely neglects to mention the stipend falling due by the twentieth of the month. For his part, Zeno never lets on that his interest in her is primarily medical. Zeno learns, however, that another person is a "complex medicine," impossible to take in doses. On one of the two days of the week he is scheduled to visit his mistress, he decides that he would be better off listening to Ludwig von Beethoven's *Ninth Symphony* (1823). The next day, however, he determines to take advantage of what is due him. He reminds himself that he must pursue a treatment "with the utmost scientific exactitude" to gage its effectiveness.

After arriving at Felicita's flat, Zeno is surprised to find there fat old Misceli, a man about his age. Regaining his composure, Zeno orders some cigarettes. Felicita's scolding of him for visiting her on an unappointed day offends him. He declares an end to their arrangement.

As he starts down the stairs, Misceli appears and announces that he, too, is leaving, having placed his own order with the tobacconist. Zeno takes considerable satisfaction in comparing his fitness favorably to Misceli's. After a discussion on maintaining health and stability, the two part.

Motivated by a sense of economy, Zeno calls on Felicita once again before the paid-up month is through. She is on her way out, and can only say that she will consider the matter. Zeno's response is an ineffectual "Ouf!"

Thus Felicita has educated him in his "present role of old man." Now he attempts to "deceive" Mother Nature simply by following women with his eyes, "trying to discover in their legs something more than a mere motor apparatus." The story closes with an episode in which Zeno's gaze at a lovely young girl on a train is met with an accusation of "Old lecher" from an aged maidservant, which he parries with, "Old fool!"

Themes and Meanings

As one of five fragments that constitute an unfinished continuation of the novel *The Confessions of Zeno* (1923; English translation, 1930), "This Indolence of Mine" treats many of the same themes: signs of health and disease, the aging process, preoccupation with death, and human motivation. Much of the narrative deliberates over medical theories and health regimes. Such deliberations dominate not only Zeno's musings but also his conversation. He even interrupts his narrative to check his blood pressure.

The marking of time is a related concern, as its loss is a reminder that one is approaching death. Zeno unsuccessfully tries to "claim" his due from Felicita before the end of his paid-up month. Following her evasions, his futile attempt to find solace in music reinforces his betrayal by time, the art of music depending on temporal relationships. Instead of the joy and harmony that he expects from listening to the last movement of Beethoven's Ninth Symphony, he senses only violence.

Presumably influenced by Freudian psychology, Italo Svevo delineates his characters by their drives: Zeno's thoughts and actions are taken up with "hoodwinking" Mother Nature into allowing him to remain alive; Felicita's every move is calculated to ensure her material well-being. Svevo also humanizes his characters, however, as he reveals the vulnerability showing through the cracks of their singlemindedness. Zeno, convinced that only surrender to love will prove an adequate health regime, is powerless to explain to Felicita how he wants her to be. Felicita, meanwhile, spoils the treatment that she is to provide by her habit of remarking that, strangely, Zeno does not repulse her.

In the story, as in other works of Svevo's later period, the author seems reconciled to human helplessness and to the inevitable dualities of character and situation, and ambition and real life. The years following World War I arguably parallel the decline of the Roman Empire, when civilization seemed threatened as much from within as from without, and people feared that the end of the world was near. At that time, both Augustinian Christianity or Stoicism offered compelling visions of the future. Zeno the Stoic characterized the world, every few thousand years, as degenerating into chaos only to rise anew, as a phoenix from its own ashes. Given his portrayal of time as an inveterate prankster, Svevo may very well have been thinking of the Stoic when he named his protagonist.

After the failure of his early novels, Svevo gave up writing for twenty years and became a successful businessman. In the 1920's, he took up his pen again, encouraged in part by his friendship with James Joyce, who had tutored him in English. In May, 1928, Svevo wrote regarding the "score of pages" he had written of his follow-up to *The Confessions of Zeno*, "I'm having a whale of a time. It won't matter if I don't get to finish it. I'll at least have one more good laugh in my life."

Style and Technique

Italo Svevo is generally considered to have pioneered the use of interior monologue as a narrative technique. Critics write admiringly of the insightful and innovative probing of character in his work. Svevo is also identified as one of the first fiction writers to experiment with psychoanalytic concepts, with which he became acquainted because of cultural ties to Trieste, his hometown, and Vienna, the center of Freudian analysis. From *The Confessions of Zeno* on, his narratives present two levels of action. The first is a loosely connected series of events linked thematically; the second takes place in the mind of the narrator.

The irony that suffuses Svevo's work derives in part from this dual structure. Motives and intentions are contrasted with the stated perceptions of others and also with their end results. Zeno is shocked when told by Felicita that she does not find him repulsive, as he has never imagined himself that way. Instead of protecting him from death and decay, Felicita ends up teaching Zeno that he is an old man. Even Zeno's ordering of cigarettes as a way of avoiding humiliation backfires: The brand, which is duly delivered to him, is one he despises. Such skillful use of irony enables Svevo to balance humor and pathos in this and other works successfully.

Svevo's style was denounced by contemporary Italian critics for its lack of polish and luster. They thereby remained loyal to the current cult of literature promoted by the poet, novelist, and dramatist Gabriele D'Annunzio and defined in his phrase, "beauty is all." Svevo's bemused and bumbling narratives could scarcely be more antithetical to D'Annunzio's virtuoso style. Thus began the "Svevo case," an extended debate among critics on the literary quality of Svevo's works. Supporters have claimed an appropriateness for his homely prose, given the transparency with which it reflects his characters' less-than-lofty preoccupations. Nobel Prize-winning poet Eugenio Montale has noted that, in translation, the "sclerosis" of Svevo's characters tends to be lost.

Svevo's "pidgin Italian," as many critics characterize his language, is reflected in his pseudonym, which means "Italus the Swabian." Here he salutes his mixed linguistic heritage: his father's in the German Rhineland and his mother's in Italy. In defense of his idiosyncratic prose style, Svevo wrote in 1925, "For me, growing up in a country where, until seven years ago, our dialect was our true language, my prose could not have been other, unfortunately, than what it is." With characteristic self-mockery, he added, "and now there is no time to straighten out my crooked legs."

Amy Adelstein

THIS MORNING, THIS EVENING, SO SOON

Author: James Baldwin (1924-1987)
Type of plot: Social realism
Time of plot: The 1950's
Locale: Paris
First published: 1960

Principal characters:

THE NARRATOR, an African American singer and actor living in Paris
HARRIET, his Swedish wife
PAUL, his seven-year-old son
JEAN LUC VIDAL, the French director of his films

The Story

On the eve of the narrator and his family's departure for the United States after twelve years of residence in Paris, the narrator is being chided by his wife and visiting sister about his nightmares. He is worried about his return to the racist United States after such a long absence and what effect it will have on his multiracial family and his career.

The story is structured around a series of social interactions. The first concerns the narrator's family and his Paris existence. He puts his son to bed in the concierge's apartment, and his wife and sister go out on the town. The narrator slips into the first of his reveries on his apartment balcony overlooking the Eiffel Tower as he revisits his first years in Paris as an expatriate and struggling artist. He speculates on the whereabouts of his old North African friends and the conditions of the current Algerian conflict. He is in love with Paris and the French because they do not judge him on skin color, but he deplores their colonial war.

The narrator has an extended flashback about his visit to the United States eight years before for his mother's funeral. He describes the boat trip on which he sang spirituals and blues for a white audience, and his arrival in New York, where he is called "boy" by a white officer as he descends the gangplank and is engulfed by the "cunning and murderous beast" of New York City.

The flashback ends and the narrator welcomes his French friend and director, Jean Luc Vidal, into his Paris apartment. Over drinks, they reminisce about the narrator's defining role as Chico in *Les Fauves nous attendent*, a movie about a young mulatto man from Martinique who dies tragically in the underworld of Paris. Vidal drew a great performance out of the narrator by forcing him to confront his own interior demons, including the hateful summer after his mother's death that he spent in the American South working as an elevator boy.

The final section of the story takes place on Paris' Left Bank. In a discotheque, the narrator is recognized and approached by four African American students on tour in

Europe. On their way to a Spanish bar, they hook up with Boona, and old Arab friend of the narrator. In a Spanish bar, one of the American girls has ten dollars stolen. Boona is accused and the narrator intercedes. Boona denies he stole the money. The matter is finally dropped, but not without an argument that forces the narrator to think about his position in relation to Africans. In the early hours they separate, and the narrator goes home to stand over his sleeping son's bed pondering father-son relationships. He awakens his son and they set out on their journey to the new world.

Themes and Meanings

The story is about an African American male expatriate who finds personal and career success in a foreign country. It shows his fears about returning to the United States after many years. He is concerned about the reception facing his interracial family, and wonders about his ability to continue his career in the United States. Examples of prejudice that he and his father experienced lace the story, giving credence to the narrator's apprehensions for his son.

The narrator is at the crux of many conflicts. He is an African American male living in Paris with an adopted language and culture. He has a white wife and mulatto son whom he loves, yet he fears for their safety. He wonders whether his successful career as a singer and actor can continue, and he debates the merits of being famous. Finally, he questions his place in French society because of France's colonial war in Algeria and his personal relationships with many poor North Africans.

At the center of the narrator's concerns is the question of color. Much of the story relates in telling detail, subtle and blatant forms of racism experienced or witnessed by the narrator. The narrator has not been able to express all of his anger. When he was asked to play a disturbed mulatto from Martinique in Vidal's film, he faltered. It was only after Vidal confronted him on his own repressed hatred of racism that he was able to perform the role with the passion it deserved.

The narrator is caught between his freedom and success in Paris and his past, marred by racism, which he is again about to confront. Using the flashback episode as an example of what he expects on his return, the narrator details the horrible feelings of helplessness and hatred generated by racist behavior. His family in the United States experienced prejudice firsthand and it damaged them forever. His father's and sister's lives were destroyed by racism, and the narrator escaped to France to avoid the same fate. Now famous, he must come to terms with his expatriate status, and find a way for his son to live without the same scars of racism.

The narrator also doubts that his identity as a black actor and singer has any validity in the United States. Having become famous in France for singing the blues, he fears ridicule in his own country, which often denigrates black creations. Coupled with this fear of failure is his suspicion of success. Fame has brought recognition, but not peace. The final section of the story deals with this conflict when the narrator is confronted by the African American tourists and finds himself absorbed into their circle. When Boona is accused of stealing, the narrator is caught between commitment to his fellow countryman and loyalty to his old, but less than honest, friend. A similar conflict is expressed in his loyalty to the French, which is strained by their colonial war. The story ends without resolution.

Style and Technique

When James Baldwin wrote “This Morning, This Evening, So Soon,” he was already famous, as is the nameless narrator of his story. The story reflects some autobiographical details much in the same way as his first novel, *Go Tell It on the Mountain* (1953), suggested the author’s early life in Harlem. As an expatriate writer, Baldwin was indebted to the French for accepting his blackness and cradling his creativity. Although Baldwin himself never married and had no son, his tormented relationship with his stepfather bothered him all of his life. Finally, success never satisfied Baldwin, and his fight against racism continued until his death.

Baldwin writes in the first person in a confessional style that manages in a few short pages to cover much historical and geographical territory. With his ability to weave flashbacks into the present narrative, he provides a picture of two cultures and demonstrates the conflicts inherent in the narrator’s ambivalent position. As an African American living in France with a white wife and a small son, he must make important choices. Baldwin expertly increases the tension by having the story occur on the eve of the narrator’s departure. Caught between two worlds, Baldwin uses a close confessional style to create tension. The narrator’s psychological dilemma is reinforced by his night on the town. Once again he is caught between loyalties and must mediate some kind of compromise. The story is a good example of Baldwin’s mature writing style, in which he is able to depict white and black characters with considerable compassion while still showing the horrible effects of racism in American life.

Stephen Soitos

THREE PLAYERS OF A SUMMER GAME

Author: Tennessee Williams (1911-1983)
Type of plot: Psychological realism
Time of plot: The 1940's
Locale: New Orleans, Louisiana
First published: 1952

Principal characters:
Brick Pollitt, an alcoholic Delta planter
Margaret Pollitt, his wife
Isabel Grey, a young widow
Mary Louise, her twelve-year-old daughter
The unnamed narrator, Mary Louise's ten-year-old friend

The Story

Brick Pollitt, a former college athlete, has married a New Orleans debutante and settled down to the life of a Delta planter. For some reason of self-disgust, the reason for which is not made explicit, he has become an alcoholic. His own excuse is that his wife, Margaret, a powerful, domineering figure, has psychologically and sexually castrated him and taken away his self-respect.

When a young doctor who has treated Brick's alcoholism dies of brain cancer, Brick befriends the doctor's genteel widow, Isabel, and her plump daughter, Mary Louise, and provides them with financial support. Although the widow becomes Brick's mistress, the reason that he turns to her has less to do with sexual desire than with the mysterious nature of Brick's need for something that remains unexplained. Much of the story centers around the croquet game that the three of them play during the summer the story takes place. It is told by a man who witnessed it all several years previously when he was a ten-year-old friend of Mary Louise.

Although Brick insists that he is curing his drinking problem and that Isabel has helped him regain his self-respect, he is not strong enough to resist the powerful personality of his wife or the strong allure of alcohol that helps him escape into a fantasy world. Before the end of the summer, Brick's self-destructive behavior increases and threatens to destroy the widow and her daughter as well. As his behavior deteriorates, Brick returns to the control of his wife and neglects the widow and her daughter, who then leave town. In the last scene of the story, the narrator reports seeing Brick, grinning with senseless amiability, being driven through town by his wife, the way some ancient conqueror like Alexander the Great might have led the prince of a newly conquered state through the streets of a capital city.

Themes and Meanings

The central thematic mystery in the story is the motivation behind Brick's self-disgust, something that Tennessee Williams has called a basic sense of unknowable dread. The narrator in the story simply says that it came upon him with the "abruptness and violence of a crash on a highway. But what had Brick crashed into? Nothing that anybody was able to surmise, for he seemed to have everything that young men like Brick might hope or desire to have." Brick says the reason for his malaise is the fact that his wife has castrated him by taking away his respect and that he must prove that he is a man again. He tells a group of painters working on the widow's house that the meanest thing that one human being can do to another is take away his self-respect. "I could feel it being cut off me," he says.

The fact that Brick tries to regain his self-respect through the passive young widow and what he himself calls the sissy game of croquet is the central irony of the story. Brick's problem is not simply sexual, or even psychological, but rather aesthetic and metaphysical. His impotence is not a reaction against the castrating Margaret but rather a revolt against the flesh itself. His flight into the chaste arms of Isabel—which have been purified by the death of her husband—is the search for truth in the basic romantic sense of its equation with beauty. It is an attempt to escape from flesh into art, to escape intolerable contingent reality into the bearable—because detached and fleshless—ideal of aesthetic form.

This attempt to escape the contingency of existence by means of aesthetic patterning and idealization is doomed from the start. His desire for a romantic relationship with Isabel, as well as his effort to play the superior game of art and form with human beings as the pawns, comes crashing up against the real physical and psychological needs of the other two players—the widow and her daughter.

Style and Technique

At the beginning of the story, the narrator establishes the metaphor that identifies the summer game of croquet with the nature of the artwork. The game, he says, seems to be composed of images the way a painter's abstraction of the game would be built of them. The wire wickets set in the emerald lawn and the colorful wooden poles stand out in a "season that was a struggle for something of unspeakable importance to someone passing through it." The formal design of the game is like a painter's abstraction; likewise, the characters become images and abstractions. They are not so much real people as stylized gestures pictorially woven within the lyrical narrative that is the legend of Brick Pollitt. The narrator says that the bits and pieces of his story are like the paraphernalia for a game of croquet, which he takes out and arranges once more in the formal design of the lawn. "It would be absurd to pretend that this is altogether the way it was," he says, "and yet it may be closer than a literal history could be to the hidden truth of it."

The narrator's engagement in the formally controlled patterning of the artwork that one uses to control the contingency of life is the same game that Brick plays with croquet. He is drawn to Isabel because her actual encounter with the contingency and horror of flesh during the time her husband was dying reflects his own fear of flesh. To engage in the summer game is thus to run out of something "unbearably hot and bright into something obscure and cool"—to run out of the unbearable world of existential reality into the cool, ordered, deathless world of the artwork.

When Brick realizes that form must inevitably become involved and entangled with the reality of flesh, he becomes caught in an unresolvable metaphysical dilemma. Because there are other players involved in his game, human beings who have real emotional and fleshly needs, the game becomes contaminated because it must be played at the expense of Isabel and Mary Louise. When Brick realizes the hopelessness of his efforts to escape life into the romantic pattern of art, he is transformed from tragic actor to clown and the croquet lawn becomes a circus ring. His desire to live within the formalized world of art and idealization is doomed to failure, and thus the mysterious metaphysical problem that plagues Brick is left unresolved. Near the end of the story, after Brick realizes the impossibility of his summer game and no longer comes to the widow's house, the narrator says, "The summer had spelled out a word that had no meaning, and the word was now spelled out and, with or without any meaning, there it was, inscribed with as heavy a touch as the signature of a miser on a check or a boy with chalk on a fence." Any attempt to spell out Brick's problem, even the attempt the story itself makes, is inadequate to get at the truth of Brick's ultimately romantic desire for beauty.

Brick's tragicomic efforts reach a climax one night when he turns on the water sprinkler, takes off his clothes, and rolls about under the cascading arches. No longer a Greek statue, he is a grotesque fountain figure and a clown. This degeneration into what the narrator calls unintentional farce is suggested by a trivial conversation carried on between Mary Louise and her mother about using ice to cool her mosquito bites. An aesthetic game that begins as an effort to transform something hot into something obscure and cool takes place among frozen stylized figures on a cool lawn of a house that itself looks like a block of ice; it finally becomes a banal banter in which the ice is reduced from its symbolic function to the practical utility of cooling Brick's drinks and easing Mary Louise's bites.

The narrator learns that when one uses human beings in an effort to play the game of art and reach the beauty and detachment of form, the result is the loss of the human. The beauty of the artwork alone can remain pure, but only because of its inhumanness.

Charles E. May

THE TIME OF HER TIME

Author: Norman Mailer (1923-)
Type of plot: Social realism
Time of plot: The 1950's
Locale: New York City
First published: 1959

Principal characters:
SERGIUS O'SHAUGNESSY, the narrator
DENISE GONDELMAN, his lover

The Story

Sergius O'Shaugnessy has tried to live entirely by his own lights, to establish the time of his time. Sergius is a sexual adventurer, a man of action asserting his manhood. He has even established a bullfighting school in Greenwich Village. He is a loner, living on the fringes of society, refusing to conform, and behaving like an artist, which means abiding by his own code and creativity.

Sergius has come by his identity the hard way. He is an orphan who grew up in a Catholic orphanage. To make himself, he has had to jettison not only the teachings of traditional religion but also allegiance to institutions of any kind. He lives in the moment, free of guilt (he claims) and any emotional baggage. His life is only as stable as his own stamina; his truths are the product of experience. He recognizes no authorities or limitations, except the ones he imposes on himself.

Sergius' conception of himself is challenged by Denise Gondelman. She is bright, Jewish, and full of the psychiatric jargon that puts off the hipster, who sees her as the typical intellectual Jew. She uses words to type people and to assert her superiority. She is obviously dissatisfied with her conventional boyfriend, and she is attracted to the nonconformist, belligerent Sergius. They become enmeshed in a love-hate affair.

Denise confesses that she has never had an orgasm. She doubts that Sergius would find her a good lover, but he takes her admission of inadequacy as a spur to his male ego and sets out to rectify her sex life by conducting a war against her frigidity. His masculine power-grabbing alienates her, yet like him, she craves intense experience, and she believes that through him she will finally achieve a sexual climax.

At first Sergius disappoints her. His own climax comes too soon for her, and she angrily accuses him of selfishness. Then they struggle in another round of sexual intercourse, each trying to pound into the other his or her own sexual rhythm. Finally, Sergius seems to triumph. Denise has an orgasm—on his terms, he believes.

Denise does reach a sexual epiphany with Sergius, but she rejects him because of his predatory code. He acts in bed like a bullfighter; his violence excites and repels her. When Sergius claims credit for satisfying Denise sexually, she retorts that he has not changed her in any fundamental way. She implies that she has gotten just as much as she wanted from him, but she has not actually put herself in his power. Sergius admits the truth of her retort when he compares the look in her eyes to that of the bullfighter ready for the kill. She has used him at least as much as he has used her. Denise's parting shot is to quote her psychiatrist, who has told her that Sergius' whole life is a lie, that he has done nothing but run away from his own homosexuality.

Sergius does not defend himself against her allegation. He simply calls it her truth. Her words define her psychological state, not necessarily what he thinks of himself or what their relationship has meant to him. He ends the story admitting that she has been a worthy opponent.

Themes and Meanings

How seriously can Sergius O'Shaugnessy be taken? Bearing a name reminiscent of a mythic Irish hero, he has come out of nowhere, so to speak, to make an impression on his times. Still, is establishing a bullfighting school in Greenwich Village really such a heroic thing to do, or is it ridiculous? Denise Gondelman's words imply there is something absurd in Sergius parading himself as a man of action defying death. He has killed bulls in Spain, but what bulls are there to kill in New York City? His real adversary is a woman and, Denise implies, himself. His tough talk and violent streak mask an uncertain identity. He is not the master of reality but its fool. He is not in control of his time but the servant of her time.

The feminine pronoun in the story's title is a profound rewriting of the romantic, heroic quest story. Denise, in some ways, displaces Sergius as the story's hero. She refuses to submit to his code of male superiority, even though he brags that she cannot experience sexual satisfaction without him. Her strength comes from knowing that her orgasm has been possible because she has fought Sergius in bed, not because she has given in to him. In effect, she expresses contempt for him as a sexual object even as he supposed she was his instrument.

Denise's truth does not displace Sergius' so much as it shows his limitations. Her comment that he has denied his homosexuality is simplistic, and is made more so because she is quoting her psychiatrist who has not even met Sergius. Nothing revealed about Sergius makes the charge of homosexuality seem relevant to his attitudes. Denise lives in the world of second-hand diagnoses. She has made real contact with Sergius, yet she resorts to jargon rather than confronting him in all of his individuality. She denies the mutuality they have shared, however briefly.

In this sense, the title is ironic and belittling of Denise. She has had the time of her time and emerged triumphant in her own mind, but where else? She has walked out on Sergius, denying him the role of conquering hero, but she also has turned him into a cliché: the macho man hiding his vulnerable side. She is, in a way, a parody of Sergius, declaring a hollow victory, slaying a bull where there are no bulls to be slain. She does not admit or wrestle with her contradictory desires to be totally in control and to abandon herself to a moment of complete ecstasy, a moment that would take her beyond her categorical view of reality. Both Denise and Sergius have been the bull and the bullfighter; their relationship is about how they constantly shift between their passive and active selves, their roles as heroes and victims.

Both characters are romantics in that they blow up experience, making of it a life-and-death battle, in which the self suffers either defeat or victory. Neither is satisfied with mediocrity or with half-success. Each sees their relationship as a duel of identities.

Style and Technique

As in "The Man Who Studied Yoga," the companion piece to Norman Mailer's "The Time of Her Time," the key to the story's meaning is the narrator. Although Sergius is Denise's antagonist, he shows remarkable sympathy and respect for her, almost as if she is his other half. He can portray her as frigid and reductionist in her judgments, yet he acknowledges her as a genuine quester to whom he feels compelled to accord a tribute, however ambivalent.

Sergius' mixed feelings about Denise do mask his own internal divisions. He wants to be strong, but he also wants to have the courage to admit his fear and inadequacy—which, in a way, Denise has done in her own case by coming to him. By allowing her to speak so clearly and boldly, he is implying not only that she is a match for him but also that he has learned something from her, grown in his ability to scrutinize himself.

The true heroism of "The Time of Her Time" is the narrator's willingness to recognize his own absurdity and powerlessness. Paradoxically, he asserts power by dramatizing how he has been stripped of it. It is not his physical prowess but his mental agility and sensitivity that triumph in the story.

If Mailer makes fun of his hero, he also gives him a full and honest voice that honors the objective of his quest: to be the best at what he does, in both the bullring and the bed. Denise has been attracted to that authentic quality, even though she seeks to deny it at the end of their affair. For Sergius, Denise is another encounter with reality, in which he simultaneously loses and gains control of himself, succumbs to and dominates his times. He makes his story, and Denise's, into a fable of all romantic quests—doomed to failure and yet assertive of self-growth.

Carl Rollyson

TO HELL WITH DYING

Author: Alice Walker (1944-)
Type of plot: Domestic realism
Time of plot: The 1960's
Locale: An unspecified Southern state
First published: 1967

Principal characters:
MR. SWEET LITTLE, an old African American man
THE NARRATOR, a young African American woman

The Story

Mr. Sweet Little was a diabetic, alcoholic, guitar-playing, tobacco-chewing, tall, thin, dark-brown man whose hair and straggly mustache were the color of Spanish moss. He lived alone on a neglected cotton farm down the road from the narrator and her family. Over a period of many years, Sweet Little and the children participated in a ritual that was an important element in the lives of all. When Mr. Sweet was feeling the worst, the bluest, the sickest-at-heart a man could be, he would take to his bed and the doctor would declare that old Mr. Sweet was dying. The narrator's father would declare, "To hell with dying, man, these children want Mr. Sweet!" and the children would swarm around the bed and throw themselves on top of the dying man. Always the youngest child would kiss the wrinkled brown face and tickle the motionless body until it began to shake with laughter. These things were done to keep Mr. Sweet from dying. The children performed the ritual naturally for many years. No one told them what to do—they played it by ear. So it was that Sweet Little was repeatedly rescued from the brink of death by love, laughter, and the innocent belief of children. As the youngest child in the neighborhood, the narrator led these revivals for the last part of Mr. Sweet's life.

Sweet Little was kind and gentle, even shy with the children—an ideal playmate. Often so drunk that he was as weak as they, he was able to act sober when drunk, a talent that enabled him to carry on fairly coherent conversations. The narrator's mother never held his drunkenness against him and always let Mr. Sweet and the children play together.

Once an ambitious person, Mr. Sweet had wanted to be a doctor or a lawyer or a sailor, but found out that black men got along better if they were not. He had loved another woman before he had had to marry Miss Mary. He was not even sure that their son, Joe Lee, was his. The narrator had learned these things about Mr. Sweet's past from the many sad and wonderful songs he made up while he played the guitar and entertained her family. She remembers how beautiful Mr. Sweet made her feel, how she listened to his songs, watched him cry, and held his woolly head in her arms, and how she wished that she could have been the woman he had loved so long ago. He was her first love. When Mr. Sweet began to cry, it indicated that he was about to die again, so the children would get prepared, for surely they would be called upon to revive Sweet Little yet again.

Mr. Sweet was in his eighties when the narrator went away to a university. On his ninetieth birthday, she receives a telegram requesting her to come home immediately because old Mr. Sweet is dying again. She is finishing her doctorate; but, sure that her professors will understand, she does not hesitate. When the dying man sees her, his eyes look spry and twinkly for a moment, but this time death cannot be stayed. The twenty-four-year-old doctoral student cannot believe that she has failed to revive the old man: He "was like a piece of rare and delicate china which was always being saved from breaking and which finally fell." The narrator sits strumming Mr. Sweet's old guitar that he has left to her; she hums "Sweet Georgia Brown," the song he used to sing especially to her; and she relives her memories of him—her first love.

Themes and Meanings

Alice Walker's first published short story, "To Hell with Dying" is an initiation story, an account of first love and first death. It depicts how, through innocent faith, laughter, love, ritual, and memory, people triumph over death. The theme of the story is that of the blues, overtly suggested by Mr. Sweet's guitar playing and indirectly suggested by the tone of the story, which is both sweet and sad, like the blues. The story also serves as the narrator's song, or celebration, of Mr. Sweet.

In an initiation story, someone—usually the main character but, in this case, the narrator—moves from a certain plane of innocence into a new realm of knowledge and, having attained knowledge, can never claim innocence again. The novice is often accompanied on the journey to enlightenment by a guide, usually an elder. Sweet Little is the narrator's guide through at least two inevitable occasions of life: love and death. The narrator identifies Mr. Sweet as her first love; he made her feel beautiful and desirable. Ultimately she learns about more than the complexion of love, for she learns the sad truth about death as well.

This story is also about ritual, laughter and celebration, and memory—the various ways people attempt to defeat death. The narrator never states that Mr. Sweet is not really dying all those countless times the neighborhood children revive him. In fact, in the final episode, she seems genuinely surprised that Mr. Sweet actually dies. The reader understands that Mr. Sweet was not really dying all those other times; he was simply drunk and depressed and was resuscitated by the devotion of the children who made him feel needed and loved. That it was the youngest child who always performed the most important part of the ritual strongly suggests that death can only be conquered through a childlike innocence and unqualified faith. Walker's account suggests that the power to stay death not only lies in the hands of children, but also exists only for those who, like Mr. Sweet, have the innocence and childlike quality to believe.

In religious terms, a revival is a renewal of faith, and some churches hold revivals often. The repeated ritual of Mr. Sweet's rescue from the brink of death is referred to by the narrator as a "rite of revival." A rite is a ceremony, a certain series of actions performed exactly the same way every time, in order to effect a particular consequence. Much religious symbolism reflects humanity's desire to thwart death. People's general need to be loved and their faith in the healing power of love are both illustrated in this story by the fact that it is the unabashed love and caresses of the children that repeatedly revive Mr. Sweet. It is through memory that humanity best defies death: No one is ever dead if he or she is remembered, that is, lives in someone's memory. When people sing the blues, they are singing of love lost yet remembered, and when the narrator tells the story of Mr. Sweet, she is reviving him. Every time someone reads this story, Mr. Sweet Little is remembered and loved. He is brought to life, again and again.

Style and Technique

In an early interview, Alice Walker offers an autobiographical source for this story and observes, "I was the children, and the old man." The story is better served by focusing on the way Walker transforms an ordinary, recognizable event—an old man thinking that he is dying—into a magical and meaningful experience about the nature of death. The title is a homey variation on the basic human rebellion against death and reverberates like the first sentence of a preacher's sermon. The story stands as a testimonial of faith. The archetypal text gives the congregation of readers an opportunity to draw from common experience. The style is repetitive in the manner of a revival meeting, yet original like a sweet, sad, wonderful song that springs spontaneously from the strings of an old blues guitar. This technique yields both ritual and impromptu experience.

Throughout the story, the narrative tone is loving and warm, compelling by its generosity of spirit. The attention is focused on the plight of the often-dying, beloved old man, while the independence and special achievements of the educated young female narrator are understated. Walker parodies the traditional formula of popular romance by making this hero poor, old, alcoholic, and diabetic—a vulnerable old man, always crying and dying.

The story derives its deep emotional power from universal values, archetypal imagery, and recurrent rhythms. The narrative style springs from an ancient oral tradition of storytelling, a spontaneous and lyric form. The text is musical in its repetition of words and sounds.

Cynthia Whitney Hallett

TO ROOM NINETEEN

Author: Doris Lessing (1919-   )
Type of plot: Psychological realism
Time of plot: The 1950's and early 1960's
Locale: London, England
First published: 1963

Principal characters:
SUSAN RAWLINGS, a wife and mother
MATTHEW RAWLINGS, her husband, a newspaper subeditor
SOPHIE TRAUB, their au pair

The Story

Susan and Matthew Rawlings are an intelligent, practical, and conventional married couple living in Richmond, a suburb of London. Their twelve-year marriage has produced four children and innumerable sensible decisions. The Rawlingses have a slightly superior attitude toward other couples who allow clichéd problems to disrupt their harmony. When Matthew, a subeditor at a large London newspaper, finally commits adultery, Susan understands and forgives.

Susan, an advertising artist before her marriage, looks forward to the moment when her youngest children, twins, begin school so that she will have some time to herself during the day. Her seemingly perfect family life, however, becomes increasingly insufficient for her, but she is resolved to avoid the typical responses to such inadequacy. She may find some meaning in work, but will wait until the children, who need an attentive mother, are older.

Susan battles an increasing depression with her intelligence, trying to find comfort in the always sensible approach she and Matthew take to everything, telling herself she regrets nothing about her life. After the twins finally begin school, Susan finds herself afraid of her new freedom and hides from her depression in cooking, sewing, and other busywork. She is afraid to be alone in her garden, where her loneliness is most likely to manifest itself. Increasingly, she considers her obligations as wife and mother to be pressures that are driving her crazy. Confused by the new Susan whom she seems to have become, she is unable to communicate her fears to Matthew.

Craving privacy so that she can be her true self, Susan retreats to a spare room at the top of her house, but soon her children and Mrs. Parkes, her housekeeper, convert it into yet another family room. After her fears take seemingly human form as a devilish young man grinning wickedly at her from her garden, she takes a solitary walking tour in Wales, but her demon follows her.

After she convinces Matthew to hire an au pair to look after the children when they return home from school each day, Susan begins spending her days in London under the name Mrs. Jones, sitting peacefully in a shabby room in Fred's Hotel, doing nothing but luxuriating in perfect solitude. Room nineteen gives her the identity that her home life denies. Suspicious of her actions, Matthew hires a detective to follow her. Because he wants it to be so, she confesses to having an affair. Matthew admits his own relationship with a friend of theirs and wants the two couples to get together. Confused over how to substantiate her imaginary lover, empty at seeing how easily Sophie Traub, the au pair, fulfills the role of mother, depressed at losing the privacy of Fred's Hotel, Susan goes to room nineteen and turns on the gas.

Themes and Meanings

"To Room Nineteen" appears in a long line of works of fiction dealing with passive resistance to conformity and the resulting mental breakdown. Its antecedents include Herman Melville's "Bartleby, the Scrivener," in which the title character's preferring not to do anything eventually leads to his death, and "The Yellow Wall-Paper" by Charlotte Perkins Gilman, whose protagonist, increasingly unsatisfied by her roles as wife and mother, gradually goes insane. This story also has some parallels to one of Doris Lessing's later novels, *The Summer Before the Dark* (1973), whose similarly alienated protagonist leaves her family to escape her depression, but eventually returns.

The story of Susan Rawlings can be misinterpreted too easily, especially because of its similarities to "The Yellow Wall-Paper," as simply a feminist parable of an unfulfilled woman driven to her death by an insensitive, male-dominated society, but Doris Lessing hardly presents the world of suburban London, in an obviously unenlightened period, so starkly. Neither does Lessing intend Susan to be simply a case history of disintegration. She is presented too specifically to be merely a type, and despite her hallucinations, she is more depressed than clinically insane.

"To Room Nineteen" is a vivid portrait of the extremes to which the sensitive individual, especially a woman, may go when the resources of everyday life prove inadequate. Susan's problem is not that being a wife and mother is not enough, although she clearly misjudges Matthew's flimsy character. Neither is her predicament so clear-cut that it can be solved by a job or career. Susan is driven to suicide because she cannot find an identity that makes sense to her. If her world makes little sense, she can exert her selfhood only by retreating from it. If this world insists upon intruding into her privacy, she loses her battle for identity.

Lessing wants readers to be moved by Susan's suicide and not try to explain it away, but recognize the limits of reason. Susan cannot accept what cannot be rationally understood and wants to consider her unease to be her fault, but blame is not an issue here: "Nobody's fault, nothing to be at fault, no one to blame."

Susan is a prisoner of her rational intelligence, refusing to acknowledge that reason cannot explain or solve everything. Unlike the protagonist of *The Summer Before the Dark*, she has no illusions about freedom because, if achieved, it would place a greater burden of responsibility for her state upon her. What she ultimately wants is not freedom from responsibility, obligations, or family, but from the inescapable—herself: "not for one second, ever, was she free from the pressure of time, from having to remember this or that. She could never forget herself; never really let herself go into forgetfulness." A portrait of such extreme alienation takes "To Room Nineteen" well beyond the limitations of any political or sociological interpretations.

Lessing underscores the universality of Susan's story when the narrator comments on the banality of thinking the individual can place all the elements of life in order, can be in complete control. Such reasonable, highly educated people are essentially dry and flat. The Rawlingses are described as "Two people, endowed with education, with discrimination, with judgement, linked together voluntarily from their will to be happy together and to be of use to others—one sees them everywhere, one knows them, one even is that thing oneself: sadness because so much is after all so little." When a thinking person such as Susan realizes the impossibility of truly imposing order upon chaos, even greater chaos results.

Style and Technique

"To Room Nineteen" opens: "This is a story, I suppose, about a failure in intelligence." This initial omniscient first-person narration provides considerable ironic distance from the characters. The Rawlingses are first seen almost as mechanical creatures of creation with their pathetic little faith in intelligence and sensibility. As the story progresses, however, this narrating sensibility withdraws, and the reader is plunged slowly into the morbid world of Susan's psyche.

The gradual progression into a desperate mind makes the presentation of Susan's dilemma less potentially didactic and more emotionally engrossing. This approach also makes the reader, who has been cleverly tricked into sharing Susan's concerns, less likely to accept easy answers to a difficult situation. The story's ending reinforces the impossibility of simplistic solutions. Because Lessing's attention to the details of Susan's suburban existence have made her an individual, the suicide is likewise too specific an act to be considered nihilistic.

Lessing employs several devices typical of psychological realism. The demon that Susan first imagines in the garden is a visual manifestation of her mental state, her "irritation, restlessness, emptiness." She fears him because he is an embodiment of all that threatens her. Lessing makes the relationship between Susan and her demon clear when the woman stares into her mirror and sees the reflection first of a madwoman and then of a demon. Susan, the madwoman, and the demon are one.

Color is used to depict the extremes of Susan's world. Her perfect house is white, suggesting sterility and oppression. She escapes from the house into the garden, whose greenness implies the freedom offered by the contrasting natural world, as does the brown river running by it. When the garden no longer provides any escape, Susan goes to Fred's Hotel, where her room has thin green curtains, a three-quarter bed covered with a cheap green satin bedspread, and a green wicker armchair. She dies lying on the green satin bedspread and drifts "off into the dark river," the ultimate escape.

Michael Adams

TOAD'S MOUTH

Author: Isabel Allende (1942-   )
Type of plot: Social realism
Time of plot: Early twentieth century
Locale: Southern Chile
First published: "Boca de sapo," 1989 (English translation, 1991)

Principal characters:
HERMELINDA, a gregarious young prostitute
PABLO, a Spaniard who seduces her
AN ENGLISH COUPLE, the owners of Sheepbreeders, Ltd.

The Story

The rocky, desolate terrain of southern Chile provides the setting for this story, which opens on a sheep ranch. The land is silent and ice cold, and has been decimated by the sheep brought by English settlers. The sheep have eaten the vegetation and trampled the remaining artifacts of the indigenous cultures.

In contrast, the impassive English couple who own Sheepbreeders, Ltd., surround their headquarters with lawns and thorny fences of wild roses. They have not adapted to their surroundings. They stay indoors, observe the formal traditions of the British Empire, and pamper themselves with whatever luxuries their ranch affords.

The South American men who work for Sheepbreeders, Ltd., are underpaid, cold, and lonely, as neglected as the sheep they herd. Their only solace is in knowing Hermelinda, a young woman who lives in a nearby shack, earning her living as a prostitute. She loves them genuinely, and they count on her for a good time. She is known for her playfulness, her enthusiastic sense of humor, and her strong, beautiful body. The only other young woman in the area is from England. The opposite of Hermelinda, the English woman is nervous, fussy, and rarely seen.

On Friday nights, men ride their horses from great distances to spend an evening drinking Hermelinda's bootleg alcohol and playing a variety of games, which guarantee her a profit without cheating anyone. The games are sexual, and the prize is Hermelinda. Sometimes the party is so wild that the English couple hear laughter as they sip tea before bed. They pretend, however, that they only hear the wind.

Hermelinda's most successful game is called Toad's Mouth. She draws a chalk circle on the floor, then lies down on her back inside of it, with her knees spread wide. Thus, she reveals the "dark center of her body" which appears "as open as a fruit, as a merry toad's mouth." The men then toss their coins toward the target. Money that falls within the chalk circle is Hermelinda's to keep. If one of the players happens "to enter the gate of heaven" with his coin, he earns two hours alone with the hostess, an event so prized it is said to transform the winner into a wise man.

One day, an Asturian man named Pablo arrives. He is lean, with the bones of a bird and a child's hands. He looks like a "peevish banty rooster" but is tenacious, and those that threaten his dignity witness his bad temper and readiness to fight. He is a loner from Spain, traveling without obligation or love, and racked by bitterness and pain. He hates the English.

When Pablo sets eyes on Hermelinda, he sees a woman with his own strength and decides life is not worth living without her. He knows that he has a single chance to win Toad's Mouth, and then only two hours to convince Hermelinda to live with him. Under his sharp gaze, Hermelinda becomes motionless on the floor and he tosses the coin perfectly. The onlooking men cheer with envy, but Pablo is nonchalant in his victory. Immediately, he pulls Hermelinda into the bedroom, and closes the door behind them.

To the astonishment of the sheepherders, the lovers do not emerge until noon the following day. They leave the shack, carrying their packed belongings. Pablo saddles the horses without glancing at anyone. Hermelinda wears riding clothes; strapped to her belt is a canvas bag with her savings. She has a new expression in her eyes and walks with a satisfied swish. She waves a distracted good-bye, then follows Pablo without looking back.

The sheepherders never see Hermelinda again. They are so distraught that the ranch managers install an enormous open-mouthed ceramic toad from London. This is supposed to cheer the men up, but they are unimpressed. Eventually, the toad ends up on the English couple's terrace. In the evenings, the bored foreigners amuse themselves by tossing coins into its artificial mouth.

Themes and Meanings

In her essay "Writing As an Act of Hope," Isabel Allende explains that she writes in order to illuminate "some hidden aspect of reality, to help decipher and understand it and thus to initiate, if possible, a change in the conscience of some readers." The reality that she describes in "Toad's Mouth" is rooted in Latin American history. In the 1500's, Spanish explorers and soldiers took over the South American continent; the impact they had on indigenous societies was prodigious.

In "Toad's Mouth," the English couple control wealth and labor in a country that is not their own. They represent any imperialist force that takes control of land and people for personal gain. Indifferent to local customs, the owners of Sheepbreeders, Ltd., maintain their prim exteriors by observing tea time and wearing fancy clothes inappropriate to the landscape. They do not interact with the peasants. They treat the native population with so little respect that they allow their sheep blindly to graze atop sacred ruins.

Much of Allende's fiction is set in Latin America, and her characters often face the duality of the poverty and wealth that can exist there. Wealth, Allende explains in her essay, is in the hands of few, yet carries with it the "pretension to dignity and civilization." In "Toad's Mouth," the English couple consider themselves dignified, but Allende depicts them as absurd and misplaced, concerned only with themselves. In contrast, the peasants live with dignity, treating one another with love and respect. It is the peasants, not the wealthy ranch owners, who form a community, work the land they love, and celebrate their passion for Hermelinda.

As a lover, Hermelinda represents the wild and generous strength of the land itself. She also mothers the men, feeding them soup when they are ill, or mending their clothes. Finally, she is their goddess, a symbol of ancient fertility rituals and the perfect recipient of their worship. She loves them as much as they love her, and the relationship is fruitful, benefiting all. Just as the land for centuries gave native people the means to survive, Hermelinda helps the men overcome their hardships.

Pablo, representing Spain, successfully seduces Hermelinda, then draws her away from her friends. He understands the game of Toad's Mouth perfectly, and wins at his first try. His passion is angry, defiant, and selfish, but strong as well, and she willingly follows him, as many indigenous people followed the customs of Spain, abandoning their native languages for Spanish and their ancient religions for Roman Catholicism.

The reserved English couple, however, misunderstand the game of Toad's Mouth entirely. They neither know nor love Hermelinda; they fear the joy she initiates and pretend not to notice the laughter that rises from her shack. Trapped in their pretensions, the ranch owners cannot feel the earthy passion of the land they attempt to control. Because they refuse to interact with the culture, they miss its beauty. They shelter themselves from what they think is barbaric and cannot see how they destroy it. In the end, they unwittingly mock their own ignorance by playing with the fake toad themselves.

Style and Technique

Isabel Allende has said that she tries "to write about the necessary changes in Latin America that will enable us to rise from our knees after five centuries of humiliations." Specifically, she writes all of her stories for a young woman in Chile whom she hardly knows. Whenever the author is "tempted by the beauty of a sentence" and "about to betray the truth," she thinks of the candid face of the woman in Chile, and then tells the story in honest, unpretentious prose.

"Toad's Mouth" typifies this style. Its descriptions are concise, playful, and rich with metaphor. Tierra del Fuego breaks up "into a rosary of islands," while the headquarters for Sheepbreeders, Ltd., rises "up from the sterile plain like a forgotten cake." The plot itself holds both humor and political commentary; Pablo's seduction of Hermelinda is both sexually outrageous and symbolically tragic.

The characters in "Toad's Mouth" represent forces larger than themselves. This encourages the reader to interpret the story on a broad scale. The peasants at Sheepbreeders, Ltd., are conquered financially by the English couple, then spiritually by the lone horseman from Spain. They are left with nothing to look forward to, because Hermelinda is gone forever. This is not just the tale of one tiny community in Chile. "Toad's Mouth" is the story of Latin America, and of what is lost when a society is dominated by outside forces.

Mary Pierce Frost

TODAY WILL BE A QUIET DAY

Author: Amy Hempel (1951-   )
Type of plot: Domestic realism
Time of plot: The 1970's or 1980's
Locale: San Francisco, California
First published: 1985

Principal characters:
A FATHER
HIS THIRTEEN-YEAR-OLD SON
HIS SIXTEEN-YEAR-OLD DAUGHTER

The Story

The three characters in this story remain nameless throughout. Instead, they are identified only by their relationships to the others: father, daughter, sister, son, or brother. Also omitted is an overt explanation of the reason these three are together in this special way on this particular day. The mother is never mentioned, yet there is little doubt that there has been a divorce and that the children are visiting their father; in fact, they are spending this night with him. The father has canceled the children's music lessons so that the three of them can spend the day together. He wants to find out how his children are doing, but will not ask them outright. He chooses simply to observe them during their day together.

The father takes his children on a long drive out of the city. Rather than attend a men's armwrestling competition, the children choose to go to a modified drive-in restaurant: Pete's—a gas station converted into a place to eat. In the car the children fall into the type of competitive banter and pseudo-arguments that siblings often share. Throughout the day the father says all the appropriate "Dad things" that fathers enjoy saying to their children, such as, "Neither of you should be eating candy before lunch."

There are two seemingly trivial but actually important incidents in the story: The girl tells a joke about three men about to be beheaded: The first two are spared because the guillotine does not work correctly, but the third dies after pointing out the device's mechanical problem. The girl learns that a family dog was not sent to a farm to live after it had bitten a Campfire Girl selling candy at their front door, but rather it was dead because the bitten girl's family had insisted that it be destroyed according to California law.

After they eat, the father lets the daughter drive home. When they reach his house, they prepare to sleep on the floor of the master bedroom in sleeping bags positioned in a cozy triangle, as if around a campfire. Nothing significant happens; yet at the end of the day, the father decides that his children are coping well, that "they are all right."

Themes and Meanings

Since readers have no guidance from Amy Hempel's narrator as to what to think about anything or anyone in this narrative, they must become more involved with the story than is typical in order to come to a conclusion. Although there are no explicit or overt explanations or evaluations, many clues are embedded in the text. The story appears to be about relationships, specifically those of a divorced father with his children, in whose lives he has been only marginally involved. It is no small matter that the title of the story coincides with the epitaph for the father's tombstone or with the general connotation of what it means to have a "quiet day" with or without others. Normally quiet time is set aside for some kind of healing, for getting in touch, for listening to inner-voices, or for trying to hear better what others are saying. In this story the day is far from being a quiet one; there is much talking going on. The quietness appears to apply to a lack of direct communication and to the soundless situations of a dismembered family and dislocated relationships.

The story also appears to be about the many ways people communicate various feelings without ever speaking the exact words, as well as how people rarely say what they really mean or really feel, but tend to fall into ready phrases, expected responses, innuendo, or euphemism—say it any other way but do not say it outright. The most obvious example of this latter theme lies in the joke that the young girl tells. Even the joke has to be "translated," and therefore is not given in direct speech. In the scenario of the joke, two people are spared execution either because they do not see the problem or because they say nothing. Only the person who recognizes the problem and, more to the point, acknowledges it aloud, suffers negative consequences—he dies. He dies for the knowing and for the telling, for the seeing and saying, for his pointing it out to others.

Many other verbal clues exist in the text of the story, clues that give meaning both to the events and to the characters' behavior, but also that reflect the methods by which this story is told. "But you could read things wrong" might refer both to the father's reading of his children as "all right" or "not all right" and to the reader's interpretation of the story. "Thinking you're invisible because you closed your eyes" might reflect the condition of thinking that pretending makes something so, or that ignoring something makes it cease to exist. There is a pun embedded in the description of the new type of arm wrestling that the family considers seeing: "The best anyone could hope to see would be dislocation." Within the new rules of the sporting event, the worst that can happen now is that someone's shoulder might be "dislocated"; in the arena of life, if "dislocation" is the best that one can hope for, then everyone in the story must indeed be "all right."

Style and Technique

A term frequently applied to Amy Hempel's short fiction is minimalism—a technique that creates fiction that is deceptively simple and realistic. At its best, minimalism creates a concentrated and uncluttered narrative. In addition, it is a style that also reflects the characteristics of the short story, the genre which best houses minimalism. Both minimalism and the short story rely heavily on figures of speech and the baggage of connotation attached to each. Metonymy is the basic trope for realism, while metaphor is the basic trope for poetry. Minimalist stories are realistic in that they use metonymy such as the joke or the arm wrestling references in this story. The joke that the young girl tells is a tiny anecdote within the short story, yet it not only reflects the whole idea of this story, it also gestures toward the larger text of a universal condition in which humanity is no longer located in strong family units and no longer able to address emotions directly. Instead, the human condition represented here disallows words and dislocates language as a means of emotional survival. The references to the arm wrestling contest and the reasons given for the trio not going to the event refer to the same sort of human condition, "The best one could hope for was dislocation"—not just of someone's arm (rather than being broken under the old rules), but also dislocation of emotions, language, and meaning.

Everything left out of a minimalist short story is as important as the things that remain. In this story, for example, there is never any mention of the children's mother (the father's former wife), but she is present as part of the dislocation caused by divorce. Likewise, the names of the characters are left out of the story; this omission gives the story a universal dimension because the characters' anonymity suggests that they could be any father and children who are characters in the drama and effects of divorce. Further, many things are not said by the narrator to the reader; many more things are not said by the characters among themselves. To omit a word, to say something indirectly, to rely on meaningless phrases for communication—all are the most emphatic means of stressing the importance of what has not been said, which in this case seems to be that a divorce has disrupted this family unit, that the father does not feel himself to be a part of his children's lives, and that he is afraid to let them know that he cares about them.

The details of the day's events are relayed by an omniscient third-person narrator, who does not intrude on the story by commenting or making any evaluations, leaving readers to watch and listen to an apparently objective report on the events of this day and the dialogue exchanged among the three characters. The readers are thus left to draw their own conclusions. In employing this type of narrative technique, Hempel presents the reader with a narrator who, in fact, practices what the story appears to preach: Do not point out the problem if you see it; just accept what is what and go on about your business. If you must say anything, say it indirectly, as with the father's assessment of his children's condition: "There is no bad news."

Cynthia Whitney Hallett

THE TRACTOR

Author: Peter Cowan (1914-)
Type of plot: Social realism
Time of plot: Probably mid-twentieth century
Locale: An Australian suburb
First published: 1965

Principal characters:
ANN, a painter, elementary-school teacher, and naturalist
KEN, her fiancé, a suburban land developer
THE HERMIT, a homeless man

The Story

Ann, a city dweller, and her fiancé, Ken, are visiting the home of Ken's parents in the outer reaches of a new suburban development. Ken reports that one of the two large tractors owned by McKay, the contractor who is clearing away trees and bushes for the expansion of the development, has been sabotaged. Ann, incredulous, cannot believe that anyone would deliberately tamper with clearing or construction equipment, but describes the preparation of marginal farming and grazing land for houses as ruthless. Ken takes pride in his business acumen and entrepreneurship: He is helping to provide people with suburban-style houses and enabling hardscrabble farm owners to realize some income from their land. As Ann acknowledges, he is more perceptive than he chooses to reveal. Ann, however, cannot imagine herself living in a development that has been carved from the bush (the Australian term for the undisturbed countryside).

Ken indicates that he and his friends know who has interfered with the tractors, and also allowed faucets on farm drinking-troughs to run continuously; they are prepared to set fire to the bush in order to flush out the hermit, who has several favorite living-spots in the region. At this, Ann realizes that she can never become one of Ken's group; she has quite different values with regard to both the environment and the homeless, the eccentrics of society, those who commune with nature rather than destroy it in the name of progress.

The summer heat becomes oppressive, and the police cannot find the hermit, who knows every feature of the bush. Ken describes the hermit as a madman, because of his total identification with nature and rejection of conventional domesticity. Although one of his camps is found, the hermit eludes police and a posse for a week. Assuming that the hermit is armed, the posse searches with rifles.

Ken and Ann acknowledge their differing values, which jeopardize their apparent love. She resorts to painting flowers, bushes, and seeds; he states his belief in making domestic use of the land and chastises Ann for being a dreamer, an impractical conservationist. While Ken is out in search of the hermit, Ann helps Ken's mother with household chores. She discerns in her an attractive quietness and insightfulness, but suspects that she has never questioned men's decisions and actions: She epitomizes the wife who accepts male hegemony without demonstration or demur.

At a local birthday party, the conversation inevitably turns to the hermit and the incompetence of the local police in apprehending him. Most people believe that the hermit should be flushed out and killed, if necessary, the way that a nuisance fox or wild dog would be caught. Because Ann's values are so different from the others', they question her qualifications to teach their children in the local elementary school.

On her return to her boarding house room after the party, Ann is introspective; her sense of anger gives way to dejection and then to fear as she realizes that the men's plan to hunt the hermit and shoot him is likely to be carried out.

A week after the sabotage of the tractor, Ann takes advantage of Ken's absence at a meeting of the posse and goes walking—ostensibly to paint wildlife, but in reality to locate the hermit and warn him of the posse's plans in the hope that he will escape. The summer heat exhausts her; although a lover of the bush, she is not experienced in traversing it and becomes lost. Suddenly she is confronted by the hermit. He is thin, his arms are sticklike, knotted and black, and he has a rifle. Ann tries to prevail upon the hermit to leave this part of the bush, but his impassivity unnerves her and she cries out helplessly. She sees that he moves in a fashion that is "liquid, unhuman . . . like an animal or the vibration of the thin sparse trees before the wind."

Later in the afternoon, Ann hears shots. Ken explains that the hermit tried to get past the line of the posse, then shot at one of them, so they had to shoot him. Ann is unable to respond. She and Ken drive back to the town.

Themes and Meanings

Almost all of Peter Cowan's short fiction treats a restricted range of thematic material, and most of these were introduced in his first volume, *Drift: Stories* (1944): the close connection of individuals to the land, farmers' loneliness without the company of sympathetic women, the incompatibility of city and country life, and the uniformity of values of small-town societies. "The Tractor" introduces all of these, although not all are explored at length. Here the despoiling of the natural environment under the pressure to extend housing and the two central characters' responses to this situation are the principal foci of the story. These, in turn, introduce a number of subsidiary considerations that challenge the thinking of the reader rather than present a set of conclusions. Is there a simple choice between conservation and development? Should the natural environment be preserved at the expense of people who wish to leave the inner cities and have modern housing far from urban blight? Is it wrong for farmers to profit from selling their land to housing developers? Should independent-minded, homeless, or eccentric characters outside the normal social sphere be allowed to wreak their individual vengeance on the representatives of social change, development, or improvement without consequences?

Because it raises so many fundamental social issues, "The Tractor," according to one critic, is a moral fable for modern times. All of its characters and events draw attention to the dominant issue, which is whether the natural environment is something to be destroyed in the interests of wealth and development—the viewpoint of the farmers and the developers—or to be maintained in the interests of nature, beauty, and tranquility—the viewpoint of Ann and the hermit. Should enforcement of the laws of community be entrusted to society itself, in the form of the police, or of the contesting parties themselves? Because Ann and Ken intend to marry shortly and declare their love despite their fundamental differences, the reader realizes that some compromises or change of belief are essential and inevitable. The solution, however, is left to the reader. Ann's belief that Ken's mother has capitulated to her husband's position makes her reconsider her own stance vis à vis male hegemony: In the interest of marriage, should she abandon her own strongly held beliefs or be strong and independent in a matter of concern to her?

Complicating an interpretation of the basic theme of the story is the fact that Ann, although at heart a naturalist, is not sufficiently versed in its ways to avoid getting lost while seeking the hermit; and the hermit, at home in the bush for a decade, has several camps (homes) and a radio (although nonfunctional) which indicates his desire to be connected to the world of commerce and materialism that he presumably disdains. It is he who sabotages the tractor, the sheep-run fences, and the cattle-drinking faucets, and, so far as one knows from the story, he fires the initial shot at the posse.

The story, therefore, invites—even demands—considerable thought on the part of the reader on matters of importance.

Style and Technique

In "The Tractor," Cowan uses the device known as metonymy: the presentation of a single case to represent a larger group; in other words, he is making use of symbolic cases. The cost of so doing is the loss of individualized emotional responses. The supposed romance between Ann and Ken is never clearly apparent, so one wonders what they really have in common. Ken's mother is neither affectionate nor markedly maternal. The birthday party is a particularly dull occasion at which jollity, friendliness, and bonhomie seem wholly alien. The posse never seems to have any true cohesiveness or social unity; even the hermit and Ann lack any real common feeling or understanding; it is as if they are as much apart philosophically as they are socially. Cowan seems to suggest that men and women cannot communicate adequately.

Cowan's talent is in showing the sincerity of his characters, although their motivations are not always explored adequately. He reveals—perhaps better than any other Australian short-story writer—the loneliness, monotony, and conformity found in the bush. Earlier writers suggested the importance of mateship—a close brotherhood between men—to the exclusion of women, and tolerance—even exaltation—of the eccentric or loner, but Cowan, a more realistic writer, questions these beliefs.

Some critics have detected a certain poetic quality in Cowan's prose, but this is rare. He has an excellent ear for incorporating everyday speech and a fine understanding of introspection or philosophical rumination.

A. L. McLeod

THE TRAIN FROM RHODESIA

Author: Nadine Gordimer (1923-)
Type of plot: Social realism
Time of plot: Mid-twentieth century
Locale: Southern Africa
First published: 1947

Principal characters:
THE WIFE, a passenger on a train
HER HUSBAND, another passenger
A LOCAL ARTIST, selling his crafts at the train station

The Story

When a train from Rhodesia stops briefly at a station, its wheels are checked, bread is delivered to the stationmaster's wife, malnourished animals and poor children approach the train for handouts, and artisans walk alongside the train's windows, hoping to sell their crafts to the passengers.

The focus soon is on a young woman (the wife) leaning out a corridor window asking to see a lion, beautifully carved by a vendor. The lion is described minutely, its detail revealing the care and love of the artisan. The young husband joins his wife as she admires the lion. The wife considers the price, three shillings and sixpence, to be too high and decides not to buy it. When the husband asks if she is sure she does not want the lion, she tells him to leave it.

She returns to her train compartment still thinking about the lovely lion with the real fur mane and the black tongue. (It seems the lion is too expensive only when considering the many other carved figures she has already purchased.) However, she also has more serious thoughts. It becomes apparent that the wife is newly married, and the train ride seems to be the end of her honeymoon journey. Her trip to all the foreign places seems unreal to her. She wonders what she will do with all the craft items she has bought on her journey; she wonders how the memories and memorabilia will fit in with her new life. Most significant, she realizes that her young husband is not merely part of her temporary journey, but will be a very real part of her new life.

As the train leaves the station, the young husband enters the compartment proudly displaying the lion. He enthusiastically tells his wife how he bargained with the vendor for fun; at the last moment, with the train moving, the vendor offered him the lion for one and six, instead of three and six. The husband threw down the coins as the train moved, and the vendor flung up the lion.

The wife is upset rather than appreciative. She tosses the lion aside and asks how he could have bargained instead of paying full price if he wanted the lion. The story ends with the train pulling out of the station, the husband looking without understanding at his wife, and the wife feeling empty and sick looking out the train window.

Themes and Meanings

"The Train from Rhodesia" deals with the contrast in the lives between the people on the train and those in the station and also between the young wife and husband. The passengers on the train represent those who have both leisure and money: The young wife on the train is on holiday; other passengers throw unwanted chocolate to dogs at the station, or sit in the dining car drinking beer. The people in the station represent the working poor: The vendors at the station squat "in the dust"; the stationmaster's children are "barefoot." The children and animals beg for handouts while the vendors nearly do so: "All up and down the length of the train in the dust the artists sprang, walking bent, like performing animals, the better to exhibit the fantasy held toward the faces on the train."

The physical setting places the white passengers above the local inhabitants: They sit inside the comfortable train and reach down to throw scraps to the animals or to exchange money for the crafts being held up by the "gray-black" hands. The interior of the train suggests luxury, but also a lack of life; artificial flowers adorn tables in the dining car, and the wife, the only passenger whose internal feelings are revealed, feels a void in her life. The train station suggests poverty but also life and creativity; the land is poor and the animals are malnourished, but the crafts of the artisans are beautiful. The meeting between the passengers and the local inhabitants is brief and unsatisfactory. The train itself is presented negatively. Each reference to the train emphasizes harsh sounds, negative power, or a lack of connection between the train and the landscape. The train brings together the two groups only briefly while actually keeping them isolated: The "few men who had got down to stretch their legs sprang on to the train . . . safe from the one dusty platform, the one tin house, the empty sand." The brief meeting highlights the disparity between the lives of both groups and suggests that such disparity is harmful to both. The young wife who lives in luxury bears internal scars, while the creative vendors live in poverty.

The young husband and wife are also contrasted. They share the same lifestyle, but apparently not the same values. The husband appears happy until the contretemps with his wife over the lion, but the reader who has access to the wife's thoughts and feelings knows that she is not content. She feels an emptiness and questions the place of her new husband in her life. When the husband proudly relates his success at buying the lion at a much-reduced price, his wife thinks not of the lovely lion but of the artisan. In anger she tries to explain her view, but her husband does not understand, and she gives up trying to explain, as if she believes the disparity in their values too large a gap to be bridged by words.

Style and Technique

Most of the story is told dramatically; its events are presented as if picked up by a camera and a microphone, with relatively little narrative intervention. Only occasionally the connotations of words—such as the negative ones describing the train—suggest interpretation. Two passages are important exceptions to the dramatic point of view: Twice the reader is allowed glimpses into the wife's thoughts and feelings.

In the first passage, the reader discovers that the wife does not buy the lion only because she already has many such memorabilia from her trip. Her thoughts also suggest that she is unsure about her feelings for her new husband. In the second passage, the reader discovers a discrepancy between how the husband and wife think and what they value. The implication of the husband and wife's failure to understand what each other feels about the carved lion suggests that these two people have different values and may therefore be incompatible. The wife finds the lion a wonderful piece of art but does not buy it because, after buying so many others already, she feels that this purchase—not necessarily its price—would be extravagant. The husband believes that she would like the lion at a lower price and does not mind haggling with the vendor for a bargain. The wife is disturbed at her husband's actions. For her, the beauty of the lion is lost at the price of what she views as the humiliation of the vendor. As she is filled with shame at her husband's actions, she feels again a void inside which she expected to be filled by marriage.

Since the train is presented negatively and the inside of the train reflects a kind of sterile luxury, the implication is that the void inside the wife may be caused not by the lack of a husband but by the lack of a life with any real meaning. Her joy at the vendor's lion suggests that perhaps she has the potential for a finer existence and that she would better rid herself of the void by participating in all of life, not just the sterile leisure life the train symbolizes. The separation of the wealthy and the poor is not a satisfactory arrangement for either group.

Nadine Gordimer builds her story on a series of contrasts: white and black, leisured and working, rich and poor, comfort and pain, above and below, sterility and creativity. Because of its dramatic point of view, most of the story is revealed through the contrasts, but on the two occasions when the reader is allowed glimpses into the wife's mind and heart, the themes suggested by the contrasts are confirmed.

Marion Boyle Petrillo

TRAVELER

Author: Ellen Gilchrist (1935-)
Type of plot: Domestic realism
Time of plot: Post-World War II
Locale: Mississippi
First published: 1980

Principal characters:
LELE ARNOLD, the teenage narrator and protagonist
BABY GWEN BARKSDALE, her cousin
FIELDING REID, her love interest

The Story

When LeLe Arnold, an Indiana high-school girl, is invited to spend the summer with her cousin Baby Gwen in Mississippi, she is thrilled. She was recently passed over in a cheerleader election because, she believes, she was regarded as somewhat overweight. She sees Mississippi as a place where she can start over and become a different and more popular person. Immediately upon arrival she begins to work on her reputation by telling her cousin that she did make the cheerleading squad and the football team saw her off at the train station.

LeLe and Baby Gwen spend their days sunbathing, playing bridge, and entertaining the boys who call on them. LeLe is attracted to one in particular, Fielding Reid, and about the time that she is beginning to believe her own publicity, that she is special, Fielding finally invites her to go out with him alone. LeLe can hardly contain her excitement but is sorely disappointed when Fielding tells her he has asked her out to talk to her about her weight, which he says is keeping her from being as beautiful as she might be. To save face, LeLe again resorts to lying, telling him that she has a thyroid condition.

When Fielding announces that it is time for his annual swim across the lake, LeLe offers to swim with him against Baby Gwen's protest that it is not a feat suitable for girls. The water empowers LeLe: She feels thin, beautiful, even perfect, and she accomplishes the swim with no trouble, her reputation as "the wildest girl in Mississippi" solidified.

When she returns home with Baby Gwen, LeLe learns that her parents are coming for her. Soon she is back in Indiana, telling a friend there that she was practically engaged to a rich plantation owner's son, while "trying to remember how the water turned into diamonds in her hands."

Themes and Meanings

A young woman's concern with her weight and popularity can be found in much of the fiction of Southern writer Ellen Gilchrist. Although LeLe's lies about herself, and her hypocrisy in befriending a girl with a wooden arm only for the sake of her own reputation, give a somewhat negative impression of LeLe, the reader is moved to sympathize with her when she is confronted about her weight by Fielding and to enjoy the clever lie about a thyroid condition that makes Fielding feel bad for bringing up the subject.

Ironically, LeLe comments earlier on how much she likes the fact that her new Southern friends are so much less competitive and more polite than her friends in Indiana. With Fielding's rude remarks, the reader realizes that this story can be viewed as part of the body of postbellum plantation fiction that tries to deconstruct images of the South as paradisiacal and all Southerners as easygoing and mannerly ladies and gentlemen. Sadly, in spite of Fielding's hurtful remarks about her weight, LeLe still wishes to impress him; that, rather than the accomplishment itself, is the main reason she wants to swim across the lake with him.

Water and swimming also are found repeatedly in Gilchrist's work, symbolizing the source of life and baptism into a new life, and usually associated with her female characters who are empowered in this medium as they are not on land. Until her swim, LeLe's reputation is based on deceit. Upon immersing herself in the water, however, a change begins to come over her. She senses her inner strength, and this time it comes from an element in which she can compete honestly. She feels weightless in the water and swims easily across the lake, thereby earning her reputation while proving that women's strength is not necessarily found only in their outward appearance.

Back on land, however, LeLe is once more engulfed by the attention paid her, in particular by Fielding, whose unqualified admiration she finally wins. When she returns to Indiana, she is again telling self-aggrandizing lies about her adventures in Mississippi; however, her wistful unspoken thoughts of Mississippi are not of Fielding or her reputation, but of how the water made her feel. That sense of true empowerment is what she is trying to recall as the story closes, reinforcing the reader's awareness of the two LeLes: the seemingly self-confident LeLe who confronts the world, and the insecure LeLe who worries about her appearance and reputation.

Style and Technique

Two complications often arise with first-person narrators: The narrator might be unreliable, and the reader is limited by the narrator's knowledge. In spite of her lying, LeLe is not an unreliable narrator. She reveals the truth to the reader at some point before lying to Baby Gwen, the maid, or Fielding. She even admits that she starts believing in her own lies and has befriended a girl with a wooden arm only for the sake of her own reputation. Such honesty to herself, while ironic given her seemingly uncontrollable compulsion to lie to others, is endearing, allowing the reader to forgive her outward dishonesty and hypocrisy.

LeLe reports at the beginning of the story that she is going to Mississippi to keep Baby Gwen company because Baby Gwen's mother has recently died. She also comments that her father tells her about the invitation just after her own mother has left him for some ambiguous reason having to do with jealousy, which LeLe does not explain. The reader wonders, therefore, if LeLe's father is actually sending her away because he does not want to be burdened with taking care of her by himself, or so that he can continue an affair. Her parents are not mentioned again until the end of the story, reflecting either LeLe's lack of concern about their problems or her desire to forget the family troubles back home. Perhaps she senses that she has been discarded and does not want to think about the implications of this. Either of the latter two possibilities shed light on her drive to be popular beyond the disappointment over her school's cheerleader tryouts. Since she is the one telling the story, if LeLe does not want to think about her parents, then the reader has no further hints to ponder.

The reader can discern the implications of other subtle details in LeLe's narrative that she does not perceive; she may not be an unreliable narrator, but she is a naïve narrator. For example, part of LeLe's joy in going to Mississippi is because her relatives are members of the Southern aristocracy, and she looks forward to taking advantage of this. From the moment of her arrival, LeLe basks in the luxuries at the Barksdale home. Gilchrist provides a brief episode that reminds the reader of the nightmarish side of this dreamlike social system: On her first morning in Mississippi, LeLe sees Baby Gwen being bathed by her black maid, Sirena. LeLe is amazed at the oddness of a teenager being given a bath and notices the contrast between Sirena's black hand and Baby Gwen's white skin, but does not comment on the social implications of the scene. The more sophisticated reader recognizes these implications: A system with an aristocracy must also have a subservient class. Again, LeLe's immature idealized vision of the South is undermined by the reader's more insightful perception of the reality.

The story's title provides another example of its multiple levels of meaning. On the surface, the title refers to LeLe's travels from Indiana to Mississippi. At a deeper level, it alludes to LeLe's swim, a trip toward some self-awareness, the realization of her strengths. LeLe's land travels may come full circle, returning her to Indiana where she is still not a cheerleader and where she continues to tell exaggerated versions of the truth, if not outright lies. Her swim across the lake, however, was a one-way journey, giving the reader hope that LeLe will not soon forget the euphoria in earning the respect of others, and herself.

The weight and water motifs employed in this story connect it to the rest of the story cycle of which it is a part (Gilchrist's *In the Land of Dreamy Dreams*, 1981) as well as the rest of Gilchrist's canon. The other stories in *In the Land of Dreamy Dreams* also focus on the issue of reputation and class, and several of them are either narrated by, or have as their protagonists, young girls similar to LeLe, which results in the sense of a composite personality as the single protagonist of the collection. LeLe is reminiscent, in particular, of Gilchrist's most well-known character, Rhoda Manning, who is the prototype for her other female characters and the protagonist of several of the other stories in this collection.

Margaret D. Bauer

A TREE OF NIGHT

Author: Truman Capote (Truman Streckfus Persons, 1924-1984)
Type of plot: Psychological realism
Time of plot: The 1940's
Locale: Alabama
First published: 1943

Principal characters:
KAY, the protagonist, a college sophomore
A WOMAN, her antagonist
A MUTE MAN, her nemesis

The Story

On an icy winter's night, nineteen-year-old Kay waits for a train. Her tall, thin figure, conservative attire, and stylish hair suggest breeding and wealth. She carries a gray suede purse, on which elaborate brass letters emblazon her name (K-A-Y), as well as several magazines and, incongruously, a green western guitar. Boarding a crowded, littered train, she finds a seat facing a grotesque couple, who share childlike characteristics. The woman's feet dangle, barely brushing the floor; on her enormous head, her dyed red hair is in "corkscrew curls." Tipsy, she behaves erratically, by turns syrupy and then mocking, rude, and rough toward Kay. Her deaf and mute companion has thickly lashed, oddly beautiful, milk-blue eyes, and he reeks of cheap perfume, looks childlike, and wears a Mickey Mouse watch.

As Kay settles in her seat, the woman begins a conversation in which she learns that Kay has been to her uncle's funeral, that she was willed only his green guitar, and that she is a college student. The woman disdains college education. Kay opens a magazine, but the woman prevails upon her good manners to talk. As tension builds between them, inexplicably, the woman becomes increasingly able to manipulate Kay. A more emotionally fraught tension bonds the girl and the mute man.

Eventually, under the guise of a polite lie, Kay anxiously tries to flee, but the woman grabs her wrist, demanding, "Didn't your mama ever tell you it was sinful to lie?" Kay denies the obvious, but hastily obeys a terse "Sit down, dear." A tangible sense of history pervading their relationship increases when the woman asks Kay about her hometown. Many cities crowd the girl's mind, but she cannot think which of them it is, then says, "New Orleans." The woman beams, telling Kay that she once ran a lucrative fortune-telling business there. The woman then explains that she and her companion have a traveling act involving the man's being buried alive in a star-studded casket.

As the woman talks, Kay gazes at the mute man, thinking that his face has the same unseeing look as that of her dead uncle. This gaze is not the first between them, for when she first sits down, he swings "his head sideways," studying her; another gaze occurs when the woman briefly leaves them. During the woman's absence, as Kay strums the guitar, the man reaches boldly and delicately to trace her cheek. Kay's mind darts in all directions as he leans closer, and they gaze, searchingly, eye-to-eye, as "keen" pity wells up in the girl, coupling with an overpowering disgust and loathing. Here, Kay feels the first stirring of primal memory.

The story climaxes when the man extracts a peach seed from his pocket. Balancing it in his hand, he catches Kay's eyes in another gaze, obscenely caressing the seed. The woman explains that it is a love charm that he wants Kay to buy for a dollar. Panicky, she refuses. When the woman will not make the man put it away, Kay flees with her purse to the lantern-lit observation platform. There, she clutches at the scant facts of her life, hopelessly seeking perspective. Kneeling down, she warms herself at the lantern's glass funnel until she senses the man hovering nearby. Looking up, Kay makes a last, lucid effort to sublimate her fear in a childhood memory that always "hovered above her, like haunted limbs on a tree of night": the memory evokes aunts, cooks, strangers spinning supernatural stories with threats of a "wizard man" who stole naughty children.

Kay follows the man back inside the compartment, where everyone is asleep—except the woman, who ignores Kay. The man merely sits with his arms folded. Kay's anxiety rebuilds. Near panic, she says that she will buy the charm. The woman does not respond, so Kay turns to the man. His face seems to "change form and recede before her" sliding under water. Immediately, the girl relaxes, succumbing to a "warm laziness," surrendering her purse to the woman, who gently pulls the "raincoat like a shroud above her head."

Themes and Meanings

Truman Capote packs "A Tree of Night" with clues for many themes, all of which relate to the fact that the story is a rite of passage piece that captures the moment when a nineteen-year-old woman passes from childhood innocence to adult sexual awareness. The peach seed, for example, is both masculine and feminine in context: The seed that a male implants in a female produces new life. This shellacked seed in the story, however, is impotent, and thus serves as a symbol of sexual union without reproduction. The mute man's handling of the seed arouses erotic and nameless responses in the innocent college sophomore, who flees to the platform of the car, only to yield compulsively to a desire to fondle the phallic lantern funnel. In doing so, she is fascinated by the tone and texture of her hands as they become luminous and warm while the funnel's heat thaws her and tingles through her.

At this same moment the mute appears. Looking up at him, his arms dangling, Kay recalls the tree of night that she feared in childhood. She remembers that adults in her youth filled her with superstitious fears by saying that a "wizard man" would steal her if she did things that she should not. Back then, a tree tapping against her window played on those fears. Identifying the mute man with her childhood, Kay, at the very edge of passage into full adulthood, follows him back into the coach, where she begs the dwarf woman (a symbol of adult authority) to let her buy the seed for a dollar. The adult influence turns its head, however, leaving Kay alone with the man to strike her own bargain. The man is the one for whom she has felt strong compassion, pity, loathing, nameless fear, and bonding. The story ends with the two characters bonded by a gaze which leads the girl to give in symbolically to her sexual desire, which is now terrifyingly aroused in her.

To understand this story more fully, it is useful to have some knowledge of the early 1940's in America, when trains were a common mode of transportation. Young women such as Kay who could afford college were typically sheltered and carefully protected from sexual knowledge of any sort. They were often kept in line by superstitious threats. A woman's vagina was called a "purse," and mothers warned their daughters to keep their purses shut. In "A Tree of Night," Kay gives up the entire contents of her purse. As was also true of sheltered young women in that period, she swoons as she lets it go. As the story ends, she is aswim in waters of sexual surrender.

Style and Technique

Capote believed that what a writer used as subject matter was not as important as how it was used. He told an interviewer that "a very fine artist" can take something "most ordinary" and, "through sheer artistry and willpower, turn it into a work of art." "A Tree of Night" proves his point. Capote makes this work universal by using a "most ordinary" 1940's situation in which there is neither realistic danger, nor tragedy, nor loss. Using psychological realism, he moves his protagonist through the sexualization process. A catalog of nouns defines the stages of her passage, as he has her exaggerate ordinary remarks and events. Her list of nouns, compatible with actual human experience, defines and parodies the universal nature of youth caught at the moment of fully adult sexual awareness.

In the rising action which provides setting, dialogue, character, and plot, Kay moves through amusement, squeamishness, timorous assertiveness, bewilderment, embarrassment, puzzlement, amazement, absentmindedness, and anger. In the story's climax, shame and fear come as she flees the peach seed scene. In falling action come compulsion, preoccupation, and realization, and in resolution come capitulation and copulation. Capote depicts capitulation as a complete "letting-go" of self (the purse identifying the brassy KAY). He depicts copulation as an innocent girl's swoon at the moment of surrender.

Capote, who said that his early stories were attempts to escape the realities of his own troubled life in a quest for serenity, seems to reveal in "A Tree of Night" his self-struggle with primal memories from a dysfunctional childhood filled with aunts, cooks, and strangers and rife with memories of sexual tensions and identity crises.

Jo Culbertson Davis

THE TROUT

Author: Seán O'Faoláin (John Whelan, 1900-1991)
Type of plot: Sketch
Time of plot: Unspecified
Locale: Rural Ireland
First published: 1948

Principal characters:
JULIA, a twelve-year-old Irish girl
STEPHEN, her younger brother

The Story

Julia, a twelve-year-old Irish girl, and her family have come to a place in the country which they have visited often before, perhaps the family's home place. Still innocent enough to enjoy childish pleasure, Julia first races to a familiar dark, dank path nearly overgrown with old laurels, which she calls "The Dark Walk." This is the first year that her brother, Stephen, is old enough to go to the Dark Walk with her, and she delights in his fearful shrieks as she races ahead of him. When Julia and Stephen return to the house and begin squabbling, one of the grown-ups distracts them by asking if they found the well. Although Julia haughtily disbelieves that there can be a feature of the Dark Walk with which she is unfamiliar, she later slips away and returns to the Dark Walk to find out for herself. After much searching, she uncovers a fern-shrouded hole in a rock, which contains about a quart of water and a desperately panting trout.

After sharing her discovery first with Stephen and then with a gardener, she returns to the house to tell the grown-ups, who begin formulating theories to explain how the trout could have gotten there. It is apparent to everyone that the fish cannot survive much longer in the cranny—the summer heat is drying up the water, and the trout already has too little room even to turn over. Julia thinks about the fish all day, returning to visit it often, bringing it bits of bread dough and a worm to eat. The trout, however, will not eat—it simply lies still, panting furiously. Although concerned about the trout, Julia does not think of freeing it; it is too fascinating, and she feels that because she has found it, it is hers to enjoy.

Stephen, apparently much younger than Julia, wants their mother to invent a fanciful story to explain how the trout got in the rock, and he delights in having her tell it to him over and over. Julia scoffs when Stephen repeats the story to her, but while in bed that night she only pretends to be reading her book while she is really listening to her mother recount the story yet again. When her mother tries to turn her story into a lesson about what happens to a naughty little fish who does not stay at home with daddy trout and mammy trout, Julia begs her not to make it a moral story. Her mother obliges by inventing a fairy godmother who sends enough rain for the trout to float safely out to the nearby river. Julia, unlike Stephen, understands that in real life no fairy godmother will save her fish. Sinking into melancholy, she is upset when she hears someone unwind a fishing reel.

Horrified that someone plans to catch—and presumably eat—her fish, Julia grabs a pitcher of water and runs barefoot down the rocky path in the moonlight, frantically searching for the imprisoned trout in the late night dark. When she finally locates the slimy crevice, she grasps the terrified fish, shoves him into the pitcher, and tears down to the end of the path, releasing her trout into the river. Returning unseen to her bed, she again hears the sounds of the fishing reel and giggles with joy at her daring rescue. The next day when Stephen wonderingly announces that the trout has disappeared, Julia suggests with an air of superiority that it must have been saved by a fairy godmother.

Themes and Meanings

A mere four pages in length, "The Trout" has deeper meanings beyond the slight anecdote that appears on the surface. On one level, it may be read as a metaphor for the Irish of the nineteenth and twentieth centuries, trapped in a small country too poor in resources to hold their burgeoning population. Seán O'Faoláin is a chronicler of Irish life and ways, and Ireland has historically been a resource-poor country with a high birth rate. The history of Ireland since the Potato Famine in the nineteenth century has been marked by periods of massive emigration. During O'Faoláin's lifetime, much of Ireland's young, well-educated population left the rural areas for the cities and suburbs, or left the country for England, the Continent, or the United States—wherever they could find greater economic opportunities.

On a more spiritual level, "The Trout" can be read as a story of a young girl's desire for mystery and her hope to continue seeing the world with wonderment, in conflict with her maturing realization that in the real world, doing nothing has its consequences. After Julia and Stephen return to the house to inform the grown-ups of their discovery of the trout, the adults begin searching for logical explanations of how it could have gotten there—such as being caught as a fingerling by a bird that then dropped it. Julia has no interest in such realistic explanations, but when her mother tries to spin a fairy tale incorporating a moral at the end, she protests and will not accept that either. She wants her trout to remain an enchanted creature that she can visit and ponder at will. Realism wins out, however, when she hears someone getting a fishing reel ready for a sure catch the next day.

By releasing the trout from the death it certainly faces, either from depleting the meager resources of its tiny well or from being caught and cooked, Julia in effect becomes the trout's fairy godmother. In doing so, she has taken a step in the direction of a self-actualizing adult, able to seize control of and change the course of a situation. She has taken a step, perhaps her first, away from being a child who believes that others—such as fairy godmothers—will save the day, and toward becoming a self-actualizing adult responsible for herself and those around her.

Style and Technique

The minimal plot of this brief story offers little opportunity for the development of conflict that might build suspense. Its point of view is that of an omniscient narrator, able to interpret the thoughts and feelings of all the characters, although, in this case, the narrator provides entrée only into Julia's mind. The story is not notable for use of irony, fantasy, emotional impact, or humor.

Although there are an indeterminate number of adults in the story, only Martin—apparently a caretaker or groundskeeper—is mentioned by name. The only character drawn in any depth is Julia, whom the reader sees as she begins her journey from childhood to adulthood, both physically and emotionally. Even she is characterized more through hints than through explicit detail—other than references to her having a long, lovely neck and long legs. Descriptions of her screaming with pleasure at the cold, dank challenge of the Dark Walk, and, at the end of the story, flying like a bird home to bed, suggest a lithe, young girl. On the other hand, she is clearly beginning her journey through adolescence to adulthood, having consciously "decided to be incredulous," since "at that age little girls are beginning to suspect most stories." She is also beginning in the smallest ways to break away from her parents: "She, in her bed, had resolutely presented her back to them and read her book. But she had kept one ear cocked."

The house and the adults are described not at all. On the other hand, the trout and the natural characteristics of the outdoors are rendered, although briefly, in some detail. Opening with his depiction of the Dark Walk as Julia experiences it, and ending with her frantic late-night journey through the walk, to the river, and back home to bed, O'Faoláin's descriptive powers give the reader a small but vivid glimpse of the Irish countryside.

Irene Struthers

TRUANT

Author: Claude McKay (1889-1948)
Type of plot: Psychological realism
Time of plot: The 1920's
Locale: New York City
First published: 1932

Principal characters:
BARCLAY ORAM, a West Indian émigré working as a railroad car waiter
RHODA ORAM, his wife, a former school teacher with social aspirations
BETSY, their four-year-old daughter

The Story

Barclay Oram is viewed by others, and views himself, as just a servant boy who is subject to moodiness. Much like an adolescent truant, Barclay is seeking to define himself in relationship to the dominant social values and to come to terms with his conflicting allegiances. When he immigrated to the United States from the West Indies in search of an education and a better life, it never occurred to him that he could have attained wisdom informally, without sacrificing the "green intimate life that clustered round his village." He was seduced by an image of the cultured life, paying little attention to how his pursuit might transform his world or what compromises he would have to make in order to achieve the trappings of success that he coveted. Thus he finds himself, at the age of thirty-six, imprisoned in a steel-tempered city, cut off from his agrarian roots, playing the role of "dutiful black boy among proud and sure white men."

Throughout his life he gladly has accepted menial jobs as a way to finance his dream. When confronted with his lack of educational preparedness, he spent a year in self-study to make sure that he could pass an entrance exam. Once at the university, however, his studies gave way to his social life. He married the pregnant Rhoda not only because he was enamored of her charm, but also because he did not want her forced to accept menial employment in order to care for their child.

Barclay has been serving as a railroad car waiter on the Eastern loop for three years. He has exhibited all the traits of the loyal employee, foregoing vacations in order to collect the tips necessary to provide for his family and never missing a day of work. Despite his devotion, he has been transferred from a run on which all the employees worked as a cohesive unit to a run on which animosity and mistrust are the watchwords.

In consequence, Barclay has grown weary and bitter. Resenting the fact that he seems "fated to the lifelong tasks of the unimaginative," he decides to abandon his regular ways and play the truant. Rather than rejoining the crew after a stopover in

Washington, he malingers, thus missing the train and earning himself a ten-day layoff for his negligence.

Like a suspended truant who revels in his newfound freedom, Barclay is elated and envisions spending his time in carefree pursuits such as parties and movies. While the thought of lost income troubles him, his concern is only momentary. His wife, Rhoda, however, is less than pleased. Rather than sympathizing with the emotions that have led him to this state, she frets about the impact of his actions upon herself, their child, and their social position.

Her concern with social standing leads Barclay into an extended reverie that results in his decision to desert his wife and child. He becomes the consummate truant. He renounces his connectedness to the Western world and swears his allegiance to "other gods of strange barbaric glory"—gods who value the substance rather than the symbols of the life that is lived. At the end of the story, he leaves the apartment bound for a destiny that has yet to define itself.

Themes and Meanings

The primary theme of "Truant" is the dehumanizing impact that modern civilization has upon the human soul. From the initial depiction of the subway's cattlelike masses speaking in staccato voices to Barclay's reflections upon his own life, Claude McKay makes it clear that in humankind's attempt to achieve progress, much that once imbued human drudgery with an inner dignity has been lost. Rather than being independent, as his ancestors were, Barclay and those around him seem to have become sycophants, enslaved to the whims of others. Because they have settled for passive roles and have become separated from one another, they expect the worst from one another and suppress their own emotional longings. For these reasons, Barclay has come to view service to others as a cruel joke and takes no pride in his own activities. Even as a father, he performs perfunctory rituals that seem to have little connection to who he is. He has so distanced himself from his fatherhood role that, more often than not, he forgets the child, unable to integrate her presence into his own definition of self.

Until he strays from his regular routine, all Barclay's actions are described in terms befitting an automaton. He kisses his wife mechanically; he mechanically accepts the tips that will allow him to support his family; he relates to his daughter in the most distracted of ways. He is a man without purpose and a man without a soul, condemned—as was the Flying Dutchman—to endlessly circle the major cities without ever making a connection or achieving a sense of personal satisfaction or achievement.

When he reflects upon his current situation against the backdrop of the life he has left behind, he finds his present sterile by comparison. He misses the verdant countryside and the will-of-the-wisp ethos that made his childhood so endurable. He resents the fact that he allowed an ill-defined dream to uproot him from his homeland and thrust him into an environment that embraces values that are antithetical to those in which he believes.

Even as he rues what he has sacrificed, he is not oblivious to the fact that modern ideals also have polluted the agrarian culture of the West Indies. He remembers watching his own countrymen return from native colleges with a new air, and with a swagger that suggested that somehow they had tapped into a superior universe. He recalls a local teacher who, afraid to admit that she had become pregnant out of wedlock, dies during a botched abortion. These memories stand in sharp contrast to his memories of those he knew during his formative years: aspiring artisans, self-sufficient tillers of the soil, and free peasant girls who, unaffected by social pretense, had gone about their labors as a matter of course.

Barclay's decision to desert his present reality is not a decision to return to the life he has left behind, but a decision to carve out a new niche, to define himself in ways alien to both his homeland and his adopted land. He now has allegiances to no society. His allegiances are strictly to himself and to his tentative set of values. His life, as he defines it, is and always has been "a continual fluxion from one state to another."

Style and Technique

From the opening of the story, McKay relies upon wry juxtapositions to underline what might best be termed societally induced alienation. As the tale opens, Barclay and his wife are safely ensconced in "Nigger Heaven," a Broadway theater that caters to those who love clean vaudeville. The show features the Merry Mulligans, a garishly proper vaudeville family who personify the popular cultural ideal of the happy family mindlessly skipping through life.

The show, in all of its mawkishness, appeals to Rhoda's sense of decorum, despite its unreality. This allows McKay ironically to contrast her reaction to Barclay's. While she is put off by the "cheap old colored shows," Barclay longs for the dynamism of the Harlem cabaret. It is therefore no surprise that when she chooses to upbraid Barclay for his irresponsible truancy, she is walking out the door to enjoy an evening of whist and dancing. Nor is it any wonder she fails to recognize the internal strife that is gradually destroying their marriage.

"Truant" revolves around conflicting personalities and mind sets. Rhoda, although a caricature of the bright woman who has used marriage as her ticket out of the workaday world, is a foil against which to present Barclay's dilemmas. Within this context, Barclay, although by no means a heroic figure, is a sympathetic character resisting the mindless and mind-numbing forces of his current environment. His decision to surrender to his own wanderlust is, finally, a decision to reclaim both his soul and his identity.

C. Lynn Munro

A TRUE STORY
Repeated Word for Word as I Heard It

Author: Mark Twain (Samuel Langhorne Clemens, 1835-1910)
Type of plot: Autobiographical
Time of plot: c. 1852-1865
Locale: Virginia and North Carolina
First published: 1874

Principal characters:
AUNT RACHEL, a sixty-year-old former slave
MISTO C——, the frame narrator
HENRY, Aunt Rachel's youngest son

The Story

At the close of a summer day the narrator sits on a farmhouse porch atop a hill. A sixty-year-old black servant, Aunt Rachel, sits respectfully on a lower step cheerfully enduring merciless chafing. After the powerful woman roars with laughter, the narrator asks her how it is that she has never had any trouble. Taken aback, she replies, "Misto C——, is you in 'arnest?" Sobered by her manner, he explains that he has never seen her other than cheerful. Aunt Rachel now becomes grave and begins her story.

She tells the narrator that even though she was once a slave, she had a husband as loving to her as he is to his own wife, and that they had seven children whom they dearly loved. She was raised in Virginia ("ole Fo-ginny"), but her quick-tempered mother was raised in Maryland and was fiercely proud of her heritage. One day when Rachel's little son Henry cut his wrist and forehead badly, everyone flew around, anxious to help him. In their excitement, they spoke back to Rachel's mother, who snapped, "I wan't bawn in de mash to be fool' by trash! I's one o' de ole Blue Hen's Chickens, I is!" She then cleared everyone out and bandaged the boy herself. Rachel adds that she uses her mother's expression herself when she gets riled.

As Rachel recalls the time when her mistress went broke and auctioned off all of her slaves in Richmond, she warms to her subject and gradually rises, until she towers over the narrator. Her recollection of the slave auction is vivid. One by one, her husband and children were sold and she was beaten as she cried in protest. When only her youngest child, Henry, remained, she held him tightly, threatening to kill anyone who touched him. Henry whispered to her that he would run away and work so that he could buy her freedom. Despite Rachel's fierce resistance, Henry was eventually taken away. Since that day, twenty-two years ago, Rachel has not set eyes on her husband or six of her children.

The man who bought Rachel took her to "Newbern" (New Bern, North Carolina?), where she became the family cook. During the war her master became a Confederate colonel, but when the Union took the town, he fled with his family, leaving his slaves behind. Union Army officers then occupied the house and Rachel cooked for them.

These officers treated her respectfully and gave her unquestioned command over her kitchen.

Remembering Henry's vow to escape to the North, Rachel one day asked the officers if they might have seen him. She described Henry as very little, with scars on his wrist and forehead, but a general reminded her that after thirteen years Henry would now be a man—something that she had forgotten. She did not then know that Henry had indeed run off to the North, worked as a barber for years, and hired himself out to Union officers so that he could ransack the South looking for his mother.

Now the Union headquarters, Rachel's house was often the site of soldier balls, during which she jealously guarded her kitchen. One night, there was a ball for black soldiers who particularly irritated her. When a spruce young man danced into her kitchen with a woman, she said, "Gid along wid you!—rubbage!" The remark made the man's expression momentarily change. Other men then came in, playing music and putting on airs. Rachel tried to drive them out, but they merely laughed until she straightened up and said, "I want you niggers to understan' dat I wa'nt bawn in de mash to be fool' by trash! I's one o' de ole Blue Hen's Chickens, I is!" Again the young man seemed to react to her words.

As Rachel finally drove the men from her kitchen, she overheard the young man tell a companion that he would not return with the others that night. Early the next morning, as Rachel removed biscuits from the oven, the same young man unexpectedly reappeared and looked her closely in the eye. Suddenly she knew. She dropped her pan and examined his wrist and forehead. It was her Henry.

"Oh, no, Misto C——," Rachel says, "I hain't had no trouble. An' no joy!"

Themes and Meanings

The essence of this tale is in fact a true story. During one of the many summers that Mark Twain spent near Elmira, New York, he heard the story from Mary Ann ("Auntie") Cord, a former slave who worked at his sister-in-law's farm. Aunt Rachel's "Misto C——" is thus "Mr. Clemens"—Mark Twain himself. In November, 1874, Mark Twain published the story in the *Atlantic Monthly*. It was his first contribution to that prestigious magazine, as well as one of the earliest stories in which he developed a fully rounded African American character and one of the few stories that he ever wrote featuring a strong woman.

At its simplest level, "A True Story" concerns human endurance in the face of terrible personal loss. Although raised a slave and violently separated from her loving husband and children, Aunt Rachel has remained strong and exceptionally cheerful. So cheerful is she, in fact, that the narrator, who presumably has known her for years, has no inkling of the troubles that she has endured.

At a deeper level, "A True Story" is a tale of revelation—the revelation to a white person that African Americans—even slaves—can share similar feelings of love and devotion. Early in her narrative, Aunt Rachel tells the narrator that her husband

> was lovin' an' kind to me, jist as kind as you is to yo' own wife. An' we had chil'en—seven chil'en—an' we loved dem chil'en jist de same as you loves yo' chil'en. Dey was black,

> but de Lord can't make no chil'en so black but what dey mother loves 'm and wouldn't give 'm up, no, not for anything dat's in dis whole world.

The fact that black people have the same emotions as other people was not taken for granted by whites during Mark Twain's time. He develops the idea more fully in *Adventures of Huckleberry Finn* (1884), in which Huck gradually understands that Jim, his black companion who is fleeing from slavery, is as fully human as himself. During their raft journey, Huck happens to see Jim with his head down, moaning to himself. Sensing that Jim is thinking about his wife and children, Huck confesses, "I do believe he cared just as much for his people as white folks does for their'n. It don't seem natural, but I reckon it's so." The frame-narrator of "A True Story" makes a similar discovery when he hears Aunt Rachel's story. The common humanity of all peoples is thus a central theme in both stories.

Style and Technique

As a story within a story, "A True Story" exemplifies the frame-story technique in which the first narrator (Misto C——) provides the "frame" within which the second (Aunt Rachel) tells the main story. By alternating the voices of his two narrators here, Mark Twain tells two different stories simultaneously. While Aunt Rachel relates the dramatic story of her family, the frame-narrator's occasional remarks quietly reveal the shifting relationship between Aunt Rachel and himself.

When the frame-narrator begins his narrative, he is sitting on a high porch, while Aunt Rachel sits "respectfully below our level, on the steps." As Aunt Rachel unfolds her story, her position gradually becomes dominant. By the time she recalls the slave auction, "she towered above me, black against the stars." Although no more is said on this subject, it is clear that the relative moral positions of the characters are reversed, with Aunt Rachel clearly in the superior position at the story's end.

The most obvious stylistic technique employed in this story is the use of realistic African American dialect. Most of the story is narrated in Aunt Rachel's own, unaffected voice. One of Mark Twain's great strengths as a writer was his ear for language and ability to render it accurately. Here again, "A True Story" anticipates *Adventures of Huckleberry Finn*, which also makes heavy use of Southern black dialects—especially for the character Jim.

In 1992, publicity surrounding the recent rediscovery of a comparatively obscure article ("Sociable Jimmy") that Mark Twain published in *The New York Times* in 1874 focused national attention on the extent to which the language of *Adventures of Huckleberry Finn* is "black." Recalling the delightfully natural and artless conversation of a young black boy whom he had met during a stop on a lecture tour, Mark Twain's article resembles "A True Story" in attempting to re-create a conversation word for word. Mark Twain wrote the *Times* article around the same time that he wrote "A True Story" and addressed similar questions about African American dialects in both.

R. Kent Rasmussen

TRUTH OR CONSEQUENCES

Author: Alice Adams (1926-)
Type of plot: Domestic realism
Time of plot: The 1930's
Locale: Hilton, a fictitious Southern city
First published: 1982

Principal characters:
EMILY AMES, the narrator
CARSTAIRS JONES, her obsession

The Story

The story opens with the narrator, Emily Ames, reading a gossip column about Carstairs Jones marrying a famous former movie star, and she decides that this man must be the same Car Jones whom she knew many years earlier. She then recounts the history of that extraordinary spring when she first met Car Jones in the seventh grade. She relives the day when she played "truth or consequences" with friends and said that she would rather kiss Car Jones than be eaten alive by ants.

Emily and her mother moved to the university town of Hilton the fall before the principal action of the story took place. Emily felt like an outsider in this town. As a recent transplant from the North to the South, she felt removed from her classmates; at eleven years of age, she was younger than her seventh-grade classmates; and the fact that her mother was rich embarrassed Emily, who felt "more freakish than advantageous." She felt socially insecure and approached the playground always with excited dread. On one particular April day, she was asked to play truth or consequences with the popular girls. After some innocuous questions, they sprang the big question on her: Would she rather be covered with honey and eaten alive by ants in the desert, or kiss Car Jones? When Emily said that she would prefer the kiss, the other children began to tease her. She did not feel overly embarrassed by the attention, however, because she felt that she had suddenly been discovered after months of invisibility.

If Emily felt socially insecure, Car felt socially removed. The quintessential outsider, he was fourteen, the tallest, the most easily bored, and the most rebellious boy in the class. He was also a "truck child"—the offspring of people living on the farms surrounding the town who sent their children to school in yellow trucks. To Emily, Car was an abnormal person. The narrator recalls him as representing dark and strange forces, while she herself had just come into the light. Although the young Emily could not afford to have anything to do with Car, her literal mind acknowledged a certain obligation. After a number of notes were sent from Car to Emily, a rendezvous was planned: They were to meet in a vacant lot beside the school on a Saturday morning.

The meeting was not what Emily expected. Car was rude and surly, his teeth were stained and his hands dirty. He pulled Emily by her hair, planted a kiss on her, and walked off with a look of pure rage.

When Emily returned home, her mother told her that a boy called. Emily worried that it was Car, but it was Harry McGinnis, a glowing, golden boy. The narrator says that she felt saved because she was normal after all and belonged in the world of light and lightheartedness. Car Jones had not altered her in any way. Emily was embarrassed about seeing Car at school the next week, but to her relief he was not there. After he demanded to be placed in another class, he took a test and was reassigned to the high school sophomore class. Emily never saw him again, but continued to hear rumors about him: He attended the university; he went "all the way" with a high school girl; he wrote a play as an English graduate student; and he turned down admission into a fraternity.

The story closes with Emily's conjectures about Car's life. She tries to imagine what his background was really like, what his innermost thoughts were. She concludes that he does not think about the past, that he never thinks about having been a truck child or one of the deprived. But the story ends with the narrator thinking that perhaps Car may be as haunted by the past as she has been.

Themes and Meanings

"Truth or Consequences" is a story about recognitions, about the discovery of truths and the consequences of actions. It appears to be a story mainly about Car Jones, but it is in fact more about the narrator and her recognition of the truths about her life. The narrator acknowledges at the end that she has no clue about the inner workings of Car's mind, or even about his background. To her he had merely been one of the truck children, greeted by his classmates "with a total lack of interest; he might as well have been invisible, or been black." Of course, Emily does take some interest in him, but she acknowledges, at least in retrospect, that she "was having a wonderful time, at his expense." She won her golden boy, Harry McGinnis, because Car's attention made her visible to her peers. She says she giggles in a "silly new way" when McGinnis asks her out because she has entered the world of normality and left behind Car's "dark and strange" world. She recognizes that her entry into the world of the "popular girls" was effected by her use of the nearly invisible Car.

After Emily is kissed by Car, she dashes from the lot; years later, she reflects that she "was learning conformity fast, practicing up for the rest of my life." She has lived what she considers a normal life for a woman of her age: three children, three abortions, and three marriages to increasingly "rich and prominent" men. Her obsessive interest in Car Jones suggests her disillusionment with the "normal world," with the consequences of her actions that were predicated on conformity, on becoming one with the crowd. She is fixated on Car and on her reinvention of him because he represents the world of rebelliousness, of saying no to the "proper course," whether it be a fraternity that he was invited to join or a career path that would have let him be one of the "rich and prominent" men.

Style and Technique

Because the characters in Alice Adams' story inhabit a larger world, the opening section of the story is devoted to a description not so much of character as of setting. The playground is discussed in terms of levels where the different ages and sexes are assigned. The reader is also introduced to the Southern university town and the intricacies of its class system even before the reader meets Car for the first time because the class hierarchies determine to a large extent the type of relationship Car and Emily can have. Given her character, her eagerness to conform and lead a "normal life," it is clear early that rigid social conventions will not allow an intimacy to develop between Car and the narrator. They are separated by too great a gulf.

If the Southern social world plays a significant role in the story, so does the Southern climate. Emily, who had recently moved from the North, witnesses her first Southern spring at the same time that she enters into society. She is "astounded by the bursting opulence" of spring, "enchanted with the yards of the stately houses of professors." This opulence and enchantment seem to conspire against any hope of attachment or communion between Car and Emily; if she is attracted to opulence and stateliness, Car can be no object of desire. He is necessary only because he allows her to have an "altered awareness" of herself. Like the Southern spring that seemed so "extraordinary in itself," Emily began to see that she could "command attention," that she was pretty and was no longer invisible.

What is interesting about the "present time" of the story, the moment when she reads the paper in which the bit of gossip about a "man named Carstairs Jones" appears, is that it is without setting, without season, without time. The present of the story encroaches on the past not at all; in fact, it is the past that is richly alive, vibrant, full of color and tension. All we know of the narrator's current life is that she is married to a "successful surgeon" and she is "haunted by everything that ever happened in" her life. She is haunted by Car's memory because of his ability to live at a distance from respectability, from conventionality, from her world.

Kevin Boyle

TWO BLUE BIRDS

Author: D. H. Lawrence (1885-1930)
Type of plot: Domestic realism
Time of plot: Early twentieth century
Locale: England
First published: 1927

Principal characters:
CAMERON GEE, a novelist and literary journalist
HIS WIFE
MISS WREXALL, his secretary

The Story

Cameron Gee, a modestly successful literary figure, has been married for several years. For the last three or four years, he and his wife have found it impossible to live together for any length of time, so his wife has taken to spending long holidays in a warmer country, where she carries on discreet love affairs. Gee makes no objections, however, and they seem satisfied with their arrangement. They have a strong attachment to each other, but simply cannot live together happily. Busy with his literary work, the husband is helped by Miss Wrexall, an efficient and adoring female secretary, and his home is run by her mother and sister. The long absences of his wife seem irrelevant to Gee, both personally and professionally.

The story focuses on an occasion when the wife is home for a short time; she considers Gee's domestic and professional arrangements and finds them disturbing. She suggests that the secretary is making things too easy for her husband, and that his work is suffering as a result of the complaisant way in which the secretary and her family make his life too comfortable. She has no wish to participate in the family, however, and finds the tepid, nonsexual nature of the arrangements between the master and his secretary depressing. When she accuses her husband of abusing the loyalty and adoration of his employee, Miss Wrexall becomes alarmed and protests that the arrangements are both acceptable and innocent, and that she is assured by Gee that he, too, finds their unfeeling relation to his liking. Gee's smug acceptance of the situation at the end of the story seems to suggest that his wife may be right to despise him, and that Miss Wrexall is not telling the full truth. Unmoved by his wife's criticism, Gee has no plan to change the way he lives, or the kind of service that he has come to expect from his servants—especially from his young secretary.

Themes and Meanings

D. H. Lawrence was always interested in problems of male-female relationships, not only in terms of their grander, more romantic implications, but also in their often subtler nuances and details. This story is particularly interesting to a late-twentieth century reader since it involves not only the difficulty of men and women learning to live together, but the nature of the roles that women and men play as individuals, both in and out of matrimony, and the ways in which male-female connections impinge upon, and sometimes distort, female aspirations.

In the early years of the twentieth century, Lawrence understood that English middle-class society expected women to be satisfied with the role of patient supporters of their husbands in their public careers. The fact that Mrs. Gee knows she is temperamentally unable to fulfill that role has something to do with her inability to live with her husband. What the story reveals, however, is that she cannot see any role for herself, other than to indulge in idle love affairs. She has, in a sense, no awareness of herself as an independent personality. She has little interest in her husband's career, although she is concerned that it is not quite as good as it ought to be, and she is sensitive to the kind of relationship with which he is most comfortable. One would think, therefore, that she might attempt to terminate this odd and somewhat tasteless arrangement. She is honest enough to know it is not what she wants, but seems to think that her only alternative is to continue as Gee's wife, if in name only, and expect him to support her, and to accept her superficial dalliances, out of sight, and out of mind. There is something ignoble about the conduct of both parties.

Miss Wrexall, the secretary, is less to blame, if her supine adoration of her employer suggests that she, too, should get out of his employ as quickly as possible. When Lawrence wrote this story the opportunities for women were limited, and the general ideas about females and careers, and about relations between men and women, were considerably narrower than they became late in the twentieth century. Lawrence was notorious for being too frank and imaginative in his exploration of sexual themes, and this simple, seemingly innocent tale of marital pusillanimity is an example of how far he was ahead of his time in dealing with the problem in one of the more banal areas of how people try to live their lives within the confines of social convention when they are obviously unsuited to do so.

Style and Technique

Lawrence uses a disarmingly simple style for this tale of marital discord. It is not only appropriate in terms of allowing for a clear-headed examination of the Gee marriage, but it is also a succinct comment upon the emotional tepidity with which the couple deal with their situation. The style reflects the lack of emotional commitment. The Gees are sensible, intelligent, and understanding; what they are not is passionate. Only at the end of the story does Mrs. Gee, for a short time, seem to have her feelings fully engaged, when she rejects the idea of being one of the blue birds fawning at the feet of her husband. The two blue-tits (an English breed of finch) may seem too obtrusively symbolic. The intrusion of battling male birds, with the suggestion of sexual competition, is an obvious symbol, made even more obvious by Mrs. Gee remarking upon it in her determination to stop any suspicion that she might want to be part of this unhealthy competition for her husband's attention.

Lawrence is less heavy-handed in his use of luxuriant flowers to suggest a self-indulgent Eden in which Gee lolls about with his adoring secretary at his feet. He is even defter in the way in which he has Miss Wrexall change into a silk dress of a color similar to that of the wife's, when she is invited to take tea with the couple. The secretary's suggestion that her dress is not quite as smart as that worn by Mrs. Gee is a juxtaposed symbol of what the contending women have to offer their lord and master. Mrs. Gee immediately retorts that smart or not, the secretary's dress was, at least, paid for with hard-earned money, while she has done nothing to deserve her own. Lawrence's wittiness, which is often overlooked, appears immediately upon this exchange, when Mrs. Gee's question about the tea, "You like it strong?" seems as much a threat as an innocent question as to how the secretary prefers her tea. There is, in fact, a good deal of threatening ambiguity in conversations, particularly in those between the Gees, which suggests that they are a match for each other in cool toughness. There is much left unsaid, which is being implied by these two sophisticated people who well know how to take care of themselves verbally—in ways that anticipate those in which playwright Harold Pinter later saw the middle classes. The Gees use language as a lethal instrument to dominate, irritate, and triumph, however empty a victory may be.

Only for a wry instant does the bird image hold possibilities of romance as Mrs. Gee catches sight of the first blue bird, but the lawn is soon invaded by the second bird, and the aptness of its arrival takes over. It is, in short, a very mean-spirited tale, and it might be suggested that its two birds are not exclusively to be seen as the two women, but sometimes as Mr. and Mrs. Gee.

Structurally, the story has three parts. It begins at a distance in the voice of a third-party narrator, who seems to be socially and morally at one with the Gees. The voice does not judge, nor is it on one side or the other. Then it becomes closely identified with the point of view of the wife, putting her reactions into context in a general consideration of the relationship, but again the tone is cool. Lawrence narrows the field once again, reverting to the third-person narrator relating the quite specific story of the encounter in the garden, with occasional intrusions into the mind of the wife. The voice is restrained, and the action reported with discretion—fastidious, watchful, and nonjudgmental.

The story has something of the shape of a scientific examination of an insect. First on the wing, then in the hand, and finally on the head of a pin—all without feeling, as befits the sour story of the Gee marriage. It is as much an exercise in tone as it is in incident, and its tone is, in part, its meaning.

Charles Pullen

THE TWO BOTTLES OF RELISH

Author: Lord Dunsany (Edward John Moreton Drax Plunkett, 1878-1957)
Type of plot: Horror
Time of plot: The 1930's
Locale: Southern England
First published: 1932

Principal characters:
SMETHERS, the narrator, a traveling salesman
LINLEY, a gentleman of leisure and an amateur detective
STEEGER, a clever and unscrupulous murderer
INSPECTOR ULTON, a Scotland Yard detective

The Story

An affable, but not very bright, traveling salesman named Smethers begins sharing a London flat with an Oxford-educated gentleman named Linley, who displays extraordinary mental gifts. (Their relationship is similar to that between Arthur Conan Doyle's Sherlock Holmes and Doctor Watson.) One day Smethers calls his friend's attention to a newspaper account of a murder case that has the police baffled and challenges Linley to solve it.

A man named Steeger is suspected of murdering a pretty blonde companion named Nancy Elth in order to get his hands on the money she had brought to their cottage in the south of England. The local police have kept the place surrounded but have been unable to find a trace of the young woman's body and cannot arrest Steeger without a corpse. Steeger claims that the woman has left the country, but he has a large amount of cash that he cannot account for.

Since Linley is constitutionally lazy, he sends Smethers to study the crime scene and talk to everyone in the neighborhood. Smethers reports back that there appears to be no way in which Steeger could have buried the body on the premises or spirited it away undetected. The most curious fact is that Steeger obtained his landlord's permission to chop down a stand of ten larch trees and cut them into two-foot logs, but he has never used the wood for any purpose. Smethers reports that two bottles of Numnumo—the brand of relish that he himself peddles as a traveling salesman—were found when the police searched the premises. Linley continues to question Smethers for the smallest details he can remember from his investigations.

Smethers reports that the local constable is suspicious of Steeger because he is a vegetarian, and vegetarians are unknown in that isolated county. Linley takes special interest in the two bottles of relish because Smethers, who knows the product better than anyone else, assures him that it can only be used with meats and savories. He has Smethers telephone to inquire whether Steeger bought the bottles of Numnumo at the same time or on separate occasions. Smethers ascertains that they were bought separately, with an interval of about six days between purchases.

After considering all the information at his disposal, Linley calls in a Scotland Yard inspector and explains the whole method of the crime in the privacy of his bedroom. Smethers, who only overhears snatches of their conversation, does not pass along all the details, but leaves them to the reader's imagination. It becomes horribly obvious that Steeger cut up the body and ate it, using the two bottles of relish to help him overcome his natural revulsion to cannibalism. Smethers relates that he overheard Linley tell the inspector that Steeger went through the trouble of chopping down the trees and cutting them into logs, "Solely in order to get an appetite."

Themes and Meanings

"The Two Bottles of Relish" is an example of the "perfect crime" story. The message in all such stories is invariably the same: "Crime does not pay." To highlight and dramatize the message, the author contrives a nearly perfect crime and makes it appear that the perpetrator is going to get away with it. Then at the last moment the criminal's nemesis, the detective, manages to come up with the answer to the problem, proving that even the most carefully contrived scheme by the most brilliant mind will fail because a nearly universal law governs matters of morality, dictating that good deeds are rewarded and wicked deeds are punished.

Readers enjoy perfect-crime stories such as "The Two Bottles of Relish" because they permit them to indulge their own fantasies about violence and antisocial behavior while receiving the assurance at the end that they live in an orderly society in which they can count upon their personal security being protected. The popular "Columbo" films on television, starring Peter Falk, were all based on the supposition that has been expressed in various ways in such comfortable homilies as "Crime does not pay," "Murder will out," and "There is no such thing as a perfect crime." In William Shakespeare's classic murder drama *Macbeth* (1606), his hero repeatedly reflects on the impossibility of getting away with murder. For example:

> It will have blood, they say; blood will have blood.
> Stones have been known to move and trees to speak;
> Augures and understood relations have
> By maggot-pies and choughs and rooks brought forth
> The secretest man of blood.

In *Civilization and Its Discontents* (1930), Sigmund Freud, the founder of modern psychoanalysis, states that modern civilization is a thin veneer and that all human beings harbor aggressive instincts which they conceal under clean linen and proper manners in order to maintain the illusion of peace, order, and respectability. Perfect-crime stories provide a sort of safety valve by giving readers a taste of blood while simultaneously assuring them that civilization is intact because it is protected by the authorities as well as by such master amateur sleuths as Sherlock Holmes, Lord Dunsany's Linley, Agatha Christie's Miss Marple and Hercule Poirot, and a host of other fictional detectives.

Style and Technique

The technique used in "The Two Bottles of Relish" resembles that of Arthur Conan Doyle in his famous Sherlock Holmes stories. Both Doyle and Dunsany were indebted to the American genius Edgar Allan Poe, who is credited with being the father of the detective story with two 1840's "tales of ratiocination": "The Murders in the Rue Morgue" and "The Purloined Letter." J. Brander Matthews, a distinguished literary critic, wrote that the history of the detective story began with the publication of "The Murders in the Rue Morgue." Branders called the story "a masterpiece of its kind, which even its author was unable to surpass; and Poe, unlike most other originators, rang the bell the very first time."

Poe invented many of the conventions of the detective story that are still in use today. He had the wisdom to tell his tales of ratiocination from the point of view of a minor character, so that it was unnecessary for him to disclose any of his hero C. Auguste Dupin's thought processes until the surprising climax of the story. Just as Dupin had his anonymous biographer and Holmes had his friend Dr. Watson, so Linley is provided with the good-natured, loyal, but slow-witted Smethers to chronicle his genius. The narrative style of Dunsany's story is conversational, deliberately amateurish, and full of slang, because Smethers has less education than Poe's or Doyle's narrators and belongs to a lower social class.

All three heroes are "amateur detectives." Poe established the useful convention that the amateur detective had to be intellectually superior to the bungling police and also indifferent to fame. Because Dupin, Holmes, and Linley are useful to the police, they are given easy access to police assistance. The ineffectual police, who usually get the credit, are so grateful that they are happy to give the amateur detectives an aegis, a cloak of authority which enables them to question witnesses, poke around crime scenes, and generally act as official detectives themselves. Without this aegis, the amateur detective would be severely handicapped, especially when investigating a murder, and stories of their exploits would be less interesting or less credible.

"The Two Bottles of Relish" is a variation of the so-called "locked room mystery," which was invented by Poe in "The Murders in the Rue Morgue" and used innumerable times by Doyle. In a locked room mystery, the central problem is how the criminal entered or exited or managed to get incriminating evidence off the premises under seemingly impossible circumstances. In "The Two Bottles of Relish," the central problem is how the murderer could dispose of the corpse under tight police surveillance.

Although Dunsany borrows from both Doyle and Poe in his nine "little tales of Smethers," as he called them, he contributes two innovations. The first is his method of dangling the most important clue right under the reader's nose. Poe and Doyle often withheld important information from the reader; Dunsany presents the vital clues on a silver platter, thereby giving readers a sporting chance to arrive at the solution by themselves. It is noteworthy that Dunsany actually used the most important clue, the two bottles of relish, as the title of his story.

His solution to the crime seems almost a parody of Poe and Doyle, who never thought of anything as weird as having a murderer eat his victim in order to dispose of the corpus delicti. The macabre humor in "The Two Bottles of Relish," another important innovation, is so characteristic of Lord Dunsany's fiction that it might be called a Dunsany trademark. Many writers have copied him over the years. Some of the classic films of director Alfred Hitchcock display a similar playful attitude toward murder which suggests that both the writer and the viewer share a secret "relish" for the details of gory crimes.

Bill Delaney

TWO KINDS

Author: Amy Tan (1952-)
Type of plot: Social realism
Time of plot: The late 1980's
Locale: San Francisco
First published: 1989

Principal characters:
JING-MEI "JUNE" WOO, the narrator and protagonist
SUYUAN WOO, her mother

The Story

A young Chinese American woman, Jing-Mei "June" Woo, recalls, after her mother's death, her mother's sadness at having left her twin baby girls in China in 1949. June has used her mother's regret as a weapon in a battle of wills focusing on what her mother wants her to be and what she wants. June wins, leaving her mother, Suyuan, stunned when she says she wishes she were dead like the twins. Although this scene characterizes the common struggle for power between mother and daughter, the story also illustrates the cultural division between an Asian immigrant and her Asian American daughter. These cultural clashes resonate throughout the short story, as does the discordant sound of June's piano playing.

Wanting her daughter to be an American prodigy, Suyuan Woo epitomizes the mother living through her child. With the American ideal that you can be anything you want, she prepares and coaches June into becoming a Chinese Shirley Temple. June believes in her mother's dreams for her and admits she was filled with a sense that she would soon become perfect.

She and her mother, who cleans houses for extra money, begin searching through the latest American magazines, such as *Good Housekeeping* and *Reader's Digest*, for stories of child prodigies. Every evening her mother tests her relentlessly for intellectual prowess, such as knowing all the world capitals and multiplying large numbers in her head. June grows resentful as she sees the disappointment on her mother's face as she fails to measure up to her expectations.

Discovering a powerful side of herself, June resolves not to become something she is not simply to please her mother. One evening while watching "The Ed Sullivan Show" on television, her mother sees a young Chinese girl play the piano with great skill. Much to June's chagrin, her mother strikes up a deal with a retired piano teacher, Mr. Chong, who agrees to give June piano lessons in exchange for weekly housecleanings. June soon discovers that Old Mr. Chong is deaf, like the great composer Ludwig von Beethoven.

Ultimately, June must appear in a talent show to display her great talent. Her mother invites all of her friends from the Joy Luck Club, a group of four Chinese women who meet regularly to play mah-jong, a card game, and socialize. Knowing she is not prepared but somehow thinking that the prodigy in her actually exists, June plays to her surprised and somewhat embarrassed parents. Only her deaf teacher applauds with enthusiasm as she completes a piece from Robert Schumann entitled "Pleading Child."

June feels that after her dismal performance, her mother's dream for her will end. A few days later while she watches television, her mother reminds her that it is time to practice. It is the final showdown between mother and daughter. June tells her mother she will never be a genius or the daughter that her mother wants her to be. Her mother explains that there are only two kinds of daughters: those who are obedient and the ones who follow their own minds. Although her mother thinks she was won by identifying which kind of daughter can live in her house, the daughter, feeling her own power, strikes the final blow by shouting that she wishes she were dead. Suyuan, because she had to leave her young twins for dead on a roadside, while fleeing war-torn China, is profoundly affected by June's outburst. Painfully, June looks back on this as an unresolved conflict that has followed her into adulthood. She believes that this was the moment that her mother gave up hope for her only daughter's success, and that she internalized this self-defeating attitude. A few years before her death, her mother offers her the piano for her thirtieth birthday. June accepts, seeing this as a peace offering, a shiny trophy that she has finally won back.

Themes and Meanings

In her essay "Mother Tongue," Amy Tan identifies the reader she envisions for her novel *The Joy Luck Club* (1986) as her own mother, because these were stories about mothers. Appearing in the novel as a chapter about the major protagonist of the entire novel, "Two Kinds" represents the central theme of the voracious love between mother and daughter and the arduous journey that one already has taken and the other will take both for herself and for her mother. It is a journey of self-discovery made through painful yet joyful connections. Just as June puts her mother's things in order for her father, she does the same for herself by gathering up her past childhood struggles with her mother, turning them over and examining them, then carefully putting them into order.

In the novel, June retraces her mother's and her three aunties' journeys from China to the United States. Initiated by Suyuan Woo's death at the start of the novel, this long pilgrimage is interwoven with the past and present lives of four Chinese mothers and their four American daughters. June's mother, as originator of the Joy Luck Club, holds a special place at the mah-jong table, which must be assumed by her daughter. To complicate June's life further, her mother's twin daughters, whom she left in China forty years earlier, have been found alive and well. Now the familial connection between China and America is made even stronger by June's desire to know her half-sisters and, by doing so, to understand both her mother and herself.

The theme of two seemingly opposite sides of a person is symbolized in the two musical pieces by Schumann: "Pleading Child," the one she plays at her first and last piano recital, and its companion piece, "Perfectly Contented." At the conclusion, June realizes that they were two halves of the same song, and that by playing both she becomes whole.

Although the self-realization completes this rich vignette, it is not without pain and loss. For June to come to this conclusion, she has had to lose her mother and revisit, through memory, the terrible moment of final conflict, betrayal, and guilt: "For after our struggle at the piano, she never mentioned my playing again. . . . The lid to the piano was closed, shutting out the dust, my misery, and her dreams." In the process of reexamining the duality of a daughter's existence—obedience versus willfulness—June reconciles and finally resolves her guilt and disappointment in herself and embraces both the memory of her mother and the strong woman she has become.

Style and Technique

Tan describes herself as a lover of language, not a scholar of English. Therefore, it is her translation into English of what she calls her mother's internal language that is at the heart of this story. Drawing the reader into the story, the narrator directs the reader through a world in which readers experience the power of a rich, colorful language. For example, when Mother Woo characterizes Auntie Lindo's daughter, an accomplished chess player at a young age, as "best tricky," the reader knows not only what it means but also how it sounds. This brand of English, often called fractured or broken, becomes a vernacular that captures the tone and color of the experience of growing up in a bilingual environment.

Further illustrating the conflict between Chinese mother and American-born daughter, the spoken language of the two creates a verbal duel. For example, when June demands that her mother look at who she really is, saying "I'm not a genius!" her mother responds with, "Who ask you be genius?" The mother's question, although incomplete grammatically, projects her confusion over being unable to understand her daughter's anger or ungratefulness.

The language also characterizes the rich, layered texture of a household built on two languages and two cultures, which often are combined to form, for example, a Chinese Shirley Temple. As her mother offers her the piano, the tense shift in her words is purposeful: "You could been genius if you want to." Even though it starts in the past, the sentence ends in the present, indicating to June and to the reader that it is not too late for June to find her genius. Ultimately, it is Tan's command of the "Englishes" that transforms the short story into one that not only captures her mother's voice but also other mothers' voices that have been silenced or, at best, standardized into an "imperfect" English that does not convey their essence, their internal language.

Cynthia S. Becerra

THE UGLIEST PILGRIM

Author: Doris Betts (1932-   )
Type of plot: Psychological realism
Time of plot: 1969
Locale: A bus traveling from Spruce Pine, North Carolina, to Tulsa, Oklahoma
First published: 1973

Principal characters:
VIOLET KARL, the narrator
GRADY "FLICK" FLIGGINS, a black soldier
MONTY HARRELL, a white paratrooper
AN ELDERLY WHITE WOMAN
MR. WEATHERMAN, a bus driver

The Story

Violet Karl is making a pilgrimage to Tulsa, Oklahoma, to have her disfigured face healed by a prominent television evangelist. Her injury resulted from a childhood accident when she accompanied her father to chop wood, and the head of the ax came off the handle, striking her in the face.

Throughout her journey, Violet keeps a journal about the things that she sees and the people whom she meets. With each settlement through which she passes, she praises the Lord for leading her one step closer to her salvation and cure. To these comments Violet adds her impressions of her fellow passengers and recounts how they pass the time during their journey from Spruce Pine, North Carolina, to her fabled Tulsa.

On the bus, Violet makes the acquaintance of three fellow passengers: an older white woman; a black soldier, Grady "Flick" Fliggins; and a white paratrooper, Monty Harrell. Each acquaintance adds to Violet's growing need for acceptance. Each shows Violet that everyone is on some sort of quest.

When she first boards the bus, Violet's only companions are the older white woman and the black soldier. She takes a seat beside the older woman, strikes up a conversation, and soon learns that the woman is on her way to visit her son in Nashville, where he works in a cellophane plant. The woman adds that she may make a permanent move to her son's home.

After the older woman goes to sleep, Violet strikes up a conversation with Grady Fliggins and begins playing a game of draw poker. Grady seems not to care that Violet's face is deformed. While they are in a snack bar during a rest stop in Kingsport, Tennessee, Violet and Flick meet a white paratrooper, Monty Harrell, who joins them on the bus and becomes the third player in the card game.

During the trip, Violet and the two young men discuss her reason for going to Tulsa. Monty seems to be most opposed to Violet's intended meeting with the television preacher. Monty freely voices his suspicion that the preacher is a "fake," but Violet will not be sidetracked.

In Nashville, the older woman leaves the bus, but not before warning Violet about her companions and men in general. She cautions Violet to be on her guard because people will recognize her weaknesses and take advantage of them. As she gets off the bus, she chats with their driver, Mr. Weatherman, about Violet, but he is replaced by another driver who shows no personal interest in his passengers.

As the journey continues, the three passengers become a closer knit group with each community through which they pass. They decide to spend the night in Memphis before resuming their journey. While she is asleep in her room, Violet has what she thinks is a dream in which Flick and Monty come into her room. From the discussion Flick and Monty have, the reader realizes that this is not a dream, but, in fact, a rape. The most telling comment comes when Flick admits that looks have nothing to do with sexual pleasure; therefore, he has no feelings, one way or the other, about Violet's appearance.

When the bus trip resumes, Violet finds herself being drawn more closely to Monty. Since no one is meeting her in Tulsa, she has her ticket changed so that she can accompany Monty and Flick to Fort Smith, with Monty making up the difference in the cost. When the bus reaches Fort Smith, Monty promises Violet that he will be there waiting when she returns from Tulsa. Flick makes no such promise, but merely says good-bye. Monty runs beside the bus promising that he will meet Violet upon her return and asking her to promise that she will return.

Violet eventually reaches Tulsa and finds the preacher's headquarters. To her dismay, the preacher is on a publicity tour, so she must deal with one of his assistants. To every question that Violet poses concerning her disfigurement, the assistant gives a canned response about her true need being spiritual. She leaves uncured and dissatisfied.

On her bus ride back, Violet refuses to look at her face. When she reaches the Fort Smith bus station, Violet hears Monty calling her name. As she turns toward the voice, she sees her reflection in a large mirror over the jukebox. She realizes that she is still ugly and tries to flee. Monty, however, will not let her escape. As the story ends, Violet, no longer thinking about her face, realizes that Monty is about to catch up to her.

Themes and Meanings

Through the trials of Violet Karl, Doris Betts continues a theme that pervades her work, most of which is concerned with people trying to find themselves within the lives in which they have been placed. Most often, this search comes in the form of an individual in search of love. Although her themes transcend geographical confines, Betts uses the isolation of the rural South to provide little obvious escape for her characters. But these characters' acquired psychological independence intensifies the need of all persons to strive to conquer their fears and low self-images.

Life is a quest or a pilgrimage. By selecting this motif for the thematic center and title for her story, Doris Betts makes the seemingly least obvious heroine the stand-in for her readers who themselves, no doubt, attempted to find meaning in their lives.

Violet Karl seeks deliverance from the physical aberration that has made her an outcast through her deep belief that the evangelist in Tulsa will be her deliverer. When she arrives in Tulsa, she finds that her deliverer is not to be found and that his assistant regales her with prepared and standard abstract responses which do not address her needs.

When Violet returns to Fort Smith and finds Monty waiting for her as he had promised, she begins to push her deformity aside and realizes that she possesses something that may indeed be attractive. Her realization that Monty is not as bothered by her injured face as she leads Violet to take the first step toward self-realization that is central to Betts's fiction. At this point, the reader understands that, although the evangelical assistant made his comments out of habit, the problem that Violet faced did, indeed, lie more within her spirit than on her face.

Style and Technique

Doris Betts's short stories are vivid examples of moments in individual lives isolated in time. Utilizing a "slice-of-life" approach allows Betts clearly to depict the epiphanic moments of realization that most humans experience at one time or another. Thus, through her brief cross-country trip in search of rejuvenation, Violet Karl becomes an "everyperson."

Violet Karl's journey is an internal journey, one which will be completed only after she accepts herself and ceases to worry whether others accept her. Betts demonstrates, through Violet's isolation because of her injured face, that psychological pains are as real as physical pains. In both cases, however, the pains can be overcome with time and proper treatment. Monty's lack of revulsion at Violet's injury goes a long way toward demonstrating that others can accept her, helping her to accept herself as she is.

The surface simplicity of the structure of "The Ugliest Pilgrim" in fact provides the work's deeper complexity. In this work, Betts allows her story's form to match its thematic function. Violet's problem seems to be simple. If she can get to Tulsa, her problem will be solved. Below Violet's surface, however, the reader finds a more debilitating problem, lack of self-esteem. The reader also finds that beneath a simple narrative form is a universal theme which is complex in both cause and resolution.

Thomas B. Frazier

THE UPTURNED FACE

Author: Stephen Crane (1871-1900)
Type of plot: Sketch
Time of plot: The late 1800's
Locale: A battlefield in an unspecified war
First published: 1900

Principal characters:
TIMOTHY LEAN, a lieutenant
AN ADJUTANT
BILL, a dead man
TWO PRIVATES

The Story

As two soldiers contemplate the body of a dead comrade, lying on the battlefield at their feet, its face turned toward the sky, the adjutant asks Lieutenant Timothy Lean, "What will we do now?" Lean decides that the body must be buried and calls two enlisted men to dig a grave. Meanwhile, the adjutant and Lean decide that the clothes of the dead man must be searched, and the task falls to Lean. Hesitant to touch the corpse, he shakily completes the chore. As the grave is being dug and the search is being performed, enemy bullets fly overhead. Finally, the two enlisted men finish their hastily dug and shallow grave. The adjutant and Lean stand almost unsure of what to do next. They decide it would be proper if they put their fallen comrade into the grave themselves rather than order the enlisted men to do it. They are careful to avoid touching the body itself as they position the corpse in the grave. Lean remembers part of a burial service and begins it. The adjutant lamely adds a word or two that he recalls. After Lean abruptly orders the two privates to begin filling in the grave, rifle fire from Rostian sharp-shooters hits one of them in the arm. Both men are sent back to their lines, so Lean, almost feverishly, fills in the grave himself. Finally, all that is left of their fallen companion is his chalk-blue upturned face. Fighting off his sense of horror, Lean takes a shovelful of dirt and swings it toward the grave. The dirt makes a plopping sound as it lands, and the story ends.

Themes and Meanings

Beginning with Stephen Crane's most famous work, *The Red Badge of Courage* (1895), but continuing through his other works, the horror of encountering death is a constant theme. Often, rather than confront death directly, Crane's characters do their best to avoid it. They walk around dead men lying on battlefields, avoid wounded, or express loathing about touching the dead or the dying. Yet in this brief tale, written less than a year before his own death, Crane forces his characters, and readers, to face death squarely. In this story there is no way to avoid the issue, just as there is no way for Lean or the adjutant to avoid it on the battlefield. The story begins with two men struggling to decide what to do. At first neither man seems exactly certain, as both grapple with emotions barely under control. At moments each man lashes out at the two enlisted men, but one senses that their anger is not really directed at the hapless privates. Rather, Lean and the adjutant wrestle with both the reality of death, and its meaninglessness.

Each man resists touching the body, but ultimately they must put the corpse into the ground. It is interesting to note that although Lean could order the privates to do the job, he instead decides that he and the adjutant should put the body in the grave. Even though it is not entirely clear whether their motivations are due to their rank, or their relationship to the fallen man, the symbolic aspect of confronting the unpleasant "face" of death cannot be ignored. Lean will not simply walk away, leaving someone else to confront the terror of death for him. What makes the issue even more immediate is the imminent possibility of any of their own deaths. Bullets continue to fly around them as they complete the funeral service.

The image of the upturned face of the dead man is prominent not only at the beginning of the story, but in several later instances. As the privates initially prepare to fill in the grave one of them hesitates, unsure where to throw the first shovelful of dirt. For some reason Lean is horrified at the thought of the dirt falling on the upturned face. As the private throws the dirt on the corpse's feet instead, Lean feels "as if tons had been swiftly lifted from off his forehead." Momentarily, when the private is wounded and Lean must continue the task himself, he fills the entire grave except for the "chalk-blue" face. Lean seems to struggle with his feelings, and even snaps an angry remark at his superior, the adjutant. But ultimately the tension releases all in a moment as the shovel swings back, then forward, and the dirt covers the face. In the end, the reality of death cannot be avoided, neither walked around nor away from. The face of death must be stared into and addressed.

Style and Technique

Crane's writing is often appreciated for its brevity, spareness, and attention to realistic detail. In "The Upturned Face" the reader may note all of these elements. The story is one of his final, and finest, efforts. What is particularly notable about "The Upturned Face" is the vivid nature of the scene created in just fifteen hundred words. For example, the reader senses that bullets are whizzing by as a continual threat, but Crane mentions only once that they "snap" overhead, bullets are "spitting" overhead, and, at the opening, that bullets are cracking near their ears. The crisp effectiveness of these concise images forces the reader not only to perceive a tangible danger, but to consider the importance of anything that requires enduring such a risk. Why is this so important to Lean and the adjutant?

Crane depicts death realistically, often describing wounds in bloody detail, or the odd positioning of a dead person's limbs, perhaps emphasizing a certain revulsion to death, perhaps reflecting the realistically alien nature of the state. In this story, however, Lean's and the adjutant's sense of horror is expressed through the spare, yet focused image of the "chalk-blue" upturned face of their comrade. The reality is not made into something alien and horrible by its unnaturalness, but by its terrible immediacy.

The tension between the lieutenant and the adjutant, as well as the tension of each toward the dead man, skillfully builds from their initial debate over what to do. The first line describes the adjutant as "troubled and excited," and it is another example of Crane's art. At first these seem like antithetical states, yet soon we discover that the body of a fallen friend, coupled with the need to bury him as bullets fly close by, make Crane's opening remark an excellent summation. From this initial tension, caused by the conflict between the need to act quickly and the inability to quite face the situation, Crane leads the two men through a series of almost meaningless rituals that serve both to delay the outcome and to heighten the anxiety caused by the delay. The adjutant lets out a strange laugh which shows his mounting tension as they are faced with the reality of actually burying the body. But first they must set it in the grave. This brings new levels of disgust to Lean and the adjutant, and they are "particular that their fingers should not feel the corpse."

In an almost comedic moment they decide that some words should be read over the body, but neither can remember the service. This further delay, coupled with the sense of futility at the few meager words finally said, causes Lean to erupt against the innocent privates as he "tigerishly" commands them to throw in the dirt.

Then, the tension which has been building to this point is momentarily released as the first dirt falls on "Bill's" feet rather than his face. Lean thinks "How satisfactory!" But the respite is brief, for the private is wounded and Lean must finish filling in the grave himself.

Lean and the adjutant have ordered for a grave to be dug, searched the body, dragged it to the grave, arranged it inside, read a snatch of scripture, and then, finally, run out of options. Crane propels the reader not only toward the inevitable point of burial, but to a release of the stresses building in Lean throughout the narrative. Finally, they are released in a shovelful of dirt which covers the upturned face of their friend and ends the story. The unadorned "plop" of the dirt as it falls adds to the realism of the portrayal, while at the same time suggesting death's finality.

George T. Novotny

THE USED-BOY RAISERS

Author: Grace Paley (1922-   )
Type of plot: Psychological realism
Time of plot: The 1950's
Locale: Greenwich Village in New York City
First published: 1959

Principal characters:
FAITH DARWIN, a wife and the mother of two boys
LIVID, her first husband
PALLID, her current husband

The Story

Faith is preparing breakfast for both her husband and her former husband, who is back from a British colony in Africa and has slept on an aluminum cot in the living room as an overnight guest. As they talk over breakfast, it is difficult to tell the men apart. Faith privately assigns them names that make them seem like twins, so that although she calls one "Livid" and the other "Pallid," they are otherwise indistinguishable. Faith derives these names from the way the men respond to the eggs that she prepares for them. One rejects the eggs in a livid way, the other in a pallid way, but both sigh in unison because they are disappointed in breakfast, and both are eager for a drink. Faith does not keep liquor in the house, however, and pointedly brings out her God Bless Our Home embroidery, which she seems to see as a protective talisman against Livid's presence. The complaints about the eggs introduce a bickering note that continues throughout breakfast.

The two men share no sense of rivalry or jealousy; they are such a convivial pair that Faith seems to be the outsider. Livid has casually ceded the children to Faith's new husband as if they are a used car he no longer wishes to maintain. Neither man takes full responsibility for the children. After establishing the shallow ties that the two rather feckless men have to the boys, the story drifts into an unsettling discussion of yet another of Faith's old lovers, a man named Clifford, who is soon to marry. While Livid and Pallid dwell on the charms of Clifford's new girlfriend, Faith's silence suggests that she has unresolved issues with Clifford.

The two children, Richard and Tonto, wake up and are delighted to find their father and breakfast. Livid expresses concern about their education and becomes enraged when Pallid raises the issue of Catholic parochial schooling. Both Livid and Pallid are lapsed Catholics, and the conversation turns to religious and political topics concerning Jews, Catholics, and the state of Israel. Faith surprises the men by speaking out against Zionism and on her identity as a Diaspora Jew, an identity that she feels she can affirm in the bohemian mix of Greenwich Village as readily as in Israel itself. For Faith, Judaism is not a nationalist identity but an exacting moral and spiritual condition. The two men are astonished, because Faith is usually more silent and subservient; as she puts it, she only lives out her destiny, "which is to be laughingly the servant of man." This clever phrase has a double edge to it, suggesting a certain mockery as well as good nature, which is why she keeps this particular remark to herself. Her two husbands continue the religious conversation and point out that Faith has abandoned her faith by marrying out of it, but she responds that she has forgotten nothing of her past, and that Judaism is a religion that does not take up space but continues in time. Taken aback by her comments, the men let go of the discussion and relax in her cozy kitchen. Faith extends the olive branch by apologizing about the eggs but, eager to see them go, reminds them of their work responsibilities.

As the men prepare to leave for their appointments, Faith happily plans a day that excludes them, involving morning housekeeping, playtime and the park with her children, and finally, as a reward for having endured beans all week, a rib roast with little onions, dumplings, and pink applesauce. She tells the two boys to hug their father. The older one runs to Livid, the younger to Pallid. Both men kiss Faith good-bye, but Pallid's kiss is the more erotic. She sends her two boyish men off into the outside world, wishing them well but with little interest in their concerns, preferring to find fulfillment in her home and children.

Themes and Meanings

This story invites the reader to share Faith Darwin's perspective. She lives apart from the men in her life, emotionally, religiously, and politically. Her children are more central to her daily life, and she devotes much time and energy to caring for them. This is a woman's world, one that the men in this story take for granted and perhaps do not fully appreciate or understand. Similarly, when Grace Paley first started to write, she worried that no one would be interested in reading about women at home with their children. Faith seems at first to exist in the margins of Paley's story, keeping her opinions, which are far more astute and mordant than the men suspect, to herself. By the end of the story, readers realize that the seemingly marginal Faith has her own purposes, which are just as important as those of the men in her life. This image of marginality applies not only to Faith's identity as a woman but also to her identity as a Jew. As is characteristic of Paley's writing, this story mixes the personal and the political. Faith celebrates herself not only as a wife and mother but also as a Diaspora Jew, described as "a remnant in the basement of world affairs" or "a splinter in the toe of civilization," images of marginality that contain a subversive moral integrity; the final image of the Diaspora Jew is that of "a victim to aggravate the conscience."

"The Used-Boy Raisers" introduces Paley's most durable character, Faith Darwin, who figures in many of her other stories. Her name, like the sardonic nicknames of her two husbands, invites interpretation. Her first name, Faith, suggests her Judaism. Unlike the men, who are associated with fixed geographical spaces, Faith affirms Judaism as a religion of seasons and days, and a religion that prevails in the home and through the offices of the mother. It is significant that this story takes place on a Saturday, the Jewish Sabbath, which Faith will observe through the celebratory meal that she is planning. During her conversation with Livid and Pallid, she admits that she lost God a long time ago, but she still has faith, that is, her own identity as a Jewish woman. Her last name, Darwin, suggests her capacity to adapt and survive in changing or challenging circumstances.

Style and Technique

Paley's style is compressed and economical, even by the standards of the short-story form. Sardonic and clever, there is also something slightly exotic about her voice, which Paley attributes to Yiddish and Russian influences. Her characters come to life through her use of odd, quirky turns of phrase. In "The Used-Boy Raisers," for example, Faith describes Livid's problems with the Roman Catholic church as his "own little dish of lava," a phrase which in an original but biting way puts him in his place.

On the surface, "The Used-Boy Raisers" is short and virtually plotless. Employing considerable dialogue, the narrative seems to be nothing but aimless and unstructured table talk. Paley circles around her themes and meanings, approaching them indirectly, under the guise of inconsequence. She is, however, pitting Faith against her two husbands as she introduces a series of topics—eggs, her old flame, the children, Israel, her plans for the day. The narrative is artfully structured so that by the end of the story, Faith's character and values have been firmly established, and important distinctions have been made between herself and the two men. Although her conversation seems to flow in a guileless, conversational way, at times Paley retreats inside Faith's mind to secure Faith's perspective as the guiding point of view in the story. Faith's sudden speech about the Diaspora Jews takes the reader in a surprising new direction. This is characteristic of Paley's stories, which often take disarming twists and turns. The conclusion imagines Faith as a woman living in a world apart from that of her husbands, underlining the series of distinctions Paley has made between her female protagonist and the two similar men.

Margaret Boe Birns

THE VALIANT WOMAN

Author: J. F. Powers (1917-)
Type of plot: Psychological realism
Time of plot: The 1940's
Locale: American Midwest
First published: 1947

Principal characters:
FATHER JOHN FIRMAN, an aging Roman Catholic priest
FATHER FRANK NULTY, another priest and his friend
MRS. STONER, his housekeeper

The Story

Father Firman celebrates his fifty-ninth birthday by inviting his old friend, Father Nulty, to dinner in the rectory. Their association goes back to their seminary days, and their conversation would turn to sentimental memories if it got the chance. The occasion, however, is thoroughly dominated by the aggressive housekeeper, Mrs. Stoner, who simply does not know her place. Mrs. Stoner has assumed the role of the priest's wife, although the relationship is innocent of any explicit sexual complications, and she has forcefully extended her authority over his life and society and opinions. She gossips about the bishop—who is not the man that his predecessor was—who cut poor housekeeper Ellen Kennedy out of Father Doolin's will, who ignored the dinner she cooked for him on his last visit, and who is coming again for confirmations this year. Clearly, there is a society of priests' housekeepers with their own gossip and social ranking, as is evidenced when she comments about the new Mrs. Allers at Holy Cross, as if she herself were the pastor there. She scolds Father Firman when he strikes a match on his chair to light the candle on his birthday cake. To him, the candle looks suspiciously like a blessed one taken from church.

The two priests have a moment to themselves when Mrs. Stoner returns to the kitchen. Father Nulty is very much aware of Father Firman's aggravation. He points out that another priest of their acquaintance, Fish Frawley, got rid of his snooping housekeeper with a clever stratagem. He told her the false story that his "nephews" (a long-standing euphemism for the children of supposedly celibate priests) were visiting him, an item that promptly appeared in the paper. Not only did Frawley dismiss her, but even made a sermon out of the event. Then he hired a Filipino housekeeper; the implication is clear that Asiatic women will be more deferential to male authority.

In laughing about how Fish Frawley painted all the dormitory toilet seats on a New Year's morning while they were in seminary, the two priests show they wish to return to a time of male bonding, when all women were in the background. When a mosquito lands on Father Nulty's wrist, he swats it and flicks it away, telling his friend that only the female bites.

Mrs. Stoner returns to the study with Father Firman's socks and mechanically reviews all the prominent converts in the news. When this subject is exhausted, she prods the others with disconnected bits of information. Do they know that Henry Ford is making steering wheels out of soybeans? Father Nulty has had enough and gets up to leave. "I thought he'd never go," Mrs. Stoner exclaims. Now that the housekeeper and Father Firman are alone, she promptly sets up the card table for their nightly game of honeymoon bridge. Mrs. Stoner is highly competitive, playing for blood, a need Father Firman recognizes by not trying too hard to win.

As Mrs. Stoner slaps down her cards in triumph, Father Firman daydreams about getting rid of her. What has he done to make God put this burden on him? In charity, he tries to enumerate her good points, but comes up with nothing except that she is obsessively clean and thrifty. She has run his life, turned away his friends, and intruded into the affairs of the parish. Although pitiable for having lost her husband after only a year of marriage, she settled in with him and never made a further attempt to remarry. Years ago she moved into the guest room because the screen was broken in the housekeeper's room, and she had never moved back. The truth of her assumed position suddenly strikes him, and long after everyone else has seen it—she considers herself his wife. He is shocked and panicked by the realization.

In desperation, he looks up the regulations governing priests and their housekeepers. Clerics can reside only with women about whom there can be no suspicion, either because of a natural bond, such as that of a mother or sister, or because of advanced age. Mrs. Stoner, however, is younger than he is. Is there some loophole in the contract that would allow him to send her packing? He recognizes, however, that she meets the spirit if not the letter of the law, and that he cannot afford to pension her off. There appears to be no way out.

A mosquito bites him in the back. He slaps at it, and it takes refuge in the beard of St. Joseph on the bookcase. He swats it again with a folded magazine, and the statue falls to the floor and breaks. Having heard the noise, Mrs. Stoner comes to his door. He tells her that he has only been chasing a mosquito.

"Shame on you, Father. She needs the blood for her eggs," Mrs. Stoner says as the priest once more lunges for the tormenting insect.

Themes and Meanings

The Catholic priesthood was a favorite subject of J. F. Powers. In "The Valiant Woman," he gives a sly and witty account of an ongoing struggle between a priest and his housekeeper. This small and ironic comedy is quite successfully set off against larger and darker issues involving human needs and limitations, and the theology that guides the characters.

Quite against his inclinations, Father Firman, a celibate priest, has "married" Mrs. Stoner by passively allowing her to assume the role of his domestic partner. Unlike the suggestion buried in his name, he has been anything but firm, and has steadily dwindled into the role of a husband. Without asking for these responsibilities he has allowed them to overtake him, and he can no longer in good conscience back away.

He cannot divorce her, just as his religion forbids divorce. In his fantasy, a Filipino housekeeper would give him the life of freedom he craves—not sexual freedom, but freedom from responsibility in his personal life. The priest is thrust into the commitment his theology teaches, and which he has no doubt preached to others.

Although the reader need not accept any particular religious view to appreciate its argument, the story is deeply rooted in its Catholic theology. None of the three characters has an unusual spiritual gift. With her garrulous and trivial nature, Mrs. Stoner is indeed a millstone around the neck of the priest. Father Firman, although conscientious in his duties, seeks only a comfortable and trouble-free life, an ideal that Father Nulty urges upon him. The author thus creates limited human beings who are confused and frustrated by their needs and fantasies. On the surface, their religion is only a social framework into which they have fallen. Yet the demands of that religion make Father Firman stand larger than he ever could on his own. Husbands, as well as priests, take vows before God. Father Firman finally begins to realize that his responsibility is not simply defined by the vows he took as a priest. In becoming a "husband," he is bound by the spirit as well as the letter of the law.

Style and Technique

The story is rich in detail and human observation, and cannot be summarized by an account of its symbolic meanings. Yet those meanings are important to understand as part of the author's wit. The symbolic use of the mosquito is clever and economical. In the course of the story, Father Firman learns two things about the mosquito. When Father Nulty tells him that only females bite, he conveys a cynicism with which Father Firman is ready to agree. They both wish to escape from the domination of females. There is another symbolic application as well: The mosquito is a part of nature, a creation of God, yet it is a persistent tormentor that we never quite manage to eliminate. It nags and gives pain and comes back again and again, representing as well as anything the inevitable frustrations of the human condition. Accepting such frustrations, and perhaps much more, is one's lot in life.

At the end of the story, when Father Firman attacks the mosquito on the statue of St. Joseph, the symbolism extends to more explicit religious parallels. Joseph, the husband of Mary, was also ambiguously involved in a marriage in a way that he did not seek. Mrs. Stoner's declaration that the mosquito needs blood for her eggs seals the argument. The female mosquito not only torments its victim, but must do so, because of its nature and inner need.

Bruce Olsen

THE VALLEY OF SIN

Author: Lee K. Abbott (1947-)
Type of plot: Fable
Time of plot: The 1970's to 1980's
Locale: Deming, New Mexico
First published: 1985

Principal characters:
DILLON RIPLEY, a prosperous banker and golf addict
JIMMIE RIPLEY, his wife
ALLIE MARTIN, a golf pro
TOMMY STEWARD, a caddy
DR. TIPPIT, the pastor of St. Luke's Presbyterian church
WATTS GUNN,
PHINIZY SPALDING, and
POOT TAYLOR, Dillon's golf companions

The Story

At a country club in Deming, New Mexico, Dillon Ripley practices his golf swing with the help of the resident pro, Allie Martin. There is little question that Dillon Ripley approaches the game as a sacred experience and not merely as an entertaining sport. On weekends he is accompanied by his wife, Jimmie, as he tries to instill in her his own reverence for the game. Golf, he tells her, is bliss and bane, like love itself. Ripley so reveres the game that he uses archaic terms such as "mashie," "niblick," and "spoon" to describe various kinds of golf clubs. Having delved into the ancient history of golf, he is familiar with its lore and minutiae.

In his daily life, Ripley is a prosperous vice president of the Farmers and Merchants Bank (loan department), and he repeatedly tells his favorite golfing partners—Watts Gunn, Phinizy Spalding, and Poot Taylor—that he intends to take his wife and four children to Scotland to play at the Old Course at St. Andrews—the home of the Royal and Ancient Golf Club. His love and enthusiasm for the sport is so profound that he once declared, on the fourteenth hole, that he had discovered "what best tested the kind we are . . . the hazards of unmown fescue and bent grass, or a sand wedge misplaced from a bunker known as the Valley of Sin." In short, what separates humans from beasts and makes them most human is how successfully they emerge from their struggles in the Valley of Sin—literally and metaphorically.

It is at the fourteenth hole on a beautiful May afternoon, however, that Dillon Ripley faces the most traumatic vision of his life when his caddy, Tommy Steward, spots a Volvo speeding toward them. In it are Ripley's golf pro, Allie Martin, and his wife Jimmie Ripley—both naked. Dillon's golf partners recognize—as does Ripley—that a corrupting agent has entered their lovely Eden and destroyed it utterly. When Ripley sees his naked wife, he immediately collapses with a heart attack.

The second part of the story takes up months after Ripley's heart attack. He seems to be on the mend, though his physician, Dr. Weems, has warned him that he is not yet ready to play golf. The Deming Golf Club has lost its Edenic glow, now that Ripley's friends realize that human beings are no more noble or charmed than "thinking worm or sentient mud." Most people accepted the view of Dr. Tippit, the Presbyterian minister, that the world is "a fallen orb." Although Ripley has seemingly accepted the terrible loss of his beloved, strange events and signs began to appear at selected places on the golf course, especially on the fourteenth hole—Deming's own Valley of Sin.

Three weeks after Ripley puts his house up for sale, apocalyptic messages begin to appear in different parts of the golf course, written in tiny script with messages such as: "We are a breed in need of fasting and praying. . . . The world is almost rotten. . . . Porpozec ciebie nie prosze dorzanin" (a quotation from a John Cheever short story). Ripley's friends interpret these hermetic statements according to their own lights and obsessions. Garland Steeples, the high school guidance counselor, views them—especially "the downward arc of time"—as foreboding signs of an imminent communist takeover.

It is Tommy Steward who first confronts the vision of horror near midnight on an early summer night. As he and Eve Spalding are making out near the fourteenth hole—the Valley of Sin morally—he beholds "the thing, wretched as a savage," leaping in front of him. It is dressed in skins, and as dirty as an orphan in a French movie, with one fist shaking overhead and the other holding a golf club heavy with sod like a cudgel. There are terrifying roars everywhere, and Tommy cannot believe the thing's blind pink eyes and its teeth as wet as a dog's. He feels as if he is staring at the hindmost of human nature.

Poot Taylor and Watts Gunn patrol the country club for a month, but the night that they cease their rounds, something begins digging pits and new notes appear: "We are blind . . . and nothing can be done about it."

In August, Dillon Ripley sells his house and moves twenty miles south into the desert, where the only sport is hunting. There is no golf course in this barren place where the winds blow constantly, as if they come from a land whose lord is dark and always angry.

Themes and Meanings

Lee K. Abbott's unique story is about the fall of a local hero in a corrupt world. Dillon Ripley embodies the high moral standards of the Deming Country Club; indeed, his old fashioned passion and reverence for golf as an ancient rite of passage make him a modern hero. He sees himself in an idealized form as "slender and tanned and strong as iron, a hero wise and blessed as those from Homer himself." Once he is betrayed by Allie Martin, his friend and guide, and his beloved wife, Jimmie, he enters the fallen world which literally and metaphorically breaks his heart. More important, the corruption of the Edenic country club takes place at the fourteenth hole—Ripley's Valley of Sin—where Allie and Jimmie appear in adulterous embrace, scandalizing the entire community. Their sin desecrates a hallowed place, a location which hitherto symbolized the highest spiritual ideals of both Ripley and his faithful entourage. His three golfing companions—Watts, Phinizy, and Poot—function as a Greek chorus commenting on the consequences of that terrible fall into reality. Abbott describes Ripley as a general and attributes to him many of the characteristics of a Homeric hero; however, his heroism is not demonstrated in his golf game. Rather it consists in his ability to mythologize the game of golf and reconnect it with its ancient origins. His use of archaic terms such as "passion and weal," "enchantments," and "bliss and bane," and the ways that he applies them to golf, revivify and reestablish ancient energies to the game by which Ripley lives his life. Once Ripley's spiritual fall takes place—and Ripley is mythically connected to that particular location—the place itself begins to show signs of its own imminent collapse. It begins to take on the look of a wasteland, and messages of its corruption begin to appear at the place of sacrilege, the fourteenth hole. Tommy Steward, "fuzzy-minded on red-dirt marijuana" believes that he sees the physical manifestation of evil appear as a demoniac figure at the very place that he is necking with a girl, who is named, aptly, Eve.

Style and Technique

The major method that Abbott uses throughout this brilliantly rendered story is what T. S. Eliot called the "Mythical Method." This narrative is about the fall of a local hero in Deming, New Mexico, but it is also an old story about the fall of an ancient local leader's fall from a condition of familial love and community into one of fragmented corruption. Most of the names of the characters, once their archaic origins are uncovered, are associated with ancient Scottish and Celtic families, locations, and clan wars. Dillon—a name that means "a spoiler, or corrupting agent"—emerges as a kind of Celtic chieftain whose spiritual health determines the health of his community. Allie Martin becomes the mythic wise guide betrayer—the one who abducts the leader's wife—very much the way that Sir Lancelot took away King Arthur's wife, Guinevere. The result is the same: the end of the communal Round Table and the destruction of Camelot.

What establishes the connection between these two worlds and stories is the archaic language—the language of those heroic Arthurian tales—which Ripley uses to define his spiritual value system. It is the language that Abbott uses that keeps those ancient ideals alive and functioning in the fallen world of the twentieth century. Oddly enough, the name Ripley means "a stripe of land or clearing," which is exactly what a golf course is. Abbott also gently satirizes the modern version of this "old story" by holding it up for comparison to the ancient one, though he is not satirizing those venerable values which golf (and other sports) embody. The Valley of Sin is also the notorious fourteenth hole on one of the courses where the British Open is played each year.

Patrick Meanor

THE VANE SISTERS

Author: Vladimir Nabokov (1899-1977)
Type of plot: Fantasy
Time of plot: The early 1950's
Locale: New England and New York City
First published: 1959

Principal characters:
THE NARRATOR, a French literature professor
CYNTHIA VANE, a recently deceased artist
SYBIL VANE, her sister, a student who committed suicide four years earlier
D., Sybil's lover, a former college instructor

The Story

The unnamed narrator, a French professor at a New England women's college, runs into D., whom he has not seen for several years, and hears about the recent death of Cynthia Vane. Four years earlier, the narrator knew D. and Cynthia in the small town where he still teaches literature. He is surprised to find D., a former instructor at his school, revisiting the site of unpleasant memories. D.'s shame is an extramarital affair that he had conducted with Cynthia's younger sister, Sybil, who was one of the narrator's students.

Cynthia once summoned the narrator to Boston and begged him to make D. end his relationship with her sister and to have D. kicked out of the college if he refused to comply. When the narrator met with D., the latter told him that he had already decided to end the relationship; he was about to quit his teaching job and join his father's firm in Albany, New York. The next day, Sybil seemed normal when she took her examination in the narrator's French literature class. Later, however, when the narrator read her essay, he found it full "of a kind of desperate conscientiousness, with underscores, transposes, unnecessary footnotes, as if she were intent upon rounding up things in the most respectable manner possible." At its end it contained what appeared to be a suicide note:

> *Cette examain est finie ainsi que ma vie. Adieu, jeunes filles!* Please, *Monsieur le Professeur*, contact *ma soeur* and tell her that Death was not better than D minus, but definitely better than Life minus D.

Immediately after reading this note the narrator phoned Cynthia, who told him that Sybil was already dead, then rushed to see her. As Cynthia read Sybil's note, the narrator pointed out its grammatical mistakes. Amused by her sister's use of an exclamation mark, Cynthia was strangely pleased by its trivialities. She then took the narrator to Sybil's room to show him two empty pill bottles and the bed from which her body was removed.

After Cynthia moved to New York a few months later, the narrator began seeing her regularly while visiting the city to do research in the public library. He disliked almost everything about her and wondered at the tastes of her three lovers, but admired her paintings.

Fearing that Sybil's spirit was displeased at the conspiracy to end her romance, Cynthia began sending mementoes—such as a photograph of Sybil's tomb—to D. She wanted to placate her dead sister because of her own belief in the spirit world. Cynthia felt herself especially susceptible to the recently dead. Although the highly rational narrator sneered at her fondness for spiritualism, he describes two of her séances at which the spirits of Oscar Wilde, Leo Tolstoy, and others appeared. He preferred these silly events to Cynthia's awful house parties, at which she was always the youngest woman present. After an argument over his snobbery, they stopped seeing each other.

Despite his skepticism, the narrator senses Cynthia's presence after her death when strange physical manifestations in his bedroom make him suspect her of staging a cheap poltergeist show.

Themes and Meanings

Stylistic techniques are never sharply separated from the themes in Vladimir Nabokov's work. "The Vane Sisters" is an excellent example of his interest in the playfulness of fiction for its own sake and his joy in the potential for deceitfulness in art. His main thematic and stylistic device here is the use of an unreliable narrator. The events of the story of the Vane sisters and D. probably occurred much as the professor says they do, but his interpretations of characters and events are not always fully accurate. In this regard, he resembles Charles Kinbote, in Nabokov's *Pale Fire* (1962), who ostensibly is explaining a poem by John Shade but is actually writing about himself.

Nabokov presents his protagonist ironically because the narrator thinks he is far more capable of understanding than he truly is. At one point, he considers himself "in a state of raw awareness that seemed to transform the whole of my being into one big eyeball rolling in the world's socket." He feels that he must ridicule others to elevate himself. Thus he emphasizes how Sybil's face was scarred by a skin disease and was heavily made up and how Cynthia's skin had a "coarse texture" masked ineptly by cosmetics applied even more slovenly than her sister's. He glories in calling attention to Cynthia's body odor and to the fading looks of her female friends. At Cynthia's parties, even though everyone is connected with the arts, "there was no inspired talk," so he amuses himself by poking "a little Latin fun at some of her guests." He will not accompany Cynthia to séances conducted by professional mediums because he "knew too much about that from other sources." He does not need to experience something firsthand to be able to dismiss it.

The narrator will not consort with two of Cynthia's friends until he is satisfied "that they possessed considerable wit and culture." How he determines this sophistication is not explained; the reader must simply take his word for it. Cynthia rightly accuses him of being "a prig and a snob" and of seeing only "the gestures and disguises of people."

Nabokov grants the sisters a measure of revenge by having them control the story that the professor thinks he alone is telling. The narrator, who once peruses the first letters of the lines of William Shakespeare's sonnets to discover what words they might form, is the victim of an elaborate literary joke. Later, the narrator vaguely recalls a message from the dead concealed in the final paragraph of some novel or short story. His own final paragraph in this story is itself an acrostic in which the first letters of its words spell out "Icicles by cynthia meter from me sybil":

> I could isolate, consciously, little. Everything seemed blurred, yellow-clouded, yielding nothing tangible. Her inept acrostics, maudlin evasions, theopathies—every recollection formed ripples of mysterious meaning. Everything seemed yellowly blurred, illusive, lost.

The dead sisters thus select the very words and images used by the pompous narrator, who has laughed at the powers of the dead. Nabokov himself explains that the sisters use the acrostic "to assert their mysterious participation in the story" in his preface to the story in the collection *Tyrants Destroyed and Other Stories* (1975).

Cynthia, whom the narrator describes as "a painter of glass-bright minutiae," does this by causing the professor to describe icicles and other prismatic images throughout the story. On a walk near a place where D. once lived, the narrator admires "a family of brilliant icicles drip-dripping from the eaves of a frame house." He tries to spot the shadows of the falling drops, but they prove as elusive as ghosts because he lacks the proper angle of vision: "I did not chance to be watching the right icicle when the right drop fell. There was a rhythm, an alternation in the dripping that I found as teasing as a coin trick." The trick played by the Vane sisters mocks his lack of perception into the true nature of what he encounters. When he arrives at D.'s former home, he finally sees what he wants: "the dot of an exclamation mark leaving its ordinary position to glide down very fast." Sybil is also present later on his walk: "The lean ghost, the elongated umbra cast by a parking meter upon some damp snow, had a strange ruddy tinge."

The pun on parking meter and the meter of language is typical of Nabokov. He enjoys playing games with his readers, whom he expects to pay attention to every detail, such as the description of the exclamation mark in Sybil's suicide note and Cynthia's delight in her sister's punctuation. This incident, like others in the story, also questions the randomness of events. Do things happen by chance or design? Nabokov and Cynthia, controlling artists, endorse the latter.

Style and Technique

Nabokov also involves his reader through literary and historical allusions. It is no accident that Oscar Wilde appears at one of Cynthia's séances: In Wilde's *The Portrait of Dorian Gray* (1891) "Sybil Vane" is a character who commits suicide for the love of a man named "D." In classical mythology, a sibyl is a prophetess who intercedes with the gods on behalf of human supplicants, just as Sybil intercedes in the professor's narrative.

The essence of Nabokov's playfulness can be seen in his allusions to Samuel Taylor Coleridge's *Kubla Khan* (1816), which the poet labeled a fragment that he dreamed until interrupted by a neighbor from Porlock. Cynthia is friends with "an eccentric librarian called Porlock" who examines old books looking for misprints—the quintessential close reader. Three days after Porlock's death, Cynthia comes across Coleridge's poem and interprets it as a message from Porlock himself. "The Vane Sisters," like "Kubla Khan," is incomplete until the imaginative reader recognizes the sisters' part in an elaborate trick. The intermingling of life, death, love, art, and the imagination is too airy a conceit for Nabokov's literal-minded narrator.

Michael Adams

VANKA

Author: Anton Chekhov (1860-1904)
Type of plot: Social realism
Time of plot: Late nineteenth century
Locale: Moscow
First published: 1886 (English translation, 1915)

Principal characters:

IVAN (VANKA) ZHUKOV, a nine-year-old boy apprenticed to a shoemaker
KONSTANTIN MAKARICH, his easy-going, bibulous "Grandad"

The Story

Ivan Zhukov, known by the diminutive "Vanka," is an unhappy orphan who has been apprenticed for three months to the shoemaker Alyakhin in Moscow. On Christmas eve, while his master and mistress and the senior apprentices are all at church, Vanka sits down to write a pleading letter to "Grandad" Konstantin Makarich in the nearby village where Vanka lived before being sent to the city. Vanka's mother, Pelageya, had been in service at a country estate, where his life had been idyllic as he roamed freely with Grandad, "one-eyed Yegor," and other servants. After his mother's death three months earlier, Vanka had first been dispatched to the back kitchen with Grandad and from there to the shoemaker. His homesickness and misery emerge heartbreakingly as he writes his letter.

As Vanka writes, he muses on his grandfather. The old man—about sixty-five—is night watchman on the estate. Vanka imagines him at his usual diversions: hanging around the kitchen, dozing, and joking with the cook and the kitchen maids before going out to walk all night around the premises shaking his rattle. Vanka knows that Grandad's dogs Kashtanka and Eel will be with him. Kashtanka is too old for mischief, but the wily Eel—long, black, and weasel-like—is sly and treacherous, snapping at unsuspecting feet or stealing chickens. For these depredations, Eel is beaten severely but his behavior is unchanged.

Vanka's most cherished memory is of going with Grandad to chop down a fir tree for the master's Christmas. The old man would preface the felling with a chuckle, a few moments with his pipe, and a pinch of snuff. When a hare bounded by, he would shout his outrage at the "stub-tailed devil."

Vanka's letter reveals how his child's world on the estate, warmed by the love of his mother and the affection of Miss Olga Ignatyevna from the big house, has been replaced by a nightmare of exhaustion and loneliness. He recalls being beaten because he fell asleep while rocking the master's baby. Whenever the older apprentices have forced him to steal cucumbers and he has been caught, he has received more beatings. His rations are meager. He gets bread in the morning, gruel at noon, and bread again in the evening. He enjoys no tea or cabbage and must sleep in the hallway, where the crying baby keeps him awake.

His song of suffering completed, the young servant turns his letter into a plea for salvation, begging his Grandad to take him away. He vows to pray for Grandad, to do the steward's job of cleaning boots, to replace Fedya as the shepherd-boy, and to protect Grandad. Moscow is a big town, Vanka laments, with many fine houses and horses, but no sheep. Its customs are unfamiliar. He cannot sing in church, and when he goes in the butcher's shop no one even knows where the game was shot. Vanka is lost in an alien land.

The letter ends with Vanka's final cry for Grandad to take him home to the village with the familiar animals and servants. He folds the letter, puts it in an envelope, and writes on it "GRANDAD," adding on reflection "KONSTANTIN MAKARICH IN THE VILLAGE." An hour after he runs to the letter box, he is asleep, "lulled by rosy hopes." He dreams of a stove, with Grandad sitting on its ledge reading his letter to the kitchen help. As the grandfather reads, the sly Eel paces back and forth in the kitchen, wagging his tail and watching for his chance.

Themes and Meanings

Many stories dramatize a young person's loss of innocence, but few embody the theme in the misery of a child so young as Vanka. Only the waifs in Charles Dickens' novels come readily to mind. Vanka's plight is especially bewildering and painful for him because of the earlier good years with his mother and grandfather and others on the estate who petted him. As Vanka sits alone on Christmas eve, watching for his tormentors to return and struggling to find words that will move his Grandad to action, he is a picture of forlornness.

Although this story has only four pages, it creates with swift characterizations a scene that goes far beyond a lonely boy's composing of a letter that will surely never reach its addressee. A whole social world opens up in "Vanka," with its rigid class system, its family life, and its cruel indifference to poor children. Much can be read into the narrative's silence about Vanka's father. Vanka describes himself as an orphan, but the story says nothing about his father's fate. Did he die by farm accident? By typhus? The unnamed father remains hidden, just one among the thousands who died early and left no trace behind except in their progeny.

Vanka's touching love for his grandfather, as well as his fond memory of bringing home a Christmas tree, suggests a kindly Grandad. Why then did the old man let the child be sent to such a cruel master? The most generous answer would be that a child with no prospects should learn a trade as soon as possible, and that a difficult apprenticeship is better than no preparation for a world that takes no interest in either its winners or its losers. From this perspective, "Vanka" is an example of the critical tradition known as literary naturalism, with its victims tossed about by forces beyond their control. The hope that buoys up Vanka as he thrusts his letter in the letter box and dreams of Grandad reading it to the servants are merely the typical hoaxes of a creation pervaded by irony.

The slight glimpse given of the Zhivarev family who own the estate comes in the person of Miss Olga Ignatyevna, Vanka's personal favorite. Miss Olga treats Vanka with sweets and would "amuse herself by teaching him to read, write and count to a hundred, and even to dance the quadrille." The word "amuse" reveals Miss Olga as one who regards Vanka as equivalent to a trained monkey whom she would exploit for her private entertainment. Her relationship to Vanka suggests what is called a synecdoche, a term for a situation in which the part stands for the whole: In this case Miss Olga's patronizing treatment of a child is the part that stands for the whole Russian class system. "Vanka" is thus a fitting document for a literary criticism that stresses a social conscience.

Style and Technique

The economy of Chekhov's style is a model for writers. The first paragraph identifies Vanka and establishes his plight in just ten quick lines. Grandad leaps to life in two sentences that fix his appearance and his habits. However, Chekhov's genius for minute observation shows up perhaps most wonderfully in his characterization of the dogs. Kashtanka is old and resigned to a dog's life, but the clever Eel is a treacherous thief animated by "the most Jesuitical spite and malice." Eel is such a romantic, satanic figure of life in the servants' quarters that Chekhov concludes the story with Eel pacing the floor, wagging his tail within Vanka's dream.

The brief descriptive passages achieve genuine poetry. The desperate Vanka, struggling with his "rusty nib" and his "crumpled sheet of paper," imagines the village on Christmas Eve: The air is still, "transparent" and "fresh" on a dark night; above the village with its white roofs, the sky is sprinkled with stars and the Milky Way stands out as clearly "as if newly scrubbed for the holiday and polished with snow." When Vanka visits the forest with Grandad to get a Christmas tree, the young fir trees coated with frost stand "motionless, waiting to see which one of them was to die."

The pathos of this story is so sharp that its depiction of childhood loneliness does not fade over time.

Frank Day

A VERY OLD MAN WITH ENORMOUS WINGS

Author: Gabriel García Márquez (1928-)
Type of plot: Fable
Time of plot: Twentieth century
Locale: A Latin American village
First published: "Un señor muy viejo con unas alas enormes," 1968 (English translation, 1972)

Principal characters:
PELAYO, a villager who discovers the old man with wings
ELISENDA, his wife
FATHER GONZAGA, a village priest
AN OLD MAN WITH WINGS

The Story

One day when Pelayo, a coastal villager, goes to dispose of crabs that have washed ashore onto his property, he discovers an old man with wings lying face down in the mud. The toothless creature is bald and dressed in rags. As Pelayo and his wife, Elisenda, carefully examine the creature, looking for clues to its origin, it responds to their questions in a tongue that they cannot identify. They suspect that he is a castaway from a ship. Other villagers who see the old man offer theories about his origins and appearance. The couple plan to set him adrift on a raft, but they first imprison him in a chicken coop. When a large crowd gathers around the coop, Pelayo and his wife decide to charge admission to view him, thereby creating a circuslike atmosphere.

The local priest, Father Gonzaga, is disturbed by rumors that the mysterious winged creature might be an angel, so he comes the next day to investigate. When the old man fails to understand Latin, the priest denounces him as an impostor. Nevertheless, curious people travel great distances to see the creature, and a carnival arrives to take advantage of the large crowds. Father Gonzaga, in the meantime, writes to the pope in an attempt to ascertain the church's official position on the creature and the apparently "miraculous" occurrences that the crowds associate with the old man. The Vatican demands to know if the old man knows Aramaic, if he can fit on the head of a pin, and if he has a navel. Meanwhile, the sick and the handicapped come to the old man in search of cures. The old man does seem to perform miracles, but these miracles are gratuitous in that they are unrelated to the sickness involved. A blind man, for example, grows three new teeth.

The crowds begin diminishing after the carnival puts on display a woman who was transformed into an enormous spider for having attended a dance without her parents' permission. Nevertheless, Pelayo and his wife have profited so greatly from their enterprise that they purchase a new house and fine clothing. After their chicken coop collapses, the old man moves into the couple's home, where he becomes a nuisance. Over the years the old man makes feeble attempts to fly, but not until the end of the story does he finally gain sufficient strength and altitude to fly away.

Themes and Meanings

"A Very Old Man with Enormous Wings" treats two issues: interpretation and invention/imagination. After the discovery of the stranger, six interpretations of his significance arise within the story. Once Pelayo recovers from his initial astonishment, he concludes that the old man is a lonely castaway. The basis for his conclusion is that the man speaks in a strong "sailor's voice." This explanation is merely arbitrary, however, because basic logic rejects the interpretation and makes Pelayo's explanation merely humorous. The second interpretation is made by a neighbor woman who is thought to know "everything about life and death." The humor of her interpretation arises in the certainty with which she pronounces that the old man is an angel.

The next three interpretations are proposed by various innocent and ingenuous villagers. According to them, the stranger may be either the mayor of the world, a five-star general, or the first of a race of winged wise men who will take charge of the universe. While Father Gonzaga believes that the old man is not an angel, it is noteworthy that as the "official" interpreter in the town, he is the only one who refuses to offer a concrete interpretation; instead he merely sends a letter to the pope.

In the final analysis, the text offers no rational explanation for the enigmatic man. If fact, the text defies rational explanation or analysis. It is suggested, however, that the old man may be purely imaginary, since he is described as disappearing in an "imaginary dot" on the horizon at the end of the story. While critics have argued that the old man leaves because of his disillusionment with the exploitation surrounding his visit, at no time is this interpretation substantiated within the narrative itself.

"A Very Old Man with Enormous Wings" thus becomes a parody of the interpretive process itself. Appearing as the first story in the volume *La increíble y triste historia de la cándida Eréndira y de su abuela desalmada* (1972; *Innocent Erendira and Other Stories*, 1979), it also functions as a kind of warning to the reader. The story's implication is that one must take extreme care when attributing rational laws of cause and effect to innately irrational occurrences. The story also affirms Gabriel García Márquez's right to invention, to the creative process, and to the life-affirming value of the human imagination.

Style and Technique

In "A Very Old Man with Enormous Wings," García Márquez makes use of several highly inventive diversions from the basic story line to make interpretation even more elusive. In these narrative diversions theme and technique become inseparably intertwined. Although the old man/angel is central to the story, and every event bears on him, his appearance, behavior, identity, fate, or effects, the attention focused on the old man is frequently interrupted by shifts of focus to other characters, who are sometimes named and described at length. The obtrusiveness of the narrator, who is both at one with and apart from the other characters, also functions to distract the reader. The story, in fact, vacillates between the perspective of the omniscient narrator and that of the villagers, individually and collectively. When Father Gonzaga enters, for example, he reveals his suspicions about the old man, his observations about him, his sermon to the assembly of villagers, and his promise to seek advice from higher authorities. A few pages later, there appears a synopsis of his correspondence to the pope about the old man, and after another few pages, the waning of the old man's popularity seemingly cures Father Gonzaga of his insomnia. Then the old man disappears from the narrative altogether.

The full history of the carnival woman who was transformed into a spider for disobeying her parents constitutes another episode and provides a similar distraction, as does the imaginative excesses of the ailments suffered by those who seek the old man's help and the cures he provides: A blind man remains blind but grows three new teeth; a leper has sores that sprout sunflowers; a paralytic does not recover the use of his limbs but almost wins the lottery. Such details call attention to themselves, rather than to their cause. Thus, the episodic structure and narrative commentary within the story combine purposefully to distract the reader from the old man, thereby making rational interpretations of his arrival and departure impossible.

The reader of the story occupies a position superior to that of its characters, who view odd persons as clowns and believe that their neighbors possess supernatural powers. This sense of superiority is important to the story's humor, but it is only a minor aspect of the reader's total response. More significant is the reader's attitude regarding the role of interpretation and invention. The reader appreciates invention in itself and learns to accept its privileged position in the story. The diversions from the main story line give invention precedence over action or closure. The reader approaches interpretation cautiously, as attributing symbolic values to either the old man or his mysterious disappearance will merely be acts of pointless interpretation. Thus, the Magical Realism of García Márquez's style—a blurring of the division between the real and the fantastic—is used to underscore the notion (indeed, the seeming contradiction) that the irrational is a natural part of life and must be accepted on its own terms.

Genevieve Slomski

THE VERY THING THAT HAPPENS

Author: Russell Edson (1935-)
Type of plot: Fable
Time of plot: Anytime
Locale: A farmhouse
First published: 1960

Principal characters:
Father, a farmer
Mother, his wife

The Story

This skewed and brief fable begins with a man, father, galloping into the kitchen of his house on an imaginary white horse. He is beating himself with a horse whip and screaming joyfully at his wife to look at what he has done: He has invented for himself a new head that is a horse's head, he roars. His wife, mother, acknowledges that he has indeed done something, but that she is not at all pleased with whatever that something might be. Father goes on to explain with delight that this new horse's head that he has created is a heroic head. It has taken the place of his intrinsic head—the man-head with which he was born—which is now in his left buttock. The inversion of the usual man/animal hierarchy is here apparent: Father's posterior seems a natural location for his man-head, as the horse's head is clearly more majestic. Also, now that father has two heads, he is compelled to repeat every phrase as though two separate mouths were speaking. Rather than serving to reinforce what he is saying, however, this repetitiveness serves only further to confuse and muddle his already muddled attempts at communicating to his wife the essential importance of his deed. In frustration mother finally yells, "Why is what is what?" Father replies in apparent justification—though in a detached manner, as if his head were not a part of himself—that his head had simply to think of a horse and it became one. That, he says, would seem to be the only explanation of how such things happen. This implication of existential ambiguity and randomness does not sit well with mother as she grows increasingly agitated. To her frenzied cries of why this has happened at all, father ends the story with the rejoinder, "Because of all things that might have happened this is the very thing that happens."

Themes and Meanings

This half-page-long story was also published as part of Russell Edson's collection *The Very Thing That Happens: Fables and Drawings* (1964). The themes that the story presents are much clearer when taken in context of the whole collection. As is evident from the above synopsis of his tale, Edson is not a fabulist in the traditional sense. His prose poems, as they are sometimes called (a description that he claims to abhor), do feature animals prominently, and they do attempt to convey some sort of lesson. It would be an exaggeration, however, to call them moral messages, as they define an amoral world that is more threatening, dehumanizing, and misanthropic than the world described in Aesop's classic fables. Instead, Edson uses the experiences of animals and objects to parallel human events as he performs a sort of ontological probing into the nature of this thing called life. Edson's primary themes here are the unstable arbitrariness of existence and the inanity of endless human attempts to make sense of it, order it, and control it.

Edson's universe may be irrational, but it is not without meaning. While poking fun at humankind's sense of superiority and the need to believe in some semblance of control, Edson also pities this human condition, and in fact justifies it. After all, without this sense of arbitrariness, there would be no process of logic. That is to say, if everything were cut and dried, orderly and sensible, there would be no need to figure things out, to draw distinctions and conclusions, or to find a niche for oneself in the universe. Self-exploration would go no further than mindless faith.

It is ironic that the search for meaning in life is what is assumed to set human beings apart from other animals. Yet it is through this search that human beings are struck by the loneliness, isolation, and meaninglessness of existence and experience such great angst that they ultimately are rendered indecisive, unadventurous, and hopeless. By conflating or interchanging father's head with the horse's head, Edson is suggesting that the typically pejorative "horse sense" is not in fact so senseless. Once humanity has embarked on its journey for wisdom and truth, through whatever ontological means, perhaps it should accept its inability to know the truth, or if that truth even exists. By accepting that its perspective cannot go beyond the arbitrary, random, and chaotic, humanity becomes free to go where its instincts and perceptions lead it—to do what it does and get on with it—like the story's horse. The human system for knowledge need not be forsaken in order to accept, and does not preclude a simultaneous realization, that any system for knowing will never fully explain the nature and workings of the universe. Things do happen. Father thinks of a horse's head and he becomes one. There comes a time for acceptance and surrender, which is necessary to struggle through the inherent search for self and meaning in life. This acceptance allows father to break out of the frozen stasis of waking, eating, and sleeping which is his function as a human.

By blurring the distinctions between man and horse, head and ass, heroic and banal, Edson manages to obviate hierarchy. Good and bad become meaningless. The playing field is leveled, and all things—both animate and inanimate—share equal weight. Importance or unimportance thus becomes a matter of perspective. In Edson's world, everything is contingent on the reference frame, or one's visual scale. Everything is part of the same reality in a skewed platonic sense. All things are shadows of images of shadows endlessly, so far removed from the absolute that it scarcely matters if the absolute even exists. Human beings are confined by their perspective and their unwillingness to stray beyond the fragile boundaries of their own psyches. This notion explains in part the animal motif, especially that of barnyard animals, in Edson's work: It offers another perspective. People tend to think of such animals as confined, as one-dimensional, and as extensions of themselves to be used as tools toward human ends. The point is that all things—people, animals, and objects—are part of the same fabric, which weaves the disparate threads of freewill, fate, and chance. It is how humans modulate these strands that determines their reality and whether their particular confined perspectives are a comfort or a curse. In this story father pushes against the false boundaries of reality and finds comfort in accepting that although unexplainable things happen, his perspective is limited only by his imagination.

Style and Technique

In Edson's surreal world, not only is the seemingly impossible possible—it literally Is. The matter-of-fact, casual tone that he employs to convey a wildly outrageous reality underscores this notion. His stories are brief snapshots of moments that are absurd, perverse, capricious, horribly grotesque, and frequently hilarious. His tightly packed stories are nutshell commentaries on the human condition, which he treats in a detached, oblique, and austere manner. His syntax is dry and elegant, and rhythmically his work has the poetic effects of fine verse. By combining quaint rhythms and subjects with grotesque images and horrible madness, he creates an imaginary world that is almost silly.

The impetuses in Edson's stories are narrative and dramatic, rather than descriptive. Description is too static as a technique to hold up against the constantly changing realities than his tales convey. His stories bleed energy, and all things are alive. Images jump off the page, changing and intertwining in a fictive realm where a character need merely entertain a possibility, and his head becomes that of a horse. Edson engages the reader, relying on the reader's ability and willingness to suspend disbelief and allow for all possibilities, no matter how great the absurdity.

Edson writes short prose pieces that blur the borders of a grossly general reality. He says his work is "always in search of itself, in a form that is always building itself from the inside out," as though the author is consumed by the story as an entity larger than himself. His is a form that discovers itself and constantly recreates itself through the act of writing.

Edson's style is experimental; his imagination revolutionary. He combines all the fantasy of Lewis Carroll's *Alice In Wonderland* (1864) with the ribald psychedelic meanderings of Hunter S. Thompson's *Fear and Loathing in Las Vegas* (1972). The resulting brew is a new genre of zany fiction that explores fundamental human anxieties.

Leslie Maile Pendleton

VICTORY OVER JAPAN

Author: Ellen Gilchrist (1935-)
Type of plot: Domestic realism
Time of plot: Mid-1945
Locale: Seymour, Indiana
First published: 1984

Principal characters:
RHODA MANNING, the narrator, who recalls a moment when she was in the third grade
HER MOTHER
BILLY MONDAY, her third-grade classmate, a rabies victim

The Story

When the story opens, Rhoda is enthralled with imagining particulars about Billy Monday's "tragedy": He is to have "fourteen shots in the stomach as the result of a squirrel bite." With ghoulish awe, Rhoda describes the ritual of the school principal and Billy's mother coming to get him everyday when it is time for his shot. Using the pronoun "we," she speaks for the whole class in her descriptions. She and her best friend Letitia joke with each other with how they themselves would react to such a situation. By contrast, Billy Monday sits on a bench by the swings not talking to anybody. He is a small, pallid boy whom everyone ignored until he was bitten.

Although Rhoda is disgusted by the fact that Billy can barely read and that his head falls on the side of his neck when he is asked to do so, she is also fascinated by him. Rhoda is the only third grader to have had an article published in the elementary school paper, and she determines to interview Billy for another article. Her first efforts at this during a noon recess cause Billy to withdraw into the shape of a human ball. Mrs. Jansma comes over to comfort him, sending Rhoda off to clean the chalkboards.

Meanwhile the school is gearing up for another paper drive to help the war effort. Rhoda jumps to her feet to be the first volunteer and to claim Billy Monday as her paper-drive partner. At home, Rhoda's mother rewards her for volunteering to be Billy's partner by baking her cookies. Rhoda feels pleased, and goes outside to sit in her treehouse with cookies and a book. As she daydreams about becoming like her mother, it becomes clear how much she wants and needs her mother's approval, especially with her father off fighting in the war. Her mother has been painting liquid hose on her legs, getting ready for a visit from the Episcopalian minister, and Rhoda thinks about what an unselfish person her mother is. Later she overhears the adults talking about her approvingly, in intimate tones. Rhoda smugly returns to her book with a fresh supply of cookies, and loses herself in the dialogue of a romance meant for adult readers.

On the Saturday of the paper drive, there is a slight drizzle, and Mr. Harmon, the school principal—who was shell-shocked in World War I—gives the children assembled on the school playground a patriotic pep talk. The third grade class is leading the drive by seventy-eight pounds.

As Rhoda and Billy begin pulling a red wagon into the neighborhood assigned to them, Rhoda interviews Billy for the article she plans to write. Billy gives her a few unsensational answers and she continues to make herself the heroine by pulling the wagon and going up to the doors by herself. They are so successful that Mrs. Jansma later says "she'd never seen anyone as lucky on a paper drive" as Billy and Rhoda. They all decide to make one more trip.

As it gets dark, Rhoda and Billy decide to try a brick house that looks to Rhoda like a place where old people live; she thinks that old people are the ones with the most newspapers. This time she urges Billy to go to the door with her because she is tired of doing it herself. A thin man about Rhoda's father's age answers the door. This time Billy asks the man for papers; it is the first time that he has spoken to anyone but Rhoda all day. They follow the man through the musty house to the basement stairs, where he says they can have all the papers that they can carry. The children feel lucky when they find a large stack of magazines. Excited about winning the competition, Rhoda eagerly goes up and down the stairs filling the wagon. When she returns, Billy beckons her to look at what is inside one of the magazines: nude photographs of young children. They leave the house immediately, not closing doors or stopping to say thank you. Outside they discover that all the magazines from this house are of the same kind. After throwing them away, they part company and Rhoda tries to comfort Billy by saying that at least he will have something new to think about when he gets his shot the next day. Then she twice urges him not to tell anybody. Uncharacteristically, he keeps his head raised and looks straight at her when he says that he will not. He also asks if she will really be writing about him in the paper.

On the way home, Rhoda struggles with the images left in her mind by the photos and picks irises in an effort to please her mother. She writes her article about Billy, and it appears in the school paper. But she never does get around to telling her mother about the magazines.

One day in August Rhoda is walking home from the swimming pool, and the man who gave her and Billy the magazines drives by and looks right into her face. She drops everything and runs home, scared and determined to tell her mother. When she gets home, however, her mother, brother, and several guests, including the minister, are crowded around the radio listening to the news. Her mother tells her to be quiet because they are trying to determine whether the United States has won the war. As they listen to news of the dropping of the biggest bomb in history on Japan, no one pays attention to Rhoda. She goes upstairs to think things over, feeling ambivalent about the war ending because it will mean the return of her father. Wrapped in her comforter, she falls into a nightmarish reverie in which she sits behind the wheel of an airplane carrying the bomb to Japan, but first dropping one on the bad man's brick house.

Themes and Meanings

The violent inevitability of both natural and social processes colliding with childhood innocence is a predominant theme in this story. The strongest treatments of this are suggested by the brutal rabies antidote that Billy must undergo, and the atom bomb itself. Although precocious Rhoda aspires to be more sophisticated than her years, her innocence is evidenced by the very romanticism with which she attempts to protect herself from the world.

The ironic source of both Rhoda's fantasies and real problems is her desire to gain status with others. The fanatical need to live for and justify larger-than-life purposes, though made somewhat comic in Rhoda's character, is also tragic when it is measured against the larger backdrop of the logic that allowed the United States to end the war by using bombs that brought with them the knowledge that humankind is capable of destroying the planet.

Through Rhoda, the story emphasizes the human tendency to feed and live off drama and suffering, whether big or small, in order to make one's own life seem more important. At the same time, it shows how Rhoda herself is victimized by such a tendency, which she has only learned from the adults around her.

Style and Technique

Ellen Gilchrist's powerful and effective use of Rhoda as a first-person narrator helps to bring out these themes without making them hackneyed or didactic. Readers can perceive the hypocrisy in Rhoda's brand of romantic idealism, but she cannot—which makes her delivery of it that much more effective. Gilchrist effectively combines character development with narrative tone that makes the telling of the story inseparable from understanding Rhoda as a character. Although she lives for such drama, the irony is beautifully rendered as her own shock at the magazines overtakes her love of the sensational, and finally, although perhaps it has affected her more profoundly than Billy's rabies shots ever did or will, she does not disclose it in the same way at all. In fact, the narrative technique is one in which the disclosure is ironic. It is revealed by virtue of the fact it was never something she could figure out how to tell her mother, unlike the other things with which she rushed home in the hope of gaining approval.

There are also images in the story emphasizing the titillating sexual disclosure more blatantly exposed in the magazines: a glimpse of underpants from the monkeybars, the liquid hose that Rhoda's mother paints on her legs, a bathing suit and towel thrown down on the sidewalk. Juxtaposed with these images of vulnerability is the rhetoric of combat used to fuel both the paper drive and Rhoda's ambitions and fears. The rabies shot and the bomb are the core images around which this juxtaposition takes place.

Maria Theresa Maggi

THE VISITOR

Author: Russell Banks (1940-)
Type of plot: Psychological realism
Time of plot: 1986 and 1952
Locale: Tobyhanna, Pennsylvania
First published: 1988

Principal characters:
THE NARRATOR, a forty-six-year-old man
HIS FATHER
HIS MOTHER
GEORGE RETTSTADT, a restaurateur

The Story

"The Visitor" is an account of how a man's past has shaped his present. As the story begins, the anonymous narrator tells of his recent trip from his home in New York City to East Stroudsburg University in Pennsylvania to deliver a lecture. The university is a short distance from Tobyhanna, where he lived as a boy; on an impulse, he drives the extra miles to visit the town.

Paragraphs about the narrator's childhood in Tobyhanna—his parents and their rage, a visit to the local bar, and the home in which his family lived—are interwoven with paragraphs about his more recent past—his adult visit to the town—both narrated from his mature perspective. The year that the narrator and his family lived in Tobyhanna was a time of frustration for his parents. His father drank heavily, womanized, and lied to his wife about how he spent his evenings. As the father's drinking increased and he spent more time away from home, he became increasingly violent. The narrator's mother was stuck with three small children in a country house five miles from town.

As the adult narrator arrives in Tobyhanna, he pulls up to the bar on the main street and goes inside. The smell, look, dampness, and dirty feel of the place are so unchanged that reentering it makes the narrator recall a visit that he, his father, and his brother made there thirty-four years earlier. This bit of memory is the beginning of a longer one about a specific Saturday during one winter; throughout the remainder of the story the remembering and telling about that visit parallels the events and details of the narrator's recent visit. The locals gathered in the bar in 1986 remind him of those present on that distant Saturday—his father and his cronies and a woman with red lipstick to whom his father gave his complete attention.

The bartender asks the adult narrator if he wants another beer; this abruptly pulls the story forward into the more recent past. The narrator declines and leaves. When he is back in his car, his story again goes back in time, and he is a young boy riding home from the bar with his father and brother. His father invents an alibi to explain their long absence to his wife and gets his son (the narrator) to support his story when his mother questions them. The father knows that of the two sons, he is the one whom his mother will question.

Approaching the same house thirty-four years later, the narrator notices that aside from its color, it is unchanged. A sign identifies the house as Rettstadt's Restaurant. Now he recalls facing the door that opened into the kitchen when he was a child. He feels weak, his heart beats hard and fast. He is going back into memory, into the past, into darkness.

On that winter Saturday those many years ago when the narrator, his father, and his brother arrive home, it is snowing, and his mother is in the kitchen. His father delivers his story: His car got stuck in the snow, and he had to do some work at the depot. Mother knows that he is lying; his threadbare excuse demands that she challenge his story. She rejects the lie, telling him that she can smell the bar and another woman on his clothes. They argue; their shouts grow louder and more pained.

Slipping from this painful memory but still on its scent, the adult narrator describes the house as he sees it in 1986—the changes made to convert it to a restaurant. A man scrubbing cooking utensils looks up, sees his visitor, and introduces himself as George Rettstadt. The narrator tells him that he used to live in the house. Rettstadt focuses his gaze and pronounces the narrator's last name; he mistakes the narrator for his father.

During a brief tour of the house, the narrator sees it as it was and steps deeper into the cave of memory of that long-ago Saturday. He remembers fleeing the kitchen, going upstairs to his bedroom, lying on his bed, his mother bursting into the room to demand the truth from him. She screams at him to admit what she already knows: that they went to the bar and that there was a woman there. The boy nods his head in assent.

The narrator declines Rettstadt's invitation to see the upstairs; instead he goes outside to look around the yard. He walks to the back of the house to stand beneath the window of his old bedroom. Thrown again into the distant past, he hears the sound of his father's steps on the stairs. The child knows what is about to happen, knows the depth of his father's rage and violence. Remembering the beating that he received from his father that day ends both this memory and his visit to the house.

From the ground below the bedroom window, the narrator leaves for the university, where he delivers his lecture to a small group of teachers and students and then dines with them at a local restaurant. Afterward he drives home to New York.

Themes and Meanings

The meaning of "The Visitor"—the problem that Russell Banks explores in this story—is expressed in its title; however, violence is an integral component of the ideas of a visitor and of visiting. While the story tells of a profound experience of one man revisiting a place and moment from his past, the narrator explicitly states that it is violence that makes his visit possible and necessary and that it is violence that makes the man a "visitor."

It is telling that the adult cannot re-create the details of his beating by his father in the same representative, clear prose that he uses to describe the incidents that preceded the beating—the bar, the drive home, and the escalating argument between his parents. Instead, his account of his father's violence against him is told with distanced language and an analytical objectivity. He does not explicitly state that his father hit him in the head, slammed him in the ribs, or threw him to the floor; rather, he says: "When you are hit in the head or slammed . . . or thrown . . . by a powerful man."

Compounding this distance, while at the same time providing a rationale for the story, is the narrator's analysis and theory of violence: that it produces "white light and heat inside the head"—an "extraordinary immolation . . . worth any price." An act of violence demands perpetuation and visitation, so that the boy who is beaten will become a man who beats, so that the boy who is beaten will become a man compelled to return to the scenes of his violence, whether he was beaten or he beat someone else there. Violence locks one into the past, into itself. It has made this man a constant visitor of places and of memories.

The necessity of anyone's return visits and participation in the perpetuation of violence is expressed in significant ways. Just as the narrator's mother felt compelled to challenge her husband rather than accept his lie, so too the adult narrator is compelled to perform violence. Banks calls violence a "narrative whose primary function is to provide reversal," so that a weak, victimized boy becomes a strong, violent man.

Illustrating the necessity of the visit, the settings in which the narrator finds himself are more powerful than he, drawing him paradoxically forward into his past. He is compelled; images plunge him into the past, into memory; light and smell affect his body, which seems to know the past and the memory before his mind does. The narrator emphatically insists on this necessity, saying to the reader, "Listen to me: you are locked into that narrative, and no other terms . . . are available."

Style and Technique

Giving the story a provocative dimension is Banks's use of images and metaphors that double. Just as the distant past of the narrator's childhood echoes his recent visit to Tobyhanna, there are several other instances that reinforce this mirroring quality. In the downtown bar the narrator orders a beer from a woman whose "double—her twin" sits on a barstool. Later he refers to this as a "doubling image" that replicates, "doubling the place itself with" memory.

As he drives up to the farmhouse, the narrator notices two stone chimneys that are "matched" by a pair of maple trees, all of this suggesting doubleness and symmetry. The child narrator and his brother share a room with a pair of windows and twin beds—the twin beds perhaps suggesting that the brother, too, was a victim of the father's violence.

More to the point, however, is the incident in which the narrator is mistaken for his father. When Rettstadt first sees him, he calls him by his father's name, and the narrator equates himself with his father, writing that he was "more likely my father than my father's son." All of this enriches the point of the story, that violence repeats itself and that because of violence the past and present must visit each other.

Julie Thompson

THE WAIT

Author: Rick Bass (1958-　　)
Type of plot: Domestic realism
Time of plot: Unspecified
Locale: Houston and Galveston Bay, Texas
First published: 1990

Principal characters:
THE NARRATOR, a bachelor
KIRBY, his best friend, a real estate appraiser
JACK, Kirby's friend, a dentist

The Story

The unnamed narrator's girlfriend, Marge, has recently left him, so he goes from Montana to east Texas to fish with his friend Kirby and Kirby's friend Jack. As they drive through downtown Houston in the early morning rain, the narrator sees the buildings as "like tall jails . . . the shutdown of a life." Depressed, he feels unable to measure up to the Texas myth that "the world can be tamed—it's a bull that can be wrestled, and with strength and courage and energy you can lift that bull over your head and spin it around and throw it to the ground." Moreover, because he is unready to take on the responsibilities of being a husband and father, he feels like an imposter, trying to live a "strong" life, "fast and free, scorning weakness." Both Jack and Kirby are married and have children, and the narrator envies them.

As they drive, they hear animal noises in a box in the back of Jack's jeep. When Jack tells them it is a coyote, the others assume that he is joking. Later, they launch a boat in Galveston Bay and notice a billboard showing a beautiful, smiling woman named Renee Jackson who is missing; the narrator finds himself on the verge of tears, presumably because he associates her with his own missing girlfriend. This time Marge has left him not for the usual reasons, but because she was tired; the narrator admits to himself that he does sometimes get really wild. Jack tells the narrator it is all right to cry over the missing woman and recalls how Kirby cried over a large pregnant redfish that they caught the previous year that died despite their efforts to release it alive. The narrator thinks that he will be ready to settle down someday and be a good husband and father, and "the wait will make it nicer," as he thinks about the missing Renee, who he hopes will return and make her parents all the happier after having waited for her.

The men's fishing is successful and even the stormy weather, which charges the sky all around them, never hits them. The only threats to their pleasure are the "popdicks," other fishermen who crowd them when they find a good spot. The narrator himself never catches a fish; when his friends fail in their efforts to help him, he concludes that "like most things, it's just something that I am going to have to work out by myself."

As the men drift back toward shore, they discuss sex, but the narrator feels uneasy about it. When Jack describes his wife as a "hellcat in bed," the narrator is relieved that Kirby does not talk about his own wife. As they near the billboard again, Jack says that he thinks they found Renee's skeleton the previous spring. This observation and the lateness of the hour make the narrator feel overwhelmingly lonely and tired.

The story ends when Jack stops the jeep and releases a coyote, which he caught in his backyard. Despite being cooped up for hours, the coyote heads north (the direction from which the narrator has come); it runs "without looking back, as if it knows exactly where it is going." The narrator sees the freed animal as "the most beautiful thing."

Themes and Meanings

Although the narrator says he thinks he and his girlfriend will get back together "because we have been together far too long *not* to come back together," he has little confidence in his own prediction because this time "it was a little different." His response is to get out of the house. Although his wildness has in the past necessitated escaping from domesticity, which may be associated here with the feminine (Marge goes back home to Virginia, a state that is symbolically feminine), the narrator has a desire for home and family, and the domesticity of his two fishing buddies is attractive to him.

In the course of the story one senses that male companionship is not sufficient. Part of what makes Jack and Kirby best friends, the narrator realizes, is that their wives are also each other's best friends. None of the feminine figures alluded to in the story are actually present, but their absence prompts desire; they include Marge, Kirby's and Jack's wives (Tricia, who has made lunches for them, and Wendy), the missing Renee Jackson, the pregnant redfish, Kirby's seven-month-old daughter (also named Kirby, which suggests a close father-daughter relationship), and Jack's dental assistant (whose "bosoms" Kirby claims he can see when she leans over the dentist's chair). Even one of the strawberry-colored artificial shrimp that they are using as bait looks "like a woman coming out of her slip." Near the end of the story the narrator describes the sky as "a lurid black, a horrible purple, like the bruise on the inside of a woman's thigh." One might question, at this point, how "wild" the narrator has been with Marge. He has never been married, and he sees himself as being even less ready to be a husband than to be a father. Perhaps his weeping over the missing Renee is not so much a display of his compassion and sensitivity as an expression of guilt.

The men in this story are generally associated with a sort of bestial wildness. The narrator associates himself with bulldogging; when he runs off into the mountains in Montana, he sees himself as lying in the sun "like a dog." Kirby tells Jack that he has dreamed that his friend was "a raccoon, banging around in the garbage." Jack, who is associated with the coyote, describes his wife as a "hellcat." Jack's seventy-nine-year-old father is mentioned at one point as ranting, raving, and "howling" when his son had engine troubles with a boat. The shameless "popdicks" who invade the men's fishing spot come from a "black squall line, savage thunderstorms, wicked cold streaks of lightning."

In short, the men in this story appear to be so concerned with not looking like "sissy-pants" shore fishermen that they risk "the shutdown of a life." Early in the story the narrator says that he feels "like an outlaw, an alien" because the two men riding in the front of the jeep are husbands and fathers. When Jack takes over the throttle of the boat, the narrator sees that he, too, has become an outlaw, but a happy one, and then he recognizes that "the longer you go without something, the happier you are when you finally get it." This truism applies to the coyote at the end of the story and may eventually hold true for the narrator as well.

Style and Technique

"The Wait" does not appear among the ten stories that make up Rick Bass's first collection, *The Watch* (1990), but it has much in common with its stories. (Kirby and Tricia, in fact, appear in three stories in that book.) Like many of them, it shares what has been called the "minimalist" style. In an article in *Harper's Magazine* (April, 1986), Madison Bell lists as characteristics of minimalism a trim or closely cropped style (which applies especially to sentence structure), concern for surface details (as opposed to elaborate or lush description), a tendency to ignore nuances in character portrayal, and "a studiedly deterministic, at times nihilistic, vision of the world." Bell does not admire the minimalist trend, which can be traced back to Ernest Hemingway, and perhaps even to Anton Chekhov, and which finds adherents in such writers as Raymond Carver, Ann Beattie, and Richard Ford. Nevertheless, this kind of spare realism has become an important mode in American fiction, and it offers an option to the fantasy and Magical Realism that have become especially popular in postmodernist and Latin American fiction.

Most of Bass's stories fit the definition of minimalism fairly well. One never sees a character vividly in his stories; one rarely knows how a character looks—in contrast to character descriptions in Charles Dickens, for example. There is a flatness to the picture's finish. For some readers, however, such surfaces are superior to one that might be described as "busy" and overwrought. Certainly, though, this story is neither nihilistic nor deterministic. As in many Chekhov stories, its ending is not absolutely resolved; the door remains open. For many readers, the open ending, the rejection of the pat conclusion, is preferable because it is more lifelike.

Ron McFarland

THE WALK

Author: José Donoso (1924-   )
Type of plot: Psychological realism
Time of plot: The 1950's
Locale: A South American city
First published: "Paseo," 1959 (English translation, 1968)

Principal characters:
THE NARRATOR, an adult recalling his childhood
MATILDE, his aunt
PEDRO, his father
GUSTAVO and
ARMANDO, his uncles
A MONGREL WHITE DOG, Matilde's pet and companion

The Story

Many years after the events related in the story, the narrator passes by the house in which he grew up and attempts to reconstruct the circumstances that led to the mysterious disappearance of his aunt Matilde. As a child, he lived in a home that included his widowed father, his unmarried aunt Matilde, and two bachelor uncles, Gustavo and Armando.

Aunt Matilde originally moved into the house in order to take care of the narrator after his mother passed away when he was four years old, but once she settled in, most of her attention went to caring for her own three brothers. Managing the household with a firm and steady hand, Matilde re-created the household in her own image—with more order than warmth, and more impersonal efficiency than human affection.

Surprisingly, one day Matilde took in a stray white dog, which she had found on a street after it was hit by a car. In her devotion to nursing the injured dog back to health, Matilde began to neglect her regular household duties and routines. Gradually the mongrel bitch replaced the brothers as her principal companion. When she stopped joining her brothers for a game of pool every evening in order to take the dog for a walk, it was clear that the life of the family was no longer the same.

This change put Matilde's brothers in the same situation as the narrator, who had always been neglected by his aunt. It was not in the brothers' nature to say anything to Aunt Matilde about the disruptive impact of her relationship with the dog. As the narrator remarks, it became "more important than ever not to see, not to see anything at all, not to comment, not to consider oneself alluded to by these events." Thus, instead of voicing their concerns, they tried to ignore the changes in their lives. As the dog became not just Matilde's companion but her "accomplice," Matilde's walks got longer and longer, and she often came home dirty and disheveled. Finally, one day she went out for a walk and did not return. Although the brothers tried to discover her whereabouts, they had no success. Nevertheless, as the narrator states, "Life went on as if Matilde were still living with us."

Themes and Meanings

A principal theme in this story, as in several José Donoso novels, is the complicated relation between order and chaos, between rationality and irrationality. Before the appearance of the mongrel bitch, the narrator's household was a perfectly ordered world in which nothing was left to chance, with no room for anything new or unexpected. At several points in the story, the witness-narrator compares his childhood home to a closed book. This comparison highlights the closure and confinement that characterize his family's life.

Once the mongrel bitch appeared, however, that "world of security" that Aunt Matilde and her brothers had so carefully constructed began to fall apart. Coming from the streets, the dog represents a worldliness that began to crack open the "closed book" of the house. The dog brought into the house the element of chance—she was a foreign body, an agent of worldliness that shattered the sanitized peace and security of the family. One evening, when the dog urinated on the floor of the room in which Matilde and her brothers gathered after dinner to play billiards, the three brothers got upset and retreated to their bedrooms. Although nobody said anything about the incident, it was clear that the family's life was no longer what it had been.

In order to dramatize the destruction of the household's order, the author insinuates parallels between events in this story and the biblical story of the Fall. For example, the narrator compares his childhood house not only to a closed book but to a "heaven," an artificial paradise shut off from the dangers of the outside world—a world that he knew only through the lights and foghorns of ships in the nearby harbor. Then, much as the serpent entered Eden and seduced Eve, the dog strayed into the house and won Matilde's affection, changing the family's life beyond repair.

The reader may well wonder, however, whether what happens in the story constitutes a fall or a redemption, as the dog's intrusion into Matilde's life also had salutary consequences. Although the rigid routines of the household kept everything in order, they also stifled feelings. As the narrator remarks about the older members of his family: "With them, love existed confined inside each individual, never breaking its boundaries to express itself and bring them together. For them to show affection was to discharge their duties to each other perfectly, and above all not to inconvenience, never to inconvenience." The other side of order, the author seems to say, is sterility. If the house is a paradise, it is also a stifling, airless one, into which the vitality of the real world cannot penetrate.

When Matilde undertook to nurse the dog back to health, she broke the house rules—choosing an elective pastime over duty, thereby inconveniencing her brothers—but she was also getting in touch with a side of her that had not expressed itself before. In caring for the dog, she displayed a warmth and tenderness that she had never shown in her dealings with members of her own family. Paradoxically, the mongrel bitch brought out Matilde's humanity in a way that her brothers and nephew never did. When Matilde abandoned the house, she may have been choosing a more vital, if less tidy, existence. The stray dog thus may not have been Matilde's temptress but her redeemer.

A related theme of the story is the fragility of excessive order. When people try to impose too rigid an order in their lives, they make themselves more vulnerable to the intrusion of disorder. If the narrator's house had been less of a closed book, the outside world would not have subverted it so easily. If Matilde had had other outlets for her human feelings, perhaps she would not have become so strongly fixated on the dog. In addition, it is clear that because they always led such sheltered lives, Matilde's brothers were not prepared to deal with the crisis precipitated by the intrusion of the dog and her subsequent disappearance. Instead of taking effective action, all they did was retreat behind the massive door of their study and discuss what had happened.

Style and Technique

As one might expect from a writer whose favorite author is the American novelist Henry James, the handling of point of view is crucial to the overall significance of José Donoso's story. His narrator's perspective on the events is affected not only by the circumstance of his reconstructing the story many years after it happened, but also by the fact that he was only a child at the time of his aunt's disappearance and thus not privy to the conversations among the adults. As sometimes happens in James's novels, Donoso's narrator has only a partial and limited access to the story he wants to tell. Indeed, much of what he reveals hc did not personally witness but only overheard by standing outside the closed door of the library, where his uncles gathered to discuss Aunt Matilde's disappearance.

For this reason, the narrator's account contains guesswork and speculation. The central mystery of Matilde's disappearance thus remains unresolved. Not only was she never heard from again, but the narrator can never learn precisely why she left. Alternatively, he may know why she left but—like his father and uncles—is incapable of coming to terms with the real reasons for her disappearance. It is significant that the first word of his account refers to her disappearance only as *Esto*, "It"—a vague, imprecise designation that may betray his difficulties with coming to grips with the disappearance of his aunt. By the end of the story, he is no closer to the truth. Appropriately, the story ends not with an explanation of the mystery, but with a confession of uncertainty: "The door of the library was too thick, too heavy, and I never knew if Aunt Matilde, dragged along by the white dog, had got lost in the city, or in death, or in a region more mysterious than either."

Although in one respect the narrator's function is to open the "closed book" of his family's life and discuss publicly the story of his aunt's disappearance, in another respect he cannot—or will not—disclose much: He opens the book only to shut it again, leaving the reader in the dark about the causes and results of Aunt Matilde's last "walk."

Gustavo Pérez Firmat

WALTZ OF THE FAT MAN

Author: Alberto Alvaro Ríos (1952-)
Type of plot: Fable
Time of plot: Unspecified
Locale: Unspecified
First published: 1991

Principal character:
NOÉ, an overweight butcher

The Story

Noé is a middle-aged man who pays precise attention to the details of his appearance—his trim mustache and creased clothing—and the details of his house, which has blue trim and a blue door that will stand against spirits. Noé's existence, however, is one of utter loneliness, with a complete lack of social and emotional contact with other human beings. His profession as a butcher brings him sadness, even though he chose this profession in an effort to do good things. Noé considers that the townspeople's polite disregard of him might be because he is overweight, but he does not think of himself as fat. He considers his body as a heaviness that has come from the inside out. He attends wakes in the town simply for the opportunity for human contact, but he receives only obligatory common courtesy from others. He simply wishes to be part of the town.

To find a release from his loneliness, Noé dresses in a blue suit and dances outside of the town. Noé dances with the faceless wind and encircles his arms around the branches of black walnut trees; the trees are as unyielding as women's arms, but they at least cannot leave to gossip about him. He feels free to let out his "thin girl"—a partner who will not ignore him. Together, they dance the dance of weddings through the night.

In an attempt to become more of a regular man and be in the mainstream of human relations, Noé begins to wear his blue suit to his butcher shop. He also devises a small plan to shake the hands of women vigorously in order to see some movement of their bodies—some indication that he is recognized as another human being. By attending wakes, he can kiss the cheeks of the bereaved, but even this clumsy attempt often meets with failure.

As a further antidote to his unwanted loneliness, Noé begins to collect clocks, even hanging them on his butcher shop walls. He collects the clocks because they have hands, "and in so many clocks was a kind of heaven, a dream of sounds to make the hours pass in a manner that would allow him to open up shop the next day." He perceives of them as women—giving them women's names—and imagines that they are beckoning and speaking to him. Despite the townspeople's objections to this strange behavior, Noé is left alone. One winter evening, however, Noé hears the blue clock, his favored "Marina," hesitate. He hurries to get to the clock that is calling to him as "a wife in pain." Even though he tells himself that Marina is only a clock, he is disconcerted, and after examining her, he wraps her up in butcher's paper like a piece of meat, an act that seems to bring him comfort.

As Noé quickly walks home in the darkness, cradling his precious Marina, he hears an oleander call to him as he passes by the stand of walnut trees where he has danced before. He hesitates as he hears his name called again, searches through the leaves, and then puts down the clock to investigate. It is a whispered voice that he recognizes, the voice of Marina, "who had made so many places for herself in his life. . . . She was the blueness inside him, the color of his appetite, the color both of what filled him and what he needed more of." The voice asks Noé if she loves him, and if so, to act like a horse. After hesitating, Noé obeys the voice, stamping and snorting, willing to do anything for Marina, the embodiment of his loneliness and desire. The laughter of soldiers hiding in the oleanders forces Noé to turn for home, without Marina, bereft of even this small comfort in his desolate existence.

The loss of Marina causes Noé to sell his butcher shop, buy a brown horse, and leave the town. He rides into the future, feeling that he has "become an exponent to a regular number." All he really wanted was to belong and for everyone and everything to be nice, for people to follow the Golden Rule of common courtesy and humanity. This, he now knows, is too much to ask. In the final section of the story, Noé meets up with a circus and feels as if he has finally found his real career with a "company of half-size men, two-bodied women, and all the rest of the animals who danced." Within this group of supposed misfits, Noé reaches a place where he is free to dance and free to be himself.

Themes and Meanings

Alberto Alvaro Ríos, a writer who has won many prestigious awards for his poetry and fiction, has said: "I was born on the border of Mexico to a Mexican father and an English mother. I write often about this background, especially the Mexican/Chicano aspects." In this story, however, the theme of loneliness transcends culture and gender to convey an archetypal portrait of an Everyperson who is at first immobilized by the abject alienation imposed upon him by others. The poignancy of the story is that Noé's desire is so seemingly simple: the need for involvement, both social and emotional, with other human beings. Because Noé is different, perhaps, overweight and viewed as suspect by others, he cannot belong in a "normal" small town. Instead, he must free himself by leaving and joining a circus peopled by beings who are viewed as equally strange, but in reality, are perhaps more humane than those considered normal in ordinary society.

Within Noé's large body, he carries characteristics that are both male and female, a fact that makes him even more identifiable as an Everyperson searching for a place to belong. This theme of androgyny can be found in Noé's dance with the wind and the trees when he is free to let his "thin girl" out, his hidden desire to socialize and make emotional contact with other human beings. Also, in two instances in the story, Noé feels as if he "were his own mother." With familial bonds absent in the story, Noé must embody this absent motherhood. In fact, Noé's large body of "slow bones" seems to encompass the desire of all humans—both male and female—to feel as if they belong.

Noé attempts to fit in by keeping a neat house trimmed in blue, wearing a blue suit to become a "regular man," and finding comfort in the hands of his numerous clocks—especially in his blue Marina. However, it seems as if this recurring blueness is a reflection of Noé's isolation; blueness does not bring him comfort or solace. Yet Noé does contain the capacity to free himself in the final section of the story when he reaches the circus people standing near the road. He realizes that they "called him without telegraph or telephone. Something stronger." Everyone, in his or her own way, is a misfit, and perhaps the ultimate satisfaction in human experience is the ability to connect emotionally with others. With the circus, finally, Noé achieves this.

Style and Technique

Ríos has said that his writing is often narrative, and he thinks of his books as "talking to each other." Furthermore, Ríos' multilingual experiences and work with translation have given him an astute appreciation for the richness and complexity of all languages. The seven short sections of this story clearly show his powers of lyricism. The language itself seems to waltz off the page, with each carefully crafted phrase contributing to fluid images. The language lends a strange beauty and complexity to the character of Noé, the fat man who is so much more than his outward appearance: the Everyperson who can succeed in a cold world.

This story also has a quality of Magical Realism; nothing is quite what it seems to be on the surface. Noé, an overweight butcher, encompasses both genders and the desire to be respected and loved. At the end of the story, he is beginning a transformation process when he catches up to the circus: "He arrived as a beast, almost, something crazed and unshaven, out of breath. Or as a beast on top of a man, as if the horse itself were more human, and asking for help." No longer confined within the parameters of what passes for "appropriate" or "courteous" behavior, Noé is released. After an existence that can only be defined by its loneliness, Noé has ridden to a new life where there is the promise of emotional bonding and the freedom to dance.

Laurie Lisa

THE WARRIOR PRINCESS OZIMBA

Author: Reynolds Price (1933-)
Type of plot: Sketch
Time of plot: A Fourth of July around 1955
Locale: Southern United States
First published: 1962

Principal characters:
AUNT ZIMBY, an aged African American woman, blind and almost deaf
VESTA, her daughter
MR. ED, the narrator

The Story

Events unfold slowly: Mr. Ed, a Southern white man, visits Aunt Zimby every Fourth of July—the date that she has designated as her birthday. His purpose is to give her a birthday present, a new pair of blue tennis shoes, although she has never played tennis and is now blind and cannot discern the color. He annually reenacts this tradition, following the example his father, who has been dead for two years.

Aunt Zimby, who was born around the time of the Civil War, has "belonged" to this family of whites through four generations, being passed down and along to them as a matter of duty, care, and heritage. In her blindness and old age, Aunt Zimby confuses Mr. Ed, the narrator, with Mr. Phil, his dead father. She sits on the front porch of the shanty, which will scarcely keep out a gentle rain, chews snuff, and reminisces about her overlong life. She retells one story from earlier years of a time when she herself was Mr. Phil's accomplice in eating mulberries against his parents' instructions. A second recollection is of a night when Mr. Phil went dancing with the white girls, and came home in the rain and mud, wearing only his underwear; he had to undress in order to protect his new clothes.

Lost in age and place, the ancient woman who survives only as a relic from the past asks when Mr. Phil will show up with her new shoes for a birthday present. Ed neither tries to explain that his father is dead nor even tries to answer her; rather, he sits silently with the new shoes in a state of contemplation and is transfigured and transposed to another time and existence. After Aunt Zimby falls asleep, Ed gives the shoes to Vesta, her daughter, and leaves, wiping tears from his eyes.

Themes and Meanings

Essentially a work of sentimentality for the South's heritage, Reynolds Price's story is at once a character sketch of a figure from the past as well as an intense expression of a contemporary Southerner coming to terms with his heritage and that past. "The Warrior Princess Ozimba" is a story in which the past meets the present, white meets black, father meets son, and youth meets age. Aunt Zimby, who is described as the "oldest thing any of us knew anything about," is one of the last surviving vestiges of the Old South. Mr. Ed, in contrast, is the modern white man replete with good intentions and symbolic gifts.

Aunt Zimby was named "Princess Warrior Ozimba" by Ed's great-grandfather, after a character in a book that he was reading during the Civil War era. After being freed, she and her own family remained connected to the narrator's family, as was the case with many slaves after their emancipation. She was then more or less handed down from generation unto generation, first as a slave, later as a servant and as an employee, and now as a relic—a kind of embodiment of an antique that does not die.

Ed, the central consciousness of the story, though not its central figure, is by all counts a good man who would not only honor family tradition, but try to do what is right by giving Aunt Zimby her due respect, as symbolized by the blue tennis shoes that he brings. He makes the annual trip out to her shanty, walking up the creek with respect, though perhaps not love, to discover that she somehow plays a role in defining his own existence. Though he evidently sees her only once each year, he enacts the family duty to her, even though she no longer even knows who he is.

Aunt Zimby has been a warrior against time itself. In her old age and confused mind, she cannot recognize that she is talking to Ed rather than his father. Somehow, the two men are intermingled, not because Aunt Zimby is mistaken, but because they are so much alike. Ed learns that he has become his father; something is thus accomplished as he comes to terms with his own identity and self-hood. It is his lot to replace his dead father; he succeeds in doing so by honoring Aunt Zimby in this yearly ritual with the tennis shoes. At first, this mixing up of characters is only a matter of confusion in Aunt Zimby's mind; but as Ed sits on the porch listening to her stories about his dead father (who, for Zimby, is not even dead), he realizes that he may as well be his father. Eventually, he realizes that for all intents and purposes he has become his father. Nothing is lost or gained in Zimby's mind and mistake. Similarly, nothing is lost or gained in Ed's new awareness that he is now his father in some sort of spiritual manner.

"The Warrior Princess Ozimba" resembles many Southern stories and novels that are dominated by characters who possess an intense longing for the past. Ed learns that he is product of that past, which is not yet dead and will not be dead even with the imminent passing of Aunt Zimby. He perceives and attains, through the character of the old black woman, a connection not only with his father, but with his grandfather and great-grandfather. His own being thus antedates the Civil War.

Similarly, revealed here is the meaningful relationship between the children of the white master and the "black mammy" figure. There is, perhaps, no racial equality depicted in this story, but there is shown interracial love and respect. For Zimby, the most important event of her life is the presentation of those tennis shoes, of value only because they prove she is remembered, honored, respected, and loved by her "white folks." For Ed, there is the fact that this woman has functioned as an archetypal Earth Mother figure for him and his forebears. Peace and love, though not equality, exist at least on some individualized basis and for these two characters.

Style and Technique

Like other Southern writers who followed William Faulkner, Reynolds Price has always tried to distance himself from the greatest of these so that his own works would not be seen merely as pale imitations of Faulkner's fiction. Nevertheless, in terms of subject matter, structural syntax, and literary sensitivity, Price's works are inescapably reminiscent of Faulkner's writing; such is especially the case with "The Warrior Princess Ozimba."

The main subject here is personality (what it means to be defined by the culture and heritage of the American South) and personhood. Although Price's technique may be independent of Faulkner's influence, it is a parallel to it. The story's confusion of the past with the present, its sentimentality for days and times gone past, its intense longing for a life that should have been but is no longer, all surface here as main elements holding this short story together. In *Intruder in the Dust* (1948), Faulkner wrote that "the past isn't gone, it isn't even passed"; remarkably and exactly, such is the case here with Aunt Zimby, a relic of the Civil War who has survived past the middle of the twentieth century.

The syntax of Price's writing also inevitably reminds one of Faulkner's own: Sentences perambulate, becoming successfully unwieldy with an occasional, out-of-place big word that momentarily throws the reader, but then is seen as appropriate, correct, and masterful. The story's first two paragraphs contain five different parenthetical thoughts and observations, all given in the manner of Faulkner; they provide insight and provoke thought. The dialogue of characters also echoes the sentimentality of the Old South rather in the same way as Faulkner would have rendered it.

These obvious and undeniable parallels to Faulkner's style do not distract from Price's own value as a writer about life, the human heart, and the South. Clearly, Price is not consciously attempting to imitate Faulkner; his own closeness to his subjects is garnered in such sensitivity that his fiction is far more than mere imitation.

Carl Singleton

THE WATCH

Author: Rick Bass (1958-)
Type of plot: Social realism
Time of plot: The 1980's
Locale: Seventy miles south of Jackson, Mississippi
First published: 1988

Principal characters:
BUZBEE, an old man who has run away from home
HOLLINGSWORTH, his sixty-three-year-old son
JESSE, a bicyclist in his early twenties

The Story

Buzbee is a seventy-seven-year-old man who has spent his entire life in a tiny community settled by his parents. Hollingsworth, his son, is only fourteen years younger; the two men have lived together primarily as friends for sixty-three years. One summer, Buzbee runs away to live in the thick, mosquito-infested woods alongside the bayou, and Hollingsworth posts an offer of a thousand-dollar reward for his father's return.

Hollingsworth is lonely without Buzbee and has to fight down feelings of wildness, especially in the evenings when the two used to talk. The town was once well populated, but epidemics of yellow fever have killed everyone but Buzbee and his son. They have buried family and neighbors in cemeteries across the countryside, and lost an edge of some sort because nothing again would ever be as intense as holding out against death. Even so, Hollingsworth is not sentimental about losing Buzbee. He does not offer a larger reward for his father because he does not want people to think he is sad.

Hollingsworth runs an old barn of a store, which attracts so little business that some cans of milk have stayed on the shelves for forty years. The Coke machine still has old-formula Cokes in bottles, and it is for these that a young bicycle racer named Jesse stops by. The first time that Jesse visits, Hollingsworth is speechless with excitement. He begins waiting for Jesse to appear, and even has the driveway paved to look like a snake in the green grass that makes a path straight to the store.

Jesse is slower than his teammates because he has an older bike. He begins each day by checking the wind; the slightest breeze means his ride will be harder, that he will slide along the roads looking for paths of least resistance. He is the only rider on his team to stop at Hollingsworth's for a cold soda; the other cyclists are too serious about their sport to take such breaks.

One day, Jesse mentions Buzbee. He has seen the reward posters, and wants the money. He tells Hollingsworth he has seen a man who looks like him, describing an old man wearing dirty overalls crossing the road with a live fish tucked under his arm.

Jesse suggests they use Hollingsworth's tractor to run Buzbee down and lasso him; Hollingsworth suggests they use the neighbor's wild hounds.

As the summer progresses, Jesse stops racing in order to help Hollingsworth catch Buzbee. He builds a go-cart so he can drive to the store, eat old cans of food, and listen to Hollingsworth talk. Even though Jesse cannot stand to listen to the man for more than twenty or thirty minutes at a time, he returns each day, growing soft and fat. Hollingsworth, on the other hand, thinks of Jesse as his true love; he hopes the cyclist has an accident so that he cannot return to racing. The older man talks endlessly about his life, and practices roping a sawhorse with a lasso, dragging it across the gravel, reeling it in as fast as he can.

Meanwhile, Buzbee knows that his son wants him home, but has no intention of returning. He has found the remains of an old settlement near the bayou, where he keeps a small fire going to ward off mosquitoes and to smoke catfish and small alligators. He hangs his food from the trees by looping vines through their jaws and stringing them up "like villains, all around in his small clearing, like the most ancient of burial grounds: all these vertical fish, out of the water, mouths gaping in silent death, as if preparing to ascend."

He brings a rooster and four chickens to his camp, and the birds locate the precious quinine berries that Buzbee's father planted long ago during a malaria epidemic. After women hear about Buzbee's settlement, they arrive a few at a time. They are middle-aged laundresses from such abusive situations that Buzbee's camp seems luxurious by comparison. They laugh and talk together, "muscled with great strength suddenly from not being told what to do, from not being beaten or yelled at."

As the women grow comfortable around Buzbee, they stop wearing clothes, and he sits in a tree above them, watching them move around naked, talking happily. At night, they all sit around the fire, eating roasted alligators and smearing the fat over their bodies to repel mosquitoes. The women begin sleeping with Buzbee, and one becomes pregnant. Another contracts malaria, but all of them prefer life on the bayou to life in town.

Several attempts to catch Buzbee fail. Hollingsworth and Jesse try to sneak into the settlement, but Buzbee and the women hear them coming and run through the swamp to hide in the trees. Hollingsworth and Jesse dig large pits and cover them with branches, hoping to catch all of them, but the women find a pit after it traps a deer. Finally, Hollingsworth borrows his neighbor's hounds. They muzzle the dogs and lead them into the swampland after Buzbee. Jesse brings an extra lariat and rope to truss him up, because he figures the old man will be senile and wild. The dogs are nearly crazed; they jump and twist at their leashes until they are too hard to hold. Then they silently and swiftly race straight into Buzbee's camp.

Jesse buys a new bike with his reward money and begins riding by himself, growing faster than ever. He now rides by Hollingsworth's store without stopping, disgusted by the sight of Buzbee chained to the front porch. Trapped by his over-talkative son, Buzbee squints at the trees in the distance and thinks only of breaking free again, for good.

Themes and Meanings

"The Watch" follows an American literary tradition of describing men who break free of responsibility to taste freedom and act young again. This freedom is poisoned by a sense of loss: The cemeteries are a constant reminder that all one's neighbors have died. In this story, even the alligators hanging in Buzbee's camp are reminiscent of a burial ground. Buzbee feels free in the silence of his camp, and the women's admiring glances make him feel young again, but at night he looks up at the moon through "bare limbs of the swamp-rotted ghost trees, skeleton-white, disease-killed." His freedom is marred by the feeling of being trapped. In constant danger of being caught, Buzbee discovers that he is not free after all.

Recurrent images of snakes in the story underscore the theme of entrapment. Hollingsworth's driveway is compared to a snake in the grass, and his porch, too, is black as a snake that has just shed its skin. Jesse is the prey in this case; Hollingsworth's driveway is the path of least resistance, and the path swallows him up for an entire summer. Afterward Jesse becomes a predator, camping with Hollingsworth in the cool grass the night before they catch Buzbee.

Buzbee's chickens disappear one by one until he finds a corn snake in the rooster's cage that is swallowing the rooster—only its thrashing feet are showing. Buzbee kills the snake, but the rooster dies when it is pulled back out. Metaphorically, the scene foreshadows Buzbee's being caught. Like the rooster, Buzbee is trapped in the woods, an easy target for a mad son with hounds. At the end of the story, Buzbee plans his final escape, sure that this time he will get away completely. This time, however, his only sure escape may lead directly to a nearby cemetery.

Style and Technique

Rick Bass learned the art of storytelling as a child in south Texas, listening to his grandfather and other relatives spin yarns at the family hunting lodge. This experience infuses much of his work with an oral quality, as though he is talking directly to the reader; critics often praise Bass for his comfortable use of a vernacular idiom. Best known for writing about the connection between man and nature, Bass often uses animals and setting symbolically, as he does in "The Watch."

The text of this story has a restless quality; although the story is long, its scenes are short. Point of view switches from one character to another, and the plot moves abruptly through time. Conflict is left unresolved. Realistic characters are confronted with bizarre situations, as when Jesse sees Buzbee with a live carp under one arm. "And listen to this," Jesse says to Hollingsworth, then suggests that Buzbee has been "eating on that fish's tail, chewing on it." Bass has said that it is important to surprise the reader with unexpected twists in the plot; "The Watch" demonstrates his agility in doing so.

Mary Pierce Frost

WAY STATIONS

Author: Harriet Doerr (1910-   )
Type of plot: Realism
Time of plot: March of 1963 or 1964
Locale: Concepción and Ibarra, Mexico
First published: 1990

Principal characters:

SARA EVERTON, a North American living in Mexico
RICHARD EVERTON, her husband, who operates a mine
KATE, their old American friend, who is visiting them
STEVE, Kate's estranged husband
INOCENCIA, an elderly beggar woman
LOURDES, the Evertons' cook
THE CURA, a local Roman Catholic priest

The Story

A train from the United States border arrives two hours late in Concepción, Mexico. Sara and Richard Everton are at the station expecting the arrival of their friends from North America, Kate and Steve. They worry that something is awry when neither friend emerges from the sleeping car. After a search, Kate is spied at the top of the train's rear platform, seemingly unwilling to disembark. Kate announces that she has come alone. Without prying, the Evertons load her luggage into their car, and they travel the road to Ibarra.

During the ride it becomes clear that Kate visited Ibarra three years earlier with her husband. Indeed, Kate is a frequent traveler who has lived in several different time zones. As Richard points out changes in the landscape since her last visit and Sara informs her that they all have been invited to attend a program for the upcoming day of the priests, Kate remains unresponsive. When she does speak, it is to inform her friends that she and her husband have separated. The reader learns that there was an accident: In an unsupervised moment Kate and Steve's two-year-old son toddled into the street in front of their home and was killed by a passing motorist. Kate's feelings of guilt and the long-lasting depression in the aftermath of her child's death have led to the breakup of her marriage.

During the first three days of her visit, Kate rises from bed only after the Evertons have gone out of the house. She spends the late mornings with the cook, Lourdes, who recognizes Kate's troubled condition and spreads talismans around her effects in an effort to reverse her ill fortune and will her spiritual redemption. Kate spends the balance of her days lying in a hammock, deep in sleep or sorrow. When Sara and Richard conspire to think of ways to lift Kate out of her depression, Sara suggests a trip by riverboat or railroad. Richard removes the hammock, and Sara takes Kate for a walking excursion to a ruined monastery at Tepozán. Kate recalls a picnic they had together at Tepozán during her previous visit with Steve.

In their continued attempts to move Kate out of her unhappiness, Richard takes her on a tour of his mine and shows her the shafts of abandoned mines in the hillsides. Sara brings her into the village, where they meet the cura and go into the newly repainted church. There they see a renovated statue of the Virgin, which came from Spain and was moved from one closed chapel to another until its arrival in Ibarra. "For her, Ibarra is only a way station," Kate observes. Sara sees this statement, along with Kate's memory of the earlier picnic, as a sign of her friend's returning abilities to remember, perceive, and feel.

Kate and the Evertons attend the priests' program as guests of honor. It is literally a watershed event. Although Kate has been repeatedly told that she will not need the umbrella that she brought with her since the rainy season does not begin until June, it begins to rain during the proceedings. Parish children perform two plays that illustrate responsibility in marriage and the various incarnations of a child who grows in faith and as he matures, commits his life to the priesthood. The plays lead Kate to question aloud the direction of her own destiny. Her itinerary lies outside the security of the Evertons' parental presence and the hierarchies of the church, in which each person has a place in a link that leads to God.

The next morning Kate brings her train ticket to the breakfast table. The story ends as it began, at the train station in Concepción. Two trains arrive at the station, one southbound and the other headed to the north. While Richard negotiates Kate's ticket inside the station office, Kate disappears. Instead of returning to the United States she takes the other train, leaving the Evertons a note saying "I've gone on." Sara and Richard imagine where Kate might go, and Sara thinks of La Chona. In that town an ambitious gardener has pruned trees into the shapes of Ferdinand and Isabella receiving Christopher Columbus, with his three ships sailing behind.

Themes and Meanings

This story is in effect a missing chapter from Harriet Doerr's 1984 novel, *Stones for Ibarra*. Set in 1960-1966, that novel chronicles the Evertons' move to Ibarra, the diagnosis of Richard's fatal illness (which is only briefly alluded to in "Way Stations"), and the couple's increasing acculturation to Mexican life and sense of belonging, ending with Richard's death and Sara's departure from Mexico. Both the novel and the short story focus on the themes of fate and chance or accident, intimacy and selfhood, multiculturalism, and the calamity and heroism of everyday life. Doerr uses "Way Stations" to explore the meanings of time and space, the nature of faith, the contrasts between modern or scientific perceptions and syncretic folk beliefs and practices, and most important, the conflicts between human will and divine plan or destiny.

Communication is an important theme, and, as in the work of Carson McCullers, the ability or inability of characters to communicate and understand is a metaphor for the essential loneliness of the individual and also for the human capacity to empathize with, relate to, and improve the lives of others. The sense of accident or fate and the blending of the secular and the spiritual, rational and magical worldviews, also are central to Doerr's work. These themes are related to the story's main metaphor, that of movement or transformation. "Way Stations," which begins and ends with a train at the station, is filled with images of and references to travel and metaphors of life as a passage or trip with several stages. Death or passing is coupled in these images with rebirth.

The many "way stations" in the story include the train station; Ibarra as a temporary place for Kate to heal from her sorrow; the church as a spiritual way station, with its stations of the cross; and the Evertons' home as a stopping point for local people passing by. Marriage has proven to be a temporary way station for Steve, while Kate thought of it as a lifelong effort. Kate is identified with the statue of the Virgin Mary, which has been moved from one country to another and then from one chapel to another, and in turn with Columbus and his voyage into the New World. Lourdes is concerned with another form of passage, the spiritual one of Kate and the Evertons' souls into heaven—in this case, the earth itself is the way station.

Style and Technique

Although not written in first person, Sara is effectively the narrator of the story, and the series of scenes unfold out of her experience of the events. The story is told in an objective tone and in episodic form, with description of events and the use of dialogue between the characters coupled with Sara's inner thoughts, feelings, and observations.

The story line of "Way Stations" in effect echoes that of *Stones for Ibarra*: Both story and novel are framed by the loss of a husband and begin and end with their female protagonists arriving at and departing from Ibarra.

The landscape is important in Doerr's work, and the tension between will and fate are reflected in it. Sara's gardening and pruning of her yard is an attempt to control her life and maintain order, in contrast to the sometimes harsh serendipity of the surrounding arroyos. Religious imagery pervades the story: For example, when Richard shows Kate the abandoned mines, Sara thinks of them as like beads on a rosary, each successive one representing a new hope or prayer.

The story follows a metaphorical path of rebirth and transfiguration. It begins with conception (at the town of Concepción), and Kate's time in the hammock at the Evertons' is a womblike period of gestation. When Kate and Sara enter the church, it is described with multiple images of water, like a baptism, or as if the two women were deep in an ocean or surrounded by amniotic fluid. The return to the train station at the end of the story is a kind of rebirth for Kate, as she chooses her own independent path and embarks upon it. Her choice involves a play on words of the story's title, as she chooses her own way at the station, accepting that the previously planned route of her life (represented in her train ticket that was purchased before the breakup of her marriage) has been changed and that she needs to go on, to her own voyage of discovery.

Barbara J. Bair

THE WAY WE LIVE NOW

Author: Susan Sontag (1933-)
Type of plot: Social realism
Time of plot: The 1980's
Locale: Unspecified
First published: 1986

Principal characters:
MAX, an AIDS victim
HIS FRIENDS

The Story

The plight of Max, a victim of acquired immune deficiency syndrome (AIDS), is told entirely through the voices of his friends. They observe his first reactions to his illness—denying that he has it and delaying a trip to the doctor for the blood test that will establish his condition definitively. Each friend reacts differently to Max's dilemma. Some sympathize with his state of denial; others worry that he is not seeking medical attention early enough. Aileen thinks of herself, wondering if she herself is at risk. She doubts it, but her friend Frank reminds her that AIDS is a totally unprecedented illness; no one can be sure they are not vulnerable. Stephen hopes that Max realizes he has options; he should not consider himself totally helpless at the onset of the disease.

When Max is hospitalized, Ursula says that Max has received the AIDS diagnosis almost as a relief after his months of anxiety. Friends wonder how to treat him. They decide to indulge him with the things he likes, such as chocolate. They visit him frequently, and his mood seems to lighten.

Does Max really want to see so many people? Are they doing the right thing by visiting him so frequently? Aileen asks. Ursula is sure they are; she is certain that Max values the company and is not judging people's motives. Friends such as Stephen question Max's doctor, trying to assess the gravity of each stage of Max's illness. The doctor is willing to treat Max with experimental drugs, but she tells Stephen that the chocolate might bolster Max's spirit and do as much good as anything else. Stephen, who has followed all the recent efforts to treat the disease, is disconcerted by this old-fashioned advice.

Kate shudders when she realizes that Max's friends have started talking about him in the past tense, as if he has already died. Several friends suspect that their visits are palling on him, while other friends argue that he has come to expect their daily presence. There is a brief respite from anxiety as Max's friends welcome him home from the hospital and observe that he is putting on weight. Xavier thinks they should stop worrying about how their visits affect Max; they are getting as much out of trying to help him as he is. They realize that they are dreading the possibility that they might also get the disease, that it is just a matter of time before they or their friends succumb to it. Betsy says that these days everybody is worried about everybody, that just seems to be the way people live now.

Max's friends think about how he has managed his life. He practiced unsafe sex, saying it was so important to him that he would risk getting the disease. Betsy thinks he must feel foolish now, like someone who kept on smoking cigarettes until he contracted a fatal disease. When it happens to you, Betty believes, you no longer feel so fatalistic; you feel instead that you have been reckless with your life. Lewis angrily rejects her thinking, pointing out that AIDS infected people long before they knew they needed to take precautions. Max might have been more prudent and still have caught AIDS. Unlike cigarettes, all that is needed is one exposure to the disease.

Friends report the various phases of Max's reaction to the disease. He is afraid to sleep because it is too much like dying. Some days he feels so good that he thinks he can beat the disease. Other days he thinks that the disease has given him a remarkable experience. He likes all the attention he is getting. It gives him a sort of distinction, and a following. Some friends find his temperament softened and sweetened; others reject this attitudinizing about Max as sentimental. Each friend clings stubbornly to a vision of Max, the story ending with Stephen's insistent statement, "He's still alive."

Themes and Meanings

"The Way We Live Now" is a brilliant orchestration of voices, showing how AIDS can change the lives of everyone who knows a victim. As Max's friends speculate about what he is going through, it is as though they are suffering from the disease themselves, trying to keep him alive in their thoughts and wishes. How they react to his disease depends very much on the kind of people they are. They argue with one another and sometimes support one another, desperately seeking ways to cope with the imminence of death. Max's approaching fate forces them to confront their own mortality, although they rarely acknowledge that they are indeed thinking of themselves as much as they are of him.

Death has many faces, many manifestations, Susan Sontag seems to be implying. For some, it is to be shunned. Some of Max's friends visit him rarely—one supposing that they had never been close friends anyway. Other friends, such as Stephen, almost seem to want to take over the fight against death—quizzing the doctors, boning up on the latest medical research, and conducting a kind of campaign against any capitulation to the disease. Very few friends are fatalistic; almost all of them hope that a medical breakthrough will come in time to rescue Max.

They live in fear. One friend finds out that his seventy-five-year-old mother has contracted AIDS through a blood transfusion she received five years earlier. No one is immune to the disease; even if everyone does not get it, everyone will probably know someone close to them who does. It is the extraordinary vulnerability of these people that makes them argue with or reassure one another and question what is the best behavior. Everyone encounters an ethical dilemma about how to lead his or her life and how to respond to those who are afflicted with the disease.

Style and Technique

Sontag allows the portrait of Max and the responses of his friends to his disease to filter gradually through the many voices of her story. No voice is dominant. Max is rarely heard speaking in his own voice, although his plight is discussed in nearly every sentence of the story. Consequently, the blending and clashing of voices reveals a society in argument with itself, testing ways of responding to AIDS, advancing, then rejecting, certain attitudes.

As in real conversation, voices overlap one another so that one statement is interrupted by another, and one speaker merges into another:

> He seemed optimistic, Kate thought, his appetite was good, and what he said, Orson reported, was that he agreed when Stephen advised him that the main thing was to keep in shape, he was a fighter, right, he wouldn't be who he was if he weren't, and was he ready for the big fight, Stephen asked rhetorically (as Max told it to Donny), and he said you bet.

In this example, the views of several friends are heard, and dialogue is recapitulated in what Max tells Donny. Sentences contain speeches within speeches, a complex layering of social and psychological observation that is emphasized by long sentences that continually switch speakers, so that a community of friends and points of view is expressed sentence by sentence.

It is the rhythm of these voices, of the ups and downs in their moods, of the phases people go through in responding to the disease, that is one of the most impressive accomplishments of Sontag's technique. She presents the tragedy of one man, yet from the first to the last sentence the story is also a society's tragedy as well. The speakers retain their individuality, yet they also become a chorus, almost like one in a Greek tragedy. They do not speak the same thoughts at once, but the syntax of the sentences makes them seem bound to one another—as enclosed by their community of feeling as the clauses in Sontag's sentences are enclosed by commas. The speaker's thought at the beginning of a sentence is carried on, refuted, modified, or added to by speakers in later parts of the sentence. The sentence as a grammatical unit links speakers to one another. Whatever their attitudes toward the disease, they cannot escape the thought of it. Thinking of it is, as one of them says, the way they live now.

Carl Rollyson

WEDDING NIGHT

Author: Tommaso Landolfi (1908-1979)
Type of plot: Fable
Time of plot: Mid-twentieth century
Locale: Northern Italy
First published: "Notte di nozze," 1939 (English translation, 1963)

Principal characters:
A YOUNG BRIDE
A CHIMNEY SWEEP

The Story

The arrival of a chimney sweep brings a wedding banquet at the bride's house to an early end. As the sweep changes his clothes and proceeds to clean out the chimney in the kitchen, slowly working his way up the chimney shaft three times, the bride exits the kitchen in embarrassment. After the sweep finishes, he changes his clothes again, eats breakfast, and sends out to the bride, who is seated outside, a gift of a small bouquet of edelweiss. The family briefly converses with the sweep after his meal; then he leaves, after which the bride places the edelweiss bouquet under portraits of her dead relatives.

Themes and Meanings

Virtually all details of plot, characterization, word choice, figurative language, and symbolism in this brief story help convey the theme that life contains a paradoxical blend of innumerable opposites or oppositions: male-female, upper class-lower class, experience-innocence, knowledge-ignorance, age-youth, life-death, daring-shyness, animate-inanimate, public-private, light-dark, bestial-refined, cleanliness-dirtiness, and white-black. The bride, whose inexperience and youth are stressed by the use of the word "young" eleven times, feels a kind of feminine shyness from the intrusion into the privacy of her home by the never-immaculate sweep, who must partially undress in order to do his job. The sweep also feels shy before his employers, however, although he knows more about them than they know about him. Concerned about his privacy, he wishes "to hide himself behind . . . words" and "let the curtain of words fall in the same way that the cuttlefish beclouds the water." Tommaso Landolfi's typical concern about whether language clarifies or obscures reality or relationships is suggested here, as well as tension between the social classes. The lower-class sweep is thus protecting himself linguistically from his employers.

During the sweep's work, the inanimate chimney comes alive for the bride, who empathizes in pain with its penetration, the "rhythm of a dull scraping which gnawed at the marrow of the house and which she felt echoing in her own entrails" and then with the sweep's cry sounding "from the stones of the house, from the soul of the kitchen's pots and pans, from the very breast of the young bride, who was shaken by it through and through." Paradoxically, what the bride first hears as a "bestial howl of agony" when the sweep finally breaks through to the roof "proves to be a kind of joyous call," suggesting a complex intertwining of opposites in life, love, and the sexual act. Moreover, the earthy sweep, never completely free from black soot and repeatedly described with animal imagery, gives to the bride the delicate, white edelweiss—a flower whose name means "noble white."

Death and life are also paradoxically mingled. Although the abundant soot's appearance and smell remind the bride of death, and the sweep standing on a pile of soot reminds her of a grave digger, the clearing out of the chimney and its penetration give it new life, just as the imminent death of her own sexual innocence will lead to the lives of her children and descendants. Ironically, the sexual act itself, leading to new life, results in a sort of death, in the participants' peaking and then decline in emotion and in physiology, as suggested by the sweep's cry of agony and joy in breaking through to the roof, his "black foot . . . of a hanged man" that emerges from the "slit" of opening to the chimney, and his appearance on the soot pile "like a gravedigger on a mound of earth" at his reemergence upon finishing the job. The sexually suggestive word "slit" is significantly repeated, implying—as much else in the story does—the influence of Sigmund Freud on Landolfi's writing. Finally, the activity of chimney cleaning, which represents two kinds of "death" to the bride, and prompts her to place her edelweiss bouquet under the portraits of dead ancestors, represents the continuation of life to the sweep and his descendants, for he reveals immediately before he leaves that he is about to bring his son into his business. A link is also suggested here with the child that the bride will likely bear as a result of her married nights, if not the impending wedding night. Though set in winter—the season of death, echoing "deaths" in the story—the actions of the plot will ultimately contribute to new life.

Style and Technique

Landolfi's word choices and sentence structures differ from some of his other short fiction in being simple in this story, helping to impart to it a fablelike quality. While some of Landolfi's other fiction uses more polysyllabic and abstract words, almost all of his work has the same kind of vivid symbolism as this story. In this tale, for example, almost all the details of the sweep's clothing are evocative, from the earthiness suggested by the brown of his corduroy suit's hue of "linseed oil" and his brown shirt, to his "two huge mountain boots." The weight of his boots also suggests the earthbound, though they also hold him "erect," counteracting his stoop, and point, contradictorily, to both aspiration and rising sexuality. The name of the material in his suit evokes aristocracy, as "corduroy" was originally thought to mean "cloth of the king"—a sharp contrast with the sweep's social class. In its liquid stickiness linseed oil suggests the by-products of lovemaking; in its hardening property, which is used for protective coating in paint and varnish, it suggests the coating of the chimney and the bride's ignorance, to be assailed by sweep and groom, respectively.

The coating that the sweep dons—ironically, in order to uncoat the chimney—is a black "gag" resembling a mask that covers his nose and mouth; it suggests the opposition between articulate and inarticulate, plus sweep and groom as masculine rapacious, intrusive robbers of a sort. The sweep's revelation that he violated prohibitions against picking edelweiss is an analogue of the groom's imminent violation of a much different sort of flower. Moreover, the bride's difficulty in summoning the courage to speak to the sweep and her difficulty in understanding his words on the two occasions that he speaks to her suggest the problems of language and communication, including their involvement in the relationship between the sexes. To maintain his own privacy, the sweep speaks opaquely obscuring sentences that resemble the cuttlefish's ink and recall his black gag.

After the bride retreats outside the kitchen the third time, the fact that she seats herself on a millstone suggests a rural setting, in which people grind their own wheat and corn; it also suggests her imminent induction into domestic life, after the wedding night. Also implied is the bride's being ground down by what lies ahead. The tool that the sweep uses to scrape out the chimney (apart from its vague phallic overtones) resembles the implement used to scrape kneading troughs. These, like the millstone, may be associated with bread—the staff of life and the focus of daily activities of family life.

In the bride's metaphoric conception, from the first moment that she meets the sweep, his "caterpillar nature" is implied his humility, or shyness, in the presence of the affluent, his ability to crawl up chimney walls, and new life and transformation after the chrysalis stage. The bride's conception, in simile, of the sweep resembling a crab louse, suggests not only his dark environment but also sexuality, echoing the caterpillar imagery. Ironically, although this caterpillar-natured person begins the destruction of the bride's insulation from the social and sexual worlds, he also gives her a flower bouquet, the beautiful edelweiss. Growing only in mountainous wildernesses, edelweiss is collected only with difficulty analogous to the difficulties of the sweep and bride. Its plucking, as the sweep admits, has been outlawed, analogous, the story implies, to the forbidden aura of the chimney sweep's and groom's activities. Finally, the flower's structure contains a protective covering of woolly bracts; this covering is implicitly related to the story's focus on penetrating the surfaces of things. This last concern is metaphysical, transcendent, and perhaps the crux of all Landolfi's fiction.

Norman Prinsky

WELCOME TO UTAH

Author: Michel Butor (1926-)
Type of plot: Antistory
Time of plot: The early 1960's
Locale: United States
First published: "Bienvenue en Utah," 1962 (English translation, 1963)

Principal character:
AN ANONYMOUS TRAVELER

The Story

"Welcome to Utah" is a chapter excerpted from *Mobile, Study for the Representation of the United States*, a larger work that attempts to render the essential quality of each American state. Like an imaginary guidebook to America, this work takes readers through all the states in the Union, in alphabetical order according to the alliance of place-names: From Lebanon, New Jersey, it switches to Lebanon, Ohio, and then to towns with the same name in Indiana and Illinois, for example. There are no characters or plot in the conventional sense; its fifty chapters—each devoted to one of the fifty states and covering a forty-eight-hour time span—provide an abundance of descriptive and interpretive material about the country. The chapters are linked by the mere invocation of town names duplicated in several states as well as by the longer continuing text of the narrator's running commentary on American history, the history of American Indians, and African American history. Comments on the time in each place and secondary material (such as catalogs, advertisements, road signs, restaurant menus, and quotations from famous historical figures) are incorporated into the text.

There is no action in the story, merely the illusion of interstate travel. The reader is carried along by the chain of associations, both temporal and spatial, provided by the narrator and by his imaginative use of quotations. The reader gains an impression of the United States that is at once startling and accurate: startling because of the frequent reminders of the suffering of America's many disfranchised peoples at the hands of white colonists, and accurate in its history and quasi-statistical evocations.

Since the chain is continuous, the complete book can be read, beginning anywhere, and readers are free to plan their own tours of the United States. "Welcome to Utah" can thus be understood on its own as a series of associative mobilizations. The town of Wellington, Utah, at sundown is the starting point for the narrator's journey of associations that propel him forward. This eventually leads to a moment early on in the chapter when Utah is abandoned for points east. Beginning with Wellington and an accompanying quote that describes the arrival of the Latter-Day Saints to the basin of the Great Salt Lake, the narration abruptly shifts to the town of Wellington, Nevada, a small town identified briefly by the presence of the Summit Lake Indian Reservation. The narrative then makes a detour back to Utah to take up the town of Huntsville, justifying this deviation with a passage quoted from textbook American history citing Huntsville as Brigham Young's chosen spot for founding his new Mormon city.

The main narrative line is then punctuated by fragments of factual information, snippets of banal conversation, quotations from road signs, and advertisements in a Sears, Roebuck and Co. catalog for a schoolbag illustrated with a colored map of the United States. Next, the history of the Mormons and their missionary zeal remind readers that they are still in Utah.

Shortly thereafter, the narrative travels in time and place to New England, where an account from the trial of Susanna Martin, one of the women implicated in the Salem Witch Trials of 1692, is presented. This account is less of a digression than a bridge leading back to the East Coast and eventually to New York City. Discussion of New York evokes a report on the numbers of European-language newspapers printed in this country, lures readers into restaurants serving French, Indonesian, Italian, and Irish cuisine, and evokes images of this city's architectural icons, the Empire State Building and the Seagram's Building. Readers are bombarded by big-city advertising, urging them to drink Coca-Cola, to fly Sabena and KLM, and to tune into WBNX for broadcasts in Ukrainian. Eventually readers are transported back in time and space to the South by way of Danville, New Hampshire, and then to Danville, Virginia. The chapter closes with several brief descriptions of the interiors of Monticello, alternating with lengthy extracts from Thomas Jefferson elaborating his belief in the inequality of race. A final associative leap jumps from Vienna, Virginia, to 11:00 P.M. in Vienna, Maryland, near Chester in Maryland. After all these imaginative deviations and detours, the welcome to Utah ends with an arrival back on the East Coast.

Themes and Meanings

In Michel Butor's travelogue of Americana, evocations of cities and cultural and political history are developed as themes on multiple levels: temporal, spatial, historical, and physical. His efforts to capture the sensation of travel transport readers backward in time, as well as forward in space, as they move from state to state, town to town, and century to century. The first word of the title of the large work, "Mobile," suggests Alexander Calder's whimsical mobile sculptures, which, like each state or historical landmark, may be read from a variety of perspectives. Road signs introducing new states and town names are reminders that America is the land of mobility in which people move from place to place in automobiles. Distilled quotations and advertising reveal other significant aspects of American culture. Recurring Howard Johnson's ice-cream flavors and advertisements from the Sears catalog echo the American mail-order catalog mentality. The names of cities that reappear in different states duplicate America's pattern of mass production. The use of juxtaposition conveys a feeling of speed as the reader travels down the highway of Americana.

This story also works as a social document of the more disturbing aspects of American history. Butor draws attention to the mistreatment of American Indians at the hands of America's white inhabitants, whom he calls "Europeans." The Indian, the "expression of this scandalous continent," posed a great menace to white colonists as they tried to replace the wilderness and build grids of roads and farmlands. To juxtapose the history of white America with its own cultural shame is, for Butor, to offer a realistic panorama of a country. It is certainly no accident that Butor pairs the name of each city with the name of a corresponding Indian reservation.

Style and Technique

Michel Butor's dedication of *Mobile, Study for the Representation of the United States* to the American painter Jackson Pollock suggests that he seeks to scatter haphazard fragments of Americana throughout his travelogue. Yet this suggestion is deceptive when one realizes how much controlled chance goes into the fabric of this story. Indeed, Butor intended *Mobile, Study for the Representation of the United States* to be composed like a patchwork quilt, piecing together the patchwork iconography of America to create his story. His purposeful juxtapositions, digressions, and quotations create the feeling of a patchwork, working rhetorically to guide the reader along prosaic roadways.

Alternating typefaces provide a crucial map for reading this travelogue. For example, geographical information, details of local flora and fauna, and advertisements are printed in roman type and serve as the story's framework. The welcoming signs that introduce different states and town names are printed in roman capital letters. County names, times, road signs, and brief physical descriptions of individual states are printed in lowercase roman letters. Around this framework Butor groups a wide selection of materials in italics. Short italicized phrases, often concerning American colonial history or containing banal dialogue, describe the natural and cultural features characteristic of each region. Longer italicized texts, including commentaries, catalogs, and selections from writings of famous Americans convey what is distinctive in American culture as a whole. The opposition of the shorter, fragmented italic elements with longer italicized texts may be viewed as dialogue or even distinction between rich local diversity and national cultural identity.

Butor's reliance on a disjointed form is much more than a compendium of impressions of America by an outsider. The quiltwork form of *Mobile, Study for the Representation of the United States* is neither symmetrical nor definitive. It is instead an experimental work that renounces a central narrative consciousness in favor of one that approximates the experience of movement through time, history, and space. The varieties of typefaces, as well as blank spaces and margins, provide readers with greater mobility as they make their way across the page over the vast American landscape. This rejection of linearity provides a compelling solution to the abundance of heterogeneous information that assails the cross-country traveler and inquiring cultural historian.

Constance Sherak

A WET DAY

Author: Mary Lavin (1912-   )
Type of plot: Domestic realism
Time of plot: Twentieth century
Locale: Ireland
First published: 1944

Principal characters:
THE NIECE, the narrator, an educated and independent thinker
HER AUNT, an older woman who respects the clergy
FATHER GOGARTY, a priest plagued by ill health

The Story

"A Wet Day" is a subtle story that explores several conflicts. The first is between the young narrator and her aunt. This young person has been to the university and has acquired ideas that are considered radical in her small Irish village. The most radical of these is her lack of respect for the Roman Catholic clergy. Her estimate of a person's worth does "not allow credit for round collars or tussore." She judges the person and not the office, and thus contrasts with her aunt, who is afraid to offend the local priest, Father Gogarty. The aunt respects the priest because of his position and never questions his moral character.

In the first scene, Father Gogarty visits the aunt to get some vegetables from her. The aunt carefully keeps her niece away from the priest so that she will not make a troublesome scene, even though doing so results in her and her niece getting wet.

The garden setting is repeatedly described as wet and sodden. This troubles the priest, who spent his early years studying for the priesthood in the balmy confines of Rome and now suffers greatly from the wet and unhealthy environment in which he lives. A diabetic, Father Gogarty can only eat vegetables—primarily cabbage and rhubarb. This wins him the sympathy of not only the aunt, but even her niece and the whole village.

Mike, the gardener, is also fond of Father Gogarty and goes out of his way to provide him with vegetables. He sympathizes with the priest's plight and encourages him to persevere. Father Gogarty occasionally despairs about his condition and diet, but, with Mike's encouragement, he comes to see that it is his duty to take care of himself.

The story changes after Father Gogarty asks Mike about a friend from his home town of Mullingar who has died recently. The young man was engaged to marry Father Gogarty's niece Lottie. During a visit the young man became seriously ill and Lottie wanted him to stay at Father Gogarty's rectory, since it would be dangerous for him to return to Dublin in a cold car. Father Gogarty revealed his selfish nature by denying the young man shelter in order to protect his own health. After everyone agreed to decide the issue by the question of whether the young man had a temperature, Father Gogarty lied about not having a thermometer and sent the sick man away in a cold car. The young man had pneumonia and soon died.

This scene revealed Father Gogarty's character. Selfish rather than pastoral, he is interested only in protecting himself. This exposure of his true nature changes the attitude of the aunt about Father Gogarty, and her relationship with her niece improves. They have fewer fights and resolve their earlier conflicts after both judge Father Gogarty to be an ineffectual priest.

Themes and Meanings

A major theme of "A Wet Day" is the contrast between the priest's official role and his moral nature. Should the priest be respected because of his clerical position, or should he be judged as others are? Eventually the story reveals that Father Gogarty lacks precisely those qualities of caring that a priest should have. Possessing no pastoral qualities, he is concerned only with selfishly preserving his own health. This judgment is rendered not in words but in the rejection of lettuce by the aunt at the end of the story. Earlier she honors Father Gogarty because of his office; at the end she sees him merely as a man—and a deficient one.

Another way the story conveys its meaning is through imagery. It is filled with images and references to wetness, sodden plants, and dripping skies. The aunt and her niece live in harmony with this wet environment. For example, the aunt keeps a dripping fuchsia bush for its beauty on the rare sunny day that comes. In contrast, Father Gogarty thinks the bush should be cut back or eliminated because he thinks it increases the danger of catching cold. He is more worried about catching an infection and disease than about caring for others.

A conflict that begins the story is between the traditional aunt with settled views and the more modern, educated niece. The young niece has no respect for institutions, especially the Roman Catholic clergy that is so important in Ireland. By the end of the story, however, she forgets about the revelation of Father Gogarty's character, which now has less significance for her. The aunt changes her own view more dramatically. She is clearly upset at Father Gogarty's showing himself to be a poor shepherd to his flock. As a result of this change, the aunt reconciles with her niece, and they agree on how to judge a person.

Another important conflict is between the "duty" that the priest feels to protect and care for himself and the necessity of being concerned with and caring for others. In obeying one dictate, he ignores the other, giving his own health and comfort priority over the urgent needs of the sick young man. The priest even goes so far as to lie about not having a thermometer in his house.

Style and Technique

"A Wet Day" is narrated by one of the major characters, the young niece, who reveals her own thoughts and observations, but no one else's. She describes the few key scenes in the story without expressing judgments on Father Gogarty.

The story's setting is also worth noticing. It is set in a small and clearly traditional Irish village. The people in the parish respect and sympathize with Father Gogarty because of his medical problems and the "cabbage" and "rhubarb" that he must eat. They endure his dry sermons uncomplainingly since they seem to conduct their spiritual lives without much help from him. They also accept the wet and cold of the church as penances that they endure for their spiritual benefit. By contrast, Father Gogarty is concerned primarily with his own comfort; he is not in tune with his setting or his parishioners. Completely oriented to the prevention of disease and infection, he has little sense of the spiritual. The aunt calls him a "martyr," but no true martyr would be willing to sacrifice the life of another to his or her own comfort and quiet.

The priest's style is clearly different from any of the other characters in the story. When introduced, he is complaining about the slugs that are ruining the lettuce on which he depends. His conversation is filled with negative comments about the weather and the possibility of disease. Self-pitying about his condition, he speaks about dying from deliberately eating a steak in order to gain sympathy from others. He is also cunning and calculating in the way that he forces the young man from Mullingar to agree to a fatal car trip. However, he seems not to be aware of the negative effect of the revelation of his character.

The lettuce is an important symbol that shows the changes occurring within the aunt. At the end, when she says "Take it away," she shows her rejection of the priest and his world of vegetables. Earlier in the story, she gladly gives lettuce to the priest to help sustain him. Now she wants nothing to do with it. In contrast, the niece could eat a "bowlful" of lettuce and is annoyed at her aunt's rejection of it. However, she does see its significance, and she and her aunt are reconciled as a result.

James Sullivan

WHAT WE TALK ABOUT WHEN WE TALK ABOUT LOVE

Author: Raymond Carver (1938-1988)
Type of plot: Domestic realism
Time of plot: The 1970's
Locale: Albuquerque, New Mexico
First published: 1981

Principal characters:
MEL MCGINNIS, a cardiologist
TERRY, his wife
NICK, the narrator
LAURA, Nick's wife

The Story

Nick, who is Mel's close friend, recounts a conversation that the two men and their wives had over gin and tonics in Mel and Terry's kitchen. The remembered dialogue is dominated by Mel, who is determined to articulate a definition of real love. Nick occasionally departs from recounting the conversation to remark briefly on the room, or on the progress of their drunkenness, or to give background information about himself or whoever is speaking. The story begins with Nick's suggestion that because Mel was a cardiologist, that sometimes "gave him the right."

Nick says, as background information, that Mel spent time in a seminary before going to medical school. Mel thinks that real love is nothing less than spiritual love. Terry recalls Ed, the man with whom she lived before she lived with Mel. Ed, she says, loved her so much he tried to kill her. She describes his brutal treatment of her, and wonders what can be done about love like that.

Mel disagrees strongly with Terry's contention that Ed's feelings for her were love. As they argue about it, Mel accuses Terry of being a romantic. Nick and Laura are reluctant to judge, but when Terry says that when she left Ed, he drank rat poison, Laura is shocked. Mel tells them that Ed is dead and begins another story about Ed's violence and his death, to which Mel was privy because he was on call in the emergency room. Mel emphasizes how Ed regularly threatened them. Laura in particular wants to know the end of the story of Ed. Terry and Mel disagree about whether it was right or not for Terry to sit with Ed when he died grotesquely as a cumulative result of his suicide attempts.

When Nick and Laura make physically romantic gestures toward each other, Terry cynically teases them, saying that only because they have been together for the short time of a year and a half do they still feel romantic. They break the tension by refilling their glasses and toasting to love.

At this stage in their drunkenness, Nick describes the yard outside as an enchanted place. Mel continues, wondering what anyone really knows about love, talking about how fleeting "carnal, sentimental" love is. Mel maintains that if any one of them died, that person's partner would go off and find someone new. Mel is also bewildered at how he could once have loved his first wife and now so thoroughly hate her. Terry worries that he is getting drunk. The situation becomes tense for a moment, and Laura dissipates the tension by claiming they all love him. Mel does not seem to recognize her as the wife of his friend, but says that he loves her too.

Getting increasingly drunk, Mel tries to illustrate the concept of real love by telling a gory story about a car accident in which a couple in their mid-seventies is critically injured. Terry interrupts him again, then tells him that she loves him, and he says that he loves her, something they repeat throughout the story as they disagree or ridicule each other. Mel goes off on tangents about wearing seat belts, finishing the gin, and wishing to be a knight. He confuses "vassals" with "vessels." His language and manner get more belligerent and careless. He is temporarily quieted by Nick's observation that sometimes knights suffocated in their armor. Laura asks Mel to finish his story about the old couple. Terry gets sarcastic about Mel's behavior and they exchange words. The room grows darker as the sun sets.

When Laura again asks Mel what happened, he makes a drunken pass at her, saying if they were not all in their present situation, he would carry her off. Terry tells him to finish his story so they can go to dinner. The story ends like a bad joke, bringing drunken despair for Mel, who still cannot explain what he is saying. He is depressed and wants to call his children. Terry talks about Mel's hated former wife, Marjorie, and reminds him that she might answer the phone. It is clear Terry also hates Marjorie, and Mel fantasizes that he would like to go to her house in a beekeeper's suit and release a swarm of bees, to which she is allergic. He would, he muses, only do this if the children were not home. He also wishes that she would get married again.

Mel is too drunk to do anything. In fact, everyone is too drunk to rise and go to eat, although Laura says she is hungry. Mel turns his glass over and spills his drink on the table. They all sit in the dark, listening to their hearts beat.

Themes and Meanings

Raymond Carver's story bears many calculated, ironic resemblances to Plato's *Symposium* (fourth century B.C.E.), a dialogue meant to showcase Socrates' views on love. Carver uses the same frame that Plato does, that of a friend recounting a story. Carver, however, twists this frame, which is meant to give added validity to the opinions expressed in the *Symposium*, to suit his own more ironic purposes. Among these is that trying to understand the nature of love through talk is at best a tale twice removed from its own point. In *Symposium*, Socrates walks away from a table of drunken, sleeping men whom he has bested with his wisdom, but in Carver's story a drunken Mel pours his gin out on the table, and sits in silence and darkness. Mel, an ironic Socrates, has bested no one and has not successfully defended his ideas about love. No one, least of all Mel, is able to walk away after the discussion is over. They are all too drunk. Mel is unable to arrive at any statement wiser than "gin's gone."

One of Carver's themes is that talking about love does not bring people any closer to understanding the experience of love. This idea is complemented by the ironic implication that talking about love seemingly inevitably involves telling stories of lovers' entanglements or situations filled with gruesome extremes. Carver cleverly dramatizes a philosophical point made by Socrates in the middle of *Symposium*: that because love seeks absolute goodness and beauty love must therefore be the state of lacking these qualities. The characters in Carver's story are examples of this lack. They seek but do not find absolute goodness and beauty. In contrast to the *Symposium*, Carver emphasizes the carnal, physical nature of love as intrinsic to its power. Carver implies that love almost never manifests itself apart from the tortures it brings.

Style and Technique

Carver's strong reliance upon dialogue gives readers a sense of immediacy. This immediacy is as deceptive and illusory as the definition of love is for the characters. The story, after all, comes to the reader secondhand; moreover, the story is modeled on a fiction that concerns itself with the truth. The emotional escalation of a conversation, masterfully rendered, emphasizes the urgency of the human need to love and be loved. The conversation shows that conversation is the medium through which love continually eludes those who would capture it and define it.

Many critics refer to Carver's writing style as "minimalist." He did not particularly like the term, given its connotations of smallness and inadequacy. Whether or not one assigns such a label or quibbles about how it should be defined, there is no question that each character is drawn sparingly, although with the essential details. For example, although Mel's drunken torpidity increases as the story develops, readers are also aware that Mel is a surgeon, and that "when he was sober, his gestures, all his movements, were precise, very careful." This observation is essential to establishing the significance of Mel's behavior during the conversation about love. A favorable definition of minimalist writing is that in it there is nothing extraneous—such a definition applies to Carver's stories.

Maria Theresa Maggi

WHAT YOU HEAR FROM 'EM?

Author: Peter Taylor (1917-1994)
Type of plot: Social realism
Time of plot: The early 1920's
Locale: Thornton, a small town in Tennessee
First published: 1951

Principal characters:

AUNT MUNSIE, an African American woman who was the nanny for the Tolliver children
THAD and
WILL, her two favorites of the Tolliver children
MISS LUCILLE SATTERFIELD, a white woman who understands her

The Story

Aunt Munsie is the town character, an old black woman who makes her way daily through the streets of town pulling a small wagon in which she collects slop to feed her pigs. Sometimes she stops traffic when she enters the square. She walks in the middle of the street, and most townspeople, when driving in town, simply call out to her until she moves out of the way. Only newcomers to town and ill-mannered high-school boys ever toot their horns at her.

As she makes her daily rounds, stopping at the houses of white women who hand her packages of garbage scraps for her slop wagon, she often calls out, "What you hear from 'em?" Her question is misunderstood by people who do not know her. Some even think she is an old beggar woman who calls out, "What you have for Mom?" Aunt Munsie knows these people laugh at her behind her back, but that does not bother her. She considers them ignorant people of "has-been quality."

The white patrons who know Aunt Munsie understand that her question is related to her history with the Tollivers, a prominent family in town. They know that she single-handedly raised the Tolliver children after their mother died. She wonders when Will and Thad, her favorites among the children, plan to return from Memphis and Nashville, where they have successful careers, and take up residence in Thornton, their hometown.

Thad and Will have made unannounced visits to Aunt Munsie's house separately over the previous ten years. During their brief visits, their children would go through her house into the backyard to see the pigs and chickens. Aunt Munsie would hug the children and fuss over them and soon be asking Thad or Will when they were coming back. They always told her that someday they would leave their businesses, buy property on the edge of town, and move back to Thornton.

Miss Lucille Satterfield, the widow of Judge Satterfield, understands Aunt Munsie's maternal feelings for the Tolliver children, and she shares any news of them when she can. At the same time, Miss Lucille and some of her neighbors are concerned that

Aunt Munsie, who is thought to be nearly deaf and blind, may be struck by an errant automobile on her daily rounds. Her refusal to stop pulling her old wagon around town leads the Tollivers and others in town to come up with a plan to stop her daily activities on the streets of Thornton. The Tollivers consult with the mayor and discover that Aunt Munsie is one of only three people in town who owns pigs. The Tollivers buy the pigs from the other two owners, and then the town passes an ordinance forbidding the ownership of pigs in the town limits.

When Aunt Munsie's daughter Crecie tells her about this new ordinance, Aunt Munsie sells her pigs to a neighbor who lives just outside the town limits. She never talks about the conspiracy to anyone. She lives another twenty years, outliving Crecie by many years. She begins to act like other old black women in town. Her character and manners become less harsh and offensive. She often reminisces with Thad and Will, who still visit her, but never again asks them when they are coming back.

Themes and Meanings

Aunt Munsie's story is in many respects a tragedy involving her loss of a clearly defined role and her loss of status as an African American in a Southern culture dominated by prominent white families. The high point of her life was the years that she spent raising the Tolliver children after Mrs. Tolliver died. Although she was an illiterate old woman, she persevered and raised the children with affection and discipline. She was proud of them, particularly Thad and Will, who became successful professional men in Memphis and Nashville. She was more than their nanny; she felt that she was almost a mother to them.

Because of her bond with the Tollivers, she thinks that she has achieved an elevated status in the town. She believes she has the right to ask about Thad's and Will's welfare and their future plans. Her constant refrain, "What you hear from 'em?" is meant to remind people of that bond. Until she is forced to get rid of her pigs, she is in charge of her destiny and has a place in the social geography of the town.

Long after Thad and Will left Thornton, Aunt Munsie harbored the hope that they would return for good. Their return would signify a recognition that her role as surrogate mother is vital and meaningful to them. Their return would mean that they respect and honor her, and still need her maternal care. When she learns that the Tolliver men have conspired to take away her pigs, she is grief-stricken. Realizing they never had any intention of returning to Thornton for good, she feels betrayed. She learns that she has no role in their lives beyond that of a nanny. She is no different to them than the other old black women on the square in Thornton who spend their days spinning yarns and "talking old-nigger foolishness." Before their betrayal, Aunt Munsie is a woman living in the present, a force to reckon with. Now she is broken by events and becomes a docile, obedient old black woman, an "Aunt Jemima" figure, wearing a bandanna around her head, a nonthreatening image of a harmless old woman who reminisces about the good old days.

The author suggests that Aunt Munsie is living an illusion in thinking that the Tolliver men will return to Thornton. In effect, she refuses to accept the social and economic realities of her life and invents a fantasy life regarding her role in the Tolliver family. When she faces the fact that Thad and Will are not coming home, she rejoins her social and ethnic group and functions in the real world for the last twenty years of her life. The narrator seems to imply that colorful town characters such as Aunt Munsie are cast aside by the forces of progress and social conformity.

Style and Technique

The narrator tells this story some thirty years after the events described. There is a bittersweet irony in his tone of voice. Apparently he represents the point of view of the townspeople of Thornton. His story is based on the strands provided by the various storytellers with access to the facts of the case. Although the narrator is sympathetic toward Aunt Munsie, he recognizes that her vision of the future was illusory and self-defeating.

The little wagon that Aunt Munsie pulls through the town functions as a symbolic object. It is shaped like a coffin, and the author writes that she pulls the tongue of the wagon as if it "were the arm of some very stubborn, overgrown white child she had to nurse in her old age." The wagon represents the death of her dream to reclaim her vital maternal role. It is like a burden she drags through town to remind people of who she was and what she has lost. She would give anything to take care of Thad and Will if they returned to Thornton, but that role has been lost, and at the end of the story Aunt Munsie is forced to give up her dream.

Robert E. Yahnke

WHY CAN'T THEY TELL YOU WHY?

Author: James Purdy (1923-)
Type of plot: Social realism
Time of plot: Several years after World War II
Locale: An unspecified American city
First published: 1957

Principal characters:
PAUL, a sickly and lonely boy
ETHEL, his widowed mother

The Story

Paul is a frail, pathetic child who lives with his mother, a frustrated and bitter woman who spends her days working and her evenings complaining on the phone to her friend Edith Gainesworth about the trouble of caring for a sick son. Paul is so desperately lonely, however, that even this kind of attention excites him. Paul has discovered photographs of his father, who died in the war, in old shoe boxes. He has transferred them to two clean candy boxes and now spends his time looking through them on the back stairs as he listens to his mother ask advice from her friend, who studied psychology at an adult center. Ethel cannot understand why Paul wants to play with these photos instead of with toys like normal children—especially since she has told him so little about his father. Despite her insistence that Paul give up the photos and overcome his obsession with his father, Paul continues to seek companionship through the black-and-white images of his father, watching him grow up from a boy his own age to a man and a soldier in the army. When his mother laments that her days at work are hard but being home in the evening with such a sick child is even worse, Paul enters the room with the pictures and attempts to distract her with airplane and bird sounds. He has been home from school for two months; Ethel is certain that his preoccupation with the photos is making him ill.

One night Ethel awakens suddenly. Paul is not sleeping in his cot and his blanket is missing, so she looks for him anxiously and resentfully. She first goes to the kitchen, but remembers Paul rarely eats anything. Finding him asleep on the back stairs with the photos, she angrily asks him why he is sleeping there, if it is to be with his photos. When Paul fails to answer, Ethel seizes his boxes of photos. She is repulsed by him; when she notices an ugly mole on his throat, she compares him to a sick bird. Paul inadvertently calls her "Mama Ethel," though she has told him never to refer to her as his mother because it makes her feel old. A black substance spews from his mouth. He has apparently tried to eat the pictures, but the omniscient narrator says that it is as if Paul has disgorged his heart, blackened with grief.

Themes and Meanings

James Purdy first published "Why Can't They Tell You Why?" in a collection of short stories called *The Color of Darkness* (1957)—a title suggesting that its stories are about emptiness and failed relationships. This story's theme is loneliness, which is reflected in both Ethel's and Paul's feelings of isolation from each other and from the rest of society. Ethel is an embittered widow who rarely even mentions Paul's father. She feels that her days of hard work with the public and standing on her feet all day are surpassed in misery only by her evenings spent caring for an ill child, yet she actually spends that time complaining to a friend on the telephone. The story's chief concern, however, is the alienation of Paul, who is denied the love that he needs from his mother and is even robbed of the surrogate that he seeks in the old photographs of his dead father. At an intense moment in his confrontation with his mother, his fear emanates from the idea that he and Ethel are the only two people in the world.

When Ethel charges Paul with preferring his dead father to his living mother, the irony is that Paul's father is more alive to him than his cold, uncaring mother. Paul's efforts to annoy his mother by looking at his father's photos while she talks about him on the phone are desperate attempts to construct the only family unity he has ever known.

The title of the story reflects the story's use of language as a marker of these failures of communication. The man to whom Ethel always refers as "your father" differs greatly from the man in the pictures whom Paul comes to think of as "Daddy." Paul is frightened by her calling him a "little man," not knowing what she means by it, but feeling that it forebodes more suffering for him. Paul cannot articulate why he is so drawn to the photos because he does not understand his own needs, the real nature of his illness. He craves love, but because he has never been shown any, he cannot explain to his mother what he seeks. Ethel insists that Paul not call her "Mama," because it makes her feel old, yet the clear implication is that she also does not want to admit that Paul is her child. When she looks at him she is revolted and cannot believe that he is her son. This denial develops into an inability even to see him as human. Indeed, she herself is dehumanizing him, robbing him of his humanity, by refusing to show him any love and by destroying the only source of love he has found in his life.

Style and Technique

Purdy's work draws much of its impact through understatement and implication. He presents little visual description but conveys vivid images through his use of metaphor. Although Ethel never actually strikes Paul in the story, its details strongly suggest that she has often locked him in the basement for punishment and that she has been physically abusive. When Ethel jerks Paul toward her by his pajamas, he pleads for her not to hurt him. She pulls his hair, and Paul winces when she raises her hand. He is apprehensive at the thought of being punished, but being sent to the basement is even more terrifying to him. That Paul is neglected is reflected in his unmended nightshirt and the strange excitement that he feels when he hears Ethel talk about him on the phone.

Paul is afraid of his mother, yet each character perceives the other as distant and even nonhuman. To Paul, Ethel is a monster; to Ethel, Paul is an animal and a burden. Purdy often describes Paul in terms of sick, starving, scared animals. Paul debases himself by pathetically petting the fur on his mother's slippers to persuade her to let him keep the photos. At the end of the story, when he goes completely mad, Paul hisses like a trapped animal. There is, Purdy tells the reader, no chance of bringing him back.

Ethel is described in equally unattractive images, often demonic, involving fire and smoke. When she takes some of the photos from him, she tells him that she will burn them. She then heads toward the basement while Paul clutches her legs and shrieks wretchedly. Ethel recoils at his touch, feeling as if a mouse were crawling under her clothes. Threatening to send Paul away to a mental institution as was his Aunt Grace, Ethel looks down at Paul crying pitifully at her feet, stroking her furry house slippers. She demands that he throw the pictures in the furnace, but after a brief period in which his fear quiets him, the boy starts running around the room in panic. His voice is strange to both of them, and unusual gurgling sounds seem to come from his lungs. As Ethel throws pictures into the fire, she turns to look at Paul, who is crouched over the pictures like a threatened, wounded animal. Her bathrobe smells of smoke; her face is lighted by the fiery furnace. Further, any suggestions of tenderness in Ethel are always qualified as being menacing or false. The candy boxes are symbolic of what the photos signify to Paul. Literally Paul is starving, as he will not eat; he is emaciated and pale. Metaphorically starving for affection, he is getting sustenance only from what he keeps in the candy boxes. Since his mother will not nurture him, he seeks his father's love. Paul's attempt to swallow the pictures completes this metaphor.

The story's omniscient point of view allows the reader to see the isolation of both Paul and Ethel from each other—she in repugnance, he in terror. They are strangers as well as antagonists. Their communication is infrequent and fraught with tension. Ethel's language is full of nuances that confuse and frighten Paul. He does understand, however, that when she says, "All right for you," Ethel is indicating that any attempt at communication is abruptly halted.

Lou Thompson

WICKED GIRL

Author: Isabel Allende (1942-)
Type of plot: Domestic realism
Time of plot: Late twentieth century
Locale: South America, probably Chile
First published: "Niña perversa," 1989 (English translation, 1991)

Principal characters:
ELENA MEJIAS, an eleven-year-old girl
ELENA'S MOTHER, the owner of a boardinghouse
JUAN JOSE BERNAL, a boarder

The Story

The "wicked girl" of the title is the main character, Elena, a nondescript, self-absorbed eleven-year-old who helps her mother run a boardinghouse. No one, including her mother, notices her unless some chore must be done. One of Elena's responsibilities is to spy on guests to ensure that their behavior conforms to her mother's standards. Elena and her mother speak to each other infrequently, but when they do, their conversations revolve around Elena's reports. Her mother, as crafty as Elena, knows when Elena embellishes on what she overhears and sees.

Their routines begin to change when a singer, Juan Jose Bernal, nicknamed "the Nightingale," comes to board with them. He is different from the usual boarders, civil servants or students who lead quiet lives. Bernal needs special food, quiet hours during the day, long baths, and extra telephone service. Knowing her mother's concern with her reputation, Elena is surprised when she rents the room to the flamboyant Bernal, but says nothing, remaining as invisible as ever.

Although dealing with Bernal's hours and demands means more work, Elena sees her mother begin to change. She wears perfume and buys new underwear, and sits opposite Bernal in the kitchen, listening to his stories, smiling and laughing. Because Elena is used to spying, nothing her mother buys or does escapes her notice. Elena begins to hate the man who has claimed her mother's attention, seeing him as a cheap scoundrel and fake artist.

One evening, Bernal appears on the patio with his guitar and begins to sing. Despite his unremarkable voice, his singing sparks a new festive air in the quiet boardinghouse. Suddenly, Elena's mother grabs her hand and pulls her up to dance. After a moment, Elena sees that her mother is entranced by the music. Elena's mother pushes her away and sways on the floor alone, absorbed in the mood of the night.

After that, Elena sees Bernal in a new way, as a sexual being who can evoke such response. She watches him even more intensely, going over and over his body in her mind. She becomes obsessed with him, waiting for him to see her, yet almost dying of pleasure if he speaks to her or touches her. At night, she stays awake thinking about him, and even goes to his room, touching his possessions and lying naked in his empty bed to absorb every bit of his essence into hers.

One day, Elena sees Bernal touch her mother and senses what the touch means. This realization so disturbs her that she begins to spy even more on her mother. She discovers that instead of singing every night, Bernal spends the night with her mother, making love. One night, she slips quietly into her mother's room and watches them. Elena notes her mother's every movement, believing that if she uses these same techniques, she can win Bernal herself.

Absorbed in this fantasy, Elena goes about her work routinely, but becomes more and more immersed in the plan she is weaving. She eats little, a fact which her mother attributes to her approaching puberty. One day, she purposely stuffs herself with peas and cheese, becoming too ill to stay at school. Returning home at a time when her mother is marketing, she goes immediately to the room of the sleeping Bernal. Removing her clothes as she has done often when alone in his room, she slides into bed with him and begins to use the techniques she saw her mother execute so successfully. Bernal responds until he feels her light body upon his. Realizing it is not his lover, he screams that she is a wicked girl, slaps her face, and leaps from the bed. The door opens to reveal another boarder standing outside listening.

Elena spends the next seven years with nuns, then goes to college and begins working in a bank. Her mother and Bernal marry, give up the boardinghouse, and retire to raise flowers in the country. Although Elena's mother occasionally visits her, Bernal does not come along. He thinks of her constantly, however, and becomes obsessed with the image of her and of all young girls. He even buys children's clothing and frequents school yards. His fantasy of that one day takes hold of his whole being.

When Elena is twenty-six years old, she and a boyfriend visit Bernal and her mother. Bernal spends hours on his appearance and rehearses every possible conversation many times in his mind. Instead of the fantasy child, he finds a shy, rather insipid young woman and feels betrayed. When the two are alone in the kitchen getting wine, Bernal tells her of his consuming passion and what a mistake he made to reject her on that morning long ago. She looks at him speechlessly. She has overcome the pain of her first rejected love. She does not even remember it.

Themes and Meanings

"Wicked Girl," with its ironic ending, focuses upon two of Isabel Allende's favorite themes: the power of passion and the strength of ordinary Latin American women such as Elena and her mother. Males dominate Latin American society. Bernal seems to have everything under control. He makes the boardinghouse adhere to his schedule of demands, because he has seduced the owner and bewitched her daughter. When he almost succumbs to Elena's seduction techniques, he calls her "wicked" for tempting him to break ancient taboos about having sex with young girls.

What he is not prepared for, however, is the effect of this seemingly inconsequential event involving a nondescript young girl. The power she has over him becomes his obsession, making him an outcast from mainstream society, sneaking around spying upon young girls exactly as Elena spied on him and the other boarders.

Elena, on the other hand, prospers. Being sent away from her oppressive home situation opens up opportunities. She goes on to college and gets a job in a bank, certainly better than waiting on roomers in a boardinghouse. When she returns to visit Bernal for the first time, she is still shy and not attractive, but the young man with her is begging to marry her, and she has a successful career. She, not Bernal, is in the position of power. She shows her real strength at the end of the story, when Bernal pours out his years of pining for her. She is astounded. She has forgotten the incident, filing it away with life's other learning experiences. This strong woman has developed coping skills that Latin Americans usually associate with men.

In the women's lives, passion is also important. Throughout the story, love transforms. Elena's mother, who had grown unattractive from years of hard work, blossoms under Bernal's caresses, acting like a young girl in love. Elena shows the immature obsession of a first awakening to sexual feelings as she stalks her prey around the boardinghouse and watches her mother make love. Love and sex are a part of women's lives. The strong woman enjoys these things, but does not let them rule her life.

Style and Technique

Isabel Allende is a master storyteller, and "Wicked Girl" illustrates her narrative abilities well. She uses an especially interesting technique, very long paragraphs that relate many events. Some cover almost two pages. All include imagery enhancing the emotions that arise from the events.

The plot begins immediately with a brief description of Elena, followed by the foreshadowing statement, "Nothing about her betrayed her torrid dreams, nor presaged the sensuous creature she would become." At the beginning of the second paragraph, Bernal enters and things move steadily along, as Allende chronicles Elena's growing obsession with Bernal. Dialogue appears only once, in the key scene in which Bernal realizes that it is Elena, not her mother, making love to him.

Images add to the sensuality of the plot. Flowers appear frequently. Before Bernal sparks the passion in the two women, the geraniums are dusty and give off no fragrance. As their passion for him unfolds, making women out of both of them, the sensations become stronger. Elena's mother wears perfume. On the Sunday evening Bernal plays his guitar and her mother dances erotically, it is hot and the scent of flowers hangs heavily in the air. The sensuous details build as Elena notices all the smells in his room when she lies on his bed, absorbing his presence with all of her senses. On the day that Elena comes to him, it is white-hot in midday.

The details are different in the last two pages, which cover the aftermath of her sexual encounter. Allende covers these events in a cool, factual style. Bernal hopes to rekindle Elena's desire on the patio where the scent of carnations hangs in the air, but the last encounter between Elena and Bernal takes place in the cool kitchen. The story ends with a twist of irony, bringing the narrative to a direct closure in the very last sentence: "She could not remember any particular Thursday in her past."

Louise M. Stone

THE WIFE OF HIS YOUTH

Author: Charles Waddell Chesnutt (1858-1932)
Type of plot: Social realism
Time of plot: The 1880's
Locale: Groveland, Ohio
First published: 1898

Principal characters:
Mr. Ryder, the protagonist, a light-skinned, socially prominent African American
Mrs. Molly Dixon, an educated, light-skinned African American from Washington, D.C.
Liza Jane, an older, uneducated, dark-skinned African American from the South

The Story

The story begins with a description of the Blue Vein Society, a social club of mixed-blood African Americans living in the North after the Civil War. While membership criteria were ostensibly based upon a person's social standing, everyone in Groveland, Ohio, knows that only those persons whose skin is light enough to show blue veins are asked to join. Mr. Ryder, a single, light-skinned man who has achieved a respected position in the railroad company over twenty-five years, is called "the dean of the Blue Veins." Possessing impeccable manners, a passion for British poetry, and a tastefully furnished and comfortable house, Ryder has arrived at the height of social standing and is ready to ask the beautiful, educated, and accomplished widow, Mrs. Molly Dixon from Washington, D.C., to marry him.

Not only is Ryder attracted to this young woman, he sees such a marriage as his social responsibility to "lighten" the race—the only means available for mixed-race people to assimilate into the larger white society. He explains that he is not prejudiced toward those of darker complexion, but that he regards mixed-blood people as unique: "Our fate lies between absorption by the white race and extinction in the black. The one doesn't want us yet, but may take us in time. The other would welcome us, but it would be for us a backward step." The joining of two such respected and accomplished mulattoes as Ryder and Molly Dixon is, for Ryder, a serious social and political obligation.

To honor Dixon, Ryder decides to give a ball in her honor; this will give him an opportunity to propose to her and also allow him to host an event that will mark a new epoch in the social history of Groveland. Only the best people—those with the best standing, manners, and complexion—will be invited. Critical of the growing laxity in social matters among even members of his own set, he wants to demonstrate to the community the standards that he considers proper to maintain.

On the day of Ryder's great ball, he relaxes on his porch as he debates which passage of Alfred, Lord Tennyson's love poetry about fair damsels would most honor

Dixon. An old black woman wearing a blue calico dress and a red shawl, who looks like a bit of old plantation life, approaches Ryder and identifies herself as Liza Jane, a former slave from Missouri. Before the Civil War she was married to a free-born mulatto named Sam Taylor, who was indentured to her master and nearing the end of his commitment. Her unprincipled master was so desperate for money that he planned to sell Taylor, although he did not legally own him. When the woman discovered her master's plan, she urged her husband to flee to freedom. Taylor promised to return for his wife, but her angry master sold her down the river and she never saw Taylor again. For twenty-five years, however, she has been looking for him: first all over the South—from New Orleans to Atlanta to Charleston—and now in the North. Liza Jane asks for Ryder's help in locating her long-lost husband.

After listening patiently and patronizingly to the old woman while examining her old daguerreotype portrait of her missing husband, Ryder tells her that he cannot help her. He promises to look into the matter, then goes upstairs to his bedroom and stands for a long time, gazing thoughtfully at his own reflection in a mirror.

That evening, Ryder's home is filled with the most prestigious of Groveland's African American citizens—teachers, doctors, lawyers, editors, and army officers. Although they are considered "colored," most of them would not attract even a casual glance because of any marked difference from white people. When Ryder finally stands to deliver his toast to Dixon, he does not quote Tennyson. Instead, he recounts his afternoon visit with the old black woman. Then, to the surprise of his guests, he poses a hypothetical question: What would any of them do if they were the young man for whom Liza Jane was looking? What if this young mulatto man had made his way in the world from his humble beginnings, had educated himself, had established himself in his community, had achieved a high social position, and had become a different person than he had been when he married as a young man? Discovering that his wife—who is older than he, uneducated, dark-skinned, and lowly—what would any of them have done? Would they have claimed their spouse?

After an uncomfortable silence, Dixon states, "He should have acknowledged her." It is then that Ryder, turning to his afternoon visitor, who is now neatly dressed in gray, and wearing the white cap of an elderly woman, announces to the elite Blue Vein Society, "Ladies and gentlemen, this is the woman, and I am the man, whose story I have told you. Permit me to introduce to you the wife of my youth."

Themes and Meanings

In "The Wife of His Youth," Charles Waddell Chesnutt presents the struggles of mixed-blood African American people in the latter part of the nineteenth century as they sought to define their place in American society. Despite their educations, their economic achievements, and their social positions, they remained at the margins of both black and white societies. A great many sentimental literary works of the post-Civil War period portray such people as tragic figures who, in their desperate attempt to pass for white and their desire to enter white society undetected, in denial of their African roots, meet a terrible end. In these romanticized tales, women sacrifice themselves to a great cause or to death, and men pose a threat to the racial purity of white society. In his story, Chesnutt rejects the tragic mulatto stereotype and insists that his readers see his characters in their individuality. Ryder and the other Blue Veins anticipate, as critic William L. Andrews has observed, the "New Negro" of the 1920's—men and women who would claim their African heritage proudly and create their own unique culture with its own art, music, literature, and philosophy. Chesnutt's characters are forerunners of African American philosopher W. E. B. Du Bois's "Talented Tenth," the top 10 percent of the African American people who would attend universities, assume positions of power and influence, and lead their people to their proper place in American society. Ryder's decision to acknowledge the dark-skinned wife of his youth is one man's affirmation of his past and his culture. Chesnutt, as Andrews points out, makes the abstract issue of racial identity a "personal ethical decision, to be judged on an individual basis in light of the social, economic, and psychological factors that most affect the persons concerned."

Style and Technique

Chesnutt first gained public attention by writing dialect stories of the South in the vein of popular writer Joel Chandler Harris' Uncle Remus tales. Chesnutt's early stories, the best known of which is "The Goophered Grapevine," present the clever former slave, Uncle Julius, who tells his new Northern master and mistress tales of voodoo, haunting, and plantation life. However, unlike Harris' sentimentalized portraits of antebellum slavery, Chesnutt's stories are accounts of courage, wit, and survival; however, Chesnutt found the dialect stories confining. "The Wife of His Youth" is his first piece using standard vocabulary and style. While the cunning Uncle Julius of his earlier stories could criticize society using wit and humor, Chesnutt's more conventional stories were not easily accepted. Readers found his discussions of miscegenation, prejudice, and class distinctions discomforting. He refused to return to the popular images of the Old South that were so profitable to him. Chesnutt insisted on examining the difficult issues of race and color, of morality and social responsibility that interested him, what he called "the everlasting problem."

The prominent novelist and editor William Dean Howells called Charles Chesnutt a literary realist of the first order. Chesnutt published sixteen short stories, along with a group of poems and essays, between 1883 and 1887. In 1899, two collections of his short stories appeared. Though he continued to write into the new century, producing three novels between 1900 and 1905, his works of social criticism never found the audience that his dialect stories had enjoyed. Chesnutt is important in the history of African American literature, initiating its short-story tradition. In 1928, he received the NAACP Spingarn Medal for "pioneer work as a literary artist depicting the life and struggles of Americans of Negro descent, and for his long and useful career as scholar, worker, and freeman."

Laura Weiss Zlogar

A WIFE'S STORY

Author: Bharati Mukherjee (1940-)
Type of plot: Social realism
Time of plot: Late twentieth century
Locale: New York City
First published: 1988

Principal characters:
PANNA BHATT, a Ph.D. candidate at New York University
HER HUSBAND, who is visiting from India
CHARITY CHIN, her roommate
IMRE, her friend, a male Hungarian immigrant

The Story

Panna Bhatt is attending a performance of David Mamet's play *Glengarry Glen Ross* (1983) in New York City with Imre, another immigrant separated, as she is, from his mate. They are not lovers, but they share the intimate friendship that only alienated foreigners in an adopted country can know; theirs is the mutual bond of strangers in a strange land. She thinks the play insults her culture and also insults her as a woman. She is so offended that she decides to write to Mamet to protest his depiction of East Indians.

She and Imre discuss her sensitivity to these issues, and he assures her that she must learn to be more flexible and adjust. Panna, however, is both resentful and disillusioned to realize that as a temporary immigrant already acculturated to certain American ways of being, she is caught in the middle, a mediator between cultures and cultural perceptions.

Panna gradually perceives differences between her old and new cultures that are in some ways freeing and expanding, and, in other ways, jarring and unnerving. For example, she is able to hug Imre in the middle of the street, an informal, spontaneous show of affection that she could not demonstrate toward her husband in India, where cultural restraints do not allow such personal displays. In India, Panna was not even allowed to call her husband by his first name.

The second part of the story briefly addresses the wide gap that separates Panna from Charity Chin, her roommate, who is a "hands" model. This short section underscores some of the emphases of the story at large, focusing on yet another immigrant who responds in her own unique way to the problem of adapting to another culture. Each immigrant undergoes the acculturation process, but it not only is different for each person, but also reflects the relativity of cultural values. In the United States, Charity is a model with high ambitions, but in India, she would just be a "flat-chested old maid."

The third sequence of the story concerns Panna's husband's visit. Panna shifts back and forth between seeing the United States from the tourist's point of view—her husband's ravenous shopping sprees, for example—and her own sense of disintegration and fragmentation. She views herself as already alienated and different from her husband and the culture and country he represents. They tour Manhattan and take the ferry to a dingy snack bar at the base of a scaffolded, and therefore forlorn, Statue of Liberty. Her husband is disappointed by the disparity between America's image and its reality; he thinks New York is no better than Bombay.

At the end of the story, Panna confronts herself naked in the mirror, a person singularly transformed by her experience as a foreigner and temporary immigrant in America. Her old life is really gone, and she recognizes this fact, not with rue or remorse, but with an exhilarating sense of metamorphosis. Yet it is a transformation both miraculous, like a butterfly, and strangely disorienting and disturbing, as she watches, simultaneously, herself and someone who is a stranger to herself: "I am free, afloat, watching somebody else."

Themes and Meanings

"A Wife's Story" is aptly titled because it is the story of one wife who finds that her sense of self—as woman, as spouse, as cultural being—is being transformed by the culture she now inhabits. Bharati Mukherjee not only indicates the particular and rarefied state of mind and being of an immigrant undergoing a definite process of acculturation within a specific culture, but also produces, through the comments and meditations of her narrator, the sense of alienation and strangeness it creates. In this story, the alienation is not merely cultural, but also takes the form of a vast alienation along sexual lines. Panna is an East Indian transforming into an American—with altered cultural awareness and values—but she is also transforming into a new woman: a female with a vision that is miles away from her husband's world and universes beyond her grandmother's restricted female being.

The other major theme addressed in "A Wife's Story" is the sometimes humiliating process of adapting to a new culture. Panna envisions herself as a new woman at the end of the story, and it is a positive, even if disorienting, expansive image. Throughout the story is interwoven the sense of irony at what the immigrant must undergo to effect a cultural transformation. The initial image of the story is the narrator watching herself being parodied and insulted by characters in an American play. She goes on to rebel at the subtle racism, the misjudgments, the stereotyping inherent in any culture clash between races and ethnic groups. She wants to write to Mamet. She will even write to Steven Spielberg to tell him that Indians do not eat monkey brains. Through the juxtaposition and, ultimately, the union of the universal theme of a global acculturation process, Mukherjee produces the picture of a mixed blessing for the individual immigrant struggling to make his or her way through a new world defined by differing and bewildering cultural codes. It is a complex and exhilarating opportunity for personal growth, but it separates the stranger in a strange land from family, spouse, and previous conceptions of self.

Style and Technique

This story carefully pairs a universal statement about the process of growth, which is often accompanied by humiliation, that occurs in any collision between cultures, with a personal statement of a first-person narrator undergoing that process. The first-person point of view is a primary means by which modern writers communicate the very nature of reality, that is, any sense of "absolute" truth actually residing in the relative world of personal perception. Thus Panna's metamorphosis, along with its disturbing elements, must be seen through her particular focused eyes. The reader is drawn into her unstable, mutating world. Through her comments, sometimes ruefully ironic, at other times determined and directed, Panna places order and meaning on this instability.

Mukherjee focuses her themes stylistically by incorporating character. It is her people who make meaning. The variety of her characters, named and unnamed, all serve to generate and further her themes. In opposition to them, Panna defines and creates herself. She is who she is—unlike them—and who she is becoming—often like them. She is estranged from a fat man in a polyester suit in the theater who "exploits her space," and yet she is like Imre when he exults in his freedom on a New York city street.

Finally, Mukherjee produces the underlying structure of her themes through her use of language. She intermixes incongruent, yet relevant terms: "Postcolonialism" (an intellectual, historical term) is somehow fitting in the same sentence with "referee" (a sports term employed metaphorically). The image of the city's numerous mixed races as astronauts possesses a certain truth. Interjected comments about her characters tend to reflect the American culture of which they are becoming a part: "Love is a commodity, hoarded like any other." Through her use of the first-person point of view, character, and diction, Mukherjee creates a world of fluctuating and transforming immigrants grounded in the personal adventure and vision of her narrator, who straddles not only two worlds, but two selves.

Sherry Morton-Mollo

THE WITNESS

Author: Ann Petry (1908-)
Type of plot: Social realism
Time of plot: Unspecified
Locale: Wheeling, New York
First published: 1971

Principal characters:
CHARLES WOODRUFF, a retired African American English professor
DR. SHIPLEY, a Congregational minister
SEVEN TEENAGE DELINQUENTS
NELLIE, a teenage girl whom the delinquents abduct and rape

The Story

Charles Woodruff, who retired as professor of English from Virginia College for Negroes, was sixty-five when his beloved wife Addie died. His wife's death has made him reluctant to pursue his former plans to spend his retirement as a homebody, so he has accepted an offer from Dr. Shipley, a Congregational minister, to work with seven troubled teens. The sole black in the white picket-fence community of Wheeling, New York, Woodruff does not enjoy his customary, exemplary success with students. After witnessing several unnerving sessions between these bright, demented young men and the authority figures they despise and antagonize (Dr. Shipley and himself), Woodruff impulsively questions their harassment of young Nellie after class. Immediately recognizing the inevitable danger to himself, and keenly aware of his well-founded fear of this devious gang, he instantaneously regrets his effort to intervene, leading as it horrifically does to their assaulting, abducting, and grossly humiliating him, as well. They imprison him in his expensive new coat, wreck his glasses, demobilize him as an auditory witness to their horrendous gang rape of Nellie, and incriminate him by forcing his imprint on Nellie's thigh after she loses consciousness. They leave Nellie in the freezing cold despite his feeble protestations, rob him, and leave him virtually incapacitated—he can hardly breathe or see, and his hands go numb as he searches for the car keys they threw at his head but which dropped in the deep snow. He realizes that as a black man, he is at the mercy of these violent youths, who degradingly address him as "ho' daddy," simply because they are white. He immediately leaves town, rationalizing his abandonment of the nightmare and of its primary victim, Nellie, as he speeds away.

Themes and Meanings

Racism and misogyny are intense themes in this story. The delinquents' willful oppression, exploitation, and abuse of both Nellie and Woodruff is institutionally sanctioned: They know, as he does, that no court will accept a black man's word over the lies of seven white males; circumstantial evidence is enough for a white jury to indict a black male, for whom white women are taboo. Nellie is reduced to a mere pawn, an object who embodies the vehicle for enactment of aggressive dominance and coercive submission. Likewise, Woodruff's humanity, professional accomplishments, and hard-won integrity are erased by inequitable power dynamics that objectify and demoralize him. Early in the story, he senses the danger that lurks around these boys when he winces at the gunshot sound their junky car makes as it approaches the Congregational church. He scurries into the building in the hope of avoiding the wrath and resentment he guesses they will express toward his expensive new cashmere coat, which even Addie would have deemed too indulgent.

Ann Petry suggests that these seven delinquents are not entirely evil or solely at fault in their extreme antagonism. They are products of superficial parents and a materialistic culture, and consumers such as Woodruff are its victims, as well. His coat, for example, Petry describes as a straitjacket: It restricts him and his movement and limits his freedom, but it takes a reversal of the authoritative power structure to demonstrate this reality. In turn, the teenage rebels against the mainstream despise the constraints imposed upon them and are too intelligent to let their own anger and disgust go unanswered. Everybody will pay for their hateful lives, especially those more disempowered than their egocentric, spiteful selves.

In addition to racial and gender conflicts, there is a generation gap pitting nonconforming teens against their elders, whom they do not respect. Petry layers the conflict and complicates the tension for, although Woodruff is black, he embodies the consumerist values these boys defy. Doubtless, they find his new-car smell, which even Woodruff agrees makes him sniff audibly and greedily, offensive, an affront to their oppositional stance. Petry metaphorically labels their dreadful car a "snarled message" to the adult world. Embittered with their meager scraps, Woodruff assumes, they resent the older generation, which gets more than its share of the goods. Perhaps this disparity is the root cause of the unrelaxed look that Woodruff notes in the eyes of children, cornered by an elusive American Dream. On a satiric level, Woodruff acknowledges that his acquisitions as an older black professional are out of line when he imagines someone calling the state police on him, the scenario of which is both sobering and comical:

> Attention all cruisers, attention all cruisers, a black man, repeat, a black man is standing in front of the Congregational Church in Wheeling, New York; description follows . . . thinnish, tallish black man, clipped moustache, expensive (extravagantly expensive, outrageously expensive, unjustifiably expensive) overcoat, felt hat like a Homburg, eyeglasses glittering in the moonlight, feet stamping . . . mouth muttering.

Style and Technique

Upon the revelation that he is a token, the protagonist demonstrates one of the most memorable narrative devices: parenthetical self-reflections particularly on words or phrases that come to mind. This is a habit fully in character with his having taught English for more than thirty years: "Nigger in the woodpile, he thought, and then, why that word, a word he despised and never used so why did it pop up like that." As Woodruff wonders about other expressions, Petry effectively calls societal assumptions into question. For example, the passage about the hypothetical police bulletin contains a parenthetical aside expressing the racist indictment that any exceptional expenditure by a black man is presumptuous and pretentious.

This technique prepares the reader for the more intense stream-of-consciousness passages touching on preconceptions that language encompasses and the behaviors that accompany them. For example, during the violent rape scene, Woodruff thinks "there are seven of them, young, strong, satanic. He ought to go home where it was quiet and safe, mind his own business—black man's business; leave this white man's problem for a white man." Immediately afterward, Petry illustrates the frustrations experienced by a respectable and educated black man who is compelled to edit himself and guardedly modulate his tone for white hoodlums. Petry's shocking description and relentless detail, especially of the rape scene, interweave poignantly with Woodruff's dismal coming to terms with this unfathomable complex. It is no accident that the pivotal scene occurs in a cemetery: Its gratuitous violence constitutes a dead end for all the parties involved. Petry's symbolism also manifests itself in Woodruff's literal blindness (he is without his glasses), which in turn reinforces his psychological justification for deserting his post and the girl in order to avoid further trouble for himself.

Woodruff is painfully and simultaneously aware of his status and his denial as both his mind and car speed him back to his proper place. Petry's skillful embedding of timeless themes raises significant questions about how this story complicates conventional perceptions of protagonists and adversaries, how the seven troublemakers differ from the students whom Woodruff describes as the "Willing Workers of America," how the boys' violent acts reflect on the community of Wheeling, how Woodruff's relationship with his wife (encapsulated in his memories) affects his decision to leave Wheeling, and how readers might identify with Woodruff's plight at the end of the story. The last question is especially resonant as readers recognize their own complicity in the crimes of varied oppression, their tacit collusion with materialist mainstream culture, and their witnessing of the destruction that ensues when the youths "blackmail a black male."

Roseanne L. Hoefel

A WOMAN ON A ROOF

Author: Doris Lessing (1919-)
Type of plot: Sketch
Time of plot: A week in June during the early 1960's
Locale: London
First published: 1963

Principal characters:
HARRY, a maintenance worker, about forty-five years old
STANLEY, a younger worker, recently married
TOM, seventeen, the youngest worker
A WOMAN SUNBATHER

The Story

This is the story of seven days during a June heat wave in London. One day, three men repairing the roof of an apartment building in the baking sun see a woman sunning herself on an adjoining roof. Taking advantage of her apparent privacy, she undoes the scarf covering her breasts. When Harry, the oldest worker, leaves to borrow a blanket to put up for shade, Stanley and the seventeen-year-old Tom let out wolf whistles at the woman, but she ignores them. At the end of the day, first Stanley, then Tom, goes to the end of the roof to spy on the woman. Stanley makes a crude remark to the others, but Tom keeps what he sees to himself.

The second day, the men look for the woman as soon as they get on the roof. She is lying face down, naked save for little red bikini pants. When Stanley whistles, she looks up, but then ignores them again. Angered by her indifference, all three men whistle and yell. After Harry calms the other two, they go to work. The sun is even hotter than the day before. That afternoon, while Harry goes for supplies, the other two men scramble over the rooftop until they are looking straight down at the woman. Stanley whistles. She glances at them, then goes back to reading her book. Stanley, furious at her rejection, jeers and whistles, while Tom stands by, smiling apologetically, trying to say with his smile that he distances himself from his mate. He dreamed about her the previous night, and in his dream she was tender to him. When the three workers make their last trip to look at the woman before leaving for the day, Stanley is so angry that he threatens to report her to the police.

The third day is the hottest yet. Harry looks for the woman first, largely to forestall Stanley, and tells the others that she is not there. The men work in the basement. Before going home, however, they climb to the roof to see the woman. Tom thinks that if his mates were not there, he would cross over to her roof and talk to her. Then Stanley screams mockingly, startling her. The fourth day they work in the basement again, but go to the roof at lunchtime for air. The woman is not there. Tom feels betrayed, for in his latest dream she invited him into her bed. The fifth day is hotter still, but the men must work on the roof; there is nothing for them to do in the basement. At midday the woman emerges and goes to a secluded part of the roof. At the end of the day, Tom sees the woman, but tells Stanley that she is not there, thinking that by protecting her from Stanley, he is forming a bond with her.

The sixth morning feels like the hottest of all. The men delay their inevitable climb to the rooftop by accepting tea from Mrs. Pritchett, the lady who has lent them a blanket. After spending an hour at her kitchen table, they reluctantly go up to the roof. There they see the woman and resent her relaxed sunbathing while they work in the brutal heat. Stanley suddenly throws down his tools, goes to the edge of the roof, and starts whistling, screaming, and stamping his feet at the woman. Harry, realizing that Stanley's wild behavior might bring them real trouble, orders the other two men off the roof. Stanley and Harry leave, but Tom sees his chance to meet the woman. He slips into the woman's building, climbs to the roof, and stands before her, "grinning, foolish, claiming the tenderness he expected from her." Tom tries to talk to her, but she dismisses him abruptly and ignores him until he goes away.

Tom wakes up on the seventh day to a gray, drizzly morning. "Well, that's fixed you, hasn't it now?" he thinks viciously. "That's fixed you good and proper." The three men now have the roof to themselves, as they plan to finish the job by the end of the day.

Themes and Meanings

Doris Lessing gives this story two levels of meaning, one individual, the other social. The individual meaning has to do with Tom's sexual and social confusion. Only seventeen years old, Tom is unsure of himself, envious of his mate Stanley's easy ability to flirt with attractive women. For Tom, the sunbather initially represents the allure of consumer society: "She looked like a poster, or a magazine cover, with the blue sky behind her and her legs stretched out." He feels a powerful sexual attraction: "He had caught her in the act of rolling down the little red pants over her hips, till they were no more than a small triangle. She was on her back, fully visible, glistening with oil."

Tom's sexual desire conflicts with his insecurity; he resolves the tension by romanticizing the sunbather. First, he fantasizes that she is tender with him. Then he dreams an explicitly erotic scene, imagined in the consumer idiom of the 1960's, but romanticized. "Last night she had asked him into her flat: it was big and had fitted white carpets and a bed with a padded white leather headtop. She wore a black filmy negligée and her kindness to Tom thickened his throat as he remembered it." Tom's imaginary trysts with the sunbather become so real to him (for his desire is so powerful) that he thinks he knows her. Moreover, he thinks that she surely must see that he intervenes to protect her from Stanley's crudities. It is all in his head, however, because to the sunbather he is just another ogling worker.

The story's social meaning has to do with the barriers of gender and class that separate the men from the woman. The gender barrier is the more obvious of the two. The woman is physically attractive, but does not respond to the men's calls, even though they think that she is signaling her availability. This angers and insults the men, for their masculinity is spurned. Their feelings relate to the class barrier between them and the woman. Stanley practices a standard of sexual morality that expects men to monitor and control their wives' behavior. His anger at the sunbather stems as much from his belief that women should not be allowed to behave "like that" as it does from the woman's actual rejection. Women who behave "like that," in his view, have husbands who cannot "put their foot down" to keep them from expressing their sexuality. Stanley's view of women reflects the prudery of the British working class.

The class barrier also appears in the theme of work. The work that the three men do is physically hard and demanding; their resentment at having to labor in extreme heat is magnified by the privileged nature of the sunbather's time. Her very presence is a reminder to them that some people do not have to work as hard as others.

Style and Technique

"A Woman on a Roof" is told by an impersonal narrator, but from the character Tom's point of view. The narrator knows what is happening in Tom's mind, what his nighttime dreams are, and what he wants from the sunbathing woman. To a lesser extent, one learns of Harry's motives in deflecting Stanley's anger so that the work can go on. Yet the narrator's perspective is curiously limited. The narrator tells of Stanley's feelings only by attaching to them labels such as "furious," "bad humour," "bitter." The sunbathing woman is seen exclusively from the outside.

Lessing heightens the story's tension by focusing on the environment of the roof. The reader learns of the basement only that it is gray and cool. The scene in Mrs. Pritchett's kitchen establishes the contrast between the cool flat and the sunbaked roof, between the friendly housewife and the indifferent sunbather. Most striking is the way that Lessing keeps the focus on the roof by revealing next to nothing about the men's lives; it is as if they have no existence beyond the roof. What little information the narrator divulges—that Stanley has been married for three months and that Harry has a son Tom's age—relates directly to the story.

Finally, Lessing uses the image of the heavy boots that the three laborers wear to draw an image of crudity. As Stanley and Tom scramble up the roof levels, they edge along parapets and cling to chimneys "while their big boots slipped and slithered." These big workmen's boots remind the reader of the class and gender contrasts between the relaxed sunbather, her sexually desirable body glistening with sweat and oil, and the three workers, whose own sweat comes from almost unendurable toil.

Lessing's control over the development of this story is superb. The story is spare in the sense that every scene is telling; there are no superfluous words or unnecessary passages. She uses words, dialogue, and description to focus attention where she wants it and nowhere else.

D. G. Paz

THE YEAR OF THE HOT JOCK

Author: Irvin Faust (1924-   )
Type of plot: Social realism
Time of plot: The early 1980's
Locale: Several American cities
First published: 1985

Principal characters:
PABLO DIAZ, an immigrant jockey from Panama
RAMONA DIAZ, his wife
RAFAEL "RAFE" LAGUNA, a baseball player and Pablo's best friend
JEFF KAHN HIALEAH, a horse trainer

The Story

Hot jock and jet-setter Pablo Diaz lives a nonstop racehorse life in the greed and lust of the United States in the 1980's. Flying from city to city, horse to horse, woman to woman, and bed to bed, Diaz's way of living parodies that of an American businessman with no morals.

Successful as a horse-race jockey, Diaz is misguidedly proud of his accomplishments and immorality. Living a hollow life with almost no friends or family values, he goes from race to race, winning most of them, only to wind up dead at the end of some sort of spiritual descent. Diaz has plenty of money, goes through women like socks, often buys expensive presents for his wife and two children, snorts cocaine, drives Mercedes and other expensive cars, and prides himself on all of the above. Perhaps with some recognition that something is wrong, he decides to take his son Lorenzo on a racing trip with him to Florida. He is unable to establish a relationship with his son, however, because he does not know how to have a friendship with anyone, and succeeds only at impressing the boy with such particulars of his lifestyle as big cars, women, and tips. He returns home with expensive presents for all, including a three-thousand-dollar Zuni Indian necklace for his wife.

Diaz loses, wins, or places in a series of races, as instructed by his trainer, Jeff Hialeah, and has a string of hotel visits with women such as Helen Stadler, a blonde he meets on a plane, and Ginny Gottlieb, his on-and-off mistress. Then the hot jock is visited by his best and only friend, Rafael Laguna. Rafe has not come on a matter of friendship, however, but of business: He asks Diaz to "pull" a race, to make his horse come in second rather than first, in exchange for $100,000. Diaz vocally refuses the offer; nevertheless, his horse does come in second. Afterward, Rafe is arrested, somehow gallantly taking the role of fall guy, and Diaz is left pretending to himself that he did not throw this race for an unknown outsider, that is, the person for whom Rafe is working.

During the next race, Diaz hears a gunshot from the stands. The horse he is riding has been shot, and as the animal collapses, so does the rider. His last thoughts are a wish that his wife Ramona will pray for him. Like a racehorse, the hot jock has simply run himself out.

Themes and Meanings

"The Year of the Hot Jock" is essentially the story of an immoral man who skids willfully to his own destruction. An embodiment of all that is negative about American society, the great jock Pablo Diaz, like the horses he rides to victory, races thoughtlessly to his own demise.

The story has little to do with jocks or horse racing; rather, it shows the end of a man who, typifying America and its values of greed and materialism, exists in a state of moral dissolution. Diaz has everything that money can buy: expensive cars; strings of women, including his wife, who satisfy his physical lust but do not give him love; children who are not subjects of love but objects whose affection is to be bought with mopeds and wide-screen television sets; money; respect and reputation as defined by this society; and total self-blindness.

As a jock—in both senses of the word—Diaz not only rides horses and women but also manifests the characteristics of the male muscle without thought or morals. As "The Year of the Hot Jock" is not about horse races or jocks, it is not about sports. Irvin Faust uses the jock here as a representative American type, much as Arthur Miller did with Willy Loman years earlier in *Death of a Salesman* (1949). It is the characteristics of the person, not the job, that are exposed and attacked.

Because Pablo Diaz's immorality is a given, he experiences little in the way of moral choices. For years, he has been following the instructions of his trainer whenever he races, finishing in whatever position he is ordered. When his friend Rafe approaches him with the same deal, he hesitates out of loyalty to his trainer and the danger of not knowing for whom he is working. When Rafe is caught, Diaz resolves to do what he considers to be the right thing, which is to give money to Rafe's wife and kids while he is in prison. Distancing himself from the actual conspiracy of pulling the race, Diaz denies what he has done; nevertheless, he places second in this race as he was asked to do by his friend.

Holding the entire story together is the overall metaphor: Life is like a horse race, and those who run fast and hard will finish close to first. This, in turn, does not mean victory and happiness, but certain and early destruction. Those who live by the sellout will die by the sellout. Diaz's way of life is not only pointless and misguided, but also stupid and evil. Not only does he work his own destruction, but he also lives a hopeless and purposeless life. Pablo Diaz, along with his race to the finish, is a comment on the proverbial "life in the fast line" of glitter-glow Americans. Ostensible success, as defined by society, is a culprit that not only destroys but also prevents a meaningful life and activity.

Style and Technique

The most noticeable characteristic of Faust's style in "The Year of the Hot Jock" is the unique syntax. Many sentences are merely fragments; all are short, and those which are longer (perhaps eight or ten words) are always broken two or three times by commas, dashes, or other punctuation. This style is used to replicate the inner workings of a jock's mind. Accordingly, readers are given snippets of thoughts that hold together and make sense, but do not cohere into any thought beyond the shallow.

The entire story is seen from a limited, first-person point of view. Readers know at all times the thoughts and perceptions of Pablo Diaz. The lies he tells others, as well as the lies he tells himself, about his life and his activities are transparent to the reader and should be transparent to the main character himself. His thoughts are on the order of stream of consciousness in a jock's mind.

Faust uses metaphors for life throughout the story. Foremost among these is the racetrack as the road of life. Similarly, women become horses, and horses become women—in a grotesque fashion, both are merely objects that Diaz rides—in this mind of the lustful male who is overcompensating for his shortness and lack of weight by becoming a stud, asserting male primitivity in the most basic of instinctual ways. The story is awash in symbols of a materialistic, greedy, and plastic society: Mercedes cars, Zuni jewelry, big-screen televisions, and so on pervade this man's life. Pablo Diaz exists not so much as a jockey who fixes races, but as a combination and culmination of crass and materialistic stereotypes.

Carl Singleton

THE YELLOW WALLPAPER

Author: Charlotte Perkins Gilman (1860-1935)
Type of plot: Psychological realism
Time of plot: A summer during the 1890's
Locale: Northeastern Atlantic Coast
First published: 1892

Principal characters:
JANE, the narrator
JOHN, her husband, a physician
JENNIE, John's sister and Jane's nurse

The Story

The story unfolds slowly over many weeks, beginning with the arrival of the narrator (whose name, Jane, is not revealed until the end of the story) at an estate in the country. Jane has gone into a gradual decline, losing interest in her family and her surroundings, since the birth of her baby. Her husband, John, and her brother believe that a long rest is what she needs to feel more like herself. Because both men are respected physicians, Jane believes that they know what is best for her and tries to put on a good face, despite her increasing suspicions that her rest cure may do her more harm than good.

At first, the colonial estate where she is the only guest appears harmless and quaint, with large gardens and spacious rooms. Jane later reveals that her windows have bars and her bed is bolted to the floor. The only people whom she sees are her husband, who comes from the city to check on her, and her nurse, John's sister, Jennie. Jane never has contact with her recently delivered child nor with friends. Her summer home takes on a more sinister tone as her mental condition deteriorates, with the very wallpaper in her room coming to grotesque life.

Jane's husband blames her thinking for all of her problems and forbids her to do anything that will employ her mind productively. Jane rebels at first and keeps a secret journal, but as she weakens, even that endeavor becomes too tiring. She withdraws into her thoughts, which form the running interior monologue of her mental collapse. Apparently accepting the separation from her infant, Jane slowly loses control of her imagination and her motivation to seek human contact. After she collapses and is forced to keep to her room, she becomes fascinated with the patterns on the yellow wallpaper, seeing in the paper's swirls faces and patterns that first amuse and then terrify her.

From her barred window, Jane begins seeing women creeping about the gardens on their hands and knees. Soon she discovers that another woman is trapped behind the wallpaper in her room, something that only she can see. At night, this woman pushes and struggles behind the paper in an effort to escape, rattling and ripping it as she fights to get free.

Jane says that the woman creeps along the walls, and she tries to help free her by gradually peeling back her wallpaper prison. Jane begins to notice signs of deterioration in her room: smears on the wall and bite marks on the bedstead. Gradually she no longer wants to leave her room; when John comes to take her home, she refuses to go and locks herself in with the creeping woman who is now free in the room.

Jane's husband and sister-in-law gain entry and find only Jane creeping around and around the room, surrounded by shreds of wallpaper. The story concludes as she creeps over the form of her husband, who has fainted from the shock of seeing her in her madness.

Themes and Meanings

"The Yellow Wallpaper" is partly autobiographical. Charlotte Perkins Gilman wrote it after she fled from her husband with her infant daughter to California. More important than the story's similarities to Gilman's own experience is the larger issue of a woman's right to be creative and autonomous. The story can be seen as advocating a woman's right to act and speak for herself; the alternative clearly leads to madness, as it does for Jane.

At the time of the story, most people believed that women were delicate and prone to madness if overstressed. A common treatment for their presumed mental illnesses combined isolation, rest, and inactivity—the very things that cause Jane's breakdown. From her own account, readers know that Jane enjoys writing and reading, yet John considers these to be dangerous activities to be avoided at all costs. At that time, it was common to remove a depressed woman from all sources of stress or sensory stimulation; women such as Jane were separated from their children, kept in bed, hand-fed, bathed, and massaged. It is precisely this type of treatment that drives Jane to begin hallucinating. The silent madness into which Jane withdraws is not only her reaction to the cure that men prescribe for her, but her only available form of rebellion against these tyrannies.

As Jane becomes more distanced from the world and from any source of sensory stimulation, she begins to hallucinate. Her visions of the creeping women and the woman enshrouded behind her bedroom's wallpaper symbolize her own binding and oppression. It is the rest treatment prescribed by physicians such as her husband and brother that metaphorically cause the women whom Jane sees to creep like infants rather than walk as independent adults. Jane's rest cure becomes her own wallpaper prison, one that simultaneously drives her insane and pushes her to assert her own rebellious selfhood. By freeing the woman from behind the wallpaper, Jane succeeds in freeing herself. Sadly, however, her mental state has deteriorated so badly that she has become truly insane and will remain utterly dependent on her husband.

At the story's conclusion, the narrator locks herself in her room and ties a rope around her waist so that she cannot be removed. Jane, the woman from behind the yellow wallpaper, creeps about the edges of her prison, a room that she will now use as a fortress. It is significant that Jane waits to reveal her name to readers until after her husband faints in horror at seeing her reduced to a crawling madwoman.

Style and Technique

The most prominent technical and stylistic feature of "The Yellow Wallpaper" is Gilman's combining of the first-person narrator and present-tense narration. By allowing readers to see only what Jane sees as she sees it, Gilman duplicates as closely as possible the feelings of entrapment, isolation, and unreality that Jane experiences. Jane's decline into true madness is so gradual and her narrative voice seems so level-headed, even when she describes events that one knows are impossible—such as the creeping women in the garden or the woman struggling to free herself from behind her room's wallpaper—that one might misread this tale as a ghost story rather than as an account of Jane's mental deterioration. By making the descriptions of the women, the room, and the malevolent shapes and faces in the wallpaper so immediate and realistic, Gilman tricks the reader into seeing Jane as simultaneously mad and in the grips of some haunting supernatural specters. This ambiguity increases the shock that readers experience when they realize that Jane has been talking in metaphors throughout her narrative, that she has been recounting her own sense of intellectual and emotional oppression, rather than seeing actual women crawling about on the ground in the gardens or moving behind her room's wallpaper.

Some readers may be content to let their interpretation of "The Yellow Wallpaper" rest with the supernatural; if left here, however, readers will miss the more important point of Gilman's tale. Gilman forces readers to reconsider Jane's entire narrative by means of the story's conclusion, when Jane finally speaks her own name for the first time as she creeps over her husband's inert body. Little of the story will then make sense unless reexamined. Gilman plants numerous clues throughout the story that express Jane's interior struggle to be herself and to reclaim her independence: her need to be creative by keeping a journal, or the existence of the woman for whom Jane demolishes the yellow wallpaper to effect her escape. Similarly, thc information that Jane offhandedly supplies readers in the story's early stages—such as descriptions of the bars on her window, the bite marks on the bed that is bolted to the floor, and her increasing lassitude—now can be reinterpreted as describing the true nature of where Jane has been staying: at an asylum. On second reading, "The Yellow Wallpaper" becomes the story of a woman who, while she may have been depressed, was not insane when she began her cure.

Melissa E. Barth

YOUNG ARCHIMEDES

Author: Aldous Huxley (1894-1963)
Type of plot: Sketch
Time of plot: The 1920's
Locale: Florence, Italy
First published: 1924

Principal characters:
THE NARRATOR, an Englishman living in Italy
SIGNORA BONDI, his landlady
GUIDO, a peasant boy whom the narrator dubs the "young Archimedes"

The Story

The narrator and his wife, a young English couple, rent a house outside of Florence because of its astounding view. When they first consider the property, the landlady, Signora Bondi, seems charming and insists that everything in the house is in perfect working order. Once they move in, however, they discover that the house has many problems. Particularly annoying is a broken pump that makes it impossible to run bathwater. Repeated visits to Signora Bondi's house bring only the answer that she is "out" or "indisposed." The couple are thus forced to communicate with her through certified letters. When even these bring no result, they have the landlady served with a legal writ. Grudgingly, Signora Bondi agrees to replace the broken pump and expresses her hope that their quarrel is ended.

When the narrator unexpectedly meets Signora Bondi's husband in town one day, Signor Bondi apologizes profusely. He knew from the beginning, he says, that the pump would need to be replaced; his wife, however, enjoys sparring with the tenants over minor repairs, and he hopes that the couple will forgive them. A short time later, the couple ask to renew their lease for a year, and Signora Bondi increases their rent 25 percent because of the "improvements" that she has made to the property. Only after extended negotiations does she agree to accept only a 15 percent increase.

Even while these problems are continuing, the narrator's four-year-old son, Robin, develops a close friendship with Guido, the son of a local peasant family. Although Guido is somewhat older than Robin, he displays patience and affection for the boy. As the narrator comes to realize, Guido is exceptionally bright. At times, he falls silent and stares pensively into the distance. Then, just as suddenly, he resumes the game that he is playing with Robin.

Signora Bondi also takes notice of Guido and wishes to adopt him. Guido's father asks the narrator for advice. He cautions the peasant against making any agreements with Signora Bondi. Her comments about Guido make it clear that she is not interested in the boy himself, but in how she can mold him. For example, she describes how she wants to dress Guido, almost as though he were a pet or doll. The peasant goes away persuaded that he should keep Guido for himself.

Shortly thereafter, the narrator's gramophone and several boxes of records arrive from England. Although Robin is only interested when his father plays marches or light music, Guido takes an immediate interest in Johann Sebastian Bach and Wolfgang Amadeus Mozart. From the first, the boy makes a practice of coming to the narrator's house each afternoon to listen to a short concert during Robin's nap. Within a few days, Guido selects favorite pieces and shows a remarkable understanding of harmony.

Impressed with Guido's aptitude for music, the narrator rents a piano and begins to give the boy music lessons. Guido progresses quickly, understanding the structure of canons almost intuitively and finding them easy to write. He is less inventive, however, when it comes to writing other types of music. Reluctantly, the narrator realizes that, while Guido is an avid student, he is not the musical prodigy that he initially appeared to be.

One day the narrator sees Guido explaining to Robin the Pythagorean theorem. Upon further questioning, Guido reveals that he has not learned the theorem from anyone else, but has discovered it on his own. The beauty that Guido finds in mathematical proofs and the ease with which he learns to compose canons cause the narrator to realize that it is in mathematics, not music, that the boy may be a genius. If Guido is not a young Mozart, he is, in any case, a young Archimedes.

The narrator explains that only geniuses such as Guido are "real men" in the world. He notes that most of the ideas taken for granted by humanity were discovered by a few dozen remarkable individuals. In the hope that Guido will grow up to be one of these few extraordinary individuals, the narrator adds lessons in algebra to Guido's ongoing study of music.

As the summer arrives, Robin's health begins to suffer from the intense heat of the Italian countryside. On the advice of a doctor, the narrator and his wife take him on an extended trip to Switzerland. After they have been away from Italy for several weeks, they receive a strange letter from Guido, who says that he is living with Signora Bondi and is terribly unhappy because she has taken away his mathematics books. He has lost his interest in playing music, although Signora Bondi forces him to work at the piano for many hours each day. He ends by begging the narrator to return with his family to Italy.

Only upon their return to Florence do the narrator and his wife learn what has occurred in their absence. Immediately after they left, Signora Bondi began pressuring Guido's father to allow her to adopt the boy. When the peasant refused, she threatened to evict him from the land that his family had farmed for generations. Eventually, the peasant acceded to Signora Bondi's demands. They agreed that Guido would live with the Bondis for several months on a trial basis. Although Guido had no desire to leave his family, he went along with the plan because Signora Bondi promised him that they would go to the seaside, a place where he had never been.

When the Bondis returned to Florence from the coast, Signora Bondi did not tell

Guido's father that they were back in the area. Convinced that Guido would become a musical prodigy only if he applied himself, Signora Bondi compelled him to practice the piano for extended periods each day and took away his other books, calling them "distractions." When Guido said that he wanted to go home, Signora Bondi told him that his father did not want him anymore. Guido's father, thinking that the Bondis were still at the seaside, never visited him, so Guido believed that this must be true. In despair, Guido threw himself from a window and was killed. Signora Bondi had the boy buried in the Bondi family tomb. When the narrator returns from Switzerland, he learns that he has arrived too late.

Themes and Meanings

A recurrent theme in many of Aldous Huxley's stories concerns a person who is trapped in a problem beyond his or her control. Most of these stories were written in the 1920's and early 1930's as fascism was spreading throughout Europe and war loomed on the horizon. The predicament in which Huxley's characters find themselves is thus symbolic of the frustration experienced by many Europeans of that period. Guido's world serves as a microcosm of European history at the time that Huxley wrote the story.

The character of Guido also represents the universal conflict between intellect and instinct, or between regimentation and unfettered genius. Standing in opposition to Guido's natural creativity are such figures as Signora Bondi herself and the fascist government to which repeated allusions are made in the story. In choosing his favorite pieces among the narrator's records, for example, Guido gives strong preference to Bach, Mozart, and Ludwig von Beethoven—who are viewed by Huxley as composers who achieved the proper balance between natural beauty and mathematical perfection—and he dislikes Richard Wagner, Claude Debussy, and Richard Strauss—who are identified by Huxley with the fascists or with debased emotionalism. In using Florence as a setting and in contrasting northern European "intellect" with southern European "instinct," "Young Archimedes" explores many of the same themes found in E. M. Forster's *A Room with a View* (1908).

Style and Technique

In a long introductory passage, Huxley sets the mood for his story and describes the continually changing countryside near Florence. This passage foreshadows the shifting moods of the story itself. From its opening account of the narrator's house and the difficulties in dealing with Signora Bondi, readers may conclude that "Young Archimedes" will be a light, comic anecdote. By the end of the story, however, the atmosphere of the work has darkened considerably and the tone has become one of pure tragedy.

The form of "Young Archimedes" is that of a character sketch or "most memorable person" narrative. Examples of this literary form include F. Scott Fitzgerald's *The Great Gatsby* (1925) and Truman Capote's *Breakfast at Tiffany's* (1958). Mixtures of comic and tragic elements are common in works of this sort. Authors use lighter moments to describe the joyous or uninhibited personalities that make their central characters memorable, and they use somber moments to suggest the voids that their characters' departures leave in the lives of their narrators. In order to give such stories greater immediacy, most-memorable-person narratives are almost always told in the first person.

Jeffrey L. Buller

MASTERPLOTS II

Short Story Series

CHRONOLOGY LIST

1808 Marquise of O——, The (Kleist)
1809 Ritter Gluck (Hoffmann)
1810 Beggarwoman of Locarno, The (Kleist)
1811 Engagement in Santo Domingo, The (Kleist)
1815 New Year's Eve Adventure, A (Hoffmann)
1816 Sandman, The (Hoffmann)
1819 Rip Van Winkle (Irving)
1819-1821 Story of Serapion, The (Hoffmann)
1820 Legend of Sleepy Hollow, The (Irving)
1824 Adventure of the German Student (Irving)
1824 Devil and Tom Walker, The (Irving)
1827 Two Drovers, The (Scott)
1829 Mateo Falcone (Mérimée)
1830 Donagh, The (Carleton)
1830 Gobseck (Balzac)
1831 Blizzard, The (Pushkin)
1831 Shot, The (Pushkin)
1831 Station-master, The (Pushkin)
1831 Unknown Masterpiece, The (Balzac)
1832 Grande Bretèche, La (Balzac)
1832 Passion in the Desert, A (Balzac)
1832 Roger Malvin's Burial (Hawthorne)
1833 Ms. Found in a Bottle (Poe)
1835 Ambitious Guest, The (Hawthorne)
1835 Diary of a Madman, The (Gogol)
1835 Minister's Black Veil, The (Hawthorne)
1835 Old-World Landowners (Gogol)
1835 Viy (Gogol)
1835 Wakefield (Hawthorne)
1835 Young Goodman Brown (Hawthorne)
1836 Nose, The (Gogol)
1837 Dr. Heidegger's Experiment (Hawthorne)
1838 Ligeia (Poe)
1838 One of Cleopatra's Nights (Gautier)
1839 Fall of the House of Usher, The (Poe)
1839 Lenz (Büchner)
1839 William Wilson (Poe)
1841 Descent into the Maelström, A (Poe)
1841 Murders in the Rue Morgue, The (Poe)
1842 Masque of the Red Death, The (Poe)
1842 Overcoat, The (Gogol)
1842 Pit and the Pendulum, The (Poe)
1843 Birthmark, The (Hawthorne)
1843 Black Cat, The (Poe)
1843 Gold Bug, The (Poe)
1843 Tell-Tale Heart, The (Poe)
1844 Artist of the Beautiful, The (Hawthorne)
1844 Purloined Letter, The (Poe)
1844 Rappaccini's Daughter (Hawthorne)
1846 Cask of Amontillado, The (Poe)
1847 Earthquake in Chile, The (Kleist)
1847 Yermolai and the Miller's Wife (Turgenev)
1848 District Doctor, The (Turgenev)
1848 Honest Thief, An (Dostoevski)
1848 White Nights (Dostoevski)
1849 Hamlet of the Shchigrovsky District (Turgenev)
1850 Ethan Brand (Hawthorne)
1852 Bezhin Meadow (Turgenev)
1853 Bartleby the Scrivener (Melville)
1853 Raid, The (Tolstoy)
1853 Sylvie (Nerval)
1855 Benito Cereno (Melville)
1858 Diamond Lens, The (O'Brien)
1859 Three Deaths (Tolstoy)
1859 Wondersmith, The (O'Brien)
1862 Nasty Story, A (Dostoevski)
1865 Celebrated Jumping Frog of Calaveras County, The (Twain)
1865 Crocodile, The (Dostoevski)

1865 Lady Macbeth of the Mtsensk District (Leskov)
1868 Luck of Roaring Camp, The (Harte)
1868 Nun, The (Alarcón)
1869 Green Tea (Le Fanu)
1869 Outcasts of Poker Flat, The (Harte)
1869 Tennessee's Partner (Harte)
1872 Little Legend of the Dance, A (Keller)
1873 Bobok (Dostoevski)
1873 Last Class, The (Daudet)
1873 Marjorie Daw (Aldrich)
1874 Living Relic, A (Turgenev)
1874 True Story, A (Twain)
1875 Jean-ah Poquelin (Cable)
1876 Peasant Marey, The (Dostoevski)
1877 Dream of a Ridiculous Man, The (Dostoevski)
1877 Herodias (Flaubert)
1877 Legend of St. Julian, Hospitaler, The (Flaubert)
1877 Lodging for the Night, A (Stevenson)
1877 Simple Heart, A (Flaubert)
1878 Suicide Club, The (Stevenson)
1879 Jim Baker's Bluejay Yarn (Twain)
1880 Boule de Suif (Maupassant)
1880 Sad Fate of Mr. Fox, The (Harris)
1880 She-Wolf, The (Verga)
1880 Wonderful Tar-Baby Story, The (Harris)
1881 Family Affair, A (Maupassant)
1881 Lefty (Leskov)
1881 Madame Tellier's Establishment (Maupassant)
1881-1882 Psychiatrist, The (Machado de Assís)
1882 Lady or the Tiger?, The (Stockton)
1882 Mademoiselle Fifi (Maupassant)
1882 Sire de Malétroit's Door, The (Stevenson)
1883 Consolation (Verga)
1883 Desire to Be a Man (Villiers de l'Isle-Adam)
1883 Piece of String, The (Maupassant)
1884 Necklace, The (Maupassant)
1885 Strange Ride of Morrowbie Jukes, The (Kipling)
1885 Two Little Soldiers (Maupassant)
1886 Chemist's Wife, The (Chekhov)
1886 Death of Ivan Ilyich, The (Tolstoy)
1886 Easter Eve (Chekhov)
1886 Horla, The (Maupassant)
1886 How Much Land Does a Man Need? (Tolstoy)
1886 Lispeth (Kipling)
1886 Misery (Chekhov)
1886 Three Hermits, The (Tolstoy)
1886 Trifling Occurrence, A (Chekhov)
1886 Vanka (Chekhov)
1886 White Heron, A (Jewett)
1887 Enemies (Chekhov)
1887 Kiss, The (Chekhov)
1887 Love: Three Pages from a Sportsman's Notebook (Maupassant)
1887 Markheim (Stevenson)
1888 Aspern Papers, The (James)
1888 Bet, The (Chekhov)
1888 Goophered Grapevine, The (Chesnutt)
1888 Lesson of the Master, The (James)
1888 Man Who Would Be King, The (Kipling)
1888 Miss Tempy's Watchers (Jewett)
1888 Steppe, The (Chekhov)
1888 Thrown Away (Kipling)
1890 Gusev (Chekhov)
1890 Town Poor, The (Jewett)
1891 Chickamauga (Bierce)
1891 Coupe de Grâce, The (Bierce)
1891 Duel, The (Chekhov)
1891 Killed at Resaca (Bierce)
1891 Native of Winby, A (Jewett)
1891 New England Nun, A (Freeman)
1891 Occurrence at Owl Creek Bridge, An (Bierce)
1891 One of the Missing (Bierce)
1891 Pupil, The (James)

CHRONOLOGY LIST

1891 Red-Headed League, The (Doyle)
1891 Return of a Private, The (Garland)
1891 Revolt of "Mother," The (Freeman)
1891 Scandal in Bohemia, A (Doyle)
1892 Adventure of the Speckled Band, The (Doyle)
1892 Désirée's Baby (Chopin)
1892 Procurator of Judea, The (France)
1892 Real Thing, The (James)
1892 Ward No. 6 (Chekhov)
1892 Yellow Wallpaper, The (Gilman)
1893 Bottle Imp, The (Stevenson)
1893 Greek Interpreter, The (Doyle)
1893 Middle Years, The (James)
1893 £1,000,000 Bank Note, The (Twain)
1894 Bontsha the Silent (Peretz)
1894 Drover's Wife, The (Lawson)
1894 Experiment in Misery, An (Crane)
1894 Hodel (Aleichem)
1894 Midnight Mass (Machado de Assis)
1894 Outlaws, The (Lagerlöf)
1894 Rothschild's Fiddle (Chekhov)
1894 Story of an Hour, The (Chopin)
1895 Altar of the Dead, The (James)
1896 Figure in the Carpet, The (James)
1896 Master and Man (Tolstoy)
1896 Tables of the Law, The (Yeats)
1897 Little Herr Friedemann (Mann)
1897 Outpost of Progress, An (Conrad)
1898 Blue Hotel, The (Crane)
1898 Boy Who Drew Cats, The (Hearn)
1898 Bride Comes to Yellow Sky, The (Crane)
1898 Death and the Child (Crane)
1898 Gooseberries (Chekhov)
1898 In the Cage (James)
1898 Lagoon, The (Conrad)
1898 Man in a Case, The (Chekhov)
1898 Man Who Could Work Miracles, The (Wells)
1898 Monster, The (Crane)
1898 Open Boat, The (Crane)
1898 Wife of His Youth, The (Chesnutt)
1899 Darling, The (Chekhov)
1899 Episode of War, An (Crane)
1899 Europe (James)
1899 Lady with the Dog, The (Chekhov)
1899 Man That Corrupted Hadleyburg, The (Twain)
1899 Sheriff's Children, The (Chesnutt)
1899 Twenty-six Men and a Girl (Gorky)
1900 Great Good Place, The (James)
1900 Tree of Knowledge, The (James)
1900 Upturned Face, The (Crane)
1902 Bishop, The (Chekhov)
1902 Deal in Wheat, A (Norris)
1902 Gladius Dei (Mann)
1902 Monkey's Paw, The (Jacobs)
1902 To Build a Fire (London)
1902 Typhoon (Conrad)
1902 Wireless (Kipling)
1902 Youth (Conrad)
1903 Adventure of the Dancing Men, The (Doyle)
1903 Amy Foster (Conrad)
1903 Beast in the Jungle, The (James)
1903 Home Sickness (Moore)
1903 Infant Prodigy, The (Mann)
1903 Julia Cahill's Curse (Moore)
1903 So On He Fares (Moore)
1903 Tonio Kröger (Mann)
1903 Tristan (Mann)
1904 Country of the Blind, The (Wells)
1904 Eveline (Joyce)
1904 Furnished Room, The (Henry)
1904 Madness of Doctor Montarco (Unamuno y Jugo)
1904 "Oh, Whistle, and I'll Come to You, My Lad" (James)
1904 Other Side of the Hedge, The (Forster)
1904 Other Two, The (Wharton)
1904 Putois (France)
1904 Road from Colonus, The (Forster)
1904 Scapegoat, The (Dunbar)
1904 Sisters, The (Joyce)

1904 They (Kipling)
1905 Editha (Howells)
1905 Gift of the Magi, The (Henry)
1905 Paul's Case (Cather)
1905 Problem of Cell 13, The (Futrelle)
1905 Sculptor's Funeral, The (Cather)
1906 Lazarus (Andreyev)
1906 Mammon and the Archer (Henry)
1906 Outrage, The (Kuprin)
1907 Kleist in Thun (Walser)
1907 Ransom of Red Chief, The (Henry)
1907 Willows, The (Blackwood)
1908 Conde, Il (Conrad)
1908 Ghosts, The (Dunsany)
1908 Jolly Corner, The (James)
1908 Silver Mine, The (Lagerlöf)
1909 In the Land of the Free (Far)
1909 Municipal Report, A (Henry)
1909 Old Woman Magoun (Freeman)
1910 Idle Days on the Yann (Dunsany)
1910 Japanese Quince, The (Galsworthy)
1910 Secret Sharer, The (Conrad)
1911 Alyosha the Pot (Tolstoy)
1911 Beckoning Fair One, The (Onions)
1911 Blue Cross, The (Chesterton)
1911 Celestial Omnibus, The (Forster)
1911 Hammer of God, The (Chesterton)
1911 Invisible Man, The (Chesterton)
1911 Odour of Chrysanthemums (Lawrence)
1911 Piece of Steak, A (London)
1911 Schartz-Metterklume Method, The (Saki)
1911 Sredni Vashtar (Saki)
1912 Death in Venice (Mann)
1912 Laura (Saki)
1912 Mote in the Middle Distance, H*nry J*m*s, The (Beerbohm)
1912 Woman at the Store, The (Mansfield)
1913 On Account of a Hat (Aleichem)
1913 Poet, The (Hesse)
1914 Araby (Joyce)
1914 Boarding House, The (Joyce)
1914 Clay (Joyce)
1914 Counterparts (Joyce)
1914 Dead, The (Joyce)
1914 Grace (Joyce)
1914 Indissoluble Matrimony (West)
1914 Ivy Day in the Committee Room (Joyce)
1914 Little Cloud, A (Joyce)
1914 Open Window, The (Saki)
1914 Painful Case, A (Joyce)
1914 Prussian Officer, The (Lawrence)
1914 Two Gallants (Joyce)
1914 White Stocking, The (Lawrence)
1915 Brains (Benn)
1915 Gentleman from San Francisco, The (Bunin)
1915 Harmony (Lardner)
1915 Metamorphosis, The (Kafka)
1915 Rashōmon (Akutagawa)
1916 Lost Phoebe, The (Dreiser)
1916 Mysterious Stranger, The (Twain)
1917 Jackals and Arabs (Kafka)
1917 Mark on the Wall, The (Woolf)
1917 Prelude (Mansfield)
1917 Report to an Academy, A (Kafka)
1917 Tale, The (Conrad)
1917 Walk, The (Walser)
1918 Bliss (Mansfield)
1919 Country Doctor, A (Kafka)
1919 Fat of the Land, The (Yezierska)
1919 Hands (Anderson)
1919 In the Penal Colony (Kafka)
1919 Interlopers, The (Saki)
1919 Sophistication (Anderson)
1919 Tickets, Please (Lawrence)
1919 War (Pirandello)
1920 Bambino, The (Sinclair)
1920 Coming, Aphrodite (Cather)
1920 Dead Man, The (Quiroga)
1920 Enoch Soames (Beerbohm)
1920 Footfalls (Steele)
1920 May Day (Fitzgerald)
1920 Miss Brill (Mansfield)

CHRONOLOGY LIST

1920 Neighbor Rosicky (Cather)
1920 Within and Without (Hesse)
1921 Adam and Eve and Pinch Me (Coppard)
1921 Arabesque—the Mouse (Coppard)
1921 Daughters of the Late Colonel, The (Mansfield)
1921 Egg, The (Anderson)
1921 Haunted House, A (Woolf)
1921 Her First Ball (Mansfield)
1921 I Want to Know Why (Anderson)
1921 Rain (Maugham)
1921 Some Like Them Cold (Lardner)
1922 At the Bay (Mansfield)
1922 Blind Man, The (Lawrence)
1922 Childhood of Luvers, The (Pasternak)
1922 Dark City, The (Aiken)
1922 Diamond as Big as the Ritz, The (Fitzgerald)
1922 Fern (Toomer)
1922 Fly, The (Mansfield)
1922 Garden-Party, The (Mansfield)
1922 Giocanda Smile, The (Huxley)
1922 Golden Honeymoon, The (Lardner)
1922 Horse Dealer's Daughter, The (Lawrence)
1922 Hunger Artist, A (Kafka)
1922 I'm a Fool (Anderson)
1922 In a Grove (Akutagawa)
1922 María Concepción (Porter)
1922 Marriage à la Mode (Mansfield)
1923 Blood-Burning Moon (Toomer)
1923 Difference, The (Glasgow)
1923 Doll's House, The (Mansfield)
1923 Esther (Toomer)
1923 Father and I (Lagerkvist)
1923 How It Was Done in Odessa (Babel)
1923 Jordan's End (Glasgow)
1923 Man Who Became a Woman, The (Anderson)
1923 Miss Cynthie (Fisher)
1923 My Old Man (Hemingway)
1923 Seaton's Aunt (de la Mare)
1923 Sniper, The (O'Flaherty)
1923 Theater (Toomer)
1924 Crossing into Poland (Babel)
1924 Grasshopper and the Cricket, The (Kawabata)
1924 Higgler, The (Coppard)
1924 House in Turk Street, The (Hammett)
1924 Indian Camp (Hemingway)
1924 Josephine the Singer (Kafka)
1924 Lyubka the Cossack (Babel)
1924 Most Dangerous Game, The (Connell)
1924 My First Goose (Babel)
1924 Outstation, The (Maugham)
1924 Wish House, The (Kipling)
1924 Young Archimedes (Huxley)
1925 Battler, The (Hemingway)
1925 Big Two-Hearted River (Hemingway)
1925 Haircut (Lardner)
1925 Return of Chorb, The (Nabokov)
1925 Soldier's Home (Hemingway)
1925 Spunk (Hurston)
1925 Story of My Dovecot, The (Babel)
1925 Three-Day Blow, The (Hemingway)
1925 Woman Who Rode Away, The (Lawrence)
1926 Absolution (Fitzgerald)
1926 Death in the Woods (Anderson)
1926 Disorder and Early Sorrow (Mann)
1926 Field of Mustard, The (Coppard)
1926 Gardener, The (Kipling)
1926 Recluse, A (de la Mare)
1926 Rich Boy, The (Fitzgerald)
1926 Rocking-Horse Winner, The (Lawrence)
1926 Sun (Lawrence)
1926 Sweat (Hurston)
1926 Winter Dreams (Fitzgerald)
1927 Alpine Idyll, An (Hemingway)
1927 Canary for One, A (Hemingway)
1927 Generous Wine (Svevo)
1927 Hills Like White Elephants (Hemingway)
1927 In Another Country (Hemingway)

1927 Jury of Her Peers, A (Glaspell)
1927 Killers, The (Hemingway)
1927 Man Who Loved Islands, The (Lawrence)
1927 Mountain Tavern, The (O'Flaherty)
1927 Two Blue Birds (Lawrence)
1928 Rope (Porter)
1928 Third Prize, The (Coppard)
1929 Big Blonde (Parker)
1929 Dunwich Horror, The (Lovecraft)
1929 Faithful Wife, The (Callaghan)
1929 Last Judgment, The (Čapek)
1929 Now That April's Here (Callaghan)
1929 Theft (Porter)
1930 Flowering Judas (Porter)
1930 Her Table Spread (Bowen)
1930 Jilting of Granny Weatherall, The (Porter)
1930 Love Decoy, The (Perelman)
1930 Mario and the Magician (Mann)
1930 Red Leaves (Faulkner)
1930 Rose for Emily, A (Faulkner)
1930 Tatuana's Tale (Asturias)
1931 Alien Corn, The (Maugham)
1931 Babylon Revisited (Fitzgerald)
1931 Burrow, The (Kafka)
1931 Dry September (Faulkner)
1931 Great Wall of China, The (Kafka)
1931 Guests of the Nation (O'Connor)
1931 Hunter Gracchus, The (Kafka)
1931 Ice House, The (Gordon)
1931 In the Basement (Babel)
1931 My Kinsman, Major Molineux (Hawthorne)
1931 Spotted Horses (Faulkner)
1931 That Evening Sun (Faulkner)
1932 After the Storm (Hemingway)
1932 Crazy Sunday (Fitzgerald)
1932 Dante and the Lobster (Beckett)
1932 Guy de Maupassant (Babel)
1932 How Beautiful with Shoes (Steele)
1932 Impulse (Aiken)
1932 Kerchief, The (Agnon)
1932 Midsummer Night Madness (O'Faoláin)
1932 Sick Call, A (Callaghan)
1932 Silent Snow, Secret Snow (Aiken)
1932 Truant (McKay)
1932 Two Bottles of Relish, The (Dunsany)
1933 Child of Queen Victoria, The (Plomer)
1933 Clean, Well-Lighted Place, A (Hemingway)
1933 Gift, The (Steinbeck)
1933 Old Red (Gordon)
1933 Roman Fever (Wharton)
1933 Summer Tragedy, A (Bontemps)
1933 Whole Loaf, A (Agnon)
1934 After the Fair (Thomas)
1934 Cinnamon Shops (Schulz)
1934 Daring Young Man on the Flying Trapeze, The (Saroyan)
1934 Deluge at Norderney, The (Dinesen)
1934 Enemies, The (Thomas)
1934 Gleaner, The (Bates)
1934 Miss Ogilvy Finds Herself (Hall)
1934 Monkey, The (Dinesen)
1934 Queen of Spades, The (Pushkin)
1934 Street of Crocodiles, The (Schulz)
1934 Supper at Elsinore, The (Dinesen)
1934 Wash (Faulkner)
1935 All the Years of Her Life (Callaghan)
1935 Basement Room, The (Greene)
1935 Children's Campaign, The (Lagerkvist)
1935 Doctor's Son, The (O'Hara)
1935 Freshest Boy, The (Fitzgerald)
1935 Grave, The (Porter)
1935 Nevada Gas (Chandler)
1935 On the Road (Hughes)
1935 Round by Round (Aiken)
1936 Astronomer's Wife (Boyle)
1936 Big Boy Leaves Home (Wright)
1936 Death of a Traveling Salesman (Welty)
1936 Leader of the People, The (Steinbeck)

CHRONOLOGY LIST

1936 Memory, A (Welty)
1936 Noon Wine (Porter)
1936 Revenant, A (de la Mare)
1936 Sense of Humour (Pritchett)
1936 Short Happy Life of Francis Macomber, The (Hemingway)
1936 Snake, The (Steinbeck)
1936 Trumpet, The (de la Mare)
1936 When the Light Gets Green (Warren)
1936 White Horses of Vienna, The (Boyle)
1936 Wunderkind (McCullers)
1937 Boy in the Summer Sun (Schorer)
1937 By the Waters of Babylon (Benét)
1937 Cloud, Castle, Lake (Nabokov)
1937 Devil and Daniel Webster, The (Benét)
1937 Di Grasso (Babel)
1937 In Dreams Begin Responsibilities (Schwartz)
1937 Many Are Disappointed (Pritchett)
1937 Official Position, An (Maugham)
1937 Piece of News, A (Welty)
1937 Sanatorium Under the Sign of the Hourglass (Schulz)
1937 Tears, Idle Tears (Bowen)
1937 Wall, The (Sartre)
1938 Bright and Morning Star (Wright)
1938 Chrysanthemums, The (Steinbeck)
1938 Flight (Steinbeck)
1938 Little Woman (Benson)
1938 New Islands (Bombal)
1938 Old Mortality (Porter)
1938 Pale Horse, Pale Rider (Porter)
1938 Peaches, The (Thomas)
1938 Profession: Housewife (Benson)
1938 Use of Force, The (Williams)
1938 Wet Saturday (Collier)
1939 Barn Burning (Faulkner)
1939 Cruel and Barbarous Treatment (McCarthy)
1939 Door, The (White)
1939 Field of Blue Children, The (Williams)
1939 Fight, The (Thomas)
1939 First Confession (O'Connor)
1939 Girls in Their Summer Dresses, The (Shaw)
1939 Petrified Man (Welty)
1939 Pierre Menard, Author of the *Quixote* (Borges)
1939 Sailor Off the *Bremen* (Shaw)
1939 Secret Life of Walter Mitty, The (Thurber)
1939 Split Cherry Tree (Stuart)
1939 Wanderers, The (Lewis)
1939 Wedding Night (Landolfi)
1940 America! America! (Schwartz)
1940 Circular Ruins, The (Borges)
1940 Fall, The (Moravia)
1940 Fancy Woman, The (Taylor)
1940 Hook (Clark)
1940 Keela, the Outcast Indian Maiden (Welty)
1940 Man Who Was Almost a Man, The (Wright)
1940 Mole, The (Kawabata)
1940 Rainy Moon, The (Colette)
1940 Saint, The (Pritchett)
1940 Summer of the Beautiful White Horse, The (Saroyan)
1940 Tlön, Uqbar, Orbis Tertius (Borges)
1940 Witch's Money (Collier)
1941 Bottle of Milk for Mother, A (Algren)
1941 Butcher Bird (Stegner)
1941 Demon Lover, The (Bowen)
1941 Eight Views of Tokyo (Dazai)
1941 Eighty-Yard Run, The (Shaw)
1941 Garden of Forking Paths, The (Borges)
1941 Leaning Tower, The (Porter)
1941 Lottery in Babylon, The (Borges)
1941 Madame Zilensky and the King of Finland (McCullers)
1941 Moving, The (Still)
1941 Nightfall (Asimov)
1941 Portable Phonograph, The (Clark)

1941 Powerhouse (Welty)
1941 Queer Heart, A (Bowen)
1941 Summer Night (Bowen)
1941 Under a Glass Bell (Nin)
1941 Visit of Charity, A (Welty)
1941 Why I Live at the P.O. (Welty)
1941 Worn Path, A (Welty)
1942 Catbird Seat, The (Thurber)
1942 Dawn of Remembered Spring (Stuart)
1942 Delta Autumn (Faulkner)
1942 Library of Babel, The (Borges)
1942 Man Who Lived Underground, The (Wright)
1942 Peach Stone, The (Horgan)
1942 Sailor-Boy's Tale, The (Dinesen)
1942 Sick Child, The (Colette)
1942 Sorrow-Acre (Dinesen)
1942 Spring Victory (Stuart)
1942 Tree. A Rock. A Cloud., A (McCullers)
1942 Wide Net, The (Welty)
1943 Ballad of the Sad Café, The (McCullers)
1943 Dark Avenues (Bunin)
1943 Kepi, The (Colette)
1943 Lions, Harts, Leaping Does (Powers)
1943 Moon Deluxe (Barthelme)
1943 Of This Time, Of That Place (Trilling)
1943 Tender Shoot, The (Colette)
1943 That in Aleppo Once (Nabokov)
1943 Together and Apart (Woolf)
1943 Tree of Night, A (Capote)
1944 Downward Path to Wisdom, The (Porter)
1944 Flying Home (Ellison)
1944 Funes, the Memorious (Borges)
1944 Happy Autumn Fields, The (Bowen)
1944 King of the Bingo Game (Ellison)
1944 Man Who Invented Sin, The (O'Faoláin)
1944 Mysterious Kôr (Bowen)
1944 Nun's Mother, The (Lavin)
1944 Old Bird, The (Powers)
1944 Secret Miracle, The (Borges)
1944 Shape of the Sword, The (Borges)
1944 South, The (Borges)
1944 Spinoza of Market Street, The (Singer)
1944 Theme of the Traitor and the Hero (Borges)
1944 Wet Day, A (Lavin)
1944 Will, The (Lavin)
1944 Wind and the Snow of Winter, The (Clark)
1945 Aleph, The (Borges)
1945 Gimpel the Fool (Singer)
1945 Her Quaint Honor (Gordon)
1945 How the Devil Came Down Division Street (Algren)
1945 It May Never Happen (Pritchett)
1945 Ivy Gripped the Steps (Bowen)
1945 Miriam (Capote)
1945 My Side of the Matter (Capote)
1945 Pacing Goose, The (West)
1945 Pearl, The (Steinbeck)
1945 Scorpion, The (Bowles)
1945 Short Friday (Singer)
1945 Story by Maupassant, A (O'Connor)
1946 Act of Faith (Shaw)
1946 Blackberry Winter (Warren)
1946 Christmas Morning (O'Connor)
1946 Cruise of *The Breadwinner*, The (Bates)
1946 Headless Hawk, The (Capote)
1946 Innocence (O'Faoláin)
1946 Legal Aid (O'Connor)
1946 Like a Winding Sheet (Petry)
1946 Prince of Darkness (Powers)
1946 Two Lovely Beasts (O'Flaherty)
1946 Winter Night (Boyle)
1947 Astrologer's Day, An (Narayan)
1947 Battle Royal (Ellison)
1947 Beyond the Glass Mountain (Stegner)
1947 Critical Introduction to *The Best of S. J. Perelman* by Sidney Namlerep, A (Perelman)

CHRONOLOGY LIST

1947 Distant Episode, A (Bowles)
1947 Drive in the Country, A (Greene)
1947 Enormous Radio, The (Cheever)
1947 Forks, The (Powers)
1947 How Claeys Died (Sansom)
1947 In Darkness and Confusion (Petry)
1947 Interior Castle, The (Stafford)
1947 Judas (O'Connor)
1947 Saturday Night (Farrell)
1947 Second Tree from the Corner, The (White)
1947 Solo on the Drums (Petry)
1947 Train from Rhodesia, The (Gordimer)
1947 Valiant Woman, The (Powers)
1947 Vertical Ladder, The (Sansom)
1947 Villon's Wife (Dazai)
1947 Wall, The (Sansom)
1948 Charles (Jackson)
1948 Children on Their Birthdays (Capote)
1948 Drunkard, The (O'Connor)
1948 Fur Coat, The (O'Faoláin)
1948 Lottery, The (Jackson)
1948 Perfect Day for Bananafish, A (Salinger)
1948 Ram in the Thicket, The (Morris)
1948 Road to the Isles (West)
1948 Shower of Gold (Welty)
1948 Signs and Symbols (Nabokov)
1948 This Way for the Gas, Ladies and Gentlemen (Borowski)
1948 Trout, The (O'Faoláin)
1948 Uncle Wiggily in Connecticut (Salinger)
1948 Up the Bare Stairs (O'Faoláin)
1948 When I Was Thirteen (Welch)
1948 World of Stone, The (Borowski)
1949 Across the Bridge (Greene)
1949 Hint of an Explanation, The (Greene)
1949 New Year for Fong Wing (Leong)
1949 Seventeen Syllables (Yamamoto)
1949 Summer Evening (Boyle)
1950 Across the Bridge (Böll)
1950 Babette's Feast (Dinesen)
1950 Big Fish, Little Fish (Calvino)
1950 Country Love Story, A (Stafford)
1950 Delicate Prey, The (Bowles)
1950 EPICAC (Vonnegut)
1950 For Esmé—with Love and Squalor (Salinger)
1950 Just Lather, That's All (Téllez)
1950 My Oedipus Complex (O'Connor)
1950 National Honeymoon (Horgan)
1950 Parsley Garden, The (Saroyan)
1950 Prison, The (Malamud)
1950 Resemblance Between a Violin Case and a Coffin, The (Williams)
1950 There Will Come Soft Rains (Bradbury)
1951 Chaser, The (Collier)
1951 Cyclists' Raid, The (Rooney)
1951 De Mortuis (Collier)
1951 Goodbye, My Brother (Cheever)
1951 Heart of the Artichoke, The (Gold)
1951 In Greenwich There Are Many Gravelled Walks (Calisher)
1951 Looking for Mr. Green (Bellow)
1951 Sentinel, The (Clarke)
1951 Time the Tiger (Lewis)
1951 Veldt, The (Bradbury)
1951 What You Hear from 'Em? (Taylor)
1951 Widow's Son, The (Lavin)
1952 Another Part of the Sky (Gordimer)
1952 April Witch, The (Bradbury)
1952 Argentine Ant, The (Calvino)
1952 Bitter Honeymoon (Moravia)
1952 Cap for Steve, A (Callaghan)
1952 Christmas Every Day (Böll)
1952 De Daumier-Smith's Blue Period (Salinger)
1952 Death in Midsummer (Mishima)
1952 Defeated, The (Gordimer)
1952 Enchanted Doll, The (Gallico)
1952 Faces of Blood Kindred, The (Goyen)
1952 Ghost and Flesh, Water and Dirt (Goyen)
1952 Mother's Tale, A (Agee)

1952 Shape of Light, A (Goyen)
1952 Three Players of a Summer Game (Williams)
1952 World Ends, A (Hildesheimer)
1953 Because We Are So Poor (Rulfo)
1953 Black Prince, The (Grau)
1953 Bound Man, The (Aichinger)
1953 Dead Men's Path (Achebe)
1953 Good Man Is Hard to Find, A (O'Connor)
1953 In the Zoo (Stafford)
1953 Lamb to the Slaughter (Dahl)
1953 Life You Save May Be Your Own, The (O'Connor)
1953 Other Paris, The (Gallant)
1953 River, The (O'Connor)
1953 Story, A (Thomas)
1953 Suicides (Pavese)
1953 Swaddling Clothes (Mishima)
1953 Tell Them Not to Kill Me! (Rulfo)
1954 Bad Characters (Stafford)
1954 Country Husband, The (Cheever)
1954 Destructors, The (Greene)
1954 Displaced Person, The (O'Connor)
1954 Empress's Ring, The (Hale)
1954 Five-Forty-Eight, The (Cheever)
1954 Gogol's Wife (Landolfi)
1954 Gonzaga Manuscripts, The (Bellow)
1954 Housebreaker of Shady Hill, The (Cheever)
1954 Magic Barrel, The (Malamud)
1954 Maiden in a Tower (Stegner)
1954 Post Office, The (O'Flaherty)
1954 Susanna at the Beach (Gold)
1955 Ace in the Hole (Updike)
1955 Angel Levine (Malamud)
1955 Artificial Nigger, The (O'Connor)
1955 End, The (Beckett)
1955 Father-to-Be, A (Bellow)
1955 Good Country People (O'Connor)
1955 Imitation of the Rose, The (Lispector)
1955 Laugher, The (Böll)
1955 One Ordinary Day, with Peanuts (Jackson)
1955 Rise of Maud Martha, The (Brooks)
1955 Star, The (Clarke)
1955 Texts for Nothing 3 (Beckett)
1955 Tomorrow and Tomorrow and So Forth (Updike)
1956 Axolotl (Cortázar)
1956 Christmas Memory, A (Capote)
1956 Don't Call Me by My Right Name (Purdy)
1956 End of the Game (Cortázar)
1956 Going Ashore (Gallant)
1956 Greenleaf (O'Connor)
1956 I Stand Here Ironing (Olsen)
1956 King Solomon (Rosenfeld)
1956 Smell of Death and Flowers, The (Gordimer)
1956 Snow-Storm, The (Tolstoy)
1956 Summer's Reading, A (Malamud)
1956 Take Pity (Malamud)
1956 Zulu and the Zeide, The (Jacobson)
1957 Adulterous Woman, The (Camus)
1957 Blank Page, The (Dinesen)
1957 Cardinal's First Tale, The (Dinesen)
1957 Childybawn (O'Faoláin)
1957 Color of Darkness (Purdy)
1957 Day Stalin Died, The (Lessing)
1957 Death of a Huntsman (Bates)
1957 First Love and Other Sorrows (Brodkey)
1957 Gentleman from Cracow, The (Singer)
1957 Guest, The (Camus)
1957 Man of the World, The (O'Connor)
1957 Reasonable Facsimile, A (Stafford)
1957 Stick of Green Candy, A (Bowles)
1957 Stone Boy, The (Berriault)
1957 This Indolence of Mine (Svevo)
1957 Why Can't They Tell You Why? (Purdy)
1958 Among the Dangs (Elliott)
1958 Blow-Up (Cortázar)

CHRONOLOGY LIST

CHRONOLOGY LIST

1971 Supremacy of the Hunza, The (Greenberg)
1971 Witness, The (Petry)
1972 Blacáman the Good, Vendor of Miracles (García Márquez)
1972 Critique de la Vie Quotidienne (Barthelme)
1972 Fable, A (Fox)
1972 Going Home (Trevor)
1972 Gun Shop, The (Updike)
1972 Hunting Season (Greenberg)
1972 Lesson, The (Bambara)
1972 My Man Bovanne (Bambara)
1972 Stalking (Oates)
1972 Steady Going Up (Angelou)
1972 Wrack (Barthelme)
1973 Everyday Use (Walker)
1973 Five-Twenty (White)
1973 Her Sweet Jerome (Walker)
1973 Innocence (Brodkey)
1973 Old Vemish (Targan)
1973 Ones Who Walk Away from Omelas, The (Le Guin)
1973 Rembrandt's Hat (Malamud)
1973 Singing Man, The (Dawson)
1973 Some of Us Had Been Threatening Our Friend Colby (Barthelme)
1973 Ugliest Pilgrim, The (Betts)
1974 Camberwell Beauty, The (Pritchett)
1974 Creature, The (O'Brien)
1974 End of Old Horse, The (Ortiz)
1974 Herakleitos (Davenport)
1974 How I Met My Husband (Munro)
1974 I'm Dreaming of Rocket Richard (Blaise)
1974 Imagined Scenes (Beattie)
1974 John Napper Sailing Through the Universe (Gardner)
1974 Killing of a State Cop, The (Ortiz)
1974 King's Indian, The (Gardner)
1974 Long-Distance Runner, The (Paley)
1974 Lullaby (Silko)
1974 Oranging of America, The (Apple)
1974 Scandalous Woman, A (O'Brien)
1974 Schrödinger's Cat (Le Guin)
1974 Signing, The (Dixon)
1974 Testimony of Pilot (Hannah)
1974 Waiting (Oates)
1974 Whore of Mensa, The (Allen)
1974 Yellow Woman (Silko)
1975 Admirer, The (Singer)
1975 Artificial Family, The (Tyler)
1975 His Son, in His Arms, in Light, Aloft (Brodkey)
1975 Rape Fantasies (Atwood)
1975 Return to Return (Hannah)
1975 Roses, Rhododendron (Adams)
1976 Englishwoman, The (Jhabvala)
1976 Going After Cacciato (O'Brien)
1976 In a Great Man's House (Jhabvala)
1976 Passion for History, A (Minot)
1976 Will You Please Be Quiet, Please? (Carver)
1977 Apocalypse at Solentiname (Cortázar)
1977 Beggar Maid, The (Munro)
1977 Collector of Treasures, The (Head)
1977 Dreamers in a Dead Language (Paley)
1977 Fat Girl, The (Dubus)
1977 Faustino (Martínez)
1977 Immigration Blues (Santos)
1977 Kugelmass Episode, The (Allen)
1977 Man from Mars, The (Atwood)
1977 Pretty Ice (Robison)
1977 Redemption (Gardner)
1977 Royal Beatings (Munro)
1977 Schreuderspitze, The (Helprin)
1977 Shifting (Beattie)
1977 Sin-Eater, The (Atwood)
1977 So Much Water So Close to Home (Carver)
1978 Child's Drawings, A (Shalamov)
1978 Home (Phillips)
1978 Rose in the Heart of New York, A (O'Brien)
1978 Silver Dish, A (Bellow)
1978 Snake Charmer, The (Shalamov)

CHRONOLOGY LIST

1978 Wild Swans (Munro)
1979 Black Tickets (Phillips)
1979 Bloody Chamber, The (Carter)
1979 Burning House, The (Beattie)
1979 Japanese Hamlet (Mori)
1979 Mr. and Mrs. Baby (Strand)
1979 Old Forest, The (Taylor)
1979 Old Light (Targan)
1979 Rags of Time, The (Targan)
1979 Silence (Bulosan)
1979 Smiles of Konarak, The (Dennison)
1979 Snow (Adams)
1980 Amish Farmer, The (Bourjaily)
1980 Black Venus (Carter)
1980 Change (Woiwode)
1980 Children of Strikers (Chappell)
1980 In the Garden of the North American Martyrs (Wolff)
1980 Moon and Madness (Singer)
1980 On Discovery (Kingston)
1980 Say Yes (Wolff)
1980 Shawl, The (Ozick)
1980 Shiloh (Mason)
1980 Soldier's Embrace, A (Gordimer)
1980 Thief (Wilson)
1980 Town and Country Lovers (Gordimer)
1980 Traveler (Gilchrist)
1980 Wissler Remembers (Stern)
1981 Anatomy of Desire (L'Heureux)
1981 Art of Living, The (Gardner)
1981 Beyond the Pale (Trevor)
1981 Black Queen, The (Callaghan)
1981 Cathedral (Carver)
1981 Coach (Robison)
1981 Damballah (Wideman)
1981 Exchange Value (Johnson)
1981 Farm, The (Williams)
1981 Greyhound People (Adams)
1981 My Warszawa (Oates)
1981 North Light (Helprin)
1981 Pleasure of Her Company, The (Smiley)
1981 Sniper, The (Sillitoe)
1981 Tommy (Wideman)
1981 What We Talk About When We Talk About Love (Carver)
1981 Why Don't You Dance? (Carver)
1981 Winter: 1978 (Beattie)
1981 Work (Plante)
1982 At the Bottom of the River (Kincaid)
1982 Firstborn (Woiwode)
1982 Graveyard Day (Mason)
1982 Greasy Lake (Boyle)
1982 Jacklighting (Beattie)
1982 Lightning (Barthelme)
1982 Lover of Horses, The (Gallagher)
1982 Miracle of the Birds, The (Amado)
1982 Overcoat II, The (Boyle)
1982 Residents and Transients (Mason)
1982 Rock Springs (Ford)
1982 Secret Lives of Dieters, The (Klass)
1982 Shoemaker Arnold (Lovelace)
1982 Sur (Le Guin)
1982 Territory (Leavitt)
1982 Truth or Consequences (Adams)
1982 Victrola (Morris)
1983 Amateur's Guide to the Night, An (Robison)
1983 Careful (Carver)
1983 Father's Story, A (Dubus)
1983 Final Proof of Fate and Circumstance, The (Abbott)
1983 Geraldo No Last Name (Cisneros)
1983 Girl (Kincaid)
1983 Glimpse into Another Country (Morris)
1983 My Mother (Kincaid)
1983 Nairobi (Oates)
1983 Not a Good Girl (Klass)
1983 Reunion, The (Angelou)
1983 Rosa (Ozick)
1983 Small, Good Thing, A (Carver)
1983 Snow (Beattie)
1983 Spirit Woman (Allen)
1983 World According to Hsü, The (Mukherjee)

CHRONOLOGY LIST

1989 Gussuk (Evans)
1989 In a Father's Place (Tilghman)
1989 Islands on the Moon (Kingsolver)
1989 Old West (Bausch)
1989 Ralph the Duck (Busch)
1989 She Is Beautiful in Her Whole Being (Momaday)
1989 Summer League (Romero)
1989 Swimmers, The (Oates)
1989 Toad's Mouth (Allende)
1989 Two Kinds (Tan)
1989 Wicked Girl (Allende)
1990 Amanda (Fernández)
1990 Big Bad Love (Brown)
1990 Dog Stories (Prose)
1990 Dragon's Seed (Bell)
1990 Ecco (Sukenick)
1990 Enero (Ponce)
1990 Esmeralda (Fernández)
1990 Flood, The (Harjo)
1990 Gravity (Leavitt)
1990 His Final Mother (Price)
1990 Leap, The (Erdrich)
1990 People of the Dog (Villanueva)
1990 Puttermesser Paired (Ozick)
1990 Sleep (Brown)
1990 Tall Tales from the Mekong Delta (Braverman)
1990 Wait, The (Bass)
1990 Way Stations (Doerr)
1991 Across the Bridge (Gallant)
1991 Deer Woman (Allen)
1991 Northern Lights, The (Harjo)
1991 One Holy Night (Cisneros)
1991 Remembering Orchards (Lopez)
1991 Slaughterhouse (Sarris)
1991 Waltz of the Fat Man (Ríos)
1992 Day They Took My Uncle, The (García)
1992 Frazer Avenue (García)
1992 In Search of Epifano (Anaya)
1992 Laughter of My Father, The (Villarreal)
1992 Man Who Found a Pistol, The (Anaya)
1992 Man, Woman and Boy (Dixon)
1992 Marijuana Party, The (Ponce)
1992 Saints (Chávez)
1993 Baseball Glove, The (Martínez)
1993 Easy Time (López)
1993 Moccasin Game (Vizenor)

KEY WORD LIST

KEY WORD LIST

GEOGRAPHICAL INDEX

GEOGRAPHICAL INDEX

TITLE INDEX

AUTHOR INDEX